SHADOW CROWN

ALSO BY KRISTEN MARTIN

THE AMAZON BESTSELLING ALPHA DRIVE SERIES

The Alpha Drive

The Order of Omega

Restitution

SHADOW CROWN

BOOK ONE

KRISTEN MARTIN

Black Falcon Press

SHADOW CROWN

For information contact :

Black Falcon Press, LLC

http://www.blackfalconpress.com

Library of Congress Control Number : 2017907237

ISBN: 978-0-9968605-9-8 (paperback)

10 9 8 7 6 5 4 3 2 1

For my Nana – I will always be your sweet girl. Thank you for believing in me.

PRONUNCIATION GUIDE

CHARACTERS

Arden: Ar-den

Rydan: Ry-den

Darius: Dare-ee-us

Aldreda: Al-dray-duh

Cerylia: Sur-lee-uh

Braxton: Brax-ten

Xerin: Zer-in

PLACES

Trendalath: Tren-duh-loth

Sardoria: Sar-door-ee-uh

Vaekith: Vy-kith

Orihia: Or-eye-uh

Ipcea: Ip-see

Chialka: Key-all-kah

OTHER

illusié: ill-oo-see-ayy

magick: magic

Caldari: Kal-darr-ee

Cruex: Crew

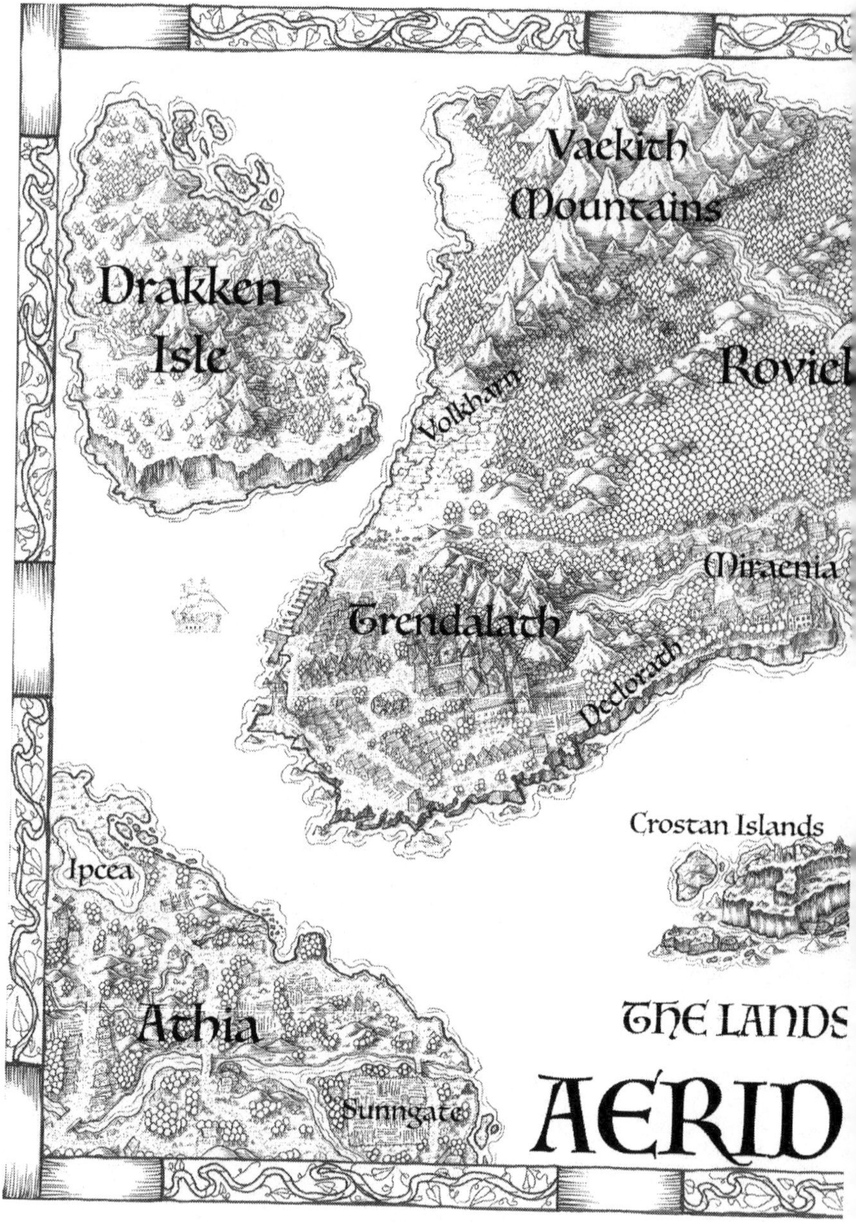
Vaekith Mountains
Drakken Isle
Roviel
Volkharn
Miraenia
Trendalath
Declorath
Crostan Islands
Ipcea
Athia
Sunngate
THE LANDS
AERID

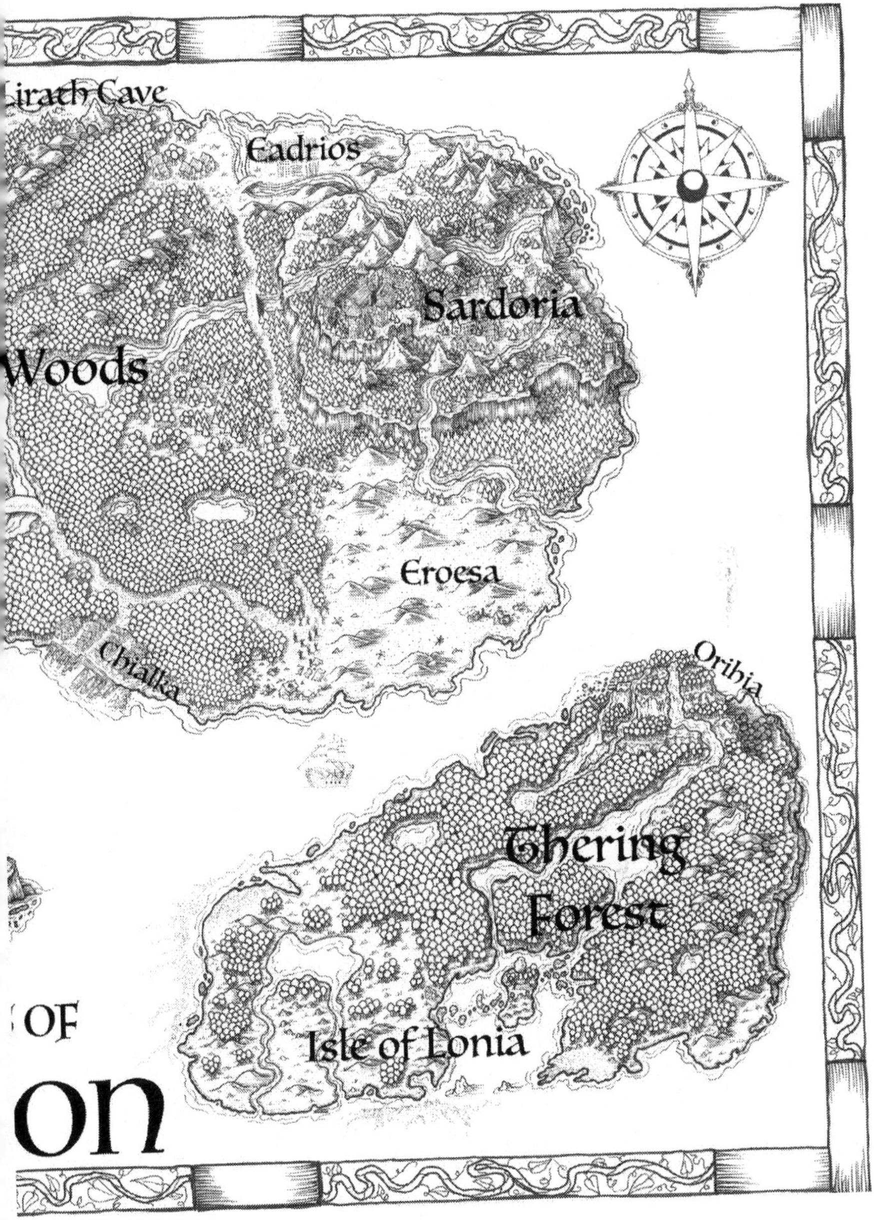

Lirath Cave
Eadrios
Sardoria
Woods
Eroesa
Chialka
Orihia
Thering Forest
Isle of Lonia
OF
on

SHADOW CROWN

ARDEN ELIRI

I WAS TWELVE years old when I took my first victim. A swift slash to the neck with a twenty-inch blade was my choice of attack, and boy, was it a good one. The man, no older than thirty-two, had dropped to his knees as crimson stained the collar of his tattered shirt, mouth parting as his final breath escaped his lips. I distinctly remember the look of fear on his face, mere moments before the light left his eyes. Fear faded into acceptance, and acceptance faded into nothing. And just like that, I had completed my first mission. It was over.

Looking back on it now, it wasn't a fair fight. How could he have seen me coming? I've been trained for the best by the best. Mercenary missions are much like its victims, here one minute and gone the next. Once King Tymond issues the decree, a member of the Cruex is assigned to carry out the sentence without question.

No doubt. No fear. Just action.

Arden Eliri.

Every time my name is called, I expect to cringe, to flinch. Maybe even bat an eye. But I don't. I know it should feel wrong to kill, to take lives, to watch life disintegrate so suddenly and know that I'm the cause of it. But it's who I am. It's all I know.

And so I continue.

I stand in front of King Tymond with the others. If my name is called, it will mark my thirteenth mission. The others in the Cruex have had a dozen more missions than me, seeing as they're ten or so years my senior—that is, everyone except for Rydan Helstrom. At eighteen, just one year older than me, he has fifteen missions under his belt. With a sideways glance, I notice that his jaw is clenched and his hands are balled into fists at his sides.

He wants this just as much as I do.

I turn my attention back to the king. Guards surround him in a flurry of chaos. Finally, they grow still, and I try not to shuffle back and forth between my feet. Waiting is my least favorite part of the process.

Just call my name.

After five excruciatingly long minutes, the king finally rises, scroll in hand. He hands it to his apprentice, who hurriedly unfurls the document, the corners flipping upward at the edges. King Tymond wets his lips and looks each of the Cruex up and down with beady eyes before speaking. His glare is potent enough to shatter the very throne that sits behind him.

I take a deep breath. A shiver runs down my spine as his lips part to speak.

"Cruex Mission CLXXVI will occur in the Isle of Lonia."

I loose the breath I've been holding. Lonia. In all twelve of my missions, I've never been assigned to Lonia. I've heard murmurings of the beauty of the village from some of the other assassins. From what I've gathered, it's much more pleasant than Trendalath, where the Cruex resides and the king reigns. Cloudless skies, deep blue oceans, cobblestone streets with no rubble or debris in sight. Lonia sounds like a dream compared to the poverty and filth that lies just outside the kingdom's walls—a kingdom headed for its own demise, thanks to Tymond.

I briefly wonder what this new target did to make it onto the Cruex hit list. Our skills are only reserved for the *truly* despicable: the murderers, the thieves, the schemers. Take my first victim, for example. This murderer was responsible for burning down an entire village—the village of Eroesa—killing all of the women and children that had settled there, ultimately leaving it to fend for itself as a wasteland with a smog-filled sky, covered in ashes and the remains of what once was. Not too long ago, Rydan was assigned a mission in Miraenia, a nearby bay village, to assassinate a thief who had pillaged half of the town's food, leaving more than twenty dead over the span of three days. Neither Rydan nor I have ever been to the Isle of Lonia.

Come to think of it, no one has.

I steal another glance at my competition. Rydan's gold-flecked eyes gleam as he adjusts his posture. He straightens his back and lifts his chin ever so slightly. One could almost mistake him for royalty if it weren't for the black Cruex uniform and unsightly scar woven along his right jawline.

His fourth mission. It'd happened before we'd grown close. The mission had gone awry in a most unpleasant way, and he'd been rushed back to Trendalath for medical attention. I shiver at the thought, not wanting to go any further down memory lane, and force my attention away from Rydan and toward one of the other assassins.

Percival Garrick. Hardly my competition, Percival's in his late twenties and has carried out twenty-four successful missions—but even so, King Tymond doesn't care to hide his dislike for the poor lad. A lifetime of ass kissing and the King would *still* assign him the most wretched missions without a hint of remorse. A shame, really.

And then there's Ezra Denholm. A stocky, brute fellow, Ezra appears to be one of the king's favorites. He's been assigned to thirty missions, all of which he's exceeded the king's expectations, and he's the same age as Percival! My empathy for Percival grows stronger every time Ezra's name is called for an assignment. Yes, Ezra's definitely one I need to watch out for.

Standing proudly next to Ezra are Elias Kent and Hugh Darby, the most annoying pair of cousins in the entire Kingdom of Trendalath. I'm still baffled as to how the two made it into the Cruex and what, if anything, the king sees in them. I've never been assigned to a mission with either of them but, rumor has it, they're absolutely ruthless. They must be good for something; otherwise the king wouldn't bother keeping them around.

And last but not least is Cyrus Alston, the most senior member of the Cruex. Undoubtedly the king's right-hand man, Cyrus has completed upward of fifty missions. Determined not to let his age get the better of him, Cyrus spends the bulk of his time in the underground training room, keeping his weapons sharp and his mind sharper. I do hope that, one day, before the king forces him to retire, we'll be jointly assigned to a mission. I'd finally get to see the real master at work.

I must admit, being the only female in the Cruex ranks was slightly intimidating at first, but I've grown fond of the situation. I get my own bedchambers, whereas the male Cruex are crammed into a space three times too small. No one fusses with me, mostly because I keep to myself, or maybe because I've frightened them. No one truly knew what I was capable of . . . until the results from my very first mission were made public.

Strike fear into the hearts of all. King Tymond's favorite saying. I would say I succeeded.

Don't get me wrong; being an outcast does come with its struggles. Rydan's really the only one who pays me any attention. He's the only one who will train with me. Eat with me. *Talk* to me. But I don't mind. I'm here to do one thing and one thing only: kill the murderers, the thieves, the schemers. I'm here to do my *job*.

My eyes make their way back to King Tymond. He's staring right at me with those light blue—almost translucent—eyes. My heart picks up pace, thumping so hard that the feeling resonates within my entire being.

"Arden Eliri."

I feel elated as the words leave his lips. *He chose me.* I try not to smile. Mission number thirteen in Lonia is *mine.*

I step forward to accept the scroll of parchment. Seeing my name scrawled across the top never ceases to give me chills. I look the king in the eye and bow as the parchment shifts from his hands to mine.

"Report back here tomorrow at 0600 hours for further details."

"Yes, sir." I nod as I step back in line with my fellow assassins. The disappointment hanging in the air is palpable.

"Dismissed," the king says with a wave of his hand.

I hurriedly roll the parchment back into its former condition and stuff it into my waistband. I turn on my heel, realizing that I'm the second to last in line to exit through the wooden double doors. Rydan stands behind me. The five other Cruex members are silent as they walk back to their chambers.

I don't know what this mission will hold. I don't know what crimes were committed or who I'm after. But these things are of no concern to me, because only one thing matters.

Lonia is mine—and I never miss my target.

RYDAN HELSTROM

WITH HIS HEART in his throat, Rydan follows closely behind Arden, trying to keep pace with her footsteps. Right foot, left foot, right, left. She seems to be running away from him, in the hopes that she'll make it to her chambers before they arrive at a chance to speak. How unlike her, to be running off like this. Typically after an assignment is announced, Arden spends the walk back poking fun at the chosen Cruex member, or in this case, flaunting her success. Whether it's bragging, pointing out flaws, or criticizing strengths, she's never been one to keep quiet. Except for today.

Today, something is different.

Rydan picks up his stride until he's walking right alongside her. With a sigh, he extends his arm in front of her, causing her to halt in her tracks.

She glares at him, then pushes his arm down with tremendous force given her petite stature. "What do you think you're doing?"

Rydan smiles. "There you are. That's the first thing you've said to me all day." His grin fades as her eyes drop to the floor. When she doesn't look up, he brings himself closer to her, his voice barely above a whisper. "Hey, what's going on with you?"

Arden's gaze slowly retreats from the floor, her piercing green eyes meeting his. "It's nothing," she mumbles before pushing her way past him.

He's seen this before. The thrill before the king announces a mission keeps the assassins intrigued, but once a name is called, the excitement begins to fizzle and reality sets in. Focus and discipline take over, and the lighthearted attitudes from before shift into something much darker. Heavier.

"This mission can't be any worse than our fourth assignment," he jokes, hoping that she'll turn around. When she doesn't, Rydan keeps his distance behind her, his focus on the back and forth movement of her chestnut brown hair, like the sway of a horse's tail. Cracking a joke to lighten the mood obviously wasn't going to work. He'd pulled her out of her own head before, on multiple occasions, but this . . . this would be a hard nut to crack. Approach number two: visceral honesty. "The Isle of Lonia, huh? I wish the king had chosen me for this one," he says with a sigh. "I've always wanted to go there."

She grunts, but continues walking. Still no verbal response.

Approach number three: ask her a question. "How do you feel about training later? I'll let you be on offense, especially with that injured shoulder of yours."

At this, Arden turns around, a coy smile tugging at her lips. "You must *really* want me to talk. And my shoulder feels fine, thank you."

Rydan shrugs. "Not really," he says, knowing that his indifference will drive her crazy. "I just need someone to train with tonight."

The smile falls from her face. "I'll train with you." A shadow passes over the hall, and he notices her eyes flicker to his jaw, to his scar. She averts her eyes the minute he catches her staring. "And I'll take you up on your offer. Being on offense, that is. Are you sure you can handle it?"

Rydan nods as silent shouts of victory ring in his ears. If there's one thing he's learned about Arden, it's that she can't stand when people act indifferent. *Feel one way or the other, there is no gray area.* Her words echo in his head as if she'd just spoken them. He finds it somewhat hypocritical though, seeing as she's the master of indifference.

"Rydan?"

He snaps back to the present. “I’ll let you get some dinner. Let’s meet in the training quarters at 1700 hours sharp.”

Arden raises her eyebrows. “You sure that’s not too late for you, old man?”

Rydan laughs, the sound echoing throughout the halls. “No, it’s not too late for me. Just because I prefer to go to bed early doesn’t mean I do so every night.”

“Sure you don’t,” she teases. “Just seven days out of the week.”

He laughs again, happy to see the return of her witty self. “Okay, you win. But training is our lifeblood. Without it, we’re out of a job, living outside these walls with nothing to our name. Gotta stay sharp, right?”

She raises an eyebrow. “Unless you prefer a swift knife to the throat.”

He can’t help but smirk at her remark. “I’ll see you in a little while.” As he turns to enter his chambers, Arden clears her throat. “Thanks.”

He meets her gaze, feeling confused. “For what?”

Her eyes wander to the ceiling for a brief moment. “I would tell you, but you already know the answer to that question.”

He almost rolls his eyes, but she’s right. For as long as they’ve known each other, Rydan has always succeeded at distracting her from her own debilitating thoughts. Some would say it’s what makes them such a good pair. “1700 hours?”

Arden cocks her head as she reaches for the door that leads to her chambers. Her *private* chambers. “Roger that.”

Rydan watches as the door creaks shut behind her, leaving him alone in the vast hallway. Voices echo further down the hall. The others are probably entering the male-designated chambers at this very moment. It’s difficult not to envy Arden’s situation. He can count multiple times where all he desired was to be alone, but the company of others was inescapable. Correction: still *is* inescapable. Just one of the “perks” of being a male Cruex member.

Rydan pushes through the doors to the chambers and heads toward the staircase. Just as he begins to climb the steps, he stops and heads back to the ground floor. He may as well enjoy what little time he has alone. It always comes to an end far too soon.

ARDEN ELIRI

BACK IN MY quarters, I stifle a scream. Holding in excitement has never been an easy task, but somehow I manage. After years of dealing with men and their lack of showing emotion, I've learned to compartmentalize my own emotions into a hidden sector of my mind, only to be accessed when I'm alone. Showing excitement around the kingdom, especially as an assassin, is a death wish. No one should be excited to kill. It's a duty, plain and simple. Complete it and move on to the next one.

But not for me. Killing is my bread and butter, my very own road to "carpe diem". And seize the day I shall.

I meander over to the far left corner of my quarters, perusing the stacks of books sitting idly on my desk. Most of them contain information about weapons, martial arts tactics, and strategizing. Not the kinds of books most would enjoy reading, but I adore them. I've found that there is nothing better to sharpen my skills and know-how except for the actual kill itself, but, obviously, this isn't always at my fingertips. For those times, these books fill the gap.

At first, I'm curious to find a book on the properties of healing, given my strange encounter earlier that day. During training, I'd severely pulled a muscle in my shoulder—to the point where I couldn't even lift my arm above my head—and Rydan's relentless jokes were no consolation. But after massaging the area for just a few minutes, the pain had completely subsided—almost as if it had healed on its own somehow. But that's impossible.

Isn't it?

I take a step toward one of the many bookshelves in my room and gently slide my fingers over their spines, leaving track marks along the way. When I reach the end, I blow the hardened dust that has collected on my fingertips into the night air. It dances around me like paper faeries first taking flight. My eyes settle back on the shelves, and I spot an unfamiliar title that appears to be out of place. *The Archmage and Illusié*. Old magick. I hesitate.

Since before I can remember, before I joined the

Cruex, it was made clear that any talk of magick was forbidden. It was considered a myth and would be treated as such. All scrolls or books mentioning magick, whether fable or fact, were ordered to be destroyed by King Tymond.

Well, it looks like they missed one.

I slide the large book from the shelf and set it on my desk. I take in its deep evergreen color as my hands cascade down the front, removing even more dust than was on the spine. I'm careful to open it, seeing as the binding has started to come undone. I flip through the first few pages, fascinated by elegant drawings of gemstones, mage robes, and masks. It makes me wonder if this particular book is based on fact or fable. As I delve deeper into the pages, the answer becomes clear. Spread over two pages is an older map of the Lands of Aeridon, where Trendalath and its surrounding villages, mountains, forests, and isles reside. I focus my attention on the Isle of Lonia, where I will be going in less than twenty-four hours.

Fact.

A loud banging at my door startles me. I jump and slam the book shut. I consider putting it back on the shelf, but now that I know it exists, I worry someone else will discover it. So I do the sensible thing. I throw it under my bed.

It's probably Rydan, arriving early to take me to training. Although, what time is it? Has it been two hours already? I flatten the wrinkles out of my trousers, realizing that I haven't changed nor eaten a proper meal since we last parted ways.

The banging continues, loud and persistent as ever.

"Just a second!" I yell as I change my tunic. I throw my hair up into a loose bun and make my way toward the door. When I open it, my heart sputters. It is not Rydan who stands before me, but one of the king's guards.

"King Tymond requests your presence in the Great Room," he says.

I try not to look caught off-guard, but my demeanor speaks for itself. "Uh, sure. The Great Room," I repeat back, sounding like an imbecile.

"Follow me," the guard says as he turns away.

I survey my quarters, trying to think of anything I might need to bring with me. Normally I'd be clad in my Cruex uniform with weapons in their holsters, but clearly there isn't time for such niceties. I decide to just go with it and follow the guard down the hall, rolling my eyes as we stop in front of the chambers housing the male Cruex.

"Sir, I believe the Great Room . . ."

He holds up a hand to silence me, then bangs on the door. "Rydan Helstrom!" he shouts, his voice powerful and intimidating.

Why is he calling Rydan's name? What is going on?

I tap my foot, waiting impatiently as the door

swings open. Rydan's hair is unkempt, his shirt untucked, and if it weren't for the vigilant look on his face, I would have assumed he'd fallen asleep after dinner. I stifle a laugh at the bewildered look on his face when he realizes I'm standing behind the guard.

"Follow me," the guard orders. "The king requires your presence in the Great Room."

Rydan smooths back his hair as he takes a step forward. "Right now?"

The guard glares at him. "Did I stutter?" Without warning, he turns on his heel and starts down the hall.

I follow suit and shortly after, Rydan is right next to me, dragging his feet like a kid whose shoes don't fit properly. He mutters under his breath so the guard can't hear. "Why are you needed in the Great Room?"

I tilt my head to the side and ask him the exact same question.

He shrugs. "Whatever it is, it can't be good."

I'm not sure why, but his statement troubles me. We are assassins. In a sense, we are the king's livelihood. And without his livelihood, the "king" ceases to exist. He needs us more than we need him. At least, that's how I see it.

"I'm sure it's fine. It probably has something to do with the Lonia mission." I swallow my words as a thought occurs to me, but I keep it to myself. *What if the king has decided to remove me from the mission?*

What if he decides to assign Rydan to Lonia instead? The thought alone makes me want to tear every strand of hair from my head. I press my mouth into a firm line as the guard leads us into the Great Room.

I guess we're about to find out.

As we approach the throne, King Tymond stays seated. Only when we stand in front of him and bow does he rise. "Eliri," he says as he addresses me with a nod of his head. "Helstrom."

"Your Majesty," we both say in unison.

Tymond waltzes down the stone steps, his black and red robe swaying back and forth with the movement. He pauses on the last step to signify that he is still above us and will always be above us. It's the first time I notice the dragon broach securing his robes.

My thoughts scatter as he speaks.

"It has been brought to my attention that the information pertaining to mission CLXXVI in the Isle of Lonia is not as explicit as we'd originally thought." He shoots a harsh glare at the guard who'd brought us here. "Given the current situation, we'll need to make some adjustments to the assignment." He pauses as he wets his lips. "We've deemed it a category eight mission."

I try not to gape at his words. *A category eight?* That would make this mission *the* most dangerous one ever assigned to the Cruex.

"Due to the nature of this mission and this

newfound information, it would be a death wish to send only one Cruex member to overcome the obstacles and expect them to successfully return."

Bile rises in my throat as the king's words echo in my ears. What he really means to say is that it would be a death wish to send a *female* Cruex member. I feel my hands clench as they ball into fists, and I bite down on the inside of my cheek to keep myself from showing any reaction. *Yet another "perk" of being the only female assassin.* I'm constantly faced with doubt, ridicule, and never being good enough. The only problem is I *am* good enough—leagues better than half of the male Cruex members combined.

My anger gets the better of me. I step forward to speak. "Your Majesty, I can assure you that I am fully-equipped to handle this mission alone. You will not be disappointed."

I hear Rydan inhale a sharp breath. He probably thinks I'm a fool for interrupting the king, for speaking out of turn. I thought that by now he knew me well enough where my rash behavior wouldn't surprise him. I suppose I was wrong.

"Be that as it may, no single Cruex member has ever even attempted to complete a category *eight* mission, let alone a category seven." The king raises an eyebrow at me. "But I admire your tenacity, Eliri."

Even though he's a step behind me, I can see Rydan's exaggerated eye roll. I step back in line beside him, anxious for the king's next words.

"I decree, as of this day, you will work as partners on Cruex Mission CLXXVI in the Isle of Lonia."

The breath Rydan was holding in slowly comes out. I'm sure the look on his face is smug as all hell, and I wish I could turn to him and slap it right off. But I maintain my composure, not flinching, not moving a muscle.

"Yes, Your Majesty," we both say in unison.

"Good," the king says. He sounds surprised, almost as though he'd expected some resistance from the two of us. "You are dismissed." He turns away from us and walks back up the steps to his throne. The guard shows us out and slams the large iron doors behind us.

In the hallway, Rydan gives me a playful nudge. "Well hey there, *partner,*" he teases.

I roll my eyes. "This is a crock of crap. You know I could complete this mission by myself with my eyes closed and my hands tied behind my back."

Rydan stops walking. "I know you could," he says, his voice almost a whisper. "But it's a category *eight,* Arden. Do you know how dangerous that is?"

I consider this for a moment. I do know how dangerous it is. Does he not remember the last mission we partnered on? The one that left him with a bruised ego and a deep-rooted scar? Or has he forgotten?

"Listen, if you don't want my help, I can put in a

transfer. I'm sure Denholm or Alston would *love* to work with you."

His sarcasm stings and I can feel myself closing up, pulling away. The truth is, I don't want to work with anybody *but* him. He's the closest thing I have to a friend. A confidante. Family. It's just that I'd prefer to go at this alone, like almost everything else. But instead of saying this and speaking the truth, I shut down, like I always do. "Do what you want. I'll either see you tomorrow at the mission, or I'll see you after I complete it. Makes no difference to me."

My response wounds him. I can see it in those sad eyes of his. I feel a flicker of remorse, but it quickly dissipates as we approach the chambers.

"If it really doesn't matter to you, then I guess *when* you find out makes no difference. You'll have to wait until tomorrow." He pulls the handle to the chamber door and sighs. "Goodnight, Arden."

I stand there like a statue as he disappears through the door. My shoulders sag at the exchange that has just taken place. Although I'll never admit it out loud, I know I've made a mistake.

I should have told him the truth.

DARIUS TYMOND

THAT EVENING, IN his chambers, King Darius Tymond stands on the balcony overlooking the Kingdom of Trendalath. A dreary combination of black, gray, and navy paints the night sky and large raindrops fall from invisible clouds. A bolt of lightning illuminates the darkness and a deafening clap of thunder follows. The shouts of people running for cover echo just outside the kingdom's walls. He can hardly understand what they're saying, but the languages are a mixture of old and new. Although he'd outlawed almost everything from the past—languages, customs, texts, and most notably, magick—he'd found that old habits were hard to break, especially when the majority of the townspeople had little to no respect for him. All things considered, it probably would have been easier had he just slayed those living under the previous king's reign; but he hadn't because that would mean starting over completely. In the interest of time, he'd chosen to spare their lives.

What a foolish choice that had been.

The screams grow louder as the thunder roars. Babies cry and women wail as the men shout to one another to find shelter. *Savages,* Tymond thinks to himself with a shudder. He places his hands on the balcony and leans over the side, gazing around at the massive walls that protect him. It honestly wouldn't come as a surprise if the entire town suddenly decided to storm the doors and overthrow his reign. Some days, he actually expects it.

As he brings himself upright, a hand lands on his shoulder. Although the touch is gentle, it's enough to startle him. He whirls around, tense, with guarded eyes, but when he sees that it's just his wife, Aldreda, he immediately softens. Plump pink lips meet his cheek as she purrs into his ear. "You should come to bed, My King. Enduring such ill-tempered weather is not a duty of the royal bloodline." She smirks at the panicked voices idly threatening to forge through the castle walls. "It's a duty of the commoners."

Darius turns his head to look at her. Strands of

long blonde hair—so blonde it's almost white—cascade over her shoulders and down her back, the ends dancing in the blustery wind. Blue eyes deeper than the oceans surrounding Miraenia gaze into his own, and although crow's feet line her eyes, she's aged beautifully, like a fine wine. He takes her petite hand in his and kisses it. "My Queen. As always, you make an excellent point."

A knowing smile crosses her face. She caresses his cheek, then leads him back into the chambers, shutting the balcony doors securely behind her. "How was the Lonia assignment taken today? Well, I hope?"

Darius shakes his head as he unfastens the brooch on his robes. He throws the garment onto the bed in a huff before seating himself. "It was, at first. Until . . ."

"Until what?"

The king sighs, running a hand through his salt-and-pepper hair. "Until I assigned two Cruex members to the Lonia mission instead of just one."

Aldreda raises an eyebrow. She clasps her hands together, her beige silk robes gliding along the floor behind her as she approaches the bed. "I see you heeded my advice to add Helstrom to the mission."

The king lets out a small laugh and shakes his head. "Don't I always?"

"I know you appreciate my counsel, but I didn't know it was a major factor in your final decision-making. Seeing as I can't be in the Great Room when said decisions are made . . ." She casts her eyes toward the floor, her words lingering in the air.

Darius stiffens at the intentional directness of her statement. "As the queen, there are many essential duties required of you every day. I don't appreciate what you're implying."

"And I am grateful, My King. Truly."

He stares at her. A flicker of something familiar darts across her eyes. Resentment? Or perhaps it's only his imagination. He waves it off, hoping to avoid *this* conversation again; one they've had hundreds of times. Asking Aldreda to let something go is like asking a knight to go into battle unarmed—pointless and dangerous. Best to tread lightly. "If you'll recall, I have requested that you be present at only the most important meetings in the Great Room."

Aldreda scoffs as she messes with the braids woven throughout her hair. "I would say a category eight mission is one of the more important meetings you've called to order during your reign, wouldn't you?"

So much for treading lightly. "The King's Guard has yet to give their approval. You know these things take time."

With a solemn nod, Aldreda moves to the other side of the bed, drawing the covers down in the process. She slips out of her robe and crawls under the thin sheets, shivering as a cool draft sweeps through the chambers. She pulls a wool blanket over her body so that it covers everything but her chin. "Of course, My King. We can discuss it in further detail at a later time. You must be tired from such an eventful day."

Darius lets out a soft exhale, relieved that Aldreda is being agreeable for once, but when he turns to face her, he realizes she is anything but. A forced smile sits on her face, her eyes colder than ice. "Goodnight, Darius." Her flat tone is enough to make any man, no matter how egotistical or strong-willed, feel like a meek little mouse. She tilts her head, eyes narrowed as a barely discernible smirk tugs at the corners of her lips. Then she rolls away from him.

"Goodnight, My Queen. Sleep well," he whispers. As he slips into bed beside her, bitter reminders of memories past creep into his mind. Sadly, he knows this is the first of many webs he'll find himself trapped in with little to no hope of escape. Consequently, he won't be sleeping well, if at all, for a long, long time.

ARDEN ELIRI

IF ONLY YESTERDAY had been a dream. I'd be waking up, preparing to go to Lonia on my own. But this is not the day that awaits me.

I stretch my arms overhead as I sit up and throw my legs over the bed. Just as my feet hit the smooth stone floor, my stomach rumbles. It's then I realize that in the midst of everything, I never had the chance to eat a proper meal last night. Feeling famished, I stumble over to my armoire and hastily throw on a pair of black trousers and a beige tunic. I grab the scroll of parchment and tuck it into the waistband of my pants. With my unfastened boots and tousled hair, I look more than unkempt, like a beggar who's been wandering the streets for months. I bend down to fasten my boots, smooth my hair down, and grab one of the cloaks hanging on the back of the door before rushing toward the mess hall.

Suffice it to say, I didn't sleep well last night, making me even more irritable than usual. As much as I wish for plates upon plates of haggis and pork, in the interest of time, a steaming bowl of porridge will do. The mess hall comes into view, just a hundred or so feet away, when an annoyingly chipper face impedes my view.

Rydan.

"Mornin', Arden," he says with irksome cheerfulness.

"Morning," I grumble back. I try to move past him, but he mirrors my every move. I let out a sigh and fold my arms over my chest. "Do you need something? I'm starving."

"Great, I was just headed that way."

I try not to groan as I let him walk beside me. The sweet smell of glazed ham and pork wafts through the doors, and I pick up my pace, hoping that maybe I'll walk fast enough to leave Rydan behind. But, much to my dismay, he keeps up with my stride as we approach the tables filled with food, and I find myself frowning as I scoop a spoonful of thick, clumpy porridge into my bowl. Rydan helps himself to a serving of the same, then follows me to one of the rickety wooden tables. Banners of all shapes, sizes, and colors sway from the rafters above us from the permanent draft in the room. I can feel the defeat of kingdoms past glaring at me as I scoop the porridge from my bowl.

We eat in silence. Out of my peripheral, I can see Rydan casting glances my way as I devour my meal, but I ignore his feeble attempts to draw my attention. Before I know it, I've finished my breakfast. I consider helping myself to a second serving, but I notice an overwhelming number of Cruex members file into the mess hall, even though it's two hours earlier than they normally eat.

Rydan interrupts my hunger-filled daze. "We need to be in the Great Room at 0600 hours. What time do you have?"

I finish the last bite of my porridge, then pull out my gold inscribed pocket watch. It was my father's—at least I think it was. I was never told what happened to him, or to my family, but the back plate of the watch is inscribed with my last name, Eliri, so it must have come from some familial line somewhere. Even if it wasn't my father's, I like to pretend it is. It makes me feel as though I have some semblance of self after seventeen years.

I almost choke on my water as I read the time. "0550."

Rydan wolfs down the last of his breakfast, finishing it off with a giant glass of milk. "I suppose we'd better get moving then."

⁂

I wrap the cloak tightly around my body as Rydan and I approach the doors to the Great Room. The same burly guard that had escorted us the night before blocks the way. "Names?" he demands in a gruff tone.

It takes everything in me not to roll my eyes. He knows who I am, but I tell him my last name, then watch as he checks his scroll. I tap my foot impatiently. Finally, he nods at me in confirmation, then turns his attention to Rydan.

"Helstrom. We have an appointment with the king at 0600 hours."

The guard waves him off as though he were an annoying insect buzzing around his ear. "You're late. Enter now."

I can tell Rydan is about to argue with the oaf of a man, seeing as he's *always* on time, but before he can open his mouth, I grab his arm and pull him along behind me. I make sure to politely utter a "thank you" to the guard. Rydan stumbles after me, cursing as we enter the Great Room. I turn around and shush him, hoping that the king didn't catch his childish outburst, but luckily for him, the king's squire appears to be holding his majesty's attention rather well.

My heart pounds in my chest as I approach the throne. As much as I wish I were the sole assassin assigned to this mission, I feel somewhat relieved that Rydan was chosen to be my partner. Anyone else would have been a hindrance, and although Rydan can, and does, get on my nerves (more often than not), he's sharp, quick, and incredibly skilled. If I can't do it by myself, having Rydan by my side is the next best option. He'll never know that, though.

King Tymond sees us approaching and dismisses his squire with the wave of his hand. An oversized amethyst ring glints in the rising sunlight, and I almost have to shield my eyes at the sight. Slowly, he rises from his throne. "Eliri." He nods at me. "Helstrom."

As if we're the same person, Rydan and I both bow and say, "Your Majesty."

The king looks directly at me. "Do you have the parchment?"

I reach behind me and pull the scroll from the waistband of my trousers. I gently set it in the squire's outstretched palm, trying not to laugh as he scurries up the steps to present it to the king.

Before he has a chance to unroll it, I say, "Forgive me, Your Majesty, but I noticed there was some missing information for this mission."

King Tymond flicks his gaze at me, then unfurls the document and browses the text. He mumbles something to the squire under his breath, then turns his attention back to Rydan and me. "I am aware. This is precisely why you are here."

Rydan looses a breath. Even though I can only see him out of the corner of my eye, I can tell he's tense, nervous. Neither of us have any idea what the king is about to say.

"Your mission is in the Isle of Lonia. I have arranged a ship to take you there. It will set sail at 0800 hours tonight." He hesitates before continuing. "Your target is the Soames household. Their residence is located in North Portside in the river valley, dwelling LVII. Take care of them however you please, it makes no difference to me, so long as they're no longer breathing." The king scrutinizes the parchment once more before rolling it back up. His squire rushes over to him and ties a royal purple ribbon around the scroll, then hurries down the steps to hand it back to me.

I gape at the king, feeling more confused than ever. This is the least amount of information I've ever received for a mission, and I can tell by the look on Rydan's face that he feels the same way. I know I should swallow my words and keep my mouth shut. That I should bow and walk away once dismissed. But, as it always does, my curiosity gets the better of me. "And what is to be said for their crimes?"

Rydan nudges me in the side. If I could see him right now, I'm almost certain his eyes would be popping out of his skull.

The king flicks his gaze from the squire. It's lethal.

It seems his rage is bubbling just below the surface, and I don't want to be here when it explodes. I swallow the lump in my throat. For the first time in a long time, I wish I'd just kept my stupid mouth shut.

"This is a category eight mission," King Tymond says through gritted teeth, "and you really think the details regarding their crimes would just be handed to you freely?"

Actually, that's *exactly* what I thought, but I know better than to say so out loud. Instead, I remain expressionless, unmoving.

"Foolish girl," the king tisks. "You swore an oath to me. You swore your loyalty. And when I order you to do something, you do it. No questions asked."

My cheeks burn as I steady my gaze. As much as I want to lash out and curse him, I hold my tongue. Instead, I say the one thing I know he wants to hear. "Yes, Your Majesty."

King Tymond doesn't smile. "That'll be all. Dismissed."

I loose the breath I didn't realize I'd been holding as I turn on my heel and make my way to the doors. Tears prick my eyes, and I shake my head to ensure they don't fall. Rydan stays a couple of steps behind me, the heels of his boots clacking on the marble surface. We're just about to reach the giant iron doors when the king clears his throat.

I turn around, slowly, so that my eyes meet

Rydan's first. His are wide with fear, as if he knows that I've pushed the king a bit too far. I take a deep breath before we break eye contact and turn to face his majesty.

Devoid of emotion, the king signals for us to come closer. We only take a few steps before he throws an open palm in the air. Rydan and I halt in our tracks. I can feel our nerves radiating off of each other, the heat between us almost insufferable. I chew on the inside of my cheek as the king's steely gaze meets mine.

"I've changed my mind," King Tymond says as he resumes his place on the throne. He taps the amethyst ring against the armrest three times before gripping the edges. "I have a specific way in which I'd like you to handle the Soames."

My throat goes dry as he continues to stare directly at me. This can't be good.

"You'll assassinate the Soames," the king says with a demonic smile, "and as proof, you'll bring me their heads."

RYDAN HELSTROM

RYDAN QUICKENS HIS pace as he exits the Great Room. He can hear the swish of Arden's trousers as she struggles to catch up to him. Only a few hundred feet until he reaches his chambers. Just a few more hallways to scurry down.

He halts as Arden's booming voice fills the halls. "Don't you dare run away from me, Helstrom!"

One would never expect such a brash, bold voice to come from someone of her stature. He chuckles to himself as he turns around, amused at her seemingly harsh tone. "And if I do?"

She moves her hand underneath her tunic and unsheathes a gold dagger from a hidden holster. "I'm not sure if you recall my aim from target practice. Care to be reminded?"

She's got him there. Impeccable aim. Today does not feel like a good day to be injured or dead, so Rydan throws his head back and with his eyes trained on the ceiling, stalks toward her. She keeps the dagger drawn until he's standing just inches from her face. He raises his hand and puts his fingers on the smooth edge of the blade, carefully pressing down on it so she'll lower the weapon. Arden resists at first, but eventually gives in. With an exasperated sigh, she sheathes the dagger back to its rightful place.

"Now, what's all the fuss about?"

"I should ask you the same question. Nudging me in front of the king like I'm some sort of child," she scoffs. "What was that all about?"

Rydan can feel his expression turn cold as he recalls the recent incident. "Do you realize what you've done, speaking out of turn like that?" he mutters under his breath. "Do you realize what this means?"

Arden shrugs. "So we have to take the Soames's heads. We've done it before."

He doesn't answer right away. Instead, he tilts his head to the left to showcase his prominent scar. She winces at the sight of it, then casts her eyes toward the floor.

"Indeed, we have done it before," he responds, his voice brusque, head still turned. "And look how well that turned out for me."

"That wasn't your fault," Arden whispers quietly. "And it wasn't my fault either."

Rydan shoots her a bewildered look. "Then, tell me, Arden, whose fault *was* it?"

She stays silent. The silence stretches on and on, until there is only tension mounting between them. The thickness of it is enough to leave them both suffocating for air.

His fourth mission. She wasn't supposed to be there, but somehow, Arden had found a way to tag along and ruin everything. Perhaps she was just observing, or perhaps she'd meant to get in the way. To this day, her intention still remains a mystery. He'll probably never know.

Rydan's fourth mission had taken place in Miraenia, a nearby bay village just a little ways south of the Kingdom of Trendalath. He'd ridden his favorite horse, Amadeus, into the town, hooves clapping against the worn cobblestone, his black Cruex cloak flapping in the wind behind him. He'd spotted his target's residence from afar. The dwelling was hard to miss: a two-story weathered wooden building with navy blue shutters falling off its hinges, and an oversized bronze knocker in the shape of a lion's head growling angrily on an emerald green door. The Langleys. The residence had matched the description on the parchment almost exactly, making it the easiest target he'd ever had to spot.

The sun had just set and he'd hurriedly tied Amadeus off to a nearby post in town. The longsword strapped to his back felt lighter than air, as though it were a part of him, as he crept toward the Langley household. He'd completed his first mission from a high peak in the Vaekith Mountains with just a bow and arrow, his second mission with an axe, and his third with a longsword. He'd had surprisingly good aim with the bow and arrow (beginner's luck), whereas the axe had felt bulky and sluggish. The longsword was, by far, his weapon of choice. It sliced through his targets with one clean sweep, and the look of it alone was enough to frighten even the most experienced swordsman.

After locating the rear entrance to the house, he'd taken a moment to wrap his hands in linen gauze. He hated the way strangers' blood felt on his skin, sticky and thick, but even more so, he despised the copper-like scent that hung in the air for hours after the slaying. It was enough to make his stomach turn.

Just as he'd finished wrapping his left hand, the rear door to the house swung open and out strolled Graham Langley. But the man wasn't alone. He was surrounded by four of his companions, none of whom were on Rydan's target list. Per Tymond's sources, Graham was supposed to be alone that day.

Trying not to panic, Rydan slowly began to slip away toward the front of the house. He silently cursed a twig as it snapped underneath his boot. The sound was enough to grab the group's attention.

What had happened from that point forward hadn't been pretty. Knowing that he'd been spotted, Rydan drew his sword and charged at the men, but they were one step ahead of him. Each held a pair of gleaming serrated knives, poised and ready to strike. A large oak tree stood behind them, and as he was charging, Rydan noticed a figure crouching on one of the branches. From underneath a cloak identical to his own, he could see long brown hair fluttering in the autumn breeze.

Arden.

Although he'd only been distracted for a moment's notice, it was long enough for one of Langley's companions to heave a knife aimed straight at his face. Rydan dove to the left, but not soon enough to avoid the blade carve a jagged line from his chin to his ear. He dropped his sword as his hands flew to his cheek, blood spurting from the gash, the linen gauze quickly soaking up the red. His hands stained crimson, Rydan averted his eyes to his fallen sword, then to his only hope, the girl in the oak tree.

Just as the men geared up to attack him, curved throwing axes, more commonly known as chakrams, had flown from the tree. Rydan watched as one sliced across Graham Langley's neck, his eyes bulging as he fell forward onto his knees. Four more chakrams skimmed through the air, skating swiftly across the necks of the others. In mere seconds, the five men lay before him in a pool of crimson.

He'd sat there in shock, clutching his cheek.

In just a few deft movements, Arden had made her way down the tree, leaves crunching underneath her boots as she landed. She'd made her way around the fresh corpses, restocking her chakram inventory with each stop. When she'd finally arrived in front of him, he didn't know what to say. What would the king think when he found out that more than just Graham Langley had been killed? And that Arden had caught him by surprise when she'd suddenly shown up? And that *he* hadn't actually killed anyone? That it had all been her doing?

She'd extended her hand, her expression grim. Reluctantly, Rydan had accepted, still clutching his cheek as she pulled him to his feet. With her eyes locked on his, she'd whispered, "This stays between us."

And it had. They'd burned the bodies of the four nameless companions, but decided to take Graham's head. "As proof," Arden had murmured as she tossed the head into her satchel. And they'd never spoken of it again.

Until now.

Rydan's thoughts scatter as he's brought back to the present.

"I suppose we need to gather our things before we set sail tonight," Arden says quietly, her eyes still cast toward the floor. "I'll come to your chambers at 0730 hours."

Rydan only nods because if he speaks, he'll choke on his words. He waits until she's turned the corner before gritting his teeth and laying his fist into the stone castle wall.

Three hours before they're due to set sail, Rydan finds himself sitting at his desk in his chambers, staring into space, shivering in the brisk evening air. Echoes from the other Cruex members bounce off the castle walls, but he hardly notices. A book lay stretched in front of him, the many pages ripped and torn. It's a wonder it's managed to stay bound for this long; the spine is falling apart and looks as though it only has a few more reads left in it. Rydan shifts his gaze from the wall back to the text in the book. *The History of Lonia.* His eyes skim the words, but of course he can't find what he's looking for. He wets the tip of his index finger to flip through more of the pages. The next page is just as useless, if not more, than the last, containing information he'd already learned as a young Cruex member. Nothing new.

Rydan slams the book shut. He takes a deep breath as he runs a thick hand through his midnight-black hair. Thoughts of earlier that morning swarm his head. The minute the king mentioned the name *Soames*, Rydan knew he'd heard of it before, but for the life of him, couldn't remember where or what importance it held. His uneasiness grows the more he repeats the name in his head. Over and over again.

Soames. Soames. *Soames.*

With a whirl of his chair, Rydan rises to his feet and marches over to the bookshelf. He runs his fingers along the edge of each shelf until reaching the one on the very bottom. A book with a similar ragged spine, just as worn as the Lonia book and navy blue in color, catches his eye. He pulls it from its spot and gently blows the layer of dust from the cover. *The History of Miraenia.* If memory serves him right, Miraenia and Lonia used to be allies before Tymond overthrew the previous king of Trendalath. Hope surges through him as he brings the book to his desk. To his surprise, a long piece of parchment unfurls as soon as he opens the cover.

What do we have here?

A childish joy lights from within him as he realizes what the scroll contains. Names, hundreds of names—essentially a roster for the villages of Miraenia and Lonia. The names do not appear to be in any sort of logical order, alphabetical or otherwise, so Rydan uses his index fingers to go through each one, line by line. As he nears the bottom of the list, the small flame of hope he first had is in danger of being snuffed out entirely. He reaches the bottom of the list and sighs.

No Soames.

Rydan slams his hand on the desk, causing the nearby lantern and copper mug to shake violently. He'd been almost certain he'd find the Soames's name on that list. He rubs his eyes with one hand and pulls a watch from the pocket of his trousers with the other. Thirty minutes of his life, wasted. He reaches for his mug of black tea, cursing as some of the liquid spills over from the top and lands on the parchment. His eyes immediately go to the wet spot on the document as it seeps through the thick paper. His eyes widen as the spot grows darker in color. *Flip the parchment over.*

Rydan blots the damp spot with the edge of his tunic, then hastily flips the piece of parchment over. There, right under his nose this whole time, is another list of names, but unlike the previous list, this one has a title. One that is dreadful enough to make him cringe.

HERESY.

Rydan knows immediately what this list contains. It's a list of households that practiced illusié, or old magick, and were deemed heretics. Traitors. Although the origin and extensive history of illusié remain largely a mystery, Rydan had heard enough over the years to know that every single person accused of practicing illusié was stoned to death. To his knowledge, this order had been fully carried out, leaving not a single heretic in the Kingdom of

Trendalath.

But it was always possible a household or two had been missed.

Rydan skims the crossed-out names, his index finger sliding down the page as he reads each one. His breath catches as he finally reaches the bottom of the second column. There's only one name on the entire list that isn't crossed out.

SOAMES.

CERYLIA JARETH

CERYLIA SITS ON her iron throne, fully alert, her dark brown eyes darting back and forth as guards rush from her side toward the main doors. As curious as she is to know what's going on outside those double doors, as well as on the outskirts of the Queendom of Sardoria, she maintains her usual air of indifference. From across the room, she can see that her most trusted advisor's eyes are narrowed, his shoulders tense, stance at the ready. Surprising for a man with only one good leg. "Delwynn!" she calls out to him with a hint of urgency in her voice.

Delwynn snaps his attention away from the doors. He grabs his white cedar staff from the pillar it's leaning against and begins to hobble over to her. It takes him a full minute to cover just half the distance, but when he finally arrives, he sinks into a low bow. "Your Greatness."

Cerylia's eyes flick to the doors. "Have you any idea what all the commotion is?"

Delwynn rises, then slowly makes his way up the steps to the throne. His staff clinks against the white marble floor with every step he takes.

Cerylia holds up her hand, knowing that if she has to hear one more clink of that staff, she'll end up berating one of her most loyal confidantes. "That's close enough."

Delwynn stops in his tracks, but leans forward as he lowers his voice. "It's another one of *them*, Your Greatness," he whispers. "And they're demanding that they speak with you."

Cerylia lets out a long sigh. She knows exactly what he's talking about. Another person claiming to be a long lost member of the Caldari. The Caldari were once the most powerful of all the illusié, or old magick folk. It was even said that some members of the illusié had magical influences greater than Mother Nature herself. The fact that yet another person desired to reveal themselves hardly came as a shock, especially after she'd announced to all of Sardoria a reward for doing so. The reward being residence in the Sardoria castle and an opportunity to become a member of the Queen's Guard.

Cerylia turns her attention back to Delwynn. "The one you speak of . . . is his behavior rash? Shall I retreat to the High Tower for the evening?"

Delwynn shakes his head. "No, Your Greatness. I wouldn't necessarily say *she's* behaving irately . . ."

Cerylia's ears perk up. "She?" *Interesting.* Thus far, only men had chosen to reveal themselves as members of the Caldari, although not much revealing had been done. She'd expected many frauds to surface, but the amount of swindlers she'd encountered as of late was truly astounding. Without another thought, Cerylia looks pointedly at Delwynn and says, "Bring her in."

Delwynn opens his mouth to protest, but closes it as the queen shifts her focus from him to the doors. With a slight shake of his head, Delwynn motions for the guards to let the girl in. Cerylia grips the edges of her iron throne as the doors open, her knuckles turning white. It's always a risk to agree to see an alleged Caldari due to their irate and unstable nature. But those could easily be rumors as well. The incentive is far greater than the risk. And so Cerylia waits.

Through the doors appears a teenage girl, no older than seventeen. She stands tall, at about 5'10", and her hair shines silver in the daylight. Stunning emerald green eyes set on a porcelain face meet Cerylia's dark brown ones. She's so stunning that the queen has to grip the armrests tighter in order to keep herself composed. It's difficult not to be completely captivated by this young girl's beauty.

The girl takes slow steps forward—confident, yet nonthreatening. Not a single guard accompanies her on her way to the throne. Clearly, they're just as mesmerized by the newcomer as the queen is. When the girl finally arrives at the bottom of the steps, she sinks into a low curtsy and nods her head. "My Queen."

Something bitter creeps up Cerylia's throat. Although the girl hasn't said anything wrong, Cerylia can almost pinpoint the malicious intent behind the greeting. She remains seated in her throne, back straight, eyes narrowed. Her white and gray robes seem dull in comparison to the girl's striking emerald green cloak, the same color as her eyes. The queen clears her throat as silently as possible, but before she can speak, Delwynn appears at her side, unannounced. "Please recite your name and tell Your Greatness what it is you seek."

The girl appears to be taken aback by Delwynn's sudden appearance, and also slightly confused that the queen hasn't spoken for herself. From the look on her face, Cerylia almost expects her to shift from one foot to the other, but the girl remains still, like a statue.

Her piercing green eyes land on the queen's. "My name is Opal Marston, a member of the Caldari," she says with unwavering certainty, "and I am here to be of service to Queen Cerylia Jareth of Sardoria." She bows her head for a moment before raising it to look at the queen again. A flicker of something darts across her eyes. Hopefulness, maybe?

Delwynn begins to speak, but Cerylia cuts him off mid-sentence. "There are many who have claimed to be members of the Caldari." She regards Opal with caution. "But they were frauds, willing to betray the trust of their queen, and sentenced to be exiled to the wastelands of Eroesa." Cerylia leans forward and folds her hands in her lap. She lowers her voice to just above a whisper. "With that being said, how would you like to proceed?"

Her words don't appear to rattle the girl. In fact, they only seem to make her *more* confident. She raises her chin with the utmost certainty and says, "I'm an inverter, Your Greatness."

Silence fills the room, the only audible sound is Cerylia's sharp inhale. *An inverter?* She reminds herself not to get her hopes up, especially after meeting the latest bunch of alleged Caldari.

Inverters, also known as time turners, had vanished centuries ago. Theirs was a powerful and dangerous gift, one that not only allowed for traveling back in time, but one that also held the capability of changing the events of the past. Only those in direct contact with an inverter would remember the time travel and the changed event; any other bystanders not in direct contact with the inverter would be just that—bystanders.

"Your claims are futile—"

"—unless I show you," Opal interrupts. "That's precisely why I'm here." She motions toward the steps with a graceful roll of her hand. "May I?"

Cerylia pauses for a moment. Does she really want to go through with this? Again? If the girl is a fraud, she'll have to face the humiliation of believing yet another one of *them.* She'd have to exile yet another person to Eroesa.

But if the girl is who she says she is . . .

"You may approach," Cerylia says without another thought. Delwynn turns to face her with wide eyes, but she ignores him.

A coy smile touches Opal's lips. "Yes, Your Greatness."

As she approaches, the queen catches a whiff of something familiar. Pine and ash. "Do you reside in Vaekith?"

Opal simply nods her head.

"How significant are your powers?"

Opal tilts her head to the side, eyes sparkling in the morning light. "I can travel back a decade."

Cerylia considers her for a moment. Secretly, she'd been hoping for a more powerful inverter, one that had the ability to travel back at least twenty years. But seeing this girl before her, and how young she is, gives Cerylia a newfound hope. The girl has potential. And with the right training and advisors residing in the castle of Sardoria, she'll have tripled her abilities in no time.

Cerylia's thoughts disseminate as Opal speaks. "If you'd like, I can show you."

The queen considers this for a moment, then extends her hand out in front of her, palm up. Opal steps forward and gently takes the queen's hand in hers. The focus in her eyes is unlike anything Cerylia has ever seen before. Opal's eyes begin to shift from emerald to a light gray, and Cerylia notices everything around them begin to shake. Images grow fuzzy, as if vibrating at the highest possibly frequency. A dark tide swells in Cerylia's stomach as her surroundings fade to black. She takes a deep breath and closes her eyes.

When she opens them, Opal is standing directly in front of her. She doesn't say a word, just moves to the side. Cerylia realizes they're standing at the top of the Vaekith Mountains, overlooking the Queendom of Sardoria, the Kingdom of Trendalath prior to Tymond's reign, Eroesa before it was a wasteland, Miraenia, Chialka, and way off in the distance, the Thering Forest, and Isle of Lonia. She can even see the tops of the trees that make up the dense Roviel Woods, their branches swaying to and fro in the breeze.

"The calm before the storm," Opal murmurs.

Cerylia turns to look at her with knowing eyes. "Before Tymond overthrew Trendalath . . ."

" . . . before he banished illusié and exiled all practicing members of the Caldari," she finishes.

A deep pang of sorrow hits Cerylia right in the chest. "Is that how you ended up here, in Vaekith?"

Opal gives a solemn nod. "But, to be frank, Your Greatness, I already like it better in Sardoria anyway." She flashes a smile at the queen, but it doesn't reach her eyes. "You truly are a great ruler, the best Sardoria has seen in a long while."

Cerylia is tempted to ask her how long, knowing that Opal has probably been around for decades, but she resists the urge. Instead, she asks, "Have you successfully changed any events in the past?"

Opal bows her head. "I wish I could say yes. But I can't go back far enough to change the things that really need changing. Not yet anyway." A sad smile touches her lips. "Perhaps one day."

In that moment, Cerylia knows exactly what she must do. "I've seen enough," she says, the words coming out much harsher than she'd intended.

Opal doesn't question the queen's sudden change in tone. She holds out her hand and the queen takes it. She closes her eyes, silently praying for her stomach not to turn as they travel back to the present. The ride back is much smoother, and when Cerylia opens her eyes, she's back in the castle, sitting on her throne with Delwynn standing right beside her.

Without hesitation, she stands. She looks Opal directly in the eye. "Opal Marston of the Caldari, welcome to your new home. Delwynn will take you to your living quarters and will provide you with your assessment and training schedule before daybreak." She glances at Delwynn, who looks as though he's about to protest. Cerylia smiles. "I look forward to seeing your progress over the next few weeks."

Opal's eyes remain trained on the queen. She doesn't smile. She doesn't move a muscle. Finally, she speaks. "Thank you, Your Greatness." She bows and with a swish of her cloak, strides toward the double doors. Delwynn takes off behind her, struggling to keep up.

Cerylia resumes her place on the throne. Excitement courses through her veins. The Caldari are here, in Sardoria, the door to their powers wide open.

And it's all hers for the taking.

ARDEN ELIRI

THE KINGDOM OF Trendalath slowly vanishes from sight as our ship sets sail. The waters are rough and my knuckles have gone numb from gripping the edge of the boat as we make our way out to sea. Rydan stands on the opposite side of the ship, strands of his once-smooth black hair flailing in the wind. He looks at me, and it takes everything in me not to laugh at how utterly ridiculous he looks.

The only other person on the ship is the captain. He doesn't appear to be much older than me, maybe in his early twenties. He stands a few inches taller than Rydan, but with a much stockier build and light brown hair with a hint of auburn. His eyes draw me in. Dark brown—so dark that his irises are engulfed in black. He's been looking at me since we set sail. Not a so much a steady gaze, but often enough where it's noticeable. Normally, I'd feel uncomfortable, but for some reason, I feel that it's okay for him to stare, like we've met before in a past life and he's trying to pinpoint where and how.

I catch him staring again, but instead of turning away to look out at the never-ending sea, I meet his gaze and decide to walk over and properly introduce myself. As I approach, I realize that he doesn't flinch or nervously shift his stance. In fact, he keeps his eyes trained on me the entire time.

I try to keep his unnervingly cool demeanor from getting to my head, but before I get the chance, he frees his right hand from the helm and extends it toward me. I pause mid-step and awkwardly receive the handshake. "I'm Arden," I manage to say as I steady my legs.

"You can call me Barlow." His voice is one that should belong to a man with many years under his belt, gruff and strong.

"It's nice to meet you," I say, quickly releasing my hand from his. He returns to his double-handed grip on the helm. The silence between us is deafening, but strangely enough, it doesn't feel awkward. In fact, it's surprisingly comfortable. "Have we met before?"

A small smile touches the corners of his lips. "I get

that a lot."

"It's just that . . ." I take in every feature of his face: the chiseled jaw, the elongated nose, the thin lips, but my eyes are instantly drawn back to those obsidian eyes. "Never mind."

"I can assure you we haven't met until now." His tone is filled with a sort of longing, something I can't quite place. Before I can ask another question, Rydan interrupts.

"It looks pretty hazy south of here. Isn't that the direction we're heading?" When he realizes he's interrupted our conversation, he blushes. "My apologies, I didn't realize you two were in the middle of something."

I nonchalantly wave my hand in the air. "Not to worry. Just introducing ourselves to one another." Truthfully, I'm irked by the interruption, but don't care to show it. "Rydan, this is our captain, Barlow." They nod at each other. "So what is this about a storm?"

Rydan shrugs. "Well, I'm not sure if it's a storm just yet, but it looks awfully dark a little ways south of here."

"I'll change course," Barlow says without hesitation. "We'll go east for a little and try to go around it. Hopefully miss it entirely."

I give Barlow a questioning look. "So you're saying it *is* a storm?"

The captain lets out a low chuckle. "Dark clouds hovering overhead always indicate rain, especially out on the open water. Chances are, we'll see a thunderstorm, although I'm not sure how severe it will be."

I don't mind storms, but I feel a flutter of panic in my chest. "How long is our voyage?"

Barlow gazes at the sky, as if it holds all the answers. "We should arrive by early morning. 0400 hours."

"Best we get some sleep then," Rydan chimes in.

"You can sleep in the mid-cabin, just below the helm." Barlow taps his foot on the deck of the ship to further his point. "I'll do my best to be quiet up here."

"Don't you need to sleep?" I ask. "Should we take shifts or something?"

Barlow turns his obsidian gaze to me. It's enough to give me chills. "I assure you, I'm well rested. I've completed many night voyages in my day." He winks at me. When I don't smile, he continues, "I'm used to it. I'll get you there safe and sound. I promise."

I still feel the urge to learn more about him, but Rydan nips that in the bud. "We appreciate it, good sir. Just holler if you need us." He throws his head in the direction of the stairwell, gesturing for me to go first.

Reluctantly, I oblige.

The mid-cabin is dank and smells of ale and rotting wood. I grab a nearby blanket from a barrel and throw it on one of the top bunks. Rydan follows quietly behind me. I can tell he wants to say something, albeit I have no idea what. We haven't talked since earlier that day when I'd brought up the Langley mission. What a mistake that had been.

I attempt to break the silence. "You tired?"

He shakes his head, but the bags underneath his eyes say otherwise.

"Yeah, I'm not either."

"We might as well try to get some shuteye," he murmurs. "We need to be at our best and fully alert for tomorrow."

I don't feel like arguing, so I just nod silently. I pull a nearby crate from across the room and use it to hop up onto the top bunk. "Well, goodnight then." The sheets are scratchy and the wool blanket is heavy, but it still feels nice to lie down.

He sighs. "Goodnight, Arden."

I close my eyes, but sleep eludes me. I keep picturing Barlow's eyes, going deeper and deeper into the blackness. There's no doubt we have some sort of connection. I felt it, and I could sense that he did, too. The creaking of the helm keeps me awake until it finally ceases and, eventually, my snores join Rydan's as the ship rocks back and forth in a steady rhythm with the waves.

RYDAN HELSTROM

WHEN RYDAN WAKES, he can't tell whether or not it actually stormed the night prior. The boat seems to be rocking less, almost as if they'd already arrived—as if Barlow had docked it. With no sense of time, Rydan swings his feet over the bottom bunk, careful to make as little noise as possible as he makes his way to the stairs. Overhead, he can hear Arden's light snoring.

He stops in his tracks and holds his breath as a mason jar appears out of nowhere and rolls across the floor. It lodges itself next to the crate Arden used to hop onto her bunk the night before. He stays still for a minute, cursing under his breath and praying she won't stir. When she doesn't move, he looses his breath and quietly tiptoes up the stairs to the main deck.

Dawn is breaking, a subdued canvas of yellow, blue, and orange, and Barlow is nowhere in sight, but Rydan finds that his assumption is correct in that the ship is indeed docked. "It must be 0400 hours," he murmurs to himself.

His stomach rumbles as he begins to search the ship for food, grunting irritably when he comes up empty-handed. Not willing to wait for Barlow to reappear, Rydan sneaks back down the stairs to the mid-cabin and throws on a pair of boots. He sweeps the room once more, checking the other bunks to see if Barlow perhaps decided to get some rest after all, but the beds are empty.

With Arden still fast asleep, Rydan hurries back up the steps to the main deck and walks over to the side of the ship. He places his hands on the sturdy wood and hops up to sit on the ledge, then swings his legs over. The dock is further away than it looks, but he braves it and pushes himself off the edge of the ship. With surprising ease, he lands on both feet. Feeling proud of himself, he fluffs the collar of his tunic and begins his walk toward the village of Lonia.

This early in the morning, Lonia is a complete ghost town, but the sights before him are absolutely breathtaking. Stone blocks with intricate carvings make up the majority of the residents and shops. The town is enclosed by a massive mountain and, at the very back, is the largest waterfall Rydan has ever laid eyes on. The water flows into separate canals that lead into the village along the stone pathways. Bridges crisscross up the mountain, and Rydan realizes that each bridge leads to a sort of enclosure. Temples, perhaps? Hundreds of them line the sides of the mountain, beckoning him to enter.

His curiosity dissipates as a low growl erupts from his stomach. The streets are completely empty except for a fresh fruit cart off in the distance. He squints, noticing a faint shadow standing behind the cart. Succumbing to the pangs in his stomach, he eagerly picks up the pace. When he finally reaches the cart, his eyes glaze over. Vibrant red, green, and yellow apples stare him in the face. They are separated by dividers, as are the bananas, oranges, and pears. So consumed by his need for food, Rydan doesn't even acknowledge the figure standing behind the cart, until he asks, "How much for a banana and an apple?"

"That depends on the color of the apple."

The voice stuns him, light and airy, a woman's. He snaps his gaze from the fruit to the source of the voice. The mystery woman is wearing a hood, her face entirely shadowed, but even still, it's hard to miss those glowing violet eyes. Never in his life has Rydan seen someone with such a captivating eye color. "Red," he says softly, sounding somewhat uncertain of his choice.

"One banana and one red apple," the woman says breathily as she picks each one from its section of the cart. "That will be six riyals."

Rydan nods his head and turns to the side as he sifts through his pocket. Different currencies of the many villages he's passed through over the years glide across his fingertips. Finally, he pulls out six amber-colored coins and places them on the cart. "Six riyals, per your request."

To his surprise, the woman brings her hands to the sides of her hood and slowly lowers it. Midnight-black hair, somehow darker than his, falls in long waves around her shoulders. The stark contrast of her eyes against her dark hair and skin makes the violet stand out even more. An innocent smile touches her full lips. "Your business is much appreciated."

Too stunned to speak, Rydan just nods his head again and gathers the food. He turns to walk away from her, but only walks a few steps before turning back around. His face falls as his eyes search the street. It's as if she's vanished into thin air. Gone. Like a ghost.

A shudder runs down his spine. Rydan blinks a few times, wondering if maybe he didn't get as much sleep as he'd originally thought. It's possible he'd just fabricated their meeting in his head. But if that were the case . . .

With purpose, he strides back over to the cart,

scanning the surface for the six riyals he'd used as payment. They're nowhere in sight. Before he can piece his thoughts together, a sharp whistle pierces his ears. He grimaces as he turns to look over his shoulder.

Barlow stands just a short distance away with an obvious smirk on his face. He walks toward Rydan, tossing a green apple in the air along the way. "Couldn't sleep?"

Rydan shrugs. "I'd ask you the same question."

Barlow gives him a knowing look as he takes a gigantic bite of his apple. The crunch of teeth into the apple's skin makes his stomach growl with hunger, and Rydan follows suit.

"I see you found breakfast," Barlow says between mouthfuls. "Come on. It's best we get back to the ship."

Rydan only nods as he takes a few more bites. It takes hardly any time for him to devour the fruit, and he hastily throws the apple core to the side of the road as he follows Barlow back to the dock. It occurs to him to ask the captain about the mystery woman with violet eyes. "Hey, did you happen to get your fruit from the same cart I was standing at?"

Barlow slows his pace, then turns around to look at him. "I believe so. Why?"

"The woman working at the cart . . ." His voice trails off as a dark look crosses over Barlow's face.

"The cart was unsupervised," Barlow says almost

a little too quickly.

Rydan gives him a questioning look. “Then how did you pay for your meal?”

“I left the riyals on top of the cart.”

His brash response leaves Rydan speechless. He’s tempted to ask *when* Barlow had gotten his meal, because the last he checked, there were no riyals sitting atop the cart, not even his own.

Before he can pry further, Barlow whirls away from him and marches onto the dock. “You should wake Arden,” he shouts from over his shoulder. “You two have a long day ahead of you.”

Not only is his dismissal insulting, it strikes a chord deep within Rydan. He turns to look back at the path from which they just came—back at the fruit cart. There is no shadowed figure standing behind it, nor is there a soul in the surrounding area. Could it really have just been his imagination, from lack of sleep? Or, could it be that there’s something Barlow isn’t telling him? Something he’s keeping secret?

His gut tells him it’s the latter. And, in that moment, Rydan decides he’ll do whatever it takes to find out exactly what that *something* is.

ARDEN ELIRI

I STIR FROM my slumber feeling awake, but not rejuvenated in the slightest. A haze drifts around my head, leaving me groggy and somewhat disoriented. From what, I don't know, but then I faintly recall that I'm on a ship. I never earned my sea legs, and it's proving to be a problem now, more so than in the past. Bile rises in my throat and I quickly slide down the bunk to the floor, racing to the nearest barrel I can find. I release my hand from my mouth as yesterday's breakfast surfaces. I instantly feel better. As I resume standing upright, a voice startles me.

"I didn't peg you as one to get seasick."

I turn toward Rydan and roll my eyes at him,

hoping that he can't see the red flush slowly creeping across my cheeks. "I'm fine."

He raises his eyebrows, then tosses me a banana. "Eat."

After tossing up yesterday's breakfast, food is the last thing I want, but the realization as to how famished I am hits me like a ton of bricks. I hungrily peel the banana and scarf it down, then throw the shell into the barrel. *How ladylike.* I flatten the wrinkles out of my tunic and trousers as I search the cabin for my boots. My eyes land on Rydan's feet.

"You're wearing my boots," I say, my voice flat.

Rydan narrows his eyes at me, then looks down at his feet. "I'm afraid you're mistaken, miss. These are my boots."

I give him a sideways look. "Do you really want to be caught assassinating someone in lady's footwear?" I tease him.

He scowls, then cocks his head toward the front end of the lower bunk. There, perched upright with the laces tied, are my boots. If I didn't know any better, I'd think they'd been polished—brand new—as if they hadn't trudged through crimson floors and muddy roads in the past.

In an attempt to avoid Rydan's gaze, and the all-knowing smirk that's surely on his face, I keep my eyes trained on the floor as I walk over to my shoes. I plop down on the lower bunk and pull one onto my left foot, then the right. When I look up, Rydan still has the same look on his face I was so desperately hoping to avoid. Another wave of embarrassment washes over me, and I can feel the heat returning to my cheeks. "All right, all right, you win," I say as I stand up and head toward the stairs.

His smirk transforms into a full-fledged smile as he rolls his hand and bows.

My embarrassment fades and all I can do is laugh. "Hey, do you happen to have any more fruit?"

A strange look crosses his face before he says, "No. But I know where we can find some."

He leads the way by climbing up the stairs. I follow him, almost running into his back when he suddenly comes to a halt on the main deck. I bring myself next to him to see what made him stop. Barlow stands just a few feet away from us, holding two red apples in one hand and a green one in the other. I notice Rydan eye him warily.

"You like red, right?" Barlow asks. His voice is almost taunting. I suddenly feel like I've missed something important.

Rydan clenches his jaw before responding. "I already ate. Give it to Arden."

I stare at the apples hungrily as Barlow shrugs and tosses them over to me one at a time. I catch them with ease. Barlow bites into his green apple, then turns on his heel and strides over to the helm. I extend the spare apple to Rydan. "I know you already ate," I start, "but you should take one anyway. You'll need your strength. We both will."

I can see the reluctance in his expression, but he knows I'm right and takes the fruit from my hand. I'm not sure what I missed earlier this morning, but I'm fairly certain I won't get any information out of Rydan anytime soon.

Barlow waves at us from the ship as we make our way down the dock to the village of Lonia. My chakrams are tucked safely at my sides in the holsters of my black Cruex uniform, and out of the corner of my eye, I can see Rydan's longsword strapped securely to his back, the edge gleaming in the morning light.

We're silent as we walk into the village, carrying not only our weapons, but also the tremendous weight of what we're about to do. It doesn't bother me as much as it seems to bother Rydan, who's continuously clicking his tongue against the roof of his mouth. Nervous habit.

"Barlow runs a tight ship, doesn't he?" I say in an attempt to break the silence.

Rydan grunts something barely audible.

Well, if that's how he's going to be, then fine. "I'm taking the lead on this one."

He stops walking and gives me a befuddled look. "Come again?"

"My name was called first. This should have been *my* mission. A *solo* mission," I emphasize. "So I'll lead."

Rydan shakes his head and lets out a small laugh. "Whether it was originally announced as a solo mission or not, it's now a duel mission *and* classified as a category eight." He furrows his brows at me. "We'll do it together."

I know that if I try to convince him otherwise, I'll never win. So instead, I slap on my best authentic smile and say, "I suppose you're right. Let's go." It fades immediately as I turn away from him and pick up my pace toward the Soames's household. I can feel his confusion trailing behind me, but I don't turn to acknowledge it.

I reach the bright red door first, the plain bronze knocker glinting in the rising sunlight. A dark cloud slowly comes into sight overhead, and I can see Rydan breathe a small sigh of relief. His preference is to complete his missions at night, for obvious reasons: not as easy to spot, and people are usually sleeping. In my honest opinion, it's the easy way out as an assassin. But after the Langley incident . . . well, I suppose I can understand where he's coming from.

I, on the other hand, couldn't care less about what time of day it is. If I have a job that needs to be done, then I'll get it done, day or night, rain or shine. The daylight does have its appeal, though: it's easier to see your targets and people are less on edge, less suspecting. Because who, in their right mind, would kill someone in broad daylight and risk getting caught?

Oh, right. I would.

I sneak around the side of the house with Rydan on my heels. A loud banging sounds from inside, and I quickly hold up my hand, motioning for Rydan to stop moving. He doesn't see it and bumps right into me. I lose my footing and fall into the side of the house. I exhale a quick sigh of relief as a canopy catches my fall, muffling the noise. I shoot him a menacing glare. Rydan extends his hand to me and helps me to my feet. "Sorry," he mumbles under his breath.

I don't say anything, but instead peek around the back of the house. A wooden ladder leans against the structure, so I motion to Rydan to follow me. He nods as we make our way across the back lawn, careful not to trip over the tools that are haphazardly strewn all over the place. Perhaps Mr. Soames is a blacksmith? Or maybe he's a tradesman of sorts? I can't be sure.

Rydan follows my lead as I climb the rungs. Once I reach the top and peek my head over the edge, a smile stretches across my face. Just as I'd suspected, the house contains a skylight, sitting half open, as if it's awaiting our arrival. I crawl across the top of the house and hurry over to the circular window, then press my ear against the opening. Shortly after, Rydan is crouched right next to me.

Voices echo from within the house. It sounds like

there are three people, but it's hard to tell. A woman speaks first, her voice soft and comforting. "You'll have no playtime, young man, until you finish your reading."

What sounds like a book falling onto a wooden surface sounds from downstairs. A young boy's voice responds, probably no older than seven or eight. "Yes, Nana. Reading first."

I jump as a brusque voice sounds from upstairs. "Radelle! Have you seen my brown trousers?"

The conversation continues for about ten minutes. Rydan and I sit on the rooftop in silence, ears pressed against the window, listening to every word. It sounds so normal, so *everyday*, that it's hard to imagine these seemingly common folk of Lonia committing a category eight crime—a crime worthy of death by the king's assassins. I look at Rydan and can tell he's thinking the exact same thing. But an order is an order, and so we must uphold King Tymond's wishes.

Rydan holds up three fingers and I nod to confirm. Three of them, two of us. It'll be one of the easier missions I've been assigned to. I lean over and pull a rope from out of the holster that's also holding Rydan's longsword, and deftly fashion it into a sailor's knot. I pull myself into a crouching position and make my way around the skylight, making sure the rope is wrapped tightly around the outer rim of the window. With a final tug, and full certainty it's secure, I pull out the chakram from my left holster. Rydan looks at me, and I give him a confident nod.

We're ready.

I begin my descent down the rope, stopping once I reach the rafters in the ceiling. I tiptoe across the beams until I have a solid bird's eye view of the kitchen. Spoons clank against bowls as the Soames family eats their breakfast. They look so peaceful, so happy. A flicker of doubt crosses my mind that maybe the king is wrong, but he wouldn't make such a grave mistake. I've learned that looks can be deceiving. This is the family responsible for a category eight crime. And so Rydan and I will do what has to be done.

Before I can process what's happening, Rydan suddenly slides down the rope, but he doesn't stop in time. He's much further down the rope, way past the rafters. I wave my hands in the hopes that I'll grab his attention, but it's no use. I hold my breath as he continues to slide down the rope, and just when I'm sure my face is about to turn blue, he lands in the living room just opposite the kitchen. Thankfully, there's a wall between the two, so the Soames family doesn't see him, and they mustn't have heard him either, seeing as their conversation carries on. I let out my breath and silently curse his antics as I creep back over to the rope, knowing that I have only one option.

To follow him.

RYDAN HELSTROM

RYDAN PRESSES HIMSELF against the wall that separates the Soames's living room from the kitchen as he surveys the area before him. Arden is nowhere in sight. A wave of panic flutters in his chest, but then the rope shifts and he looks up to see his partner snaking her way down to the floor. She lands quietly on her feet, a less-than-pleasant look on her face.

"I thought you came down before me," he says under his breath.

She rolls her eyes and points up to the ceiling. "The rafters, Rydan. Always hide and survey in the rafters first," she whispers before bopping him in the side of the head.

He's about to scold her when chairs scrape across the kitchen floor. Arden jumps at the sound and joins him against the wall, flattening herself like a pancake. Footsteps draw near. Rydan raises his arm to his right shoulder, his hand gripping the hilt of his longsword. He glances at Arden who is armed and ready with chakrams in both hands.

A blonde head of hair emerges first. The young boy. Rydan slowly releases his grip on the hilt as he hears Arden's breath catch. Her stance softens and he finds his own posture reflecting hers. The boy bounces through the living room, heading over to a window by the front door. Arden nudges Rydan, and he's not sure whether he should take it as *"Well, what are you waiting for?"* or something else. He glances at her again and shrugs, but her eyes tell all. Arden, the killing machine and rogue assassin, does not want to kill this little boy. And honestly, neither does he.

In that moment, Rydan's faith in King Tymond begins to waver. What could this little boy possibly have done to deserve death at such an innocent age? Surely he wasn't involved in the category eight crime. Impossible . . .

His thoughts scatter as the woman, Radelle, rushes into the room. "I thought I told you to stay away from the window." Her long black hair is speckled with gray and her petticoats are ratty and torn, but there's something different about her.

Something that's a little . . . off. If it weren't for her vibrant, youthful face, one would think she's much older than she appears.

The woman turns and spots Rydan, her mouth opening in shock, but, in just a few swift movements, Arden is across the room and behind the woman's back with her hand over her mouth. Radelle's shrieks are muffled as she struggles to get away from Arden, but she holds strong. The young boy scurries to the side of the room and hides underneath an end table, eyes wide, lips trembling in fear.

Rydan remains pressed against the wall as heavier footsteps make their way through the kitchen. "Radelle? Is everything all right? I thought I heard something—"

The moment he steps foot through the living room, Rydan also moves forward, longsword unsheathed and extended in front of the man's neck. The man halts in his tracks, eyes wide with both anger and fear as they shift over to Rydan. He's tall—gigantic, actually—and Rydan has to make a conscious effort to inhale and exhale normally.

"What is the meaning of this?" the man bellows.

It appears he wants to take another step forward, but Arden's voice stops him. It's cooler than ice. "I wouldn't do that if I were you." With the woman still tight in her grip, she flashes him the Cruex emblem on the sleeve of her uniform.

By the look on the man's face, he knows exactly who they are. His tone shifts. "Please, this is a mistake. You have the wrong house."

Rydan speaks up. "Are you Erle Soames?" He catches Arden's eye. She seems surprised that he knows their first names. "And is the woman across the room Radelle Soames?"

The man closes his eyes before opening them again. He remains still, unmoving.

With the sword still extended, Rydan steps in front of Erle. He leans into his stance, pressing the blade harder against the man's neck. "Answer me."

His eyes flick open, but they don't land on Rydan. Instead, they land on Radelle.

Arden has a chakram resting on the woman's cheek, the other at her side. She almost looks relaxed, but Rydan knows that in one deft movement, that woman would be lying on the ground, spurting blood.

Arden narrows her eyes at the man. She tightens her grip and brings the chakram closer to Radelle's ear. "Answer him."

The man breaks eye contact with Radelle and shifts his gaze to Arden. Slowly, he nods.

"Then we have the correct household," Rydan growls. "By order of King Darius Tymond of Trendalath, you are accused of committing a category eight crime and are hereby sentenced to death." In the background, the boy begins to cry and scream, but Rydan only raises his voice. "Do you have any last words for one another?"

Erle and Radelle look at each other, and it's in that moment that Rydan senses something strange. It's almost as if there is some sort of unspoken communication between them. Almost immediately, the energy in the house shifts from warm and inviting to something darker.

Much, much darker.

He wants to call out to Arden to run, but he stands firm, keeping his sword steady against the man's neck. What happens next is completely out of his control. The woman breaks free from Arden's grip and, with sheer force, throws her against the back wall. Indigo sparks ignite from her hands as she turns her ferocious gaze toward him. The realization hits Rydan like a punch to the stomach.

The Soames are illusié.

ARDEN ELIRI

THE JOLT IS enough to knock the wind out of me. I try to take a deep, steadying breath, but I end up coughing profusely instead. I turn my head, watching as specks of blood spray from my mouth onto the wooden floor. My vision goes in and out as black and white dots fill the space that is supposed to be the Soames's living room. For an older woman, Radelle's got some serious strength.

But then I see it. The indigo sparks flying from her fingertips. And they're pointed directly at Rydan.

I briefly wonder if perhaps I'm hallucinating. Maybe I hit my head much harder than I realized. Before I can rally another explanation, I see Rydan swing his longsword at Erle's neck. I cringe as the man's head goes flying across the room. The body falls lifelessly to the floor.

Normally, it would be me doing the dirty work, slashing limbs and twisting necks, but something feels wrong here. Very, *very* wrong.

Radelle screams in agony as Erle joins the deceased, and I watch, in and out of my haze, as Rydan dodges her line of deadly sparks. The boy is still curled up underneath the table, rocking back and forth with his head in between his knees. I have no idea what is going on or how things went awry so quickly, but I know I can't just lay here. I push myself up onto my hands as Radelle sends another blast of sparks toward Rydan, the room illuminating in a shade of cobalt.

I begin to process my thoughts as my mind comes back to reality. The Soames are illusié. Magick has been banished ever since King Tymond began his reign over Trendalath, but not once was it ever made clear that the use of magick was punishable by death, nor that the assassination would be completed by a member of the Cruex.

Bile rises in my throat as the truth rains down on me. How many people have I killed because of their status as illusié? How many people did I murder, simply for being born into a magickal bloodline? How hypocritical am I, especially after the strange things

I've recently discovered I'm capable of? My hands ball into fists as I look from the terrified boy to the ongoing battle between Radelle and Rydan. I have to do something. It's either her or him. Rydan is my partner, my friend. He's my family.

I stand and raise my hands, chakrams at the ready. I step back to fling one at Radelle, but something stops me. I try again to release my weapon, but my body feels stuck. Frozen. Everything's frozen except for my eyes. They shift to the little boy. He's staring at me.

I can't move.

I'll be damned, the child is illusié, too.

Rydan seems to notice my predicament and rushes toward Radelle with every ounce of strength he has left. He shoves her into the wall with the window, the glass shattering upon impact. Radelle screeches, but her eyes close shortly after, her head lolling to the side.

I try to move my legs, but it's no use. The boy is still staring at me when Rydan steps into his view. His concentration breaks, causing me to unfreeze and stumble backward, my arms flailing wildly in the air. I let out a strange flurry of sounds until I find my balance again.

The child scurries out from underneath the table, panting as he makes his way to the center of the living room. Rydan raises his blade. Before I have the chance to stop him, he brings the blade down. My eyes grow wide as the pommel is brought down onto the boy's head, knocking him out cold. I shudder as the child falls to the ground. Only when his chest rises and falls do I breathe a sigh of relief.

The boy is still alive.

I rush over to Rydan, looking over my shoulder to make sure Radelle is still unconscious. When she doesn't move, I forcefully grab him by the shoulder. "What the hell was that?" I hiss.

I can see the adrenaline leave his body, his face calming and returning to normal. He furrows his brows as he surveys the room. His eyes land on Erle's decapitated head. All he says is, "King's orders," as if what just happened was completely normal.

I can feel my rage building, boiling to the surface. "King Tymond was *wrong*. These people," I say as I gesture around the room, "didn't do anything wrong. They are innocent."

Rydan's eyes flick to me. The potency in his expression is enough to make me want to curl up and hide. "They're illusié, Arden."

I can't believe he's holding steadfast on this. Does he really feel this way? Does he actually agree with King Tymond's views? "They're innocent!" I exclaim. "They were eating breakfast!" Tears threaten to fall, although I'm not entirely sure why. I point to the boy. "He was going to read and then go out to play! He wasn't doing anything wrong!"

A soft groan escapes Radelle's lips. Rydan shifts his attention away from me and marches over to her.

"Rydan? Rydan, what are you doing?" I shout.

The woman puts her hand out with her palm facing up. "Just not the boy."

Rydan raises his sword overhead. I yell for him to stop, but by the time I make it over to him and grab his shoulders, it's too late. Radelle's head rolls onto the floor next to my feet. Her mouth is still open with one final unspoken plea.

I shove Rydan harder than I've ever shoved anyone. I press him against the wall and bring my chakram to his neck. "Is this what you want?" I scream. "Trying to prove that you're the tough guy, that you didn't need my help with the Langley mission?" My voice grows louder and I almost choke on my own words. I press the chakram harder into his neck. A drop of crimson rolls down the blade.

Rydan's eyes are wide, not with fear, but with confusion. He doesn't wince as the blade begins to slice into his skin. "Arden." Somehow, his voice is soothing and calm, but not enough to get me to back down.

I am livid.

"Arden, we don't get to *feel* things. We are assassins, members of the Cruex." He scoffs, then rolls his eyes. "I swear, what is going on with you lately? It's like you're a completely different person."

I inadvertently lower my weapon as his words sink

in. I know he's right. I don't know how to explain it, but our mission—*this* mission—feels wrong. Twisted in some way.

"Come on," he urges. "We're not done yet."

I quickly learn what he means as he stalks over to the young boy who's still lying unconscious on the floor. A pool of blood seeps from his head. "No," I whisper under my breath. My eyes scour the room for something heavy. A metal lantern on the end table catches my eye. I grab it and rush toward Rydan. With one giant swing, I hit him on the back of the head. He jolts forward from the impact, the lantern dropping to the floor at the same time his body does.

Without thinking, I rush over to the boy and carefully lift his head off the ground and into my lap. I comb through his hair to try to find the wound, to see just how deep it is. It doesn't look too bad, but then again I'm no doctor. I place my hands on the boy's chest and close my eyes. I sit there for a few moments, feeding off the silence in the room. I try not to think about the look on Erle's face as he met his end. I try not to think about Radelle's last shrieks of panic. I try not to think about their decapitated heads lying at opposite sides of the room. I just focus, allowing the quiet and stillness to wash over me.

I open my eyes. And gasp.

Shining from my own two palms is a sort of white light. It hovers over the boy's chest and as I move my hands to his head wound, I notice his eyes begin to flutter.

Holy lords, I'm illusié.

The boy awakens, his expression eerily calm. I was expecting him to be frightened and eager to harm me, but he just stares at me with glimmering golden eyes.

He looks down at his chest, noticing the aura emanating from my hands. "You're a healer," he says. His voice catches me off-guard. It sounds much older, wiser, than it did earlier.

"I wasn't sure illusié still existed. I can't believe I *am* one," I say more to myself than to him.

"You're more powerful than you think," the boy responds. "There are more out there like us. Many more." He has an all-knowing smile on his face that reminds me of Rydan's usual demeanor. I glance over my shoulder at my partner's unmoving body and sigh; but when I turn back around to ask the boy a question, he's gone.

Panicked, I look back and forth across the room, but he's nowhere in sight. My heart thumps in my chest as unsettling thoughts run through my mind. He saw everything, knows everything that happened here today. What if he tells someone? Who would he choose to tell? Who *is* he? I don't even know his first name. I look over again at Rydan. He would know the boy's name, but I'm not willing to wake the beast any time soon.

I pick myself up off the floor and dust the debris from my pants. It's a good thing the Cruex uniforms are black—I'm sure there's blood splattered on every inch of my clothes. And, for the first time, I realize I had nothing to do with it.

I sheathe my chakrams, then walk over to where Rydan lay facedown on the ground. I kick his shoe with the toe of my boot, but he doesn't flinch. A multitude of thoughts whirl through my head, but only one undeniable truth repeats itself over and over again.

I can't go back.

The more I repeat it, the more staggering it becomes.

I can't go back.

I gaze down at Rydan, then look at the decapitated heads of Radelle and Erle.

Lords help me.

Without another thought, I hurry into the kitchen, throwing cupboards open and searching every inch of the space. Finally, I spot an oversized sack labeled *GRAINS*. It's empty.

Perfect.

I take the sack and rush back into the living room. With a deep inhale, I look down at my feet, Erle's wide eyes staring up at me. I grab the decapitated head by the wisps of gray hair, or what's left of it anyway, and throw it into the sack. It lands at the bottom with a sickening thud. I walk around Rydan's body to the opposite side of the room and repeat the process with Radelle's head. I twist the top of the sack until it closes, then secure it with a nearby clothespin.

I pause at the front door and take one last glance at Rydan. A pang of guilt hits me as my eyes land on his body. I can see that his chest is slowly rising and falling, so I know he's still alive, just knocked out.

I can't go back.

With the sack thrown over my shoulder, I turn the doorknob and step outside into the warm sun. The door slams shut behind me. And that's that. My decision is made.

Where I'm headed, I have not a clue. I'm not sure what awaits Rydan when he wakes up and returns to Trendalath without evidence of the Soames's death. There is one thing, however, that I *do* know.

I won't be there for any of it.

RYDAN HELSTROM

RYDAN SITS IN the middle of the Soames's living room, trying to recall the events from earlier that day, but his pounding head makes it difficult. He lays back down on the floor and stares up at the ceiling. A piece of fabric hangs from one of the rafters, fluttering in the breeze. He watches it for a few minutes, swaying back and forth, back and forth when . . .

He remembers.

He shoots up into a sitting position as the events of the morning become clear. Barlow. The ship. Their mission. Arden's face as he swung his sword. Radelle and her . . . magick.

Illusié.

Rydan surveys the room, looking for any sign of Arden, but she's not there. Neither is the boy. The Soames's bodies lay lifeless and unmoving. Erle's sideways on the ground and Radelle's slouched against the broken window. Their decapitated heads . . . they're missing.

His hands curl into fists and he brings himself upright, feeling woozy as he straightens his legs. His knuckles are bruised and bleeding and the left side of his head is throbbing uncontrollably. He winces as he touches the open wound on the back of his skull. His eyes travel down to his feet, on an iron lantern scattered just a few inches away. It doesn't take long to put the pieces together.

Arden.

He kicks the lantern across the room and lets out an angry scream. He walks over to Radelle's headless body and rips a swatch of fabric from her ratty petticoats. He swipes his longsword from the floor and spits on the rag, cleaning the now-dried blood from the blade with a quick slide of his hand. He sheathes the longsword and straightens his shoulders, his eyes dead-set on the front door.

Arden couldn't have gone far. Rydan vows that he *will* find her and return the Soames's heads to Trendalath, no matter how long it takes.

DARIUS TYMOND

"THEY SHOULD BE back by now." Darius paces back and forth across the Great Room, his strides growing more rushed with each step. Aldreda sits on the throne adjacent to his, tapping her fingers impatiently with each breath the king takes. The look on her face is enough to make the autumn leaves shrivel up and wither away.

"Just because they haven't returned doesn't necessarily mean something's gone awry."

Aldreda always seems to be the voice of reason, but he won't allow it. Not today. He gestures toward one of the castle windows. "I should have at least heard something by now. They should have returned this afternoon." An orange glow lights the room as the sun continues its descent behind the hillside. "It's nearly nightfall and still no word. How does one explain that?"

Aldreda just sits there in silence, her lips pursed.

The king runs a swift hand through his salt-and-pepper hair. "Well?"

Aldreda slowly rises from her seat and makes her way down the marble steps. Her white-blonde hair sways gently with the movement and seems to billow in an invisible breeze. Her cobalt eyes stay locked on his until she reaches the final step. She gently places her hand on his forearm and gives it a light squeeze. Like a gentleman, he leads her down the last step.

His wife turns to face him, bringing both of her hands to his cheeks. "When was your last meal, My King?"

Darius has to think back. It *had* been a while, probably since breakfast, or possibly even dinner the night before. He starts to respond, but Aldreda's knowing smile stops him. She already knows the answer.

Of course she does.

"If you would follow me," she purrs, "a feast awaits."

He doesn't have much of a choice, seeing as she's already leading him toward the doors of the Great Room, but her chipper tone catches him by surprise, especially after witnessing the harsh expression she held through his mini tirade. "What's the occasion?" he asks as the double doors swing shut behind them.

A spark of excitement flashes across her eyes. "You don't recall?"

For a brief moment, all he can think about is how he's probably forgotten something important. He swiftly counts through the months in his head. His panic subsides knowing that it's not their anniversary he's forgotten, so what event is she speaking of?

A coy smile tugs at her lips. "A decade ago, you strode into Trendalath with due force and declared your reign over this kingdom, banishing all illusié from this land."

Ah, yes. Darius smiles at the memory, although it's hard to believe ten years have passed. Even more surprising that he hadn't remembered it until just now, seeing as it is, by far, his greatest accomplishment. "A historic day," he says with a nod.

They continue their walk down the hall leading to the banquet room. It's quiet—almost too quiet—but knowing his wife, she's got something up her sleeve. The doors swing open as they approach. Atop the long banquet table are platters upon platters filled with savory meats, cheese, bread, and fruit. The servants scurry around the room, hurriedly placing gigantic carafes of wine around the table. A fire crackles in the corner and violet embers simmer below the burning wood. The scent of pine and rosemary fills the room.

Paired with the meal, it's enough to make his mouth water.

One of the servants bows and leads them to their seats. He pulls out a seat for the queen and she takes it graciously, then fluffs her napkin onto her lap. Another servant appears from the shadows and pulls Darius's chair out for him. The king takes his seat, noticing that there aren't any other guests in the room. Usually when Aldreda plans a feast, the entire castle is invited, but tonight is different.

A lone candle burns between them. Aldreda motions for the servants to leave. They scatter like wind-blown leaves, and Darius finds himself alone with his wife. The silence goes on for a few minutes, his comfort level diminishing with each passing second. He clears his throat out of discomfort, then reaches for a carafe of wine and leans over the table to pour them both a glass. "I must say, this is unexpected."

Aldreda chuckles under her breath. "It's a great accomplishment you've sustained for years and years. A decade is something to be celebrated." She raises her glass with a twinkle in her eye. "To you, My King. And to this glorious kingdom we both can call home."

He finishes pouring himself a glass, then raises his cup, the red liquid sloshing with the movement. "And to you, My Queen, for sticking by me, for better or for worse." A lump catches in his throat as a memory surfaces, but he takes a deep breath and pushes it back down where it belongs.

Aldreda seems to notice his distress. “Cheers,” she says. She brings the glass to her lips but doesn’t drink, her eyes trained on the king the entire time.

He follows suit, taking a much larger gulp than intended. Just as he’s about to call for the servants, Aldreda stops him. Her voice comes out just above a whisper. “You were thinking of him, weren’t you?”

He sighs. Damn her for always knowing. Hiding anything from her is useless, seeing as her ability to sense things is uncanny. He’s not sure why he still tries to keep things to himself. Any sense of privacy he once had was lost years ago.

When he’s certain his voice won’t crack, he replies, “It’s hard not to.”

Aldreda runs her finger along the outside of the goblet. “I know you prefer not to discuss it, but I am open to it,” then hurriedly adds, “but only if you want to.”

“What is there to say?”

“I don’t know. My point is we’ve never talked about it.”

Her accusation and curt tone get the better of him. “Our only son ran away and we’ve never been able to find him,” he spits out. Hearing the words out loud sounds so foreign that he can’t help but slam his hands on the table.

Aldreda catches her wine glass right as it’s about

to tip over.

"I think about this, all of this," he exclaims with a wide sweep of his arm, "all the sleepless nights and men we've lost over the years in battle. How we have no one to continue the Tymond reign." His breath catches. "It makes me wonder if any of this was worth it, or if it was just a waste of time. It's beginning to feel like the latter."

"Darius, stop," Aldreda scolds. "You cannot possibly think that." If he didn't know better, he could have sworn her eyes were glimmering with fresh tears. But not Aldreda. Not the ice queen. "Braxton will return to us one day. I'm certain of it."

"How dare you speak his name!" He rises from his chair and slams his hands onto the table. The dishes clink and shake, but Aldreda doesn't move. She holds her stone-still gaze. Then, in an even tone, she says, "He is my son and I will speak his name as I please. I am his mother and I will hope for his safe and timely return, as any mother would."

Darius narrows his eyes. "He made his choice seven years ago to leave this family and strip himself of the royal name," he growls. "You've lost your mind if you think I'd ever let him return."

Aldreda purses her lips. "Well, if that's the way you feel about our only son, then perhaps I should end this right here, right now." She rises from her chair and claps her hands twice, a signal to the guards.

Darius lowers his gaze as the guards appear from

the shadows. They surround the table ten-fold.

"Aldreda, be reasonable. You know I would never hurt you."

"It's not me I'm worried about."

Darius raises his head and looks her right in the eye as it becomes clear.

Her hands move from the table to her lower abdomen. "I'm pregnant."

ARDEN ELIRI

IT'S DIFFICULT TO say exactly what time it is, but the sun overhead indicates that I've slept longer than expected, which I suppose is a good thing after yesterday's events. I silently curse myself for not bringing my pocket watch with me, even though I never bring it on Cruex assignments. Call me sentimental, but it'd tear me up inside if anything ever happened to it.

I pick myself up off the forest floor, brushing the dirt and dried leaves from my uniform. A film of dust lingers, but I ignore it, checking to make sure my chakrams are still secured in their holsters. I spot some thorny brambles in the distance. I squint my eyes, trying to make out the color and the shape of the fruit. When I realize what it is, I grin.

A blueberry bush. My favorite.

I grab the sack containing the Soames's heads and jog over to the bush, picking as many blueberries as will fit in my palm. I know I should save some for later (who knows how long I'll be out here), but I find myself devouring them by the handful. They're perfectly ripe—not too tart, not too sweet.

When my stomach starts to feel on the verge of being full, I slow down and rip a small square of fabric from the sash on my uniform. I pick another handful of berries and place them inside the square and wrap it up, then tuck it safely into the outer pocket on my sleeve.

That'll probably be lunch. Possibly even dinner.

I gaze overhead through the canopy of tree branches at the blindingly white sun. Luckily, the seasons have just begun to shift, so the heat isn't overbearing. I lick my lips, realizing that both my mouth and throat are drier than usual, and immediately begin my quest for a fresh water source. I try to discern animal tracks in the fallen leaves and look for wet spots along the ground, hoping that one of the two will lead me to a river or a stream.

After an hour of searching, and probably walking in circles, it dawns on me that I am parched to the point where I'm beginning to hallucinate. Passing out due to lack of hydration is a real possibility. Before I can fully register what's happening, my legs go numb and I stumble into a nearby tree. I slide down the trunk and my legs splay out in front of me, the sack falling from my fingertips. My breathing grows ragged as black dots fill my vision. I close my eyes, swaying in and out of consciousness. I try to hold on for as long as I can, but my efforts are futile. It only takes a few seconds for the darkness to swoop in and take me.

I'm not sure how long I've been out for, but when I open my eyes, the first thing I notice is a shadow lurking in the distance. Although groggy from my unconscious spell, I suddenly feel alert and concerned for my own safety. I lift my back from the tree and force my eyes to stay open, but every inch of my being aches and throbs, most noticeably my head. With a groan, I lean back into the trunk, feeling ashamed of my weakened state.

The figure grows closer. My vision still isn't back to normal, but I can tell it's a woman. And, if my eyes aren't deceiving me, a seemingly beautiful woman.

I take a few deep breaths, filling my lungs with as much fresh air as I can manage, hoping that maybe my vision will clear for just a few minutes and allow me to focus, to concentrate. It seems to work, if only briefly, and I'm not sure if I'm imagining the sound of sloshing water as the woman draws nearer.

"I'm not going to hurt you," a silky voice calls out. The woman puts her hands in the air with her palms facing me. A surrendering motion.

I try to pull my back away from the tree again, to sit upright, but it's no use. I'm too famished and too weak to do anything besides sit here like a rotting log. I have no choice but to let her approach.

When the woman finally reaches me, she kneels so that her eyes are level with mine. A slosh of water sounds again and my throat silently screams as she pulls something from behind her back.

A canteen.

Before she can even offer it to me, I grab the life source, guzzling every last drop of refreshing clear liquid. I pant, thirsty for more, as I lower the canteen, then smile sheepishly and hand it back to her. She smiles back. It's genuine and warm.

"Thank you," I manage to say. My throat is still dry and scratchy, but I can already feel a huge difference in my focus.

"How did you end up here in the Thering Forest?" Her tone isn't accusatory—how can it be when it sounds as smooth as aged wine being poured for the very first time? With the effortless way her words roll off her tongue, I'd almost assume that she's an escort for the royal court, but the way she carries herself is different than those girls. Poised and powerful with a silent confidence.

Suddenly feeling insecure in my own skin, I try to straighten my posture. I make it halfway when she tisks and gently presses my shoulders back against the tree. “Don’t exert any more energy than you need to, Arden.”

My breath catches and I force myself to mask my surprise as I look her square in the eyes—eyes that are the most vibrant hue of violet I’ve ever seen. *Stunning.*

She smiles, and I find myself wholly entranced by her beauty. Her mocha skin, silky obsidian hair, and again, those violet eyes. Perhaps she *is* an escort after all.

I silently scold myself for losing focus. *How does she know my name?*

As if she can read my mind, she says, “There’s no need to be concerned. I’m Estelle Chatham.” Her lilac eyes glimmer in the afternoon light. “I must say I’m surprised we’re meeting this way. Frankly, it’s not what I expected at all.”

I let out a laugh that sounds slightly more crazed than I’d intended. This is definitely a hallucination. That, or she’s an angel who’s been summoned to bring me to the afterlife. Neither sounds half bad given my current state. Anything to take my mind off the hunger, thirst, and pain I’m in is a welcome distraction.

“How do you know my name?”

Her mouth twitches as she begins to say

something, then thinks better of it. She pulls something from the inner pocket of her cloak and holds it out in front of me. I blink a few times to make sure I'm actually seeing what she's holding.

It's a pocket watch, exactly like the one I own.

"Where did you get that?" I ask. My heart picks up speed and I begin to feel lightheaded again.

The pocket watch dangles from her fingertips, spinning round and round in a clockwise motion. "Let's just say we're alike in more ways than one."

I open my mouth to ask what she means when I notice a small creature creeping up behind her. "Look out!"

Estelle turns, her obsidian hair whipping wildly behind her. She jumps to her feet, looking out into the forest then up at the canopy of trees.

"Not up there, by your feet!" I yell.

Estelle looks down at her feet as a ball of black and white fur approaches her. I cringe, thinking it's probably a skunk that's about to spray its goodness all over us (thanks to my loud ass), but instead I hear Estelle laugh then coo. "Juniper, there you are. Come here, girl."

I lean my body to the side so I can see around her. I can hardly believe my eyes. It's not a skunk. It's a fox.

The woman has a pet *fox*?

Juniper passes right by Estelle. I freeze as I realize

she's headed straight for me at an alarming speed. "Estelle . . ." My voice trails off as the animal grows closer. I bring my arms into my chest and close my eyes, but nothing happens. My lap grows warm and when I open my eyes, I look down to see Juniper curling into a ball right atop my thighs. I gaze at Estelle in amazement, but she just shrugs as if she's seen this a million times before.

"She's taken an immediate liking to you," Estelle says.

"She's beautiful." The fox stays still, more than comfortable in a stranger's lap.

Out of nowhere, Estelle says, "She's yours. Consider her a welcome gift. I can never keep track of her anyway." She swiftly returns the watch to the inner pocket in her cloak. "I'm a terrible pet owner."

I look down at Juniper just as her bright blue eyes gaze up into mine. I release my arms from my chest and gently graze her fur coat, fascinated by the black and white marble design.

"She's a marble fox," Estelle clarifies. She joins me on the ground and pulls some berries from another pocket within her cloak. Juniper gobbles them up as if she hasn't eaten in days.

"Where did you find her?" I ask.

"One day I was walking through the woods and she sort of just appeared," Estelle says as she takes her free hand and scratches behind Juniper's ears. "She started following me around day after day and never left."

I continue to stroke the glossy coat as the little fox finishes her meal. "Why Juniper?"

Estelle grins, pulling another handful of fruit from her cloak. "Juniper berries. I can't get her to eat anything else."

"I've never heard of those before." I take one of the berries from her outstretched palm to examine it. "Are they any good?"

Estelle shrugs. "They taste like a cross between blueberries and raspberries."

"Well count me in," I say as I pop the berry into my mouth. "Blueberries are my favorite."

Estelle doesn't respond. Instead she just looks at Juniper, then pulls her pocket watch out again to check the time. The look on her face says she needs to leave and, although I can't place my finger on why, I don't want her to go just yet.

"That reminds me," I start, "before Juniper showed up, you said that we're alike in more ways than one. What did you mean by that?"

"I meant that I'm illusié, as are you." She says this so nonchalantly that one would think we're chatting about something as diminutive as the flavor of tea over Sunday brunch.

"How did you know . . . ?" My voice trails off, not wanting to give too much away, but apparently Estelle knows everything there is to know about me. The thought alone is frightening. My chest constricts and I suddenly feel as though I can't breathe.

Estelle senses my discomfort immediately. "Breathe in and out, Arden," she soothes. "One, two. One, two."

I nod as I do what she says, but my breathing only gets sharper. My lungs feel as though they're on fire, the flames growing and rising with each inhale.

"You know, you can actually heal yourself, seeing as that *is* your power and all."

I look at her with wide eyes as the young boy's words from yesterday echo in my head. *You're a healer.*

With Juniper still sitting comfortably in my lap, Estelle takes both of my hands and places them palm-down on my chest. "Focus," she instructs. "Like you did yesterday."

If I want to focus, I'll have to ignore the fact that she has some sixth sense and seems to know everything about me. How, I don't know, but that's a question for another time—a time when my lungs *don't* feel like they're about to explode.

"Focus," she repeats, keeping her hands pressed against mine.

I close my eyes, trying to channel the same energy as yesterday with the Soames boy, but whatever I seem to be reaching for isn't there. It's like reaching into a dark abyss, a void where nothing exists. My eyes shoot open. "There's nothing there," I manage. It hurts to speak, to breathe. To just *be*.

"Look at me," Estelle says. "You can do this. You will be fine. Now focus."

I let myself fall into her gaze, into those deep violet irises, the beating in my chest growing as she continues to press. Deep within her gaze I find something, albeit I'm not sure what exactly. My fingers begin to pulse with energy. An electrifying shock sparks from my fingertips as an overwhelming and unexplainable sadness washes over me. I don't dare to look down at the glow emanating from my hands.

"Breathe," Estelle soothes. "Breathe and focus."

I close my eyes and do as she says. After a minute, my breathing slows, my chest loosens, and my body relaxes. I feel her hands release from mine and the pounding in my chest vanishes. *Finally.*

A rustle in the brush distracts me from my calmed state. My eyes fly open. Juniper hops off of my lap as I immediately shift from a sitting position to a crouch. I scan the area before me, quickly realizing that Estelle is nowhere in sight. Perhaps the rustling came from her, although it seems unlikely she could get over there so quickly. "Estelle," I hiss. "Where are you?"

I jump as a figure suddenly appears right next to me. I fall back on my heels, almost losing my balance completely. She grabs my arm and steadies me, bringing me back to my crouch. Just as an obscenity is about to fly from my mouth, she brings her index finger to her lips, her grip still tight on my arm.

Four men on horses reveal themselves from the brush, swords at the ready. My eyes are immediately drawn to their black and red armbands. I wouldn't miss the Tymond House symbol if it hit me between the eyes. Apparently, Estelle also knows who they are and where they're from. She mumbles something under her breath that sounds like "traitors", but I can't be sure.

My foot twitches as I attempt to move backward and hide behind the tree, but Estelle squeezes my arm with tremendous force. I grimace in pain and stay put. "We need to hide," I urge. But she just shakes her head and puts her finger to her lips again to silence me.

I try not to panic, but the guards are closing in. Surely they've seen us by now; we're out in the open, clear as day crouching by this darned tree. One of the guards dismounts his horse and walks directly toward us. The leaves on the ground crunch mercilessly beneath his feet. I stifle a breath as his steel boots land just an inch from my own. I lean back against the tree, confused as to why he hasn't motioned to the other soldiers to come over and take us hostage. Or kill us.

Knowing King Tymond, it'd probably be the latter.

"Here!" one of the other guards shouts. "There are tracks in the leaves."

The guard standing in front of me looks right at

me. My eyes widen as my breathing stops. Surely we've been caught. But then he averts his gaze and turns away from me—from us—and rushes back over to the group of guards. He nods at his fellow comrade as he mounts his horse. "We have a lead. This way!" he shouts, and before I can even register what's happening, they take off. The sound of hooves becomes quieter and quieter until it's so silent that no one would ever guess they were here in the first place.

Estelle finally releases her death grip on my arm and it's in that moment I understand exactly what just happened. "You shielded us so they couldn't see us. Your power . . ."

Estelle grins. "I'm a Cloaker. I have the ability to cloak myself as well as those I touch, making us invisible to the human eye."

"Cloaker." The word feels odd on my tongue.

Estelle nods, then puts her fingers in her mouth and whistles. Juniper comes flying out of a nearby bush and lands back in my lap, just like before.

"I suppose I should thank you," I say, feeling weirdly at ease now that Juniper is back in my lap, "for showing me that I can heal myself and for cloaking us from those guards."

Estelle jumps to her feet and fluffs her cloak. "You're welcome."

I gently pick Juniper up and place her next to me as I stand. Although I still feel weak, I'm in a much better position than I was an hour ago. "Well, it was nice meeting you," I say. I look to my left and locate the bag containing the Soames's heads. I can feel Estelle's eyes on me as I pick it up, then begin to retreat further into the Thering Forest.

"Where do you think you're going?"

Her voice stops me. I turn around to look at her. "To find a cliffside and dump this bag. And then . . ." I shrug, not knowing what to say next.

Estelle takes a few steps in my direction. "I know of a cliffside. I'll take you there." Her eyes flick to mine as she passes me, grabbing the sack along the way.

"Hey!" I shout, but it's too late. She's already opened it.

I'm almost sure she's going to turn around and berate me, to tell me how disgusting it is for a person to kill and then carry around the heads as a trophy. But instead, she does the *last* thing I'd ever expect.

She *laughs.*

"Come on," she says, swinging the bag so that it barely misses the ground. "I have a feeling you're going to fit in just fine."

RYDAN HELSTROM

A PEBBLE SHOOTS through the air as it leaves the toe of Rydan's boot and lands just a few feet in front of him. He approaches the pebble again and kicks it harder this time. A sharp pain shoots from his foot to his knee, and he curses under his breath as he hops on one leg, squeezing the toe of his boot to make the stinging go away. The pain subsides and he continues to hobble along the cobblestone path leading into the town of Lonia.

Yesterday, he'd searched for hours trying to find Arden, well into the evening, as well as all day today. He assumed Barlow would be worried, but boy was that assumption wrong.

Rydan narrows his eyes as he makes his way down the road to the docks. He scans the area before him, quickly realizing that the ship they'd arrived on is gone. Barlow left without them. Correction: without *him.*

Bastard.

Bringing himself to the edge of one of the piers, he plops down onto the uneven wood planks. He hastily pulls both of his boots off, tossing them carelessly to the side. Tiny fish swarm the area as he dips his feet into the water. He gazes out at the clear blue sky and emerald green sea. The combination of the two immediately reminds him of Arden and her piercing green eyes.

He shakes the image from his mind, feeling momentarily foolish for trusting in someone like Arden. The girl was damaged beyond repair before he'd ever even met her. He'd known it, too. And yet, he'd still befriended her, still trusted her, when no one else in the Cruex would. Perhaps *they* were the smart ones after all.

Rydan slowly lowers himself onto his elbows and leans all the way back so that his body is perfectly horizontal, except for his legs. Rays of sunlight shine through every inch of his body. The heat is so intense that he has to shield his eyes with his arm. But with the sun on his face and his feet in the water, it's the most at ease he's felt in years.

His thoughts turn as Tymond's voice invites itself

into his head. *You'll assassinate the Soames. And as proof, you'll bring me their heads.*

He can't go back to Trendalath, not after everything that had happened here. There's every possibility he'd be exiled from the Cruex, and it's even more likely that a worse punishment awaits him. But where to go? He's miles away from Trendalath, miles away from the northern lands. Besides the Thering Forest, Lonia appears to be his best option. But how could he expect to assimilate into their society when he's a trained killer? His track record isn't even close to flawless, and the townspeople would probably hang him before he'd even found a place to live and settle in.

Quite the predicament.

As Rydan weighs his seemingly limited options, he notices from behind closed eyelids that the sun is not nearly as bright as it was before. In fact, it seems as though a dark cloud has rolled over it, or perhaps it's disappeared altogether. But then the sound of metal clinks, and his eyes shoot open. Standing over him is a burly Trendalath soldier, and by the sound of multiple swords being drawn, he's not alone.

"Rydan Helstrom?" the soldier asks, his tone gruff.

Rydan gulps, but doesn't respond. This could either end very badly for him or . . . well, very badly. Options don't seem to be on his side these days.

"Answer me and you will be spared," the soldier says. "Are you Rydan Helstrom?"

He closes his eyes as he nods his head. "Yes."

"And your partner?"

They want to know about Arden. Rydan stays silent, trying as fast as he can to formulate a believable story, but the words won't come.

The soldier kicks him in his side. He lets out a small yelp. "Where is Arden Eliri?" he roars.

Rydan slowly brings himself upright, clutching his pulsating ribs. He looks up at the soldier and motions for him to come closer. As he lowers, Rydan grabs him by the collar of his uniform and pulls him in. "She's dead," he snarls as his fist collides with the man's temple.

"Arden Eliri is dead."

CERYLIA JARETH

CERYLIA APPROACHES THE door to Opal's chambers. A breeze makes its way through the hall, sending a shiver down her spine as she raises her hand to knock. Cerylia stares at her hand, fingers curled into a fist, then lowers it. It's late, well into the evening. Surely after a few long and gruesome days of training, Opal is sound asleep. With a shake of her head, she turns away from the door and retreats down the hall.

If Delwynn had been more thorough when it came to explaining Opal's progress, the queen wouldn't be roaming the corridors at all hours of the night. Nope, just a few updates every here and there, with little to no detail regarding the progression of her current powers or development of any new ones. Sometimes it felt like he simply "forgot" to give her an update at all. Unacceptable. "I'll have to demote him and find Opal a new trainer," Cerylia mumbles to herself.

Just as she's about to turn the corner back to her quarters, a door creaks open. She whirls around just as Opal's head pokes through a narrow crack, her silver hair gleaming in the moonlight. Her eyes look darker in the dim lighting—a forest green as opposed to emerald—and her pupils are large enough to swallow most of the hue.

"Your Greatness?" she asks as she rubs one of her eyes. "Have I missed something? Do you require my assistance?" There is urgency in her voice, although she's fighting a yawn as she speaks.

Opal steps through the door, the hinges creaking behind her as it shuts. Her white nightgown just barely brushes the floor. The delicate lace sewn into the hem seems to clash with the seemingly harsh, yet confident woman Cerylia has come to know. As Opal takes a few steps forward, the queen imagines her as a child whose innocence was too quickly ravaged by reality—a doe-eyed lamb wholly exchanged for an unforgiving warrior. *She's always had to be tough, to build her walls higher and higher. Just like me.*

Opal stops just a few feet away as Cerylia raises her hand. "Not here," the queen whispers. She rushes toward Opal and grabs her by the arm to lead her back into her rooms. The door slams shut behind them and a chill immediately runs down her spine. She glances at the open window, the curtains billowing in the crisp night air. Opal seems to sense the queen's discomfort because she hands her a wool blanket, then wraps one around herself. "I like the cold," she murmurs with a sheepish smile. "If it's unpleasant, I can close the window."

Cerylia shakes her head. "No, it's quite all right." She pulls the blanket tighter around her, soaking in the immediate warmth it provides. "If I'm being perfectly honest, I, too, enjoy the cold."

Opal tries to stifle another yawn, but her exhaustion wins. "Apologies, Your Greatness. I wasn't expecting any company this evening and my sleep schedule is a little off due to—"

"—your training," Cerylia finishes. She purses her lips before speaking again. "That's precisely what I was hoping to speak with you about."

Opal tenses. An unusual expression crosses her face, one that Cerylia hasn't seen from her yet: fear. "Have I failed you in some way, Your Greatness?"

Cerylia smiles as she shakes her head. "No," she soothes, her voice light and airy, "that's not it at all."

The girl immediately relaxes at the response, her shoulders releasing their former tension, but her mouth twitches. She's still slightly on edge. "I'm pleased to hear that."

Cerylia bites the inside of her cheek as she attempts to properly word what she wants to say next. "I came tonight . . ." She trails off as Opal leans forward, her undivided attention on the queen. "I came tonight because I need you to do something for me."

Opal bristles at the request, but keeps focus. "I'm listening."

"There's somewhere I need to go . . . somewhere in the past." Cerylia stumbles with her words, feeling foolish for not having rehearsed this earlier.

"To change something?"

Opal's candor leaves Cerylia speechless. What a brave soul, to directly ask the queen of her intentions. She shakes her head.

"Apologies," Opal starts, realizing just how direct she'd been. She fiddles with the ends of her hair then says, "It's just a question I always ask. When people want to change things, I want to know why. I'm sure you understand how risky it can be to change past events."

This feels more like an insult—unexpected and accusing—but Cerylia maintains her air of calm. "I don't desire to change anything, rather I need . . ." She looks out the window, her eyes landing on the bright yet solemn moon. "Clarification."

"You have uncertainty about the past?" Opal presses.

Cerylia pauses, unsure as to just how much she wants to share with the girl. "About some events, yes."

Opal's eyes seem to glow at her response. "Just say when and where and off we'll go."

Cerylia lets out a small laugh. "Oh my dear, how I wish that were the case." She chuckles again, not taking her eyes off the cream-colored moon.

Opal furrows her brows, but doesn't ask the question. Cerylia can see it in her eyes, in her face. She knows. She knows she's not powerful enough. Not yet, anyway.

BRAXTON HORNSBY

BRAXTON HEAVES THE last sack of grains atop an already monstrous pile, his breathing labored from the effort. Just as he bends over to catch his breath, a window swings open and a brusque voice shouts from inside the Hanslow Inn. “Hornsby!”

Braxton jumps to his feet, feeling sluggish and exhausted as he drags himself toward what is sure to be yet another set of chores. Ever since he arrived in Athia seven years ago and took the position at the inn, Hanslow hasn’t wasted any time. It’s one chore after another after another. Not that Braxton minds—after all, he knew what he’d signed up for from the beginning—but his original title had been ‘barkeep’. To tend to guests—normally weary travelers who'd spent the last week or so aboard a ship—pour their ale, serve their food, listen to their stories. These are things he doesn't mind doing. It's the hundreds of *other* chores Hanslow seems to come up with, completely unrelated to his barkeep duties, that have started to get under his skin.

Braxton approaches the window and pokes his head inside. Sure enough, Hanslow has disappeared—probably off doing something of little to no importance, but to him, if left incomplete, would be the end of the world *and* his business as he knows it. For that, Braxton does respect the man. As senile and scatterbrained as he can be, Hanslow's got a knack for holding things together.

A white head of hair pops up in the window, startling Braxton half to death. He jumps back and curses, then runs a hand through his unkempt golden hair. "What did I tell you about suddenly just appearing like that?" Braxton scolds. He shakes his head. "If you do that one more time, I swear . . ."

"I know, I know, you'll keel over dead from shock," Hanslow finishes with a shake of his head. "Have the grains been unloaded?"

Braxton nods, then gestures toward the back of the inn. "Unloaded and stacked right next to the shed, just as you requested."

Hanslow gives him a crooked smile, one that

pronounces the wrinkles lining his eyes more so than usual. “Well done. I’m expecting a large number of guests to arrive tonight. I assume the duration of their stay won’t last more than a fortnight, but it’s best to be prepared.”

Braxton tries not to roll his eyes, and somehow succeeds, but can’t keep the weary sigh from escaping his lips.

Hanslow immediately notices his contempt. “I suppose I can always find another barkeep, one that is actually *willing* to do my bidding,” he scoffs. “It’s not like I compensate you for your work or anything.” A pang of guilt hits Braxton right in the chest as Hanslow tosses him a small sack of silver coins. “Do you accept, or shall I find myself another workhand?”

Braxton bites his tongue before speaking. “I accept.”

The old man’s eyes gleam in the morning light. “Good. Now if you’ll come inside, I’ll get you started on the downstairs rooms . . .”

Hanslow’s voice trails off, leaving Braxton outside by himself with his guilt and the satchel of silver. It crosses his mind to just leave—he’s made enough over the past few months to go somewhere new, perhaps start a new life, a new job . . .

He pulls one of the coins from the bags and rolls it through his fingers. If only Hanslow knew that he was actually royalty, the son of King Darius Tymond, heir to the Tymond throne, perhaps he never would have hired him in the first place. If he hadn't left those ten long years ago, he'd be sitting with his mother and father in the Great Room, deciding the fates of those who entered, just like his father had unknowingly decided his own son's fate. The thought sends a shudder down his spine.

At least money wouldn't have been an issue.

Braxton sighs as he returns the single coin to the pouch, then heads inside, the silver jingling with each step he takes.

Nightfall. Braxton's favorite time of the day. After hours of being indoors—sweeping the floors, changing the linens on the beds, and stocking the bar—the appearance of stars in the sky is a welcome sight. He steps through the door of the inn, careful not to slam it shut behind him, and lets out a small breath as he gazes upward. The constellations always remind him just how trivial his problems really are.

With nothing more than a satchel, a bow and arrow, and a canteen of water, he begins his trek down the main dirt road, the dimly lit lanterns stationed near each house serving as his guide. He walks for about twenty minutes until civilization eventually tapers off, leaving him with only starlight to go by. He takes a quick look around him before entering the brush. Twigs snap underneath his sturdy boots and fallen leaves crunch with every step. A few minutes pass, and he begins to worry that maybe he took a wrong turn somewhere. As often as he comes out here, he'd think each journey would get easier, but it's quite the contrary—especially in a night as pitch black as this one.

He wipes the beads of sweat forming along his brow, his confidence wavering. *I should turn around and retrace my steps.* The thought is dismissed as quickly as it first appeared.

Off in the distance, not more than thirty feet away, is a canvas of still blue water. It gleams in the moonlight, the stars twinkling in the mirror-like reflection. He looses a breath and smiles. Why he ever doubts himself eludes him. He adjusts his bow, then makes his way to the lake.

Lake Ipcea. One of the only bodies of water in Athia that isn't a surrounding ocean. Braxton's always had a preference for freshwater fish—something about the taste leaves his mouth watering for more. His mother and father used to require that only freshwater fish be served in the Kingdom of Trendalath; any other catch could be thrown to the townspeople as scraps. His father thought himself generous for doing so.

One day, when his mother and father had left on official business for more than a few hours, Braxton had seized a rare opportunity: to catch his own food. He'd rigged together a long stick with a piece of string and fastened an iron hook from the kitchen onto the end. Without saying a word to the servants, he'd left the castle, climbing through a back window that appeared to serve no other purpose than decoration. Seeing as the castle was built on a hill that overlooked the Great Ocean, Braxton had no choice but to sidestep down the steep grassy knoll.

When he finally made it to flat ground, he'd dug for worms and placed them in a small tin he'd also found in the kitchen. He'd sat there for hours until a saltwater fish—a rainbow trout—had tugged on his line. And so, he'd brought it inside for lunch. Phillipa, one of the housemaids, had been appalled at the time but, because of her soft spot for the boy, had cooked up the trout anyway.

Braxton could remember the way the saltwater trout tasted as if it had happened yesterday—and it wasn't good. Simply put, it was fishy and pungent, like a piece of salmon that had gone bad. From that point forward, he understood why his parents preferred freshwater fish and never complained again at a meal.

And that's precisely what he plans to do tonight in the stillness of Lake Ipcea. Hanslow is a saltwater kind of fellow, meaning that anytime seafood is served at the inn, it's brought in from the Great Ocean. Braxton skips out on those meals when he can and heads straight for the lake. What can he say, old habits are hard to break.

In the moonlight, he spots a nearby set of branches and breaks off one of proper length. Like old times, he ties a piece of string at the end and fastens the hook. With a reel that he handcrafted himself, he loops the string round and round. He situates himself close to the shore and casts the line. Sitting in the peaceful stillness never ceases to clear his mind. It's almost as if time stands still, if only for a few brief moments.

The stillness is suddenly disrupted as something rustles in the bushes at the same time his line pulls. He drops the line and jumps to his feet, readying himself in a defensive stance. He swiftly pulls his bow from the holster on his back and draws an arrow. He gazes blindly into the dark with his weapon pointed at the forest. His heart thumps in his chest as the rustling grows louder. What appears through the brush is something most wouldn't be afraid of, but he keeps his weapon raised, the tip of the arrow aimed right at the heart.

Eyes the color of crimson stare back at him.

It's a young boy.

RYDAN HELSTROM

THE SHIP COMES to a halt as the captain docks it, the underbelly shaking from hitting the port over and over again. Rydan sits in a corner on the lower deck, his hands bound behind his back, feet tied together, a musty rope pressed between his teeth. His jaw aches from clenching for so long, and both his mouth and throat have gone dry, making it even more difficult to breathe.

One of Tymond's guards sits on a barrel from across the room. He stares at Rydan, like he's being doing all day (and well into the night), but surprisingly it doesn't bother him. If he really wanted to, he could escape from these shackles in seconds. But where would he go? He'd considered taking down all the men on the ship and steering it far, far away from Trendalath, but the effort seems too great.

So he'd sat there, holding the guard's gaze for long as he could, until he'd finally broken his stare and leaned his head back into the wood panels lining the lower deck of the ship. He'd closed his eyes, only to find that when he opened them, they'd arrived at their destination. The journey back felt much shorter than the journey there. Not surprising.

Two guards seize him and cut the rope binding his ankles, but don't bother with the one around his wrists or the one in his mouth. Rydan tries to spit it out, but one of the guards slaps him across the head. "Knock it off," he growls.

As much as Rydan wants to curse the oaf, he maintains his composure and lets the guards lead him up onto the main deck and off of the ship.

The town of Trendalath is bustling with activity, and as they walk toward the castle, Rydan notices various merchants actually have the courage to approach the king's guards in an effort to try to sell their goods. The guards, however, remain indifferent and simply wave away the townspeople as if they're pesky gnats. Rydan's steps falter as one particularly brave soul spits on the ground before them, shouting obscenities—but shockingly, the guards ignore the boisterous young lad. This is surprising, especially since Tymond is known for doling out punishments for almost everything, no matter how trivial the crime.

The scent of spices and herbs fills the air and brightly colored silks and linens line the dirt streets. While the people seem to be in good spirits, it's obvious that many of them haven't eaten in days. Rydan notices one family in particular—a mother with two young children, one that isn't even old enough to walk. She holds the child to her bosom, her eyes wet with tears. Her husband is on the streets, hustling, doing everything he can to sell his woodenwares.

A chill creeps down Rydan's spine. That could have been him. If King Tymond hadn't taken him in as a member of the Cruex ten years ago, there's no doubt in his mind that he'd be bartering for food and working ridiculous hours just to make end's meat. As hard as it is to admit, Rydan will always be grateful to King Tymond; even if his decisions seem brash at times or don't fully make sense, that man had seen something in him and saved him—had chosen him.

Rydan's thoughts flicker to the day prior, to the Lonia mission with Arden; to the appalled look on her face when she'd tried to stop him from killing the Soames family and failed. In hindsight, he probably should have told her that the Soames were illusié, but knowing Arden, it probably wouldn't have mattered anyway. Bullheaded and stubborn, once she's made her mind up, there's no changing it, so when she'd set out to save the Soames instead of assassinate them, he should have known that it'd end poorly for him. Although, he never could have guessed—never *would* have guessed—that she'd knock out her own partner to save the very people they were assigned to assassinate, and then flee, but Arden's also full of surprises. Never a dull moment with that one.

Rydan snaps back to the present as they approach the castle, its monstrous stone walls stretching as far as he can see. Up on the right, Rydan notices a fruit cart, much like the one in Lonia—the one with the mysterious violet-eyed woman. He points his gaze straight ahead as mocha-colored skin and obsidian hair drift across his memory. His breath catches. There's something about her he can't quite put his finger on. Something familiar. When he looks back over at the cart, the sight almost stops him in his tracks. It can't be.

Felix Barlow, the *original* captain of their ship to Lonia, stands just next to the wooden cart. He tosses a green apple into the air with an all-knowing smirk plastered on his face. Rydan blinks, just to be sure he's actually seeing Barlow, when a commotion to the left steals his attention. Two young boys are fighting over what appears to be a loaf of bread. One of the guards surrounding Rydan breaks from the circle formation they'd been walking in and approaches the scuffle. A sword is drawn. The boys stop fighting and stare up at the guard with wide eyes, then drop the bread and run for their lives. The guard sheathes his sword and retreats back to his original position.

Rydan diverts his attention back to the fruit cart. His shoulders sag at the realization that as quickly as Barlow had appeared, he's gone. Rydan silently curses himself for not keeping a closer eye on the lad. He was probably his only chance for escape at this point.

Rydan and the guards go as far as they can, reaching the moat that separates the castle from the rest of the town. A guard at the top of the watchtower motions to another to lower the drawbridge. Rydan winces as the hundred-year-old chains moan. After what seems like an eternity, the bridge lands on the ground with a loud thud. The ground rumbles, but the guards take little notice as they drag him forward across the walkway. Rydan looks up at the many men guarding the castle, bows drawn at the ready, dozens of iron-tipped arrows pointed directly at his skull. He lowers his head, afraid that one false move could be the deciding factor in whether he lives or dies.

The castle smells just as he remembers it—damp and musty with a side of death. The hallways are dimly lit with barely any light seeping through the windows. The thunderstorm Barlow had predicted hasn't hit yet, so perhaps today will be the day. They approach an all too familiar room, one that Rydan was hoping he wouldn't have to see for a while.

The Great Room.

He locks his knees, knowing that this won't stop

the guards from bringing him inside, but at least it will give him a few extra seconds of peace. The double doors swing open and he takes a deep inhale as the guards push him forward. He walks solemnly toward the king, eyes cast downward, until the guards stop him.

He slowly lifts his head and immediately wishes he hadn't. The usual light blue of Tymond's eyes is completely engulfed in black, and his salt-and-pepper hair has strayed from its usual comb over. Eyes alight with rage, he looks like a demonic creature sent from another world. Rydan tries to restrain a shudder, but the king's dreadful glare makes it almost impossible to do so.

Tymond presses his lips together before speaking. "Rydan Helstrom." The bitter expression on his face says it all.

"Your Majesty." When Rydan doesn't bow, one of the guards elbows him in the side, causing him to keel over in a semi-bow.

Tymond taps his fingers, the sound deafening in the quiet space. "This is not how I expected our next meeting to go. I thought we'd be joined by your partner." His expression grows even darker than before, something that Rydan didn't think was possible. "Care to enlighten me?"

A multitude of scenarios run through his head. He could lie, like he had to the soldiers, and tell him that Arden's dead. Already highly unbelievable, seeing as the soldiers found small, petite footsteps leading *away* from the Soames's residence.

He could say that they'd lost tabs on each other once they'd arrived in Lonia. He could also say that just as they'd been about to complete the assassination, the tables had turned, leaving Arden no choice but to flee and leave the rest of the dirty work to him. Oh, how he wished that were what had actually happened. But, most likely, Tymond already knew the truth, so there would be no use in lying. No sense in digging an even deeper hole for himself. "I do not know where Arden is." The words fall out of his mouth almost too easily. "But the assassination is complete."

Tymond narrows his eyes. "And where's my proof?"

Rydan swallows. *Oh right, that.* "I don't have it, Your Majesty, but I give you my word that the assassination was carried out just as you'd requested."

Tymond rises from his throne, walking down the steps ever so slowly. He keeps his gaze pinned on Rydan the entire time. When the king finally reaches him, it takes everything in him to maintain eye contact. The urge to look away is strong, but his desire to remain dignified is stronger.

"I have your *word*?" the king hisses.

Rydan's body goes stiff as a board.

"Tell me, Helstrom, what good is your *word*?"

The king's face is just inches from his own, his hot

breath blazing across Rydan's cheekbones. "Your Majesty, I am an honorable man." His voice wavers. "You can trust my word, I swear it."

Tymond takes a step back. He slowly shakes his head and looks . . . disappointed.

Not good.

"I had high hopes for you Helstrom," the king says with a sigh, "but unfortunately, you are a traitor and a liar."

The words hit him right in the gut. Rydan squeezes his eyes shut, wishing that this were all just a dream. A twisted, backwards nightmare of a dream.

"You see, Helstrom, my guards infiltrated the Soames's household, and while the bodies of Mr. and Mrs. Soames were indeed decapitated, the *whereabouts* of said heads were nowhere to be found." Tymond tisks under his breath. "In addition, the body of the Soames *boy,* nor his head, were present. So it appears that you completed a little more than half of your mission, which, as you are aware, is considered a failure in my book."

Rydan opens his mouth to protest, but one of the guards kicks him in the back of the knee, forcing him to kneel.

"Rydan Helstrom, I hereby sentence you to one year in the dungeons, at which time the royal court will deem your worthiness of a trial."

He clenches his jaw to keep it from dropping, but it disobeys. *Well, that turned rather quickly.*

The guards yank him to his feet and whirl him toward the double doors. With much intended force, Rydan manages to break free, if only for a moment, and runs up a couple of the steps leading to Tymond's throne. The king watches him approach with beady eyes, raising a hand to cease the guards from attacking.

Rydan's fierce gaze meets the king's. "You are not worthy of the throne you sit upon and I will no longer serve under your reign." He spits on the ground at Tymond's feet. "Consider this my formal resignation."

Tymond's gaze hardens. "Make it two years." He motions to the guards. "You are dismissed," he snarls.

One year, two years, what did it matter? It was all the same to the king—Rydan would wind up dead and his remaining scraps of flesh would be fed to the buzzards.

The guards seize him and turn him back around to face the double doors. Rydan notices a black falcon perched on one of the windowsills, watching him, observing him. He scowls, then allows himself to be led through the double doors and down the hallway that leads to the dungeons. He takes one last glimpse of his life—his old life—before ducking into the stairwell. Even in the dim light of Tymond's underworld, his new home for two years, Rydan manages to keep his head held high. The guard throws him into an empty cell. The iron door slams shut.

DARIUS TYMOND

DARIUS REMAINS SEATED on his throne, staring at the double doors to the Great Room. Whispers of what a dreadful king he is consume his thoughts, but he forces them away with a quick shake of his head. He did what was right. He'd been left with no other choice. The boy had to be locked up, seeing as he poses a potential threat not only to the Cruex, but also to his reign as king. Even still, a lump forms in his throat. Failure will not sit well with his Savant; the thought of facing them is enough to fill him with dread.

The glinting of his amethyst ring briefly catches his attention, but his focus shifts as one of the doors creaks open. A head of long white-blonde hair pokes through. With a quick nod of her head, Aldreda enters the Great Room and closes the door behind her. Her shoes clack across the marble floor, her black and red robes slithering along the smooth surface. She looks absolutely stunning, as she always does, and Darius catches himself holding his breath as she approaches.

Aldreda curtsies then says, "My King."

Darius rises and steps toward her, taking her hand in his. "My Queen," he responds as he bows and kisses the top of her hand.

Aldreda seems to hardly acknowledge the gesture. "The Helstrom boy," she starts without hesitation as she gazes back at the double doors, "I saw the guards leading him toward the dungeons."

The king drops her hand, suddenly feeling insecure with his decision-making capabilities.

Aldreda turns back toward him with an icy glare. "Did you not consider consulting me first?"

Darius just stares at her, uncertain how to respond.

"Apparently, my counsel is of little to no importance to you, but I'm going to express my opinion anyway." She brings her hands to her lower abdomen, cupping the small bump that is seemingly more visible from underneath her robes. "Seeing as you haven't given it much thought, condemning the Helstrom boy could have serious repercussions."

"On the contrary, I have considered it," Darius

shoots back. "Not only does he pose a threat to the Cruex, he also poses a threat to my reign over Trendalath."

Aldreda raises an eyebrow. "How so?"

"If I don't severely punish Rydan for disobeying the terms of his mission, then I will lose the respect of the remaining Cruex members. And without the respect of the Cruex, *my* assassins, I am powerless."

Aldreda tilts her head back and forth as if weighing the statement. "Did you not consider how respected Helstrom is among the Cruex?"

Darius bites his lower lip. In all honesty, he *hadn't* considered that. Aldreda was the one who maintained closer relationships with each of the Cruex members. She'd observed them for quite some time, learning of their internal ranks with little to no interference. In this scenario, her word is probably better than his, but Darius isn't about to let her win so easily. "Even so, their respect for their king and the obligation to do the right thing should outweigh their respect for a disloyal member of their group, no matter how deep the ties run."

"*Should,*" Aldreda scoffs, "but that doesn't necessarily mean it *will.*"

Darius keeps his eyes on hers. Impossible woman. If it weren't for her beauty, he probably never would have married her. As brilliant as she is, her need to constantly challenge his every statement is downright exhausting. It makes him appear weak, and that is something the reigning King of Trendalath cannot, and should not, stand for.

His expression turns cold. "It seems we've reached an impasse."

Aldreda holds his gaze. "It seems we have."

"And what of Arden? Do you suggest we allow her to roam the castles freely with Rydan, too? Two traitors with free rein! A truly inspired idea."

Aldreda bristles at the mockery in his voice. "It seems unjust that you would lock up one and not the other, especially when they were on the mission together."

Ah, so the queen doesn't know. Either she was misinformed or uninformed, but either way, Darius realizes he now has the upper hand. Not that he'd ever intentionally *try* to make his wife feel stupid, but she'd been rather irritating lately.

Too irritating.

"Interesting point of view," Darius remarks as he rubs his thumb over his chin. "And how would you suggest I lock up Arden when she never returned from the mission?"

Aldreda regards him with wide eyes, clearly shocked by this discovery. "Arden . . . did she not return with Rydan?"

Darius shakes his head, his face stoic. "She did not."

Aldreda bows her head. "My sincerest apologies,

My King. It appears I do not have all the details to provide proper counsel."

As much as Darius wants to revel in the moment, he can't find it in his heart to make a mockery of his wife. It's rare for her to make mistakes, and this is certainly no exception. Belittling her will prove nothing and will only make his reign more difficult in the days to come. With this in mind, he decides to take the high road. "It's quite all right, My Queen. You were misinformed to no fault of your own."

"Your forgiveness is greatly appreciated and will not be forgotten." She gazes back up at him with eyes a deeper blue than the Great Ocean itself. A small smile tugs at the corner of her lips. "May I ask how you plan to proceed?"

"First and foremost," Darius says as he takes her hands in his, giving them a light squeeze, "we must find Arden Eliri."

ARDEN ELIRI

IT TAKES A few days to travel to wherever Estelle is taking me, but I don't utter a single complaint. After stumbling upon me in my wounded condition in the forest, she took it upon herself to lead me to a nearby cliff where I could finally dispose of the Soames's decapitated heads. I said a quick prayer before throwing the bag into the abyss, hoping that Erle and Radelle Soames have found peace in whatever realm they now reside in.

Estelle is a decent guide, and I can tell she enjoys sharing her knowledge with me. She's constantly pointing at trees and bushes, informing me of the plants I can eat and ones I should stray from. Her affinity for nature is something I've quickly come to admire. Juniper trots happily beside me, constantly glancing in my direction to make sure I'm okay. If I'm being honest, the little fox is growing on me. I sneak her berries every chance I get, as long as Estelle isn't looking.

We approach a thick brush, probably the densest one yet, and Estelle advises me to stand back. She pulls out a dagger with an enormous blade and begins swiping at the branches, quickly forming a walkable pathway. Her determination is commendable, and I find myself drawing my chakrams to help. Estelle glances at my weapons, then at me. She smiles. We continue carving off the branches until a path forward makes itself clear.

I've come to learn that Estelle is not fond of superfluous conversation, so I've tried to keep my talking to a minimum, but I have so many questions that need answering. First of all, it'd be nice to know *where* she's taking me. "I didn't know the Thering Forest went this deep," I say in an attempt to strike up conversation.

Surprisingly enough, my tactic works.

"Do you travel to Lonia often?"

That's probably a rhetorical question. I bite my tongue and mentally slap myself in the forehead. This is my first time in Lonia *and* the Thering Forest, and I'm guessing Estelle already knows that. *Nice going.*

She must sense the hesitance in my response because she stops walking and turns to face me. Her violet eyes bore into mine. I know better than to lie, so I drop my head and mutter, "No, this is actually my first time to Lonia. And to the Thering Forest."

She lets out a small laugh. "I know you don't actually care about how deep the forest is, so if there's something you want to say or ask, then just do it already."

Blunt much? "I just . . ." The words are there, but they don't want to come out.

"You just what?" she presses.

I sigh. "I'd just really like to know where we're going, that's all."

She raises a perfectly arched eyebrow. "You don't trust me, do you?"

"It's not that," I fib, "but I did just meet you, and you seem to know a lot about me and my . . . abilities." I struggle to get the last word out. "I'm sure you can understand why I'm hesitant."

Estelle stands taller and lifts her chin ever so slightly. Her midnight hair dances in the wind. *Radiant* is the one and only word that comes to mind. "If you don't trust me, then we should go no further." I narrow my eyes, and Estelle mirrors my expression. "Really. I'm being serious. We should part ways this instant if you can't find a way to trust me."

Trust. Such a small word that carries tremendous weight. I trusted King Tymond all these years and look where that got me. Okay, so maybe I didn't *fully* trust him, but I loyally served under his reign—something I wish that, now, I could take back. Same with Rydan. Where had that *trust* gotten us? Oh, that's right. To a breaking point where I had to bash him over the head with a lantern on a mission that was intentionally designed to destroy us.

He'll probably never see it that way, though.

I push my thoughts of Rydan and King Tymond aside. Estelle is still standing in front of me, blocking my path. "Can you just give me something? Some sort of inkling as to where we're headed?"

She smirks. "You'll be safe. That's all I can tell you."

For a moment, I think about turning to run, of abandoning ship and starting over by myself. But something in me tells me to stay, to trust this mysterious woman who already knows so much about me. I give a slight nod of my head. "Well," I say, looking from Juniper back to Estelle, "I suppose that'll have to be enough."

CERYLIA JARETH

CERYLIA STARES AIMLESSLY through a window from the top floor of the Sardoria castle. She shudders as a crisp breeze floats inside, ruffling her wavy chestnut hair. She pulls a blanket from her bed and wraps it around her, immediately soaking up the warmth it provides.

She closes her eyes, feeling grateful that she stood her ground all those years ago when Delwynn had advised that she be easily accessible, in case of an emergency, and had suggested she reside on the ground floor of the castle. Much to his dismay, Cerylia had wholeheartedly negated this idea. As queen, she deserves the best view in the castle, and it just so happens the best view is on the top floor, where she can oversee not only Sardoria, but the surrounding areas: the once-thriving Eroesa (sadly now a wasteland due to King Tymond's tirade), Chialka, Miraenia, Declorath, and off in the distance, the Isle of Lonia. The Vaekith Mountains in the north are also a sight to be seen, especially in the winter months—nothing like white snow-capped mountains to make one revel in nature's beauty.

A knock on her bedchamber door startles her. Who would be disturbing her at such an early hour? The sun hasn't even started its ascent yet. She quickly walks toward the door, tightly securing her robe along the way. She opens the door only a crack, then pokes her head into the hallway.

Delwynn stands before her with one hand holding a torch, the other in the pocket of his trousers. One look at the grim expression on his face is all it takes for her to slip through the doors and follow him down the hall. They reach the main stairwell and rush down the castle steps. She notices that he's not hobbling—on the contrary, he's moving a lot faster than usual.

"Delwynn," Cerylia pants in the middle of descending the staircase, "I can tell that something urgent has happened, but you need to brief me on the situation so that I know what I'm about to walk into."

Delwynn stops in his tracks and turns to face the queen. "Of course, Your Greatness. Please forgive my brash behavior." The words flow so easily from his mouth, but his hasty glance down the stairwell says otherwise. "It's just that we need to get to the healing ward immediately."

All the color drains from Cerylia's face. "Is it Opal?" she asks, her voice barely above a whisper.

Delwynn nods solemnly.

"Let's not waste any more time," she snaps, even though their stopping was of her own accord. "Take me to her immediately."

There's no mistaking that he hears the urgency in her voice because he takes her through secret passageways, unbeknownst to her or any of her guards. He leads her through chambers, bobbing, weaving, and turning, rushing through areas of the castle that she didn't even know existed until now.

When they finally reach the healing ward, Delwynn flings the door open and ushers Cerylia through. There, in the dim morning light, lies Opal, stark white and unmoving. Cerylia rushes to the girl's side and reaches to grab her hand, but thinks better of it. She looks around the room until she spots the castle's healer, his back facing her. He appears to be making some sort of tonic, taking herbs and spices from different areas of his workstation and mixing them together with a mortar and pestle.

"Healer," Cerylia calls out, her voice strained.

He immediately turns to face her, mortar and pestle still in hand.

For a brief moment, Cerylia feels guilty for not knowing his name, but quickly dismisses the thought. There are greater things at stake here. *Much* greater. "What happened?" she presses.

The healer takes his time finishing the tonic mix, then pours it into a mason jar. He studies the liquid for a minute and, only when he appears to be happy with it does he walk over to them. The only thing keeping her from lashing out at the boy is the mysterious tonic he holds in his hands.

The healer sits on the ground next to Opal, across from the queen, and sets the tonic down beside him. "As you're aware, Opal has been working diligently to expand her abilities and improve upon them." His eyes flick toward Delwynn. "She doesn't want to disappoint, Your Majesty, so she's been working longer and harder every day. Early this morning, she pushed herself too far."

Cerylia averts her gaze from the healer to Delwynn. "As much as I want her to expand her abilities, I never ordered that she work herself to the point of being harmed." She narrows her eyes. "Explain."

Delwynn's mouth falls into a frown as he shakes his head. "I have been pushing her, but this . . ." He gestures to Opal's lifeless body. "This was her own doing."

"It would appear that her desire not to disappoint

you is far greater than her own well-being," the healer states.

His condescending tone is enough to make Cerylia want to backhand him across the face, but she resists the urge and takes the dignified approach. This healer, whoever he is, may be Opal's only hope for survival. "What is this . . . state she appears to be in?"

"She's still alive, but she's asleep in a sort of paralysis state."

"And how did she come to this state?" Cerylia pries, trying not to meet the healer's intense gaze.

Delwynn chimes in. "She attempted to travel back further than she ever has before."

A lump forms in Cerylia's throat as her mind wanders to the last conversation she had with Opal. The unspoken words. *She's not powerful enough yet.*

The room starts to sway even though she's sitting on the ground. "How far back?" she croaks.

The healer stares at her with narrowed eyes, as if he already knows that this is all her fault. "Fifteen years."

His response is enough to make the room go black.

BRAXTON HORNSBY

SNEAKING THE YOUNG boy into the Hanslow Inn hadn't been an easy feat. Thankfully, the darkness had helped some, but not when it came to actually *entering* the inn. The lack of burning lanterns made it difficult to see, and there were a few times where Braxton had almost knocked dishes and other various items over. He'd knocked the boy unconscious, so maneuvering through the tight spaces throughout the inn proved to be even more challenging than usual.

Not much later, Braxton sits on a nearby crate in one of the spare bedrooms, his eyes fixed on the still-unconscious boy. With the way he'd placed him on the bed, it would appear to an outsider that the boy had fallen into a deep sleep, peaceful and undisturbed. Of course, this couldn't be further from the truth.

Braxton tenses as the boy stirs. With a groan, his eyes flutter open and his hand immediately shoots up to the black and blue bruise that's already started to form along his temple. Braxton's doing, no doubt. The boy's crimson eyes meet his own, but instead of looking angry or fearful, he looks . . . tranquil. Relaxed. Almost as if he knew all along that this was going to happen and that he's meant to be here.

The thought unnerving, Braxton stands from his crate, his hand clutching the handle of a knife he'd hastily shoved into the back of his pants on his way upstairs. "Who are you?"

The boy continues to stare at Braxton. He doesn't say anything, just continuously massages his bruised temple.

Braxton straightens his posture and clears his throat. "Who are you?" he demands again, this time more brusque.

The boy remains silent. He closes his eyes and starts murmuring something under his breath. Just as Braxton is about to ask again, a soft yellow glow appears around the boy, as if fireflies were intently outlining every angle of his body. The boy moves his hand from his temple to his face so that his eyes are completely covered. The glow becomes more and more vibrant until the entire room is encased in an eerie shade of yellow. A gray mist appears from overhead and Braxton watches in awe as the boy shifts shape into a . . .

Into a *different* person.

A young man, right around his age, has taken the place of the young boy. The sudden transformation is enough to make Braxton lose his footing, and he stumbles backward into the crate, falling straight onto his behind. In a somewhat compromising position, he finds the nerve to repeat his question, albeit this time his voice comes out as merely a squeak. "Who are you?"

The man stands from the bed, the paleness of his face accentuating his blood-red eyes, spikes of blonde hair sticking up in every direction. "Xerin Grey." His voice is raspy, like sandpaper on wood.

"Why were you in the forest tonight? Who sent you?"

Xerin shrugs. "I suppose you could say I sent myself."

Braxton regards him with narrowed eyes. "What do you want?"

"To recruit you," Xerin says simply. He glances toward the door as though there's somewhere else he needs to be.

"Recruit me?" As soon as the words leave his mouth, the pieces come together faster than a bolt of lightning in a thunderstorm. "You're one of them," he whispers, backing further into the crate so that his back is pressed against the wall.

A voice bellows from down the hall, making both of them nearly jump out of their skin. “Hornsby!”

“You’ve got to be kidding me.” Braxton looks from Xerin to the door then back to Xerin, but his new accomplice is already darting for the half-open window.

Braxton pushes himself up from the crate and rushes over to the other side of the room, but it’s too late. He watches in distress as Xerin lands on his feet and takes off down the all too familiar dirt road.

Hanslow bursts into the room wearing only a bathrobe and some slippers. “I thought I heard voices.”

Braxton swiftly shuts the window, making sure to lock it in place. “Pesky raccoons,” he mutters in an effort to play it off.

Hanslow’s jaw drops open. He rushes over to the window and opens it, undoing everything Braxton just did. He pokes his head out into the night and squints his eyes. “They didn’t get the grains, did they?”

“Huh?”

“The raccoons? They didn’t get the grains, or did they?”

Braxton snaps back into his lie. “No, I shooed them away before they had a chance.” Probably better to keep the façade going than to tell Hanslow what had really happened. Finding Caldari this far south? The man would have a cow.

"Good thing you were up, even at this ungodly hour." Hanslow shuts the window and locks it, then turns to face him. "Why exactly are you awake?"

Braxton shrugs, willing his cheeks not to turn pink. "Couldn't sleep."

"Ah yes, I understand," Hanslow murmurs. "Well, you ought to try. Busy day we have tomorrow."

Braxton nods absentmindedly and keeps his eyes focused on the floor. "I'm looking forward to it." He remains still until Hanslow exits the room and shuts the door quietly behind him. The innkeeper's footsteps fade off into the distance, and when Braxton is sure he's gone, he darts over to his armoire and pulls on his hunting boots. He swipes his bow and arrows from the top shelf and strides over to the window, the locks clicking as they switch positions one last time. He gazes out at the vast expanse before him. He takes a deep breath.

And then he jumps.

ARDEN ELIRI

I ALMOST DROP to my knees as I follow Estelle through the entrance to a hidden cave. We're so far into the forest that I've lost any sense of direction I once had—north, west, east, south—I haven't a clue. The only thing I do know is that what we've just walked into is absolutely magnificent. Breathtaking. Surreal.

At first, the cave is absent of almost all light, dim and dark. A deep blackness surrounds us to where I can't even see my own two hands in front of me. Estelle doesn't bother to light a lantern or conjure any other light source for that matter; it makes me wonder if her violet eyes inherently carry some sort of night vision. My trust wavers, but I follow her further into the darkness, almost tripping over my own two feet.

Further and further into the darkness we go. My breathing is labored, although I can't tell if it's from physical exertion or from fear. Maybe it's both. I tell myself that there's nothing to be afraid of, that Estelle promised I would be safe—but the deeper we climb, the more I doubt her word. I'm almost certain I'm hallucinating when we reach what appears to be the end of the cave.

But it's only the beginning.

I shield my eyes as a bright white light floods my vision. It's enough to make my head pound and my eyes burn, so I keep them shut until it feels safe to open them again. That time feels like it will never come, but, eventually, it does. I slowly lift my eyelids and allow the light to seep in. When my eyes finally focus, my heart just about leaps out of my chest.

Deep within this cave we've wandered into is another *world*. Trees of all different shapes and sizes shoot up from the ground, their branches entwining and interconnecting to form pathways that lead to various structures built into them—a sort of tree village. Streams of fresh water run in winding paths at the bottoms of trees, and plants of magnificent colors—magenta, ruby, and lilac—dot the surface. The entrance to the cave, to this *tree village*, is miles above the surface, so it's difficult to see what else resides on the ground floor. Falcons with yellow, orange, and green-tipped wings fly overhead, along with smaller colorful birds and insects with vibrant shells and wings.

I'm sure Estelle can sense my amazement, seeing as it's written all over my face. As if to surprise me even more, she says, "Follow me!"

Before I can respond, she suddenly jumps over the edge, disappearing from my sight. I dart to the edge of the cliff and look over to find her bouncing up and down on an enormous mushroom-like plant, laughing hysterically.

Confusion begins to replace my awe. "What is this place?" I ask out loud, even though she clearly can't hear me.

"Are you coming or what?" Estelle calls from twenty feet below.

I scoop Juniper up and take a deep breath as I bring myself closer to the edge. I focus on the giant mushroom that Estelle is rolling off of. Just as I'm about to jump, I notice a dark mist slowly starting to take shape around me. Juniper jumps from my grip and scurries back into the depths of the cave, to somewhere I can't see. I call out to her, but she doesn't come.

When I turn back around, I watch the beautiful backdrop of the tree village fade, faster and faster, until I'm enveloped in nothing but darkness. A figure in a crimson cloak floats before me with its head pointed down toward the ground. A shiver runs down my spine as a cool draft sweeps through the cave-turned-abyss.

I can't help but feel panicked. *Where is Estelle? And Juniper? Where is the tree village? More importantly, what is this thing floating in front of me and how the hell did it get here?*

"Come, my child." The sound is enough to make the hair on the back of my neck stand. It sounds like a male, but could easily be an older woman with a deep voice. The figure extends its arm and beckons for me to approach, its spindly fingers curling in and out. "You do not belong here."

I remain rooted to my spot, as if I'm one of the long-standing trees I'd just witnessed moments ago in the cave—a place I desperately wish I could go back to.

"Who are you?" Even though my heart is pounding in my chest, my voice comes out confident and harsh, which is surprising, even to me.

I can almost hear the figure's lips crack as its mouth twists into a grimace. "You don't know who I am?"

Anger churns deep within my belly, although I'm not sure exactly what's causing it. "Of course I don't know who you are," I shoot back. "That's why I'm asking."

A low guttural sound emerges—it sounds like a laugh, but could easily be mistaken for a cry of pain.

"You belong with *us*. Your powers are too strong for *them*. Don't be foolish."

A strange sensation washes over me and a tingling erupts in my fingers and toes. I suddenly feel drawn to this figure, creature—whatever it is—and I find myself taking a step closer.

"That's it," the figure purrs. "Keep walking."

I stop in my tracks. "I will not be taken for a fool."

A snarl. "That's sinister news for your dear friend. Should you tell him or should I?"

My mouth opens to respond, but before I can say anything, a seemingly *real* image of messy, matted black hair and tired gold-flecked eyes appears, wrists and ankles bound in chains. My hand flies over my mouth as the realization hits me. *Rydan.*

"This should change your mind." Another gruff sound erupts from deep within the figure's throat.

Even though I'm angry, hurt, and appalled by Rydan's recent actions, seeing him in such a vulnerable state—weak and defenseless—is enough to make me cringe in disgust. And it's enough to make me think twice about whatever proposal I'm about to hear. "Let him go," I growl.

"You assume this is my doing?" Another spine-tingling laugh. "Incorrect, but thanks for playing."

"Let him go!" I say again, louder this time.

But the figure just stands there next to the image of Rydan. Rydan and his pleading eyes. Begging me. *Save me, Arden.*

I don't know what comes over me, but my anger suddenly neutralizes. "You don't deserve to be saved," I say under my breath.

The cloaked figure turns its head to the side, as if in shock. "My, my. There she is. I've been waiting for you."

I stand still, my eyes flicking back and forth between the *thing* and Rydan. *He doesn't deserve to be saved.*

"Join us," the figure hisses. It extends its gangly fingers toward me once again.

I reach out to take the figure's hand, but just before I do, both it and the image of Rydan vanish into thin air. My eyes roll into the back of my head as my body thuds to the ground.

I'm not sure what to think when I regain consciousness. My head pounds in rhythm with my heartbeat, which is rapidly accelerating as I recall recent events. Darkness. Crimson cloak. Lanky fingers. Reaching . . . reaching for me.

You don't belong here. Join us.

The whispers circulate through my head like a flock of birds flying south for the winter, desperate to get away from the cold. Desperate to be anywhere but here.

A familiar feeling.

The thumping in my chest begins to slow as I focus on the person in front of me. Violet eyes. Midnight hair. A calm, yet concerned expression.

Estelle reaches a hand out to me and pulls me up from the ground. "Are you okay? That was a pretty nasty fall you took." Her eyes travel at the same time mine do, up to the edge of the cliff I allegedly fell from.

I lightly rub the back of my head. "So, I didn't jump? I fell?"

Estelle shrugs her shoulders, then bites down on her lip. Concern, mixed with something else I can't quite put my finger on, is written all over her face. "It looked like you were going to jump, but then . . ." Her voice drifts off. I can tell she's struggling to find words to explain what had just happened.

"I must have lost consciousness from the adrenaline and all," I say quickly, hoping it'll end the conversation. "I'm okay though." I look down to my left, then to my right, suddenly feeling panicked. "And Juniper?"

Someone whistles behind me, and it's then I realize we're not alone. "I've got her right here," a familiar voice says.

I whirl around to find Juniper happily curled up in Barlow's arms, eating some berries from his open palm. Felix Barlow, ship captain. The same ship captain that took both Rydan and me to Lonia for our mission.

I gulp down the memory as I look back and forth between these two strangers, feeling confounded at the realization that somehow they *know* each other. "But you . . ." I point to Felix, unable to finish my sentence.

"Welcome to Orihia," Felix says. He wipes the berry remnants from his hand onto the side of his trousers, then makes a grand gesture at the tree village surrounding us. "Home to the Caldari."

My thoughts immediately shift to my quarters at Trendalath Kingdom and the many books I scoured, the many rumors I tried not to pay attention to. But they're true.

They're all *true.*

"The Caldari," I whisper. "So, it's not a myth."

Estelle and Felix stay silent, surely to let this baffling piece of information sink in.

"Your abilities?" It comes out as a half-statement, half-question, but Estelle and Felix seem to catch my drift.

A coy smile tugs at his lips. "Would you like us to tell you or show you?"

Is he being serious? Obviously, show me! I open my mouth to respond, then quickly shut it. *On second thought . . .* "It depends on what your abilities are."

He chuckles. "Smart girl."

Estelle shakes her head with a grin. "She's already witnessed my abilities. Isn't that right, Arden?"

I blush as I recall the almost-encounter with

Tymond's soldiers.

Estelle raises an eyebrow at Felix. "That means it's your turn," she says with a sly grin.

Felix nods before gently setting Juniper on the ground. The little marble fox immediately runs to my side. "I will forewarn you, my talent isn't quite as discreet as Lady Chatham's." I don't say anything. I just stare at him, hoping he won't say the one thing circling my mind. "And it will require your participation." I lower my head and close my eyes.

He said it.

Felix walks a number of steps in front of me and readies himself. He rolls his neck and cracks his knuckles, two things that never help to put my mind at ease. "Are you ready?"

I take a deep breath and nod. I'm the one who asked, who wanted to know, and now, I'm about to find out.

"Right then," Felix says. "I need you to attack me."

It's hard to stifle my disbelief. A cross between a snort and an awkward laugh escapes. "Come again?"

But Felix isn't laughing nor is he smiling. His eyes are dead-set on mine, his expression grim. "I said, *attack me.*"

I look at Estelle for confirmation, just to make sure Felix hasn't completely lost his mind. When she nods, I turn my gaze back to him.

"Um, okay," I manage to say. I pull my chakrams from their holsters and position myself in my throwing stance. "Are you sure about this?"

"Wow, Eliri, I didn't take you for such a . . ."

I know exactly where he's going with that one and I don't allow him to finish his sentence. Just as I gear up to throw the chakrams, something incomprehensible happens. My weapons drop from my hands, clinking together as they fall to the ground behind me. And somehow, a little boy stands before me.

The Soames boy.

Rydan stands next to him, drops of crimson falling from his skull. "You must complete your mission."

My hands shoot to my throat. I feel like I can't breathe. *What's happening?* My heart thumps in my chest, faster and faster, as the world grows dim. Tiny spots dot my vision, threatening to take over my full state of consciousness.

"You must kill him. Innocent or not."

The pool of red grows larger at his feet, and it's the first time the sight of blood makes me queasy. I fall to my knees, one hand clutching my throat, the other holding my stomach. This feeling is not one I'm used to, not one that surfaces often. My stomach twists as though I've been stabbed with multiple knives and someone is turning the handles over and over again. There's no denying what this feeling is.

Fear.

"I can't," I gasp. But my body and mind refuse to

align. I find myself crawling toward the Soames boy. He's docile, like a deer in the middle of a quiet meadow. I continue to crawl toward him until I reach his feet.

When I look up, the boy is still staring straight ahead, but Rydan is looking down at me, his lips twisted in a sickening grin. "Do it," he whispers.

I break free from Rydan's gaze and slowly bring myself to my feet. I open my palms and extend my hands toward the boy's throat. Instead of looking *at* me, he seems to be looking *through* me, as if I'm not even there. *Don't do it*, a part of me whispers. *He can live. He doesn't need to die.* But the other part of me is urging, pleading. It's stronger. It's telling me to kill, that I must complete this mission.

I do it all the time. Why should this be any different?

I can feel my pupils dilate as I bring myself closer to the boy. My breathing becomes more rapid as my hands land on his neck and I squeeze, pressing my thumbs and fingers harder and harder against his skin. I'm almost positive they'll leave an indentation. The boy's now-bulging eyes finally land on mine as he begins to gasp for breath. But he doesn't flail. He doesn't fight.

I'm strangling him and he's . . . *he's letting me.*

A deep current of longing and retribution washes over me. Thoughts of power and justice consume me. I lick my lips as the boy's gasping becomes louder and louder. My hands are shaking, but I continue to press, continue to squeeze. I can feel Rydan watching me, devouring every move, every breath I take. This is me. This is who I am. A killer.

And I *enjoy* it.

Just as the boy's eyes are about to roll into the back of his head, panic seizes me. My hands retreat from the boy's throat to my own. I begin to hyperventilate as I stumble backwards. I fall to the ground, gasping for air. My airways are closing and the only thing keeping me conscious is what little oxygen I'm getting. I can't breathe.

My hands fall to my chest, my eyes darting back and forth, looking for some sign of Estelle or Felix. As luck would have it, both Rydan and the Soames boy begin to fade as a head of black hair rushes toward me.

"Arden!"

Estelle—at least I *think* it's Estelle—lays me down onto the ground. She presses my hands onto my chest. "Shhh, shhh. You can heal yourself, remember?"

In my head, I nod, although I'm not sure if the motion comes across, and I try to still my gasping. I put more pressure on my chest, doing everything I can to channel my healing energy. A soft glow appears, illuminating the features on Estelle's face, and I can tell by her smile that I'm doing something.

I'm healing.

My breath begins to even out and my chest falls back into its regular rhythm. Estelle leaves my side and darts over to the other side, where Rydan and the Soames boy had stood. I can't see what she's doing, but as I gingerly prop myself up on my elbows, I notice that Felix is lying on the ground.

Gasping.

Even though I feel weak and short of breath, I rise and rush over to him. There's fear in his eyes as they land on mine. His breathing becomes even more labored, his chest pumping up and down at a terrifying speed. I furrow my brows as I try to calm him, but it's not working. And then he gives me a look, one that says *back-off-now-or-I'll-kill-you.*

"Move!" Estelle shouts as she barrels toward us. I shuffle out of the way as she kneels to Felix's side. She moves his hands from his throat to his chest, just like she did for me. "Focus on me, Felix," she whispers. "Focus."

"I can help," I say, still trying to wrap my head around what had just happened. "I can heal him."

Estelle shakes her head. "You've done enough for today."

I open my mouth to respond, then close it. I scoop Juniper up from the ground and walk over to the nearest tree. I slide down the bark slowly with the fox securely in my arms, my eyes trained on both Estelle and Felix.

It doesn't take long for Felix to sit up, and when

he does, I push myself up off the ground. Estelle helps him to his feet. His head lifts and, with a snarl on his face, his eyes meet mine. He storms over to me until he's just inches from my face. Surprisingly, I don't flinch.

"What the hell was that?" he shouts. "Who do you think you are?"

With a bewildered expression, Estelle runs over to us and places her hand on Felix's shoulder. "There's no need to shout."

Felix pushes her hand away. "You," he growls, shaking his index finger at me, "are not one of us. We're hardly ever wrong, but this time, we are."

I keep my mouth shut, too afraid to speak.

He lowers his finger and cocks his head. "You should just leave."

"Felix," Estelle pleads, "please don't."

I look at him with a pained expression. I try to find my words. "Felix, I have no idea what just happened. Whatever I just did, or didn't do, I didn't mean to, I just . . ." My words are jumbled, just like my thoughts. "Can you explain to me what just happened?"

My apologetic tone seems to sway him, if only slightly. "I'm an amplifier." The words come out just above a whisper. "I can amplify fear and other emotions in my attackers." He shakes his head. "But you . . ."

His silence is brutal. "But what?"

Felix sighs. “As much as I tried to amplify your fear, I couldn’t.”

“Why not?” I press.

“Because there was an emotion greater than fear.” His gaze is menacing. “One that I couldn’t control.”

I gulp, knowing exactly what he’s about to say next. Looks like the cat’s out of the bag, but I ask anyway. “And what emotion is that?”

Felix looks at me for a moment. He shakes his head. Then, with a shaky breath, he says the one thing I’ve tried so hard to keep hidden.

“Your desire to kill.”

RYDAN HELSTROM

WITH NO CONCEPT of day or night, Rydan is sure he's already lost his mind. Three days, three weeks, three months could have passed, and it would all feel the same. No sunrise. No daylight. No sunset.

Just darkness.

Rydan brings his head between his knees as a cool draft sweeps through the room. The hair on the back of his neck prickles as the current flows over him, causing him to shiver. He squeezes his arms around his legs, hoping that maybe if he applies enough pressure, his body will somehow just implode. But no such luck.

He's still alive—barely surviving. Stuck in this miserable, lonely cell.

A clatter sounds in the distance. His ears perk up. A door, perhaps? Has someone come for him?

He crawls to the front of his cell and grabs onto the iron bars with both hands. He narrows his eyes in the dim lighting, expecting to make out the shape of a burly guard, but instead, a figure with a small frame moves toward him. A faint light glows in one of her hands; in the other is a small tray.

Rydan keeps his eyes trained on her as she moves closer, noticing her clothing, a peasant skirt and ratty tunic, accompanied by long blonde braids. Her facial features are gentle and innocent, like a tiny mouse, and her lips are the lightest pink he's ever seen.

As she draws nearer, her blue eyes meet his. "Your dinner." She holds out the tray, then crouches down to push it between the bars.

Without uttering a word, Rydan grabs the tray and begins devouring the stale bread and bland meat.

The girl gives a small smile, then stands and turns to walk away. He stops, mid-bite. Even though he's a prisoner, he's still a human being, and a gentleman at that. No need to act like an animal. "Thank you." The words come out as a croak.

The girl turns around to face him. "You're welcome."

Now that he has her attention, Rydan sets down his tray. "I'm Rydan. What's your name?"

She bites her lip, then looks behind her as if she's expecting someone. "I really shouldn't."

He furrows his brows at her response. "I take it you're the one who will be bringing me my meals on a daily basis?"

She stays silent and nods.

"Right then," he confirms as he takes another bite of his bread, "so I can assume that we'll be seeing a lot of each other. Is that correct?"

The girl shifts uncomfortably from one foot to the other. "I suppose."

Rydan flashes her a toothy grin. "Then I would love to know your name so that I can thank you properly."

The girl hesitates before falling into a well-versed curtsy. "Elvira. But you can call me Vira for short."

"Elvira." The word flows so smoothly off his tongue. It's a pretty name, one he hasn't heard before. "It's nice to meet you."

"Likewise."

Silence falls between them.

He doesn't want her to leave, but the tension is thick and uncomfortable. "Well, I suppose I shouldn't keep you, but I appreciate you bringing me my dinner."

"It's no problem, really," she says, looking over her shoulder again. "I best get going."

He gives her a nod and she curtsies again, then

scurries up the stairwell from which she came. He turns his attention toward his tray, realizing that he's no longer hungry enough to finish his meal, so he scoots it to the opposite side of the cell. He crawls to the back where strands of hay and leaves had been gathered, undoubtedly from the last prisoner. He briefly wonders how long that person was in this very cell, until the thought of them dying in that very spot floats across his mind. Morbid, indeed.

He shakes the thought away as he lies down on the ground. The hay and leaves don't do much in the way of comfort, but at least it's *something.*

With a yawn, he closes his eyes, mumbling Elvira's name as he drifts into a deep sleep.

DARIUS TYMOND

DARIUS DIRECTS A harsh gaze at the six men kneeling before him. “You may rise.”

The men stand in unison and, if the situation weren’t so dire, the sight would be enough to make a shiver run down his spine. *I’ve trained them well.*

“What is the status on Arden Eliri?”

The soldiers remain silent for some time.

Darius narrows his eyes. “When your king asks you a question, you respond.”

One of the soldiers, a younger lad, looks up from the ground. “The girl is still missing, Your Majesty.”

Darius balls his hands into fists. He takes a deep breath and rises from his throne as he focuses on the soldier who will soon discover he's made a mistake in delivering bad news. "What could possibly be hindering the six of you from finding this girl? She's a *girl*, for lords' sake! It's been a week!"

The men shuffle their feet and mumble, clearly afraid to look their king in the eye.

"I've had enough of your blatant incompetence. Each and every one of you can consider yourselves discharged from duty." Darius waves his hand dismissively in the air. "Get out of my sight."

With their heads bowed, the soldiers retreat to the Great Room doors and exit one by one. Darius lets out a long sigh before heading toward his throne. Just as he turns to take his seat, an intoxicating scent hits him—lavender and neroli—and he knows immediately who it is. Aldreda.

"By the glum look on your face, I surmise the guards still haven't located Arden?" she asks.

Darius does not respond, only shakes his head.

Aldreda purses her lips. "I see." With her hands resting comfortably on her abdomen, she takes several long strides across the Great Room. For a woman with child, she moves gracefully and elegantly, as if gliding through the air like an eagle. She floats up the marble steps without making a sound, then stands confidently next to her husband. Her eyes drift to a window at the back of the castle, her gaze fixed on a black falcon perched on the sill. Darius notices a small smile tug at her lips as she places a hand on his right shoulder.

"You know what this means."

He looses another breath before nodding. "I'm afraid I do."

She removes her hand as quickly as she'd placed it there. "Shall you send for them or shall I?"

Darius stands, his back turned to her. If she sees the look on his face, there's no doubt she'll try to take over and control the situation. And if there's one situation he needs complete control over, it's this one.

"I'll do it." He wavers. "I should be the one to initiate."

Aldreda straightens and, without even looking at her, Darius knows she's sensed it. His weakness.

"When?" she demands.

His voice cracks. "At dawn."

"Hmm, we'll see" his wife purrs.

Darius closes his eyes, fully aware that she's about to pounce and take full advantage of this opportunity.

"My King, you have more than enough on your plate. And this is an urgent mission, is it not?"

He remains silent, doing everything in his power to remain standing on what little ground he has left.

"It's only logical to make contact immediately, wouldn't you agree?"

With a deep breath, he whirls around to face her. His expression is stoic, like a statue. "Then I shall make contact this evening. Would that please you, My

Queen?"

His harsh words seem to fall on deaf ears. "Better yet, allow me to do it for you."

"Aldreda."

Her hands leave the comfort of her stomach and fold across her chest. "Darius."

His mouth presses into a firm line. "I will take care of it. You need to tend to the baby." He gestures to her growing bump. "The state you're in is fragile enough as it is. You do not need the extra burden."

Her stone-cold gaze indicates that she's not going to give in, but, much to his surprise, she does.

"Fine, if that's how it must be." Her words are quiet, but she's not defeated. "I just figured I'd have better luck with them anyway given my . . . history."

Darius sucks in a quick breath, then shoots her his best *don't-even-go-there* look. "I would prefer for you to leave now."

Knowing that she's won, Aldreda bows her head to hide her smile, but Darius sees it, bright as day. He clenches his jaw as she slowly begins to exit the room. When she reaches the doors, she turns to look back at him for a brief second, then slips through them, shutting them quietly behind her.

His shoulders drop and the muscles in his face relax. Unwelcome images of Aldreda gallivanting around town with a member of his Savant creeps into his mind. "No," he mutters as he closes his eyes, trying to think of anything other than another man's hands all over his wife, another man's mouth caressing his wife's lips, another man's . . .

"Enough!" he shouts to himself as he stands and flings his arm, knocking a goblet of wine clear across the room. Red covers the once pristine white marble. He allows his head to fall into his hands as he tries to push the memories further and further from his mind.

And then it occurs to him.

Maybe this is exactly what he needs—anger, adrenaline, and confidence—to reach out to his dear old friend. Maybe he'll be able to face him again without feeling the need to kill him, once and for all.

CERYLIA JARETH

DAWN IS JUST breaking as Cerylia roams through the castle halls. A grumble erupts from deep within her stomach and she realizes she'd fallen asleep without eating supper the night prior. She approaches Delwynn's chamber, wondering why he hasn't arrived at her rooms yet with her breakfast, but then she remembers.

Opal.

With a quick pivot of her foot, Cerylia turns around and rushes down the hall. She makes a swift left turn and continues her long strides until she reaches a window overlooking the courtyard. Sure enough, Delwynn and Opal are positioned in the middle of the yard, training and practicing per her original orders. This was before Opal's . . . *incident.* The sight angers her, even though the healer had advised her fit to continue her training. Cerylia had been convinced that her prodigy needed at least a fortnight's rest, but Opal had also insisted that she was fine to carry on. And so, much to her dismay, Cerylia had approved the request to continue training.

She discreetly watches as Delwynn instructs Opal to sit down on the ground, legs crossed, palms facing upward and resting on her knees. Delwynn imitates the movement until they're both sitting ducks in the middle of the courtyard.

When they remain still for a few moments, Cerylia can't help but roll her eyes. She gathers the front of her cloak and scurries down the stone steps that lead to the courtyard. Although her footsteps are barely audible, Delwynn immediately senses her approach. He opens one eye and quickly rises to his feet. Opal follows suit.

"Your Greatness," he announces as he drops into a bow. Opal lowers herself into a half-curtsy and then, as if she's changed her mind, rises before quickly dropping into a bow. "What can we do for you this fine morning?"

Cerylia brushes a strand of chestnut hair from her face before responding. Although irritable from not having breakfast, she's determined not to let it show.

"How are you getting on with your training?" She directs the question to Opal.

Before the girl has a chance to respond, Delwynn's hands fly to his cheeks. His eyes grow wide. "Your breakfast!" He shakes his head. "My apologies, Your Greatness, I had a late start and have been so focused on Opal and her training. Let me run to the mess hall right away—"

"Delwynn," Cerylia interrupts, "There will be no need. I can handle retrieving my own breakfast." She gives him the warmest smile she can muster. "You two keep to your training schedule. Your dedication has been noted." She winks at Opal, who gives her a large grin before turning her attention back to Delwynn.

"I can assure you, it won't happen again!" Delwynn shouts as the queen heads back up the stone steps into the castle.

Once inside, Cerylia doesn't head to the mess hall, but instead goes for a stroll along the hallway perimeters. It doesn't take long for her to reach another set of windows that overlook the courtyard. Due to the direction of these windows, Delwynn's back now faces her, so she can clearly see Opal's front. She watches them for a few moments, noticing how brightly Opal's emerald eyes shine in the growing morning light. Laughter echoes throughout the courtyard. Cerylia smiles. She seems to be enjoying her training—a good thing, no doubt.

But her smile fades as a realization surfaces; the

truth she'll have to eventually face—and what she'll force Opal to face as well. Another memory works its way into her head, and Cerylia closes her eyes, shoving it far, far away, into the depths of her subconscious. But the pain feels fresh. The hurt lingers. And the agony of what once was screams.

She only came to be Queen of Sardoria a mere decade go, although it feels longer, and it certainly wasn't of her own accord. The townspeople nor the royal court would ever presume her widowed status—given her poise, demeanor, and governance. She'd built Sardoria from the ground up, for those seeking refuge from Tymond's barbaric reign.

Her mouth presses into a harsh line. *Tymond.* The precious diadem that sits upon his graying head is nothing but a shadow crown. If only the people of Trendalath knew who their real king and queen were, they would rejoice!

The lies, betrayals, and deceit surrounding Tymond's reign are not known amongst his people, if at all, which is why it has become her sole purpose to expose the man for who he truly is.

A murderer. A thief. And a coward.

But before she can act, there is one question that must be answered. What *truly* happened to her husband those fateful fifteen years ago?

For over a decade, a past riddled with uncertainty, with hurt, with longing, is all she's known. Trendalath was once her home, her safe haven—a place where she would raise a family and produce the next heir to the throne, the next king. But it had all been taken away from her far too quickly in a cowardly tirade.

Cerylia narrows her eyes as her gaze lands once again on Opal. But this girl . . . this girl is the key to finally releasing the ghosts of her past. And when she's ready, Cerylia will finally have her vengeance. She will finally uncover whether or not Darius Tymond killed her beloved husband.

BRAXTON HORNSBY

IT'S WELL INTO the evening the next day, and still no sign of Braxton's covert visitor. He's almost certain that Xerin couldn't have gotten very far by foot, but the further he ventures into the woods, the more he realizes what a rash assumption that is.

He stops at a nearby tree and pulls a canteen of water from his belt. The canteen is nearly dry, giving him two options: either turn around and head back to the inn, or search for a freshwater source. Seeing as he's the furthest he's ever gone into these woods, it would make sense to retreat back to the safety and security of Hanslow Inn, but he's never been one to give in so easily. Having spent a large portion of his life outdoors, tracking animals and their trails is just one of the many skills he's picked up over the years.

A fresh set of deer footprints catches his eye, so he turns left, his focus trained on the newfound trail. He's thrown for a loop a few times—apparently the deer had a muddled sense of direction—but after five minutes, he notices something glimmering through the brush.

A lake.

He pushes his way through the thorny bushes and branches, the bottom of his trousers catching on a nearby bramble. He shakes his leg in an effort to free the stubborn shrub, but it doesn't budge. With an exaggerated sigh and two hands clasped tightly over his knee, he pulls. His eyes widen at the sound of fabric ripping.

He immediately releases the grip on his knee and lowers his head, shaking it, then lifts his half-clothed leg away from the shrub. As he's walking away, his temper gets the better of him and he whirls around to kick the darn thing. Tiny green leaves explode into the air and the plant sways back and forth from the impact.

"Damn plant," Braxton mutters to himself as he smooths down his trousers. He adjusts his vest and satchel before continuing onward.

Based on the setting sun, he surmises it's probably close to 1900 hours. He'll have to turn back soon in order to retrace his steps to the inn, whether he finds the lad or not.

When he reaches the lake, he loosens the cap on his canteen, smiling at the canvas of purples, blues, and pinks reflecting off the water. With a deep inhale, he takes the sight in for all it's worth. He lifts his gaze to a nearby conifer tree just across the lake. A black falcon is perched on one of the branches. And for some reason, Braxton can't help but feel like the bird is *watching* him.

He tilts his head to the side, watching in bewilderment as the bird mimics the movement. Braxton straightens up and fluffs his vest. The bird's head returns upright as it ruffles its feathers. This bird . . . it has to be . . .

Impossible.

The falcon takes flight from the tree and soars toward him. A majestic creature, Braxton watches in awe as it flies overhead, then swiftly turns around and takes a dive straight at him. In defense, he ducks and throws an arm over his head so that his forearm is facing the sky. A couple of seconds later, he feels a pricking sensation as talons grip his skin. As someone who's fond of nature and animals, normally this wouldn't frighten him, but there's something strange about this particular bird. It's almost as if it can think and understand—like it somehow has *intentions.*

Slowly, Braxton brings himself upright from his crouch so as to not disturb the creature. The bird turns its head so that it's looking *right at him.* A shiver creeps down his spine. "Who are you?" he whispers.

As if to not torment him anymore, a familiar yellow glow appears, causing Braxton to scurry backward as the falcon hops from his arm onto the ground. Once again, he watches in amazement as the falcon shifts into a boy and then a man—but it isn't the same man he'd met in the woods. No, this person is older . . . much older. Salt and pepper hair. Strong jawline. Thin lips. And eyes the same icy blue as his own.

Braxton jolts backward and sucks in a breath as if he'd just had the wind knocked out of him.

His *father,* Darius Tymond, stands before him.

Braxton's initial shock is quickly replaced with anger. His eyes narrow and his jaw clenches. Normally, he would speak, but he keeps his mouth shut. This man, his so-called *father,* doesn't deserve his words, his breath. So he remains silent, waiting to be spoken to.

Darius slowly lifts his gaze from the ground, cold eyes meeting his own. His lips part to speak.

"Failure."

His words sting.

"Disappointment."

Braxton balls his hands into fists.

"Disgrace."

That last one is enough to make him lunge toward his father, all the pent-up rage from years of hatred pulsing throughout his body. He cries out as he's about to pin his father to the ground, but finds himself falling alone onto the dirt into a light gray mist.

When the haze finally settles, he finds none other than Xerin Grey standing before him. With crossed arms and narrowed eyes, Braxton can tell he isn't happy.

Xerin whistles in disbelief. "I knew it," he mutters with a shake of his head. "I don't know why I never trust my instincts. They're always dead-on."

Braxton regards him with wide eyes as what just happened sinks in. His father was never here. It was all an illusion. And now this *stranger* knows his deepest, darkest secret.

Who he is.

"What the hell was that?" Braxton hisses.

"Why don't you tell me, *Prince Tymond*?"

His words knock Braxton back on his elbows. They ring unpleasantly in his ears. "This stays between you and me, you hear?"

Xerin chuckles as he shakes his head. "Your identity is the least of my worries. Trust me."

Braxton studies him for a moment. *If he doesn't care who I am, then what does he want?*

"Back at the inn, you said you knew who I was." The words linger in the air as Xerin adjusts his stance. "So? Who am I?"

Braxton hesitates, unsure whether or not this is a trick question. "You're . . . illusié."

A wide grin stretches across Xerin's face. "Ding, ding, ding, we have a winner."

Braxton looses a breath, feeling relieved at his reaction. But his relief morphs back into panic when Xerin says, "And so are you."

Realizing he's still on the ground, Braxton pushes himself up and dusts the dirt from his pants. He looks at Xerin and casually shrugs his shoulders. "I don't know what you're talking about."

Xerin rolls his eyes. "You're really going to try to pull that?"

Braxton considers it, but decides against it. "No, I suppose not."

"You're Prince Braxton Tymond of Trendalath, son of King Darius Tymond and Queen Aldreda Tymond. You fled the kingdom seven years ago because your father banished illusié." Xerin gives him a sideways smile. "How am I doing so far?"

It takes everything in Braxton to maintain eye contact. "But how . . .?"

"I told you I came to recruit you. Don't you remember?"

Oh. Braxton stumbles backward and leans into a nearby tree for support. " That means you're . . . you're . . ."

"Yes, you're so close," Xerin taunts. "Come on, spit it out."

"Caldari."

The weight in the air seems to grow heavier and

heavier, as if anvils were dropping from the sky.

"Correct you are," Xerin says with a wink. "I am a member of the Caldari, so that just leaves us with one piece of unfinished business."

Braxton's breath catches. "Which is?"

Xerin takes a step closer to him. He rolls his neck and then cracks his knuckles, one finger at a time. "Will you or will you not be joining us?"

ARDEN ELIRI

I FIND MYSELF sprinting faster than I ever thought possible. My feet hit the ground, one after the other, with each stride I take, my arms pumping at my sides. I take a quick glance behind me, making sure that Estelle and Felix aren't following me.

No sign of them.

I continue to run through the Thering Forest, away from Orihia, away from the truth. They know my secret, and lords only know what they plan to do with it.

I reach a familiar cliffside; the one Estelle had brought me to. The one where I'd dumped the Soames's heads. I come to a screeching halt as a pebble catapults over the edge into the abyss. I need to think. I need to let everything soak in.

And I need to do it alone.

I take a seat, allowing my legs to dangle over the cliff. It's a long, long way down. I scoot back a little so that my knees are aligned with the edge.

Dawn is just breaking and the view is breathtaking. Yellows, oranges, and whites light up the lower part of the sky, but the top remains dark as night. It's one of my favorite parts of the day, although it only lasts for a few moments. Eventually, the sun carries on with its inevitable rise, illuminating the entire sky with its vibrant hello.

My gaze travels to the uppermost part of the sky, and I block out the bright colors below. The darkness is what I'm drawn to, what I've always been drawn to. It's an integral part of me, like the beating of my heart or the air I breathe. It's terrifying and disturbing, yet intriguing and indispensable.

It is all that is *me*.

Trying to explain that to another person? Impossible, stupid, and downright foolish. No one will ever truly understand, nor do I want them to. I'm not here to be understood. I'm here to be unapologetically myself, the good *and* bad parts of me.

My eyes lower as the sun's greeting fills the dark spots in the sky. Lightness always overcomes darkness. It's an absolute. So what does that say about me?

I shake my head, pulling myself from the farthest reaches of my mind and clear out every single solitary thought. I sit in silence, staring at the opaque sun as it rises into the morning sky. Goodbye, night. Goodbye, darkness.

We'll meet again soon.

If I had to guess, I've probably been sitting here for an hour or so, when I hear footsteps approaching. Instead of jumping up to hide behind a tree or large rock, I remain seated, still as stone. It's taken me a long time to accept myself for who I am, and it's something I'm still working on, so if Estelle and Felix don't accept it right away, that's understandable. I get it.

I just wish they'd leave me be.

"Arden, there you are!" Estelle gushes as she runs toward me. In her arms, she holds Juniper, who looks both frightened and relieved to see me.

"Are you okay?"

I nod my head, but stay quiet.

I hear another set of footsteps, heavier than Estelle's, and it's obvious that they belong to Felix. If anything, I was sort of hoping that Estelle would show up alone. *Wishful thinking, indeed.*

Estelle takes a seat beside me and, just as I suspected, Felix appears next to her. He doesn't say anything, just throws his legs over the edge of the cliff, until Estelle nudges him.

"Felix has something he needs to say." I can't see her face, but I'm sure she's giving him a pointed stare.

"I'm sorry," he mumbles.

His apology is barely audible, so I decide to make him work for it. "What was that, Felix? I couldn't hear you."

Estelle stifles a laugh.

He glares at her, then back at me. "I said I'm sorry. I was caught up in the moment and shouldn't have said the things I did."

"Oh, what? You mean the part where you said you were wrong about me? And how I'm not 'one' of you?"

He lets out a long sigh. "I reacted based on my emotions which, at the time, were full of confusion. You have to understand, I've always been able to amplify fear in others." He shrugs his shoulders. "But not with you. That was a strange and uncanny experience for me."

I loose a breath, relieved that he doesn't think I'm some psychotic, cold-blooded killer, even though—technically—I suppose I am. "Felix, I'm an assassin. All I've known my whole life is killing. I can thank King Tymond for that." I sigh. "When you're forced to do something long enough, it only makes sense to adjust and to learn to enjoy it."

Estelle turns her gaze from Felix to me. "Okay, well seeing as that's slightly morbid, I'm going to end this conversation right here." Juniper hops from her lap as Estelle pops up from where she's sitting and extends her hand to me. "Come on, get up."

I take her hand and stand up at the same time Felix does. "Where are we going?"

Estelle winks at me. "Back to Orihia."

Felix starts to open his mouth in protest, but one look from Estelle silences him.

"I'm not so sure that's a good idea," I say. I lower my gaze to the ground. A part of me hopes she'll just agree with me and let me go in peace, but another part of me has a stronger pull, and it desperately wants to go with them. Besides, where else would I go?

"You're coming with us," Estelle says, her voice harsh, "and that's the last I'll hear of it. Understood?"

I nod my head, happy to hear that she hasn't changed her mind. Unfortunately, it appears Felix doesn't seem to feel the same way.

As she turns to head back into the Thering Forest, I make sure to follow closely behind her. I don't turn around, even though I can distinctly feel Felix's fiery gaze searing a hole into the back of my head.

When we arrive in Orihia, it's nearly sundown. I don't remember the journey taking this long last time, but then again, those travels were broken up with bouts of unconscious spells and confusing memories. Hell, I was probably either knocked out or asleep half of the time, if not more.

I follow Estelle back into the depths of the tree

village and into a small hut. Its appearance is certainly deceiving. On the outside, it looks like a standard hut made out of the usual materials: clay, straw, hay; but on the inside, the walls are made of stone and the living space is as up to date and modern as my chambers in Trendalath castle. Albeit it's not as large as the rooms in the castle, it's surprisingly spacious. Estelle removes her cloak and throws it on a nearby chair that's positioned next to a cozy fire, then kicks off her boots. She falls into the leather and lets out a loud sigh, her eyes trained on the orange embers.

Felix removes his satchel and sets it by the door before taking a seat at a wooden table. He checks a couple of canisters for wine, slamming down the empty ones, until he finally picks one up that's full. I can hear the liquid sloshing around in the metal container as he pours it into a goblet. He lifts the glass and says cheers to the open window before taking a giant gulp.

Feeling uncomfortable and wholly out of place, I remove my boots and make my way over to an empty chair across from Estelle. She doesn't seem to notice my arrival, so I close my eyes and let the events of the day soak in. The fire feels warm and soothing on my face and it's enough to make me want to fall asleep. It's been a while since I've had a proper night's rest.

I open one eye and steal a look at Estelle. Her eyes are now closed, and it appears she's in the beginning phases of drifting off into a peaceful sleep. I shift my gaze to Felix, who is now facedown on the table, goblet in hand.

Just as I'm about to drift off to sleep, something catches my eye in the corner of the room. I quietly lift myself up off the chair and tiptoe over to the draped piece of furniture. It's tall and rectangular and I'm almost positive I know what it is. I slip the drape off the mysterious object, trying not to cough as a cloud of dust bounces from the fabric into the air around me. I smile as the object is revealed.

It's a bookcase. And behind that is . . .

Another, and another, and *another.*

I'm almost certain my eyes deceive me as I lean to the side, counting how many bookcases they've seemed to stash in this hut. I count twelve, but it's possible there are more hidden somewhere. I turn back around to check on Estelle and Felix—who are both now snoring—before facing the bookcases again.

I can't help but feel even more astonished at the size of this hut. Before I slipped the drape off the first one, it appeared that a single bookcase sat against a single wall. But as soon as I uncovered it, almost a dozen more seemed to appear out of nowhere, the room stretching on for miles. Yes, this hut is quite deceiving to the naked eye and it makes me wonder what other secrets are hidden here.

I grab a lantern off the table Felix is now drooling on and make my way through the aisles of shelves. I hold the lantern up to each row, hoping to get a better view of the titles. I almost drop the lantern as my eyes skim across the first row, then the second. Every single book pertains to illusié.

Which means I'm in the presence of Tymond's entire banned book collection.

The realization is almost enough to make me squeal with delight as I run my fingers over the worn spines. I pick one at random, then replace it as another more intriguing title catches my eye. How am I going to read all of these?

There isn't enough time.

I can't even begin to fathom how much knowledge surrounds me, how many questions I can easily have answered, how much *trouble* this could potentially cause for Tymond if the public finds out. That last thought makes me giddy, and I can feel my heart pick up pace as I set the lantern down and lower myself to the floor. I flip open the book I'd chosen and begin to read as fast as I can, trying to absorb as much information as humanly possible. The pages feel old and worn against my fingertips. I feel so privileged. Elated. All the secrets of the illusié and the Caldari are here, in this room. I am in the presence of *everything.*

It's enough to make my head spin.

Just as I'm getting to the good stuff, I hear someone stir. I slam the book shut and return it to its proper place on the shelf. I silently hope that it's Estelle who's stirred and not Felix, but my optimism fades as I hear heavy footsteps approaching the bookshelves. There's no use in hiding, seeing as they're already uncovered. I stand still, waiting for him to appear.

He finishes checking the second aisle, finally coming to the one I'm standing in. I raise the lantern so I can see his face more clearly. He holds his hand up to cover his eyes, his voice groggy. "What are you doing back here?"

I shrug. "I like to read."

Felix stifles a yawn before saying, "You shouldn't be back here." He grabs my hand and leads me to the front of the hut. I watch despondently as he throws the black drape back over the bookshelf, returning the hut to its original size. Personally, I don't know why they cover those shelves. It adds a certain zest to the room, having all those books out in the open like that; but seeing as they're banned books, I suppose I can understand why they have them hidden.

"Can I ask you a question?"

Felix smiles. "You just did."

I roll my eyes. "Seriously. Where did you get all of those books? You're aware that King Tymond banned them, right?"

Felix nods his head. "It wasn't easy, but we couldn't allow our entire history to be reduced to mere ashes and dust. Especially when we're discovering so many newcomers, brothers and sisters, like you."

I stick my lower lip out in a pout. "Then why did

you pull me away? I have so much to learn. You said so yourself."

Felix sits down at the table and pours himself another drink. I can tell by the way he sets the goblet down that he doesn't want to answer my question. "After what we experienced earlier . . ." He trails off, but I know exactly what he means.

I sit down next to him and look him in the eye. He shifts uncomfortably but holds my gaze. "You can trust me," I tell him. "You weren't wrong about me. I *am* one of you. Whether you want me to be or not, I know I am."

Felix taps his fingers against the table before taking another drink. With the goblet in one hand, he says, "You're right. But that doesn't excuse what happened earlier. We need to sort through your . . .," he struggles to find the right word, "desires. We've been plagued by darkness for too long and I'll be damned if we let it back in."

I know he doesn't mean me, but I still cringe. I *am* darkness. My thoughts from earlier repeat in my head: *It's all I know.* I don't dare say that aloud though, not at a time like this.

He stares at me for a few minutes before glancing over at Estelle. "We should probably wake her."

I follow his gaze. "Nah, let her sleep."

Out of nowhere, a *click-clack* and wing flaps fill the room. Felix and I both jump from our seats, our eyes flitting to the source of the noise. There, on the windowsill, is a black falcon.

My hand flies to my chest. I can feel my heart thumping at double its normal speed. “Holy lords, that scared me half to death,” I say. I look at Felix, but he doesn’t seem all that surprised.

He turns to look at me and gives me a crooked grin. “Yeah, we definitely need to wake Estelle for this.”

RYDAN HELSTROM

RYDAN SITS IMPATIENTLY in his cell, his knuckles turning white from gripping the iron bars. It feels as though it's been days since he last saw Elvira, and not knowing whether or not she's okay is really starting to eat away at him. He keeps his eyes trained on the dimly lit stairwell, hoping and waiting for a flicker of a lantern. Somehow, he'd missed his last meal, so not only is he hungry, but also concerned for his newfound friend's well being.

Something clanks in the distance, immediately causing his ears to perk up. A swish of clothing catches his attention, and he looses a breath as a shadow of a petite figure comes into view. "Vira, I'm so happy to see you. I was starting to get worried." He bites his tongue, realizing just how clingy and desperate he sounds.

A small laugh echoes in the distance. "Worried? What for?" She brings the tray closer to him and slides it through the bars.

Not wanting to seem eager for both her company *and* the food, he takes his time reaching for the bread before sinking his teeth into it. It's stale and hard and glorious all at the same time.

"Don't mind me," Vira says as she pulls a stack of hay from a nearby corner. She fluffs her skirt before sitting on it. "And I'm sorry for missing your last meal. You must be ravenous. No need to mind your manners." She gives him a wide grin as she crosses her legs.

Rydan smiles back. "Thank the lords because you're right. I am ravenous." With gusto, he digs into the meat and other piles of slop, even those that he normally wouldn't dare touch. His stomach rumbles in approval as he finishes every last morsel. "Ahhh," he says with a long exhale, "that's just what I needed."

"May I take your tray?"

He nods, but immediately wishes he hadn't. It dawns on him that she may take the tray and scamper off to whatever's next on her list of duties—but to his delight, she takes the tray and returns to the haystack. "So, have I missed anything?" she asks.

He knows it's a rhetorical question, but in the

hopes of making her stay a little while longer, he decides to take a stab at his humor. "Well, Joseph came by the other day with a rare collection of handcrafted bowls that he swears are made from the finest oak in all of Trendalath." He tries to gauge her response and when she giggles, he keeps going. "And Lady Napoli just won't give her seamstressing skills a rest. Says she can fix my tunic and trousers right up and make them look like new again."

A sad smile drifts across her face. "Do you think they'll ever let you out?"

Rydan's shoulders sag as he realizes his attempt at making her laugh has already come to its inevitable end. "I don't know," he whispers in response. "I sure hope so."

They sit in silence for a few moments, their breathing the only audible sound throughout the dungeons.

"Enough about me and my situation," Rydan says with a faux smile, "tell me about you. I want to know more about the girl who brings me my food. It's the highlight of my day, you know." He blushes as he stumbles over his words. "Have you always lived in Trendalath?"

Vira smiles again, but it doesn't reach her eyes. "No," she says quietly. "I haven't always lived in Trendalath."

Rydan can tell he's losing her, so he jumps in with

another question. "Miraenia then? With that beautiful blonde hair, I can picture you strolling about the markets in that seaside village."

She laughs, and Rydan is relieved to hear it's a *real* laugh, one coming from joy and not from pity.

"Chialka, actually. I grew up there." She hesitates before continuing. "I moved to Trendalath somewhat against my will. My family, was . . . well, we were split up."

Rydan sits back on his heels as he digests this information. "Oh, I had no idea. I'm terribly sorry to hear that."

"It's quite all right. I've grown accustomed to Trendalath. I hardly even think about Chialka anymore." Her voice cracks and Rydan can tell she's trying to keep her emotions at bay.

"Vira," he soothes, "this is a safe place. You can tell me. I promise I'm not going to tell anyone." He smirks, then jokingly says, "Well, maybe Lady Napoli. She's unusually inquisitive, that one."

Vira's shoulders relax as she looks up from the ground. "After the fires of Eroesa, Chialka was evacuated to higher ground. My mother and I were sent to Trendalath, and my brother and father . . ." Her voice catches. She doesn't finish her sentence.

"You don't know where they are?" he asks, trying to finish for her.

She nods.

"Well, I'm sure they're safe somewhere, maybe

even here in Trendalath."

She shakes her head sadly. "I highly doubt that. They couldn't be here." She bites her lower lip as if she's purposely trying not to say anything further.

Rydan wishes he could break out of his cell and give this poor girl a hug. He essentially forced her to open up to him and now she's sitting on a haystack, alone, with no one to comfort her.

Nice going.

"Tell you what, when I get out of here," Rydan says, "we'll search every inch of the Lands of Aeridon for your father and brother. We'll even journey to other cities if we have to."

Her eyes gleam even in the dim lighting, and he can tell she's on the verge of tears. "That's kind of you, but I think it'll be near impossible to find them. Best to just move on."

Rydan knows not to press any further so he says, "Well, if you change your mind, the offer still stands."

Vira gives him a nod. "Thank you." She looks over her shoulder as if she hears something. "I should probably be on my way out."

"Vira?" Rydan says her name a little too quickly. "It was really nice talking to you and getting to know you. And I apologize if I made you feel uncomfortable."

She waves her hand flippantly in the air. "It's not that at all. I just have bad memories of . . ." She trails off again, a faraway look in her eyes.

"No matter," Rydan says, breaking her from her trance. "I look forward to our next encounter."

She sinks into a half-curtsy before picking up the empty tray. "As do I."

Rydan watches as she leaves, feeling both better and worse at the same time. Who knows when he'll see her again, especially after going on and on with question after question about her family and her past. He wouldn't be surprised if she requested a change in her duties, one that didn't require serving *him* his meals. That thought alone causes him to suck in a sharp breath.

No, she'll come back. They connected. She wouldn't leave him alone to rot with no social interaction. Not to mention, she seemed just as lonely, if not lonelier. *I have nothing to worry about.*

But the more he repeats those words, wishing them to be true, the more they feel like an empty promise—one that, sadly, will never come to pass.

DARIUS TYMOND

AFTER A FULL day's travel, Darius finds himself standing on a doorstep he thought he'd never have to approach again in his lifetime. A burnt orange door stares him in the face, beckoning him to knock. *Go on, burn yourself. It couldn't possibly be worse than last time,* the nonexistent voices whisper.

Darius swiftly turns to look over his shoulder at the carriage and horses that brought him to this retched place. Declorath: the city of lying, deceitful, cowardly men. Or perhaps that was just from his own past experiences.

He could turn around and leave. Head back to Trendalath. Lie to Aldreda. Find another way out of this stupid mess. But Aldreda would find out, and she'd either have his head for it, or do it herself. Best not to awaken the beast.

With a reluctant raise of his hand, Darius raps his knuckles against the door. A few seconds go by and no one answers. Relief washes over him, but the feeling is quickly replaced with dread. He has to be here. Where else would he be?

Just as he's about to knock again, the door swings open. Darius takes a step back, startled by the sudden shift of stillness to movement. His eyes meet those of the man standing before him.

Clive Ridley. The leader of his Savant. He hasn't aged a day and looks exactly as Darius remembers. His copper hair is still wound in tight curls around his head, his hazel eyes lively and bright. Wrinkles are scarce and there's not a mark on his face, not even a freckle. He smiles wide, showcasing his jagged teeth before saying, "Darius! The last person I ever expected to see. How have you been, my old friend?"

Darius gives him the once-over before forcing a smile. "I have been quite well. Is this a bad time?"

"For *King* Tymond? It's never a bad time!" Clive gives him a sturdy slap on the back as he ushers him inside the house. "Do come in. Sit, sit. Can I get you anything? A cup of tea?"

Darius watches him intently as he hurries over to the cupboard and pulls out a wooden cup, then proceeds to the fire with a pail of water. He really isn't in the mood for tea, but Clive seems to be purposely trying to keep busy, so Darius keeps his mouth shut.

It's hard not to like Clive. He's charming, amicable, and charismatic. A loyal confidante. A trustworthy advisor. That was, of course, until the affair with his wife.

Darius takes a seat at the table as Clive pours the water into a cup and begins to steep some strong scented herbs. He brings the concoction over to the table and sits down across from him. "So," Clive says as he cracks his knuckles, "what can I do you for?"

Darius glances down at the steaming beverage before pushing it to the side. "First and foremost, I need to make it clear that my trip here is strictly business." He cocks his head toward the tea, implying that it's something old friends would do, which they are not. "I've come to you because I'm facing a dilemma in Trendalath."

Clive nods his head as he scoots the cup of tea back to his side of the table. "I understand. Proceed."

Darius hesitates, weighing how much information to provide. "One of my assassins has gone missing, and the other Cruex members are starting to grow restless. I've had my men searching day and night for her, but to no avail." He pauses. The next few words are hard to get out. "I need you. And the Savant."

Clive regards him with interest as he strokes his beard. "I see."

While this short response angers Darius, he doesn't let it show. "I need you to find her. She has . . . abilities. I'm not sure she's discovered them just yet."

"Well, we *are* the King's Savant. You say the word and we'll be there."

The statement should fill Darius with comfort, but instead, it does just the opposite. Every time Clive opens his mouth to speak, he imagines the words that were spoken to his wife. The way his tone caressed her ears. His charm. His charisma. His allure.

It was strong enough the first time for Aldreda—who's to say it wouldn't be even stronger the second time?

On the ride over to Declorath, Darius had gone back and forth in his head as to whether or not pulling the Savant into this was a reasonable idea. He'd exiled his Savant to Declorath specifically after learning about Clive's affair with Aldreda. The King's Savant used to live in the Trendalath castle, and that's where it'd all happened—right under his nose. He'd been too blind to see it.

So inviting the Savant back into his life seems utterly absurd; but finding Arden is of the utmost importance. And to do that in the time allotted, Darius needs the Savant where he can keep a watchful eye on them.

In Trendalath. In his castle. In his *home.*

Knowing that he's about to invite Clive back to the very place he'd forcefully removed him from is a difficult pill to swallow. But there is no other choice. It has to be done. And quick.

Clive is busy talking about the shortage of crops in Declorath when Darius interjects, "I need you to gather the other members of the Savant and make your way to Trendalath castle." He spits the words out; they taste like poison on his tongue.

Clive raises a thick eyebrow, obviously thinking the exact same thing Darius is, but keeps his shock to himself. "When?"

"Immediately. If you can ride in tonight, that would be preferable."

Clive looks around his house, his forehead creasing. "It's short notice, but we will make do. Let me notify the others."

Darius nods his head as he scoots his chair back from the table. "Your sense of urgency is recognized and appreciated." He extends his arm for a handshake, but finds himself being pulled into a bear hug instead. He grunts as Clive pats him on the back with a little too much force.

"I'm so glad we can put this all behind us. Don't forget what I said. We are *your* Savant. Just say the word and we'll be there. That will never change."

Darius gives him a half-smile. "I look forward to seeing everyone again."

Clive lets out a low chuckle. "As do I, My King." He sighs longingly. "As do I."

And just like that, Darius wishes he could reverse the last twenty minutes, and kill the damn rat bastard instead.

CERYLIA JARETH

"YOUR GREATNESS, YOU shouldn't have."

Cerylia grins as Opal's excitement radiates from across the room. She watches as she pulls piece after piece of fine silk from the box. "Do you like them?"

"Do I *like* them?" she squeals. "They are exquisite. Magnificent." She clutches the robes tightly and brings them into her chest. "I don't think I've ever received such a thoughtful gift."

"Hard work deserves to be rewarded," Cerylia says. She rises from the chair in Opal's chambers and glides over to the bed. Gently, she takes a seat next to the girl, who is still admiring her new robes. The look on her face—one of pure joy—is familiar, an emotion that Cerylia wishes she could still summon, but sadly, it was taken from her some time ago. "You've been pushing yourself harder and harder each day. I want you to know that it has been recognized. These robes are a token of my appreciation."

Opal shifts her gaze from the robes to the queen. "They're stunning, but hardly necessary, if I may say so, Your Greatness. You've given me shelter, food, training, and companionship. You have given me more than enough." What looks like a tear threatens to fall from her eye, but she takes a deep inhale and it disappears.

"On the contrary, I hardly think I've done enough. Without your courage to approach me, none of this would be happening, and my questions would remain unanswered. Because of you, I will finally have clarity."

Opal blushes just as a knock sounds on the door.

Cerylia lets out an exasperated sigh. "Who is it?" she calls out.

"Your Greatness, my apologies," Delwynn says hurriedly from behind the door, "I had no idea you were visiting with Opal. I've come to take her to training."

Cerylia turns to Opal and gives her a small smile. "No need to apologize. Come in, Delwynn."

Her advisor scurries into the room, looking disheveled and embarrassed. He sinks into an awkward bow as he addresses the queen, then faces

Opal. "I can come back at another time."

Opal eyes Cerylia, who shakes her head. "No, that's quite all right. We were just finishing up."

He eyes the intricate silk robes that Opal is stuffing back into the box. "What marvelous robes," he points out. "A gift, I presume?"

Opal nods her head.

Delwynn fixes his gaze on Cerylia. "No doubt. What a fine gift for someone who's showing such tremendous progress. As her mentor—"

Cerylia holds her hand up. "I didn't forget about you, Delwynn. You've been a loyal advisor and an effective mentor."

Delwynn beams at the compliment. "Thank you, Your Greatness."

"Which is why," she turns behind her and pulls something from the other side of the bed, "I got you this." She extends a staff made of white marble to him. "It's about time we got rid of that old thing," she says with a nod toward his white cedar cane.

"But how—?"

Cerylia already knows what he's about to ask. "The marble is lighter than a falcon's feather. I had the healer conjure a mixture using dragon scales before it was sculpted into its final form. Give it a try."

Delwynn takes the staff from her, his eyes widening as he realizes how light it is. "This is truly remarkable, Your Greatness. But it would be selfish of me to accept."

"And it would be disrespectful of you not to." Cerylia gives him a knowing smile. "It will never need replacing and the support will be like no other."

"It would appear I have no choice but to accept then. Thank you, Your Greatness," Delwynn whispers. "I am wholly grateful."

"Now," Cerylia says as she swiftly rises to her feet, "I suppose I should check on our supper. It should be served at 1800 hours. As our guests of honor, please arrive on time."

Both Delwynn and Opal nod as the queen takes her leave. Just as she's about to walk down the hallway, whispering catches her attention. Opal and Delwynn seem to have carried on a separate conversation.

"Have you asked her yet?"

Cerylia sneaks back toward the door and presses herself against the wall. The door is still cracked, enabling her to eavesdrop.

"I'm afraid not," Opal responds, her voice quiet.

"Why not?" Delwynn presses.

"I haven't found an opportune moment, but I'm sure one will come along. Any day now."

Cerylia bristles at her response. *Opportune moment? To ask me what?*

"Well, when you find out, please make sure I'm the first to know."

"Delwynn," Opal says, "I understand. I will come

straight to you."

"It's critical that we know exactly what she needs to clarify and soon."

Cerylia sucks in a sharp breath as if she's just been shoved into a wall. *Opal is confiding in Delwynn?*

"If the queen finds out that you've been able to travel back to her desired timeframe all along, lords only know what she'll do with us. We definitely won't be seeing anymore of these," he says half-jokingly, and Cerylia immediately presumes he means the gifts.

Her hands curl into fists as rage ignites within her. Not wanting to hear another word, she takes off down the hall, trying to be as quiet as possible until she rounds the corner. With her head in her hands, she slinks against the stone down to the floor, her robes overflowing into a pool around her body. *She's been able to travel back all along. Why did she lie to me?*

The question repeats itself over and over again in her head, and still, she cannot find the answer. She desperately tries to remember everything she's shared with Opal—what information she's dished so freely to this newly discovered conspirator.

And as for Delwynn, his betrayal is far more surprising than Opal's. For years, Cerylia had convinced herself that her advisor worshipped her and would never do anything to put her trust in him at risk. How terribly wrong she'd been.

Feeling foolish, but knowing not to dwell on the matter for too long, Cerylia pulls herself to her feet. She marches toward the dining hall, just as she'd planned to do originally when someone runs into her. Her brows furrow as she realizes who it is.

Delwynn?

Impossible. He was just in Opal's chambers, on the opposite side of the castle. The sight is enough to leave her lightheaded. She stumbles backward, almost falling over, but Delwynn drops his cane and rushes to catch her just in time. "Your Greatness, is everything all right?"

"How are you here? I just saw you . . . in Opal's room . . ."

Delwynn gives her a concerned look. "Your Greatness, I do not know of which you speak. I've been in the Great Room with the counsel for the past few hours."

Cerylia looks him straight in the eye. Delwynn wouldn't lie to her. He would never betray her. He *is* loyal. He *is* her most trusted confidante. She draws in a sharp breath as the reality sinks in. Delwynn wasn't in the room with Opal.

A Caldari was.

"Delwynn, alert the guards," Cerylia says through gritted teeth. "There's an imposter in the castle."

BRAXTON HORNSBY

BRAXTON SITS AT the bar top at the inn, his hands wrapped around a lukewarm cup of tea. Hanslow is behind the bar, making a racket as he moves dishes around—the same dishes Braxton had put away just an hour prior. He sighs as plates and cups clink together, breaking his concentration.

It's been three days since Xerin left. Braxton had hoped things would become clearer as the days wore on, but everything has only become more confusing. Xerin invited him to join the Caldari, the strongest standing members of illusié. At first, all Braxton wanted to do was laugh in his face. Xerin had tricked him into revealing that he was King Tymond's son, and then asked him to join the very group that his father had banished from Trendalath—the very reason he'd fled the kingdom seven years ago.

Confusion doesn't even begin to cover it. Not even close.

Braxton takes another sip of his tea before pushing his chair back and standing up. He runs a hand through his blonde hair and lets out a long exhale.

Hanslow seems to sense that something is bothering him. "My boy, what troubles you?"

Braxton slides his hand to the back of his head and presses firmly against his skull. The pressure feels good—exactly what he needs. "I'm fine."

Hanslow shakes his head and whistles as he wipes down the counter. "You most certainly are not. You haven't talked my ear off like you normally do. And when I've asked for you to finish your assignments, you've done so without question." He shakes his head again and makes a clucking sound. "No, sir, you are not fine."

Braxton shrugs, knowing that unless he says *something* to Hanslow, this conversation could go on for hours, and, at this junction, all he wants is to be left alone. "I just had a strange conversation with someone today. It rubbed me the wrong way, put me in an off mood. That's all."

Hanslow eyes him warily.

"I swear it," Braxton says as he raises his hands,

palms facing out. "No need to worry. I'll be better tomorrow."

"I'd advise you to get some rest. You look like you could use it."

Braxton doesn't say anything in response, just nods his head as he walks into the main room and through the front door. There's no time to rest. Not when a decision as heavy as this is weighing on his shoulders. Xerin said he'd return in one week for his answer and by the way he'd said it, Braxton understood he'd only get one chance at this.

Yes. Or no.

There would be no turning back, no do-overs.

A long sigh escapes as he walks along the dirt path to the forest. Four days isn't nearly enough time to make such a life-altering decision. He needs more information, more facts, just *more* . . .

His thoughts trail off as he reaches a fork in the road. Without even realizing it, he's wandered off to an area completely unfamiliar to him. The sun is beginning to set and night is closing in. He turns around and looks back the way he came, suddenly feeling disoriented. *Did I come from that way? Or was it this way?*

With a mind so cluttered, it's hard to think straight. A task as simple as turning around and going back home feels like an impossible feat. Maybe Hanslow's right. Maybe he *does* need sleep.

He tries again to decipher which direction he came from, but it's no use. His mind is mush and his thoughts feel like frantic butterflies flapping their wings every which way. A barrel of hay near a seemingly abandoned farmhouse catches his eye. Without a second thought, he heads straight for it. The doors to the barn are locked, so the barrel of hay will have to do.

Hanslow will probably worry about him. The old man's probably crazy enough to come looking. Hopefully that's not the case. Being alone is exactly what he needs right now.

He leans back onto the haystack, his eyes trained on the navy canvas above him. Nightfall came fast. Brightly lit stars already dot the sky, and he has to commend himself for recognizing a few of the constellations. The more he stares into the sky, the more at peace he feels, but a few questions still circle in orbit around his mind.

Why wouldn't I join the Caldari? What's stopping me? After all these years, why am I still concerned with disappointing my father?

The last question haunts him. It's haunted him ever since he can remember. He shouldn't care what his father thinks, not after the way he's treated him—his *only* son. And especially not after the way he's mistreated those who dare to challenge him, for the sheer purpose of instilling fear in an entire population of innocent, good-hearted people.

No, his father is not a decent man, nor will he ever be. It's time for everyone in Trendalath to know that, and there's only one way Braxton can help.

He makes his decision right then and there.

ARDEN ELIRI

WATCHING SOMEONE morph from a bird-like state to a human being is much more disturbing than I imagined it would be. Not that this is something that comes to mind frequently—it doesn't—but still, it's surprising, to say the least.

I knew there was something odd about that bird when I first saw it looking at us from the windowsill. At the time, it appeared to be a normal falcon with its pointed beak and sleek black feathers, but there was something off-putting about it.

Its eyes.

They were crimson, almost as if its brain were bleeding into its eye sockets. Felix had shot out of his seat to wake Estelle, who'd swatted at him repeatedly. She'd been amidst a seemingly terrible nightmare. When she'd awoken, Felix had informed her of the falcon's arrival. She'd seemed both anxious and excited.

I'd had no idea what was going on.

But then the falcon had morphed into a man with blonde hair and those same crimson eyes. He'd introduced himself as Xerin Grey and that's when I'd understood. He was also a Caldari, one of them.

Correction: One of *us*.

Now, an hour later, I'm intently listening to Xerin and his precocious stories. Being a Shaper (that's what they call illusié who can morph into other people and animals) has its advantages. Xerin gets to fly from town to town, discovering truths and revealing secrets. I feel a tinge of jealousy toward him and his freedom. He's not tied to anyone or anything. No king to obey. No rules to abide by. No reigns holding him back.

But what makes me most jealous is the fact that he receives no judgment. Felix and Estelle seem to accept him for who he is, as do I, and I *just* met the guy.

I snap out of my trance and back to the conversation as Xerin turns to me.

"And how is our newcomer enjoying Orihia?"

I raise my glass to toast both him and the beautiful tree village. "It's truly remarkable. I've never seen anything like it."

Xerin nods his head sadly. His spiky blonde hair doesn't budge an inch, and it makes me wonder if it gets windblown when he's soaring over the cities. "If only everyone saw it that way."

The room falls silent.

I'm not sure if we're having a "moment"—or what a "moment" would even entail—so I hesitate before breaking the speaking. "How do you mean?"

"Tymond," my three new friends say in unison.

"Ah, right. The exiler of illusié," I say glumly. "If only he could see this place, and see all of you. Maybe then he'd come to his senses."

They stare at me as though I'm firing missiles and missing my target on purpose. "Or not," I say quietly, suddenly feeling uncomfortable.

"You were making a joke," Estelle confirms, trying to clear the air. "It was just a joke. That's all."

I notice both Felix and Xerin exhale as their shoulders drop.

More silence.

I try to cut through the tension, yet again. "So, how long have you all known each other?"

"Well, Xerin's been around for quite some time," Felix says. "One may even say that he's the originator of the Caldari."

"Really? That's fascinating." I'm pleased that Felix answered so quickly and it makes me hopeful that the last awkward silence of the night is over and done with. “What about you, Estelle?”

Estelle regards me thoughtfully. “Let’s see. I joined the Caldari after Xerin and Felix. Felix was actually the one who found me.” She winks at him. “And thank goodness for that.”

I tilt my head and eye her questioningly. “Why is that?”

“I’d lived in Lonia my entire life until Felix found me. It’s a beautiful village with plenty to do, but I learned pretty early on about my abilities. I was too afraid to show my family because I was afraid that they’d reject me. Just when I’d planned to leave, Felix found me.” A hint of a smile tugs at her lips. “He showed me that there was nothing to be afraid of and that I wasn’t alone—that we could create a new kind of family and share everything. And so I left, but not alone.” She punches Felix playfully in the shoulder, making their brother-sister relationship clear as day.

“So you came back here with Felix? To Orihia?”

Estelle nods. “I sure did. Xerin was waiting here for me, too. I knew the minute I walked in that this is where I was meant to be all along.” She pauses, her eyes full of longing. “If only I’d found it sooner.”

Xerin clucks his tongue. “There’s no use dwelling on the past, Stelle. You’re here now and that’s what matters.”

My heart swells as I watch them exchange looks. They seem like such a tight knit group—like a family.

Although I wouldn't know what that feels like because I never truly had a family.

Except for the Cruex.

Really just Rydan, though.

Rydan.

I close my eyes as the floodgates open, memory after memory pouring through my mind. I hate the way we left things. I hate that I had to see that side of him. Rydan was always good and pure and untainted in my eyes. An example of who I should be. But now I know the truth.

He's exactly like me.

I can feel the darkness swooping in. I squeeze my eyes shut and try to focus on something else—on the three incredible people surrounding me. Just as I think it's about to pull me under, and win, Estelle saves me.

"What do you think of the Caldari so far?"

Xerin chortles. "You're basically asking her what she thinks of us! Not forward of you at all."

Estelle waves her hand absentmindedly. "I'm serious. I want to know."

I look into those deep violet eyes and say, "I agree with everything you've said, especially the last part."

Estelle furrows her brows and looks at Felix and Xerin. It's clear she's trying to remember what that was. They just shrug, unable to recall either.

I give a half-smile before saying, "If only I'd found you sooner."

RYDAN HELSTROM

RYDAN IS DISMAYED to see a burly shadow walking toward him. It's been two days since he's seen Vira, and he's hoping that today she'll visit. He worries that something's happened to her, or that perhaps she's been assigned elsewhere now. Had someone eavesdropped on their conversations? Had he unknowingly gotten her into trouble?

Rydan gulps as the shadow, which happens to be a hefty man, comes into view. He recognizes the guard almost immediately. It's the same one who led him off the ship from Lonia and to his fate in this wretched dungeon.

"Happy to see me?" the guard grunts as he

fumbles with his key ring.

Rydan bites his tongue, afraid that if he answers, he'll only get himself into more trouble. Something he *really* doesn't need right now. Or ever.

After a few tries, the cell door opens. "Hands," the guard orders. Rydan does as he says and extends his hands, watching despondently as heavy metal clinks around his wrists, locking securely in place. The guard yanks him from the cell, causing him to stumble over his own two feet. "This way."

Feeling weak on his feet from lack of food and sleep, Rydan trudges up the stairs. Seeing as the guard's hand is resting heavily on his shoulder, his pace is slower than normal. More and more energy is exerted, leaving Rydan partially out of breath as they reach the top of the stairs.

"Keep going," the guard orders as he changes position to lead the way. Rydan is pulled forward, and he quickly realizes he's heading toward a familiar area. The Great Room.

Hope flickers within his mind, but is quickly extinguished as multiple scenarios begin to infiltrate his thoughts. Tymond had made it clear that his trial wouldn't be for at least two years. Hadn't it only been a few weeks? A month at most? His stomach turns as another thought surfaces. *What if this has something to do with Elvira?*

As they approach the Great Room, Rydan can't help but feel lightheaded. He stops walking, but having fallen behind the oaf of a man, the guard tugs on the metal to keep him moving forward. Rydan howls as he loses his balance and falls flat on his face.

"Get up!" the guard yells. With one hand, he grabs Rydan by the scruff of his neck and pulls him up.

"Forgive me," Rydan pants. "I haven't eaten in a couple of days."

The guard eyes him warily. "I suppose that would explain your inability to walk straight or stand upright. I thought you were just drunk."

Rydan guffaws out of exhaustion and hunger, but mostly disbelief. "Believe me, I wish that were the case. Tell me, have the other prisoners been getting special treatment? Have I been ruled out for some reason?"

The guard rolls his eyes, ignoring his jest. "Follow me."

Much to Rydan's delight, they pass the Great Room and head straight for the dining hall. His eyes glaze over at the sight of trays and trays of croissants, sausage, ham—even the bowls of clumpy porridge look appetizing. The smell is enough to make his mouth water, and he realizes right then and there how truly hungry he is. *Starving* is actually the proper word for the situation.

"Any requests?" the guard asks.

Rydan takes a step back. That was a question he wasn't expecting. He wishes he could take back all the negative thoughts he'd had about the guard. Maybe the guy has an empathetic side after all.

"Honestly, I want everything," Rydan says greedily.

The guard wags a finger. "Choose wisely."

Internally Rydan pouts, but he keeps a straight face. "Croissants, please. With extra glaze."

The guard retrieves a basket of croissants and brings them to a nearby table. The dining hall is completely empty, so he assumes from this, and the position of the sun just outside the window, that it's between 1400 and 1600 hours.

Rydan can feel the guard eyeing him in disgust as he scarfs down each and every crumb. When he finishes, he pushes the basket to the side and gives the man his most genuine, appreciative smile. "Thank you."

The guard yanks on the chains and pulls him up from the table, and just like that, his empathetic friend has disappeared. "Not a word of this to the king. Am I understood?"

Rydan gives him a hasty nod.

"Good. Now, come on. We're already late enough as it is."

Rydan reluctantly follows the guard down the hall into the Great Room. The minute he enters through the double doors, he can tell something isn't right. The air is stale and smells of copper—as if there's just been a slaughter.

No.

He squeezes his eyes shut, trying to push images

of Elvira's headless and bleeding body far from his mind.

You're jumping to conclusions. She's fine.

He keeps his eyes glued to the ground as he walks behind the guard. When they reach Tymond's throne, Rydan lifts his eyes from the ground, feeling surprised to see that the king isn't seated. His eyes drift to the window, where a figure cloaked in black and crimson robes stands, his gaze on the scenery outside. Rydan coughs, and the king swiftly turns his gaze to him. "Helstrom."

The words come out ice cold and send a shiver down Rydan's spine. "Your Majesty."

King Tymond throws his robe behind him as he marches over to his throne, but instead of sitting down, he pushes past the guard until he's eye to eye with Rydan. "Are you finding your accommodations . . . pleasant?"

It seems more like a jab than a question.

Rydan remains silent, but doesn't break eye contact.

"I'll take that as an affirmative," the king huffs. "I must say, it's a shame about your little lady friend . . ."

Rydan's ears immediately perk up. The king notices almost instantly. *Way to be nonchalant.*

"I've come to learn—from credible sources, of course—that you've been participating in illicit behavior with one of the handmaidens."

Rydan can't help but snort. "If you mean casual conversation, then yes, I'm guilty. But that's hardly *illicit* behavior."

King Tymond narrows his eyes. "For a prisoner it is."

For a moment, Rydan thinks he must be joking, but the king's expression doesn't shift. It's as rigid as a statue. *He's serious.*

Tymond turns away from him and slowly walks toward his throne. "Elvira is a handmaiden, a servant. Her duties involve serving our prisoners their meals and then returning to the dining hall to wash and dry the empty trays. But Elvira . . ."

Rydan gulps. He can feel beads of sweat forming along his hairline.

"Elvira has been late on more than one occasion. And we've determined that the culprit," he turns to give him a crooked smile, "is you."

Rydan's breath catches in his throat, but he manages to think on his feet. "She's been serving my food and making polite conversation," he says a little too quickly. "I swear, if I had known that talking to her would have gotten her into trouble, I would have kept my mouth shut. I wouldn't have so much as looked at her."

Tymond clucks, his tongue tapping the roof of his mouth. "Well, you did."

Rydan's heart sinks. *What have I done?*

"Seeing as she can't deign to do the *one* thing I've asked of her, I have no use for her services anymore. She shall be punished."

The smell of copper appears again, and all Rydan can think about is her perfect head of blonde hair being smashed into a pulp. The ground beneath him is suddenly tinged with red, and he has to blink a few times to clear the disturbing hallucination.

Tymond claps his hands twice, and Rydan looks behind him as the double doors to the Great Room open. Two guards enter—burlier than the one that brought him here—and behind them is a petite girl with matted blonde hair. Elvira. Her tunic and skirt are ragged and torn, and her feet are black with soot.

Rydan's jaw clenches at the sight of her. He turns his gaze from his battered friend to King Tymond. The guard stumbles as he takes an abrupt step forward, then spits at the tyrant's feet. "This isn't her fault. She didn't do anything!"

The king's eyes lower to the wad of spit on the ground, then back up to Rydan. "Precisely," he hisses, "she didn't *do* anything."

The irony takes Rydan aback. He looks at Elvira, but her focus remains on the floor.

"Well, Mr. Helstrom, you've certainly made it much easier on me to decide her punishment." He flicks his hand at the guards. "Lock her in the cell in the south corridor. I don't want to make any rash decisions."

Rydan's eyes widen as the guards begin to drag Vira away. "Please! Let her go."

At the sound of his plea, Vira's head snaps up, if only for a brief moment. Her blue eyes meet his. They're eerily calm, as if she's accepted all of this—as if it's her fault.

As if she *deserves* this.

I'm sorry, Rydan mouths, afraid that if he says it aloud, she'll hear how weak he really is.

Vira gives a single nod of her head, then drops her gaze back to the floor. The guards drag her out. She doesn't flinch—not even the slightest movement can be seen. She is completely still.

Rydan blinks back his rage as the Great Room doors shut behind them.

"Her punishment will be decided before tomorrow at dawn. But first, I need a proper meal." With a jovial hop, Tymond excuses himself from his throne and heads for the doors.

Rydan watches him with vengeful eyes. "Coward," he mutters.

With one hand on the door handle, Tymond turns to face him. "I'd keep that mouth of yours sealed shut. It only seems to get you into trouble."

Rydan bites his tongue.

"Take him off the meal schedule for a week," he directs the guard. "And after that week, let Gladys know that she'll be his handmaiden."

The guard nods and Tymond opens the doors. They slam shut behind him, the sound reverberating throughout the entire room.

Rydan can feel his heartbeat thumping in his ears. He doesn't know who Gladys is, but from the way Tymond just said her name, he knows he's just gotten into something *way* over his head.

DARIUS TYMOND

WITH A BAD taste in his mouth from the last encounter, Darius finds himself on yet another doorstep in Declorath. Fortunately, the resident of this dwelling is one he's looking forward to seeing.

He knocks on the door and waits a few moments. Footsteps scurry on the other side and before he realizes what's happening, the door swings open. Before him stands a pale, lanky man with disheveled auburn hair and deep set brown eyes. He extends a bony hand toward the king.

"Landon Graeme," Darius beams as he meets his grip. "It's been a while."

"Darius Tymond," Landon says with a smile.

The king pulls his hand away after a surprisingly firm handshake, then says, "May I come in?"

Landon throws his hands up in the air. "Pardon me, where are my manners? Of course, do come in."

Darius follows him inside the quaint household, motioning for his guards to stay outside.

"I'll be brief," he says as Landon shuts the door. He gestures toward a seat, but Darius refuses. "I have no doubt that Clive will be reaching out to you shortly, but I wanted to come here first and break the news."

Landon's face falls. Darius turns to see a stout woman appear from behind one of the walls, carrying a stack of dishes. "A moment," Landon snaps. The woman sighs and sets the dishes down on a nearby table before marching into the other room.

"Servant?" Darius asks.

"I wish," Landon responds with a roll of his eyes. "Wife."

Darius gives him an empathetic smile. "As I was saying, I won't be too long, but there's a situation in Trendalath I'd very much like to discuss with you . . ."

By the time Darius finishes his story, Landon is sitting in a chair, rubbing the bristles on his half-shaven beard. "So you want me to come back with you?"

"Not want," Darius says firmly. "*Need.*"

Landon's eyes flit to the room his wife had walked

into earlier. "I can't just leave on such short notice."

Darius gives him a coy smile. "Oh, I think you can. To be frank, I can't imagine why you'd want to stay."

Landon tilts his head back and forth, weighing the validity of the statement. "You do have a point."

He gets up to show Darius the door, but the king stays put. "There's one other thing," he whispers under his breath.

Landon looks at him intently.

"I need you to befriend Clive."

Landon groans. "You know that's a poor idea."

"I need you to watch him. And I need you to watch . . ." He doesn't realize until now how difficult the words are to speak. "I need you to keep an eye on Aldreda, but mostly the two of them. I need reports if and when you see them together, for how long, what their conversations consist of, and so on." He takes a deep breath, not sure how his request will be received.

Now it's Landon's turn to give him an empathetic smile. "I understand. And I will do just as you ask."

"Good." Darius nods. "Now pack your things."

Landon looks taken aback. "We're leaving *now*?"

"Clive and the others should arrive by tonight. You need to be there beforehand."

Again, Landon's eyes flicker to the other room. "Well, can I just . . . I just need a moment."

"Certainly. I will meet you outside at the carriage."

Landon shows him to the door and hurriedly

packs his things. Even from outside the house, Darius can hear his wife yelling. He feels slightly guilty for a moment, then immediately better knowing that he's taking Landon away from such a miserable situation.

He's going to be living in a castle, for lord's sake.

Upon their arrival at the castle, Darius is dismayed to see another carriage already parked outside the drawbridge. His lips tighten as they draw nearer and a familiar object comes into view. Eloquently detailed serpents have been carved into the wood of the carriage, and the cover is a deep emerald green.

As the royal coachman is about to park the carriage next to it, Darius pokes his head out the side and yells, "Carry on and release the drawbridge!"

The coachman turns over his shoulder and, with a confused look, continues onward. The drawbridge lowers slowly. Only once it's completely lowered does Darius pull the upper half of his body back inside the moving carriage.

"Unbelievable," he mutters, the fact that he has company briefly slipping his mind.

"What's that, Your Majesty?" Landon asks.

"Oh, don't mind me. Just talking to myself."

Landon nods and averts his eyes out the window.

When the carriage finally comes to a stop within

the castle walls, Darius swings the door open and jumps out, straightening his robe behind him as he hurries toward the entrance. Landon can barely keep up. “Come along now, we have no time to waste!”

As they enter the castle, Darius stops for a brief moment. His ears are on high alert as he attempts to hear any conversations that might be coming from other rooms, although it’s hard to hear anything with Landon’s excessive panting. “Hush, will you?” he snaps.

And then he hears it.

Laughter. Just down the hall.

“This way,” he commands as he marches in the direction of the noise. They arrive at the Great Room just moments later. Muffled voices continue to converse on the other side of the doors. There’s another bout of laughter, one that’s easily recognizable.

His wife’s.

He gathers his nerve, then pushes through the double doors into the Great Room. There, sitting at the oversized table are his wife and, not surprisingly, his dear old friend, Clive Ridley.

Darius looks directly at Clive. “Impeccable timing,” he says, his tone overflowing with sarcasm. He glances around the room, realizing that no one else has arrived yet. “And where are the others?”

Clive gives him a sinister smile. “They’re on their way. Aldreda saw my carriage from the tower window and let me in. She's been quite hospitable, something I truly appreciate after my long travels." Aldreda blushes, and Darius can feel his own face burning. Clive changes the subject and says, "Landon Graeme, is that you?"

From the hall, Landon pokes his head around the doorframe. Darius didn't even realize he hadn't followed him into the room. Landon steps through the double doors. "Clive Ridley. How long has it been?"

"I would dare to say at least six years!" Clive says as he grabs his shoulder and slaps him across the back. "When I went to find you, you weren't home. I should have known Darius was on top of it though." He winks at the king.

Darius looks up at the ceiling in an attempt to keep his eyes from rolling. He repeats his question that Clive so rudely ignored. "Where are the others?"

"No need for unease, Your Majesty," Clive responds with a condescending chuckle. "The remaining Savant members should arrive before midnight."

Aldreda pipes up, "It'll be nice to see everyone together again."

Her face immediately falls as Darius shoots her a sharp look. "Right. Well, Landon and I are weary from our travels and we could use a meal. Have you two eaten supper?" Aldreda slides a goblet closer to her, clearly trying to hide some evidence. "I see you've already started on the wine," Darius comments, his tone crisp. He turns to Landon. "Well, come on, pull up a chair. Let's all have a meal."

Aldreda and Clive exchange a glance before joining the table. Darius pretends not to notice it, but beneath the surface, his blood is boiling. Aldreda sits next to him, with Clive across from her, and Landon takes the seat just across from him. He calls out to the servants, and they head straight for the galley to prepare the meal.

He reaches for the half-empty bottle of verdot and pours a hefty glass. With three giant glugs, the goblet is empty. Silence surrounds them, but he quickly changes that as he slams his goblet down on the table. "Why the somber undertone? This is to be a joyous occasion!" He bangs his other hand down on the table, rattling his guests' goblets and dishes.

Aldreda slides her hand underneath the table and gently places it on his forearm. Darius turns his steely gaze on her. The words come out as a growl. "Do not touch me."

Without hesitation, she removes her hand from his arm. Darius takes another look around the table as he refills his goblet.

Yes, tonight will surely be interesting.

CERYLIA JARETH

ALERTING THE GUARDS to search the castle for a rogue Caldari seemed like a bit of a stretch, even to Cerylia, but, at the time, she hadn't had much of a choice. Unfortunately, the guards had found nothing after a full week of monitoring and searching. She'd ordered they discreetly keep an eye on Opal for several days—and in this aspect, they'd managed to succeed.

As if her stress level isn't already high enough, Delwynn has become increasingly more frustrated with her for not disclosing *why* she alerted the guards in the first place. Days have passed without speaking to Opal, and she knows if she doesn't talk with her soon, the girl will likely sense, if she hasn't already, that something is wrong. In tense situations, Cerylia normally confronts the problem head-on; however, this particular situation calls for a delicate hand—a thoughtful, and certainly methodical, approach.

The queen sits quietly in her chambers, deep in thought over the prior week's events. Trying to understand and piece things together only makes things more confusing and, on more than one occasion, she's wanted to take the easy way out. To rid the castle of Opal and her secrets and start fresh with a new Caldari.

The problem is . . . whomever Opal was talking to seems to know more about Cerylia's situation than she ever would have wished. And, *if* that person is a Caldari, then it's likely *all* Caldari members now know her plans.

Trust has been shattered.

Cerylia runs her fingers through her long chestnut hair, working out a tangle or two in the process. After a couple of deep breaths, she decides it's time to face one of her two counterparts. Delwynn's incessant whining is starting to get on her last nerve, but the thought of confronting Opal is equally as taxing. She drums her fingers on the side of her bedframe.

Be done with it. Go straight to the source.

Without a second thought, she leaves her room to walk to Opal's bedchambers. It's late in the evening, so she should already be winding down from her training and supper. She knocks on the door and Opal answers quickly, as if she'd sensed her arrival. Feeling surprised, Cerylia takes a step back, and then steps back again after just one look at her supposed protégé.

The girl looks *awful.*

Her hair is knotted and unkempt, the bags under her eyes are a dark violet, and she appears frailer than before, as if she's made the foolish decision to forego food for the past week. She looks damaged, broken. Disheartened, even.

"May I come in?" Cerylia asks gently.

Opal hesitates, but eventually opens the door wider and gestures for her to enter. "What can I do for you, Your Greatness?"

Cerylia sits in a chair across from the bed and motions for Opal to join. With an exhausted sigh, the girl trudges over to the bed and plops down. She looks her dead in the eye. "I need to discuss something of great importance with you."

At this, Opal straightens up a little. "Will it explain why you've been ignoring me for the past week?"

Cerylia blushes, feeling foolish. "Yes, most likely."

Opal nods. "Proceed."

"Several days ago, I overheard something I wasn't supposed to. And as much as I'd rather not know, I need clarification." Cerylia studies the girl's face before continuing. "I heard you speaking with someone . . . about me. They were asking about my situation and what I want from you."

Opal's face falls.

"At first, I heard Delwynn's voice. But as I was leaving, I happened to run into Delwynn. He explained that he'd been with my counsel for two hours. That's when I knew it couldn't have been him." She leans forward as Opal falls back. "There's only one group who can enter this castle undetected. You and I both know who they are."

Opal lowers her head, but not fast enough for Cerylia to miss the guilt written all over her face. "You were speaking to another Caldari, weren't you?"

Her voice comes out as a squeak. "Yes."

The answer sends a chill down Cerylia's spine. "Who was it, Opal?"

The girl gives her a pleading look. "Your Greatness, I wish more than anything that I could say, but I can't."

Cerylia narrows her eyes. "What do you mean, you *can't*?"

"I have to protect his identity. There is so much I need to tell you, but I need to know that you still trust me."

The queen feels a sudden urge to laugh, but, with great effort, remains silent. *Trust* her? How could she tell Opal that that ship had already sailed?

Although . . . it *could* be in her best interest to lie to the girl, and see what other information she might reveal. Being conniving has never been Cerylia's strong suit, but she'll have to make do if she ever hopes to uncover the truth. In the most unwavering tone she can manage, she says, "Yes. I still trust you."

Opal studies her for a moment, and Cerylia can't tell if she's relieved, nervous, or maybe a little of both. "Okay, here it is." She pauses as if she might change her mind again.

"Go on," Cerylia urges with a forced smile.

Opal nods. "Trendalath is in a state of complete chaos. I can't go into too much detail, but things are about to get worse—much worse. The Caldari plans to intervene and they . . . they needed to know where you stand."

Cerylia bites her lower lip as she absorbs the information. It isn't much, but it's something. And yet, it still doesn't explain the *other* half of the conversation she'd overheard. She gives Opal a small smile. "If you think I'd ever side with Darius Tymond, you have much to learn about me."

Opal grins, then lowers her gaze. As if she can read Cerylia's mind she says, "I'm guessing you heard the entire conversation. About my abilities?"

Cerylia gives a slight nod of her head, afraid that if she interrupts, Opal might change her mind and stop talking.

"It's true. I have been able to travel back to the timeframe you'd originally requested. I'm actually able to go back as far as twenty years."

Cerylia feels her heart drop into her stomach. “Why did you deceive me?”

“I know what information you seek, and I don’t think you’ll find solace if we go back.”

Cerylia’s heart thumps in her chest. *Does this mean Tymond had nothing to do with my late husband’s death?* The thought is enough to make her head spin. She clears her throat, then says, “I am not looking for solace, I am looking for answers. In order to rebuild the trust that you’ve broken, I demand that you show me what you know.”

Opal shifts uncomfortably. “I must forewarn you, Your Greatness, that the truth may come as a shock.”

Cerylia looks straight into those emerald green eyes and, without a second’s hesitation says, “Try me.”

BRAXTON HORNSBY

OVER A WEEK has passed and still no sign of Xerin. Braxton's gotten into the habit of checking the upstairs and downstairs windowsills every couple of hours, just to be sure; but there's been no sign of a falcon. No sign of Xerin.

After completing his outdoor duties for a few hours, Braxton decides it's time to take a well-deserved break. He does a quick once-over of the inn, just to make sure no birds—nor their droppings—have decided to make a last minute appearance. The inn is pristine, spotless. He wipes the sweat from his brow and decides he can spare a few minutes to relax, maybe even doze off. Just as he's closing his eyes, the clopping of hooves catches his attention. His eyes shoot open, focusing on the figures a few miles down the dirt road that leads to the inn. He can't tell who or what is approaching, but from the sound of the many hooves, they mean business.

He dashes to the front of the inn to alert Hanslow. The innkeeper hurries through the front door to peer down the dirt road.

"Are you expecting anyone?" Braxton asks.

Hanslow shakes his head. "No, but they seem to be headed our way." He runs back inside the inn in a tizzy.

Braxton follows, watching as his superior begins tidying up at an alarming pace. "What's going on? Is there something I need to know?"

Hanslow shakes his head, but continues dashing back and forth across the galley. He begins wiping down an already spotless area on the bar top, and it's then Braxton knows something is truly wrong. He rushes over to his Hanslow and places a gentle hand on top of his.

The back-and-forth movement stops. "The flag," Hanslow whispers.

Braxton looks at him questioningly before heading back out the front door. The pounding of hooves is even closer now, and the mysterious guests are coming into view. So is the flag Hanslow's talking about—thick black and red stripes with an emblem of a serpent in the lower right-hand corner sways in the breeze.

Braxton gulps and rushes back inside. “It’s the King’s Savant.” He tries not to look panicked so as to not give anything away, but Hanslow seems just as shaken up as he is.

The innkeeper motions for him to come behind the bar. As they kneel out of sight, he whispers, “We must close up shop. We are closed—better yet, we’re not even here. Understood?”

Braxton nods his head, relieved that Hanslow isn’t going to greet the Savant or let them inside. He rushes toward the front door and closes it, quickly pulling blocks of wood to secure it in place. Hanslow covers the windows with the darkest linen he can find and Braxton follows with more strips of wood. After a few minutes, every opening is covered. Honestly, it could be more secure, but it’ll have to do given the last minute notice.

Hanslow points upstairs before climbing the small staircase. Braxton follows closely behind him. They divide and conquer, covering as many of the windows as possible with the same dark linen.

A sudden knock on the door startles both of them. Braxton looks at him, then quickly finishes securing the last window. They both duck down, and Hanslow puts his index finger to his lips. Braxton nods as the knocking continues. It grows louder and louder, until it turns into a violent banging. Before Braxton can process what’s happening, Hanslow jumps to his feet and makes his way to the staircase.

Braxton stumbles as he rises from his crouched position. He catches Hanslow by the shirt just as he's starting to descend the stairs. "What are you doing?" he whispers harshly.

"I'm going to talk to them and inform them that we have no vacancy."

Braxton makes a wide gesture with his hand as his eyes bulge out of his head. "But clearly we *do* have vacancy! More than enough!"

"Shhh," Hanslow hushes. "Keep your voice down, will you?"

"They're going to see that we have no horses and no carriages outside. They'll see right through it. They'll know you're lying!"

Hanslow waves his hand dismissively in the air. "Let me handle this."

Braxton tightens his grip on the old man's shoulder. "Hanslow, what's going on? I thought you'd be happy to house the King's Savant." He tries not to spit the words, but the sarcastic undertone is blatantly obvious.

Hanslow gives him a knowing look. "You need to leave. Now."

Braxton's jaw drops. "What? Why?" He shakes his head. "No, I'm staying here."

Hanslow turns to face him and puts both hands on his shoulders. "Son, sometimes I wish you'd just listen to me."

Braxton stands firm. "I'm not leaving."

"I *know* who you are," he gives Braxton a sad smile, "Your Highness."

Braxton stares at him as a tornado of emotions rips through him. Fear, relief, overwhelm—all at the same time. His grip loosens on the old man's shirt. "I don't understand. How do you—?"

"There isn't any time," Hanslow interrupts. "I've known all along. And I'm telling you, for your own good, you best get going." His attention shifts to the door as the banging resumes. "Right now."

Braxton struggles to find his words. "But what about you, Hanslow? What will they do to you?"

"As far as I'm concerned, they don't know you're here. Which is why you need to go. *Now.*" His eyes say it all. "I need you to trust me."

With a shaky breath, Braxton nods and releases Hanslow's shoulder from his grip.

"Find the ones who are like you," Hanslow urges in a hushed voice. "You belong with them. And together, you will do great things."

Before Braxton can ask another question, Hanslow bolts down the stairs and marches to the front door. Braxton looks behind him and darts to the room at the furthest corner of the inn. He uncovers the window he'd previously sealed shut, then spots an empty bag in the corner of the room.

Without a second thought, he rifles through the

armoire, stuffing the bag with clothes and whatever else he can find. He grabs the bow and arrows that are perched against the wall and throws them over his shoulder. He pauses, listening for any indication as to how it's going downstairs.

Against his better judgment, he tiptoes out of the room toward the top of the stairwell. Loud voices boom from outside. Wood pops and snaps, and he winces as the door is steamrolled by what sounds like dozens of men. It lands with a thud on the ground. Hanslow yells at them to leave at once. Sinister laughter echoes from downstairs.

Braxton readies his bow and arrow. If only he could shoot the men from the top of the stairs—but there's no way for him to get a clear shot.

Hanslow is on his own.

With a grunt, he lowers the bow and arrow and returns it to his back. While he can't hear what is being said, he does hear Hanslow say one thing. "The boy isn't here!"

It's then he realizes that it's time to go. There is nothing left for him here. And by the sounds of it, pretty soon there will be nothing left for Hanslow either. It pains him to turn away, to leave such a loyal and decent man behind, but he knows this isn't the time to think.

This is the time to act.

He hurries to the window and swings his legs over the ledge, ducking so that he can fit his upper body through the tight opening. If he had known he'd be escaping through windows so frequently, he would have made it a point to practice more often.

Clattering and clanging, followed by yelling, sounds from downstairs. Braxton pauses to think twice about his decision. As much as he wants to help Hanslow, he knows that if the Savant find him, they'll likely assume he's been staying with Hanslow the entire time. Who knows what the punishment would be then?

Braxton inches the rest of the way through the opening, then pushes off the ledge. He falls two stories and, even after flailing a little in midair, somehow manages to land on his feet. He takes off toward the forest, feeling relieved as he makes his way further and further into the shrubbery. He stops mid-step as loud wailing sounds from behind him, from the inn.

Hanslow knows who he is. The old man had known his secret all along. And yet, he *still* protected him, still took him under his wing.

I owe him my life.

But turning around would be the nail in both of their caskets. Hanslow had told him to find his people. The Caldari. *And that's exactly what I'll do.*

The wailing is hardly audible twenty minutes later as he delves further and further into the forest. As much as he wants to forget this entire day, Braxton knows that this scarring memory will forever be etched

ARDEN ELIRI

A FEW WEEKS in Orihia and I already feel like I'm settling in with my new Caldari family. The tree village is a wonderland that I never want to leave. There are other creatures that reside here, but as far as people go, it's just me, Felix, Estelle, and Xerin (when he's not flying around the world).

At first, I thought I might get bored and have trouble filling my time, but that's not the case at all. There are so many hidden areas to discover in Orihia and an abundance of new creatures to befriend and learn about. Every now and again, when I want some peace and quiet, I head into the Thering Forest with Juniper and pick assorted berries and nuts to contribute to our meals. Estelle and Felix seem to appreciate it.

They've mentioned a few times already that they want to start me on my training. I have no idea what this entails, but apparently I have to go through some preparation before I can become a full-fledged Caldari. I suppose it makes sense, though, seeing as I honestly don't know the strength of my own abilities. Felix has offered to assess my gifts, and Estelle jumped at the opportunity to be my mentor. We haven't started yet, but I'm hoping we will soon.

I'm starting to get restless.

For the time being, each of us has been assigned to our own little huts to use as living quarters. Estelle has big plans for remodeling and rebuilding to make the dwellings larger, but for now, these will do.

After a long day of walking around the Thering Forest with Juniper, I kick off my boots, lie down on my bed, and gaze up at the ceiling. Juniper curls up at the edge, right by my feet. Although I love it here, I feel as though my mind hasn't been stimulated in a while. As an assassin for the king, I'm used to training every day—not only my body, but also my mind. It takes more focus and discipline—more mental capacity—imaginable to be a full-time assassin for the royal court.

I think back to my first full day in Orihia in Estelle's dwelling and my discovery of the hidden bookshelves. After had Felix caught me, I hadn't dared venture back over there, but I'm feeling bold and adventurous tonight.

I sit up from my bed and pull my boots back on. There's no way of knowing whether or not Estelle is back for the evening, so I'll have to be stealthy. I open my front door and close it quietly behind me before making my way down the flower-lined path in front of the residences.

It's so beautiful here, I almost can't take it.

I walk as casually as I can until I reach a set of rocks that signal the path is about to come to an end. By this point, I've already passed Estelle's residence, but I want to get a feel as to where Felix is. I don't see him lurking about in the shadows (a good sign), so I make a quick left turn to walk behind the houses. Luckily, our row backs up to a line of trees, so if someone sees me, I can easily hide. It's quiet and still, though, and the sun is just setting—it's getting dark enough where hiding is unlikely.

I continue along behind the houses, stopping once I get to Felix's. I crouch as I make my way through the backyard and onto the patio. I peek inside the window. It appears to be empty, but then I spot him with his feet up on the couch, asleep.

I grin to myself as I take off, my eyes trained on the gold and brown building that houses Estelle and her many eccentric belongings. I can only hope that she's either asleep or off doing something else in

Orihia.

As I approach, I get a sense of unease, but I push the feeling as far away as I can. I peek through the window. My lips are dry and my breathing is ragged, but adrenaline pumps through my veins as I take in the sight before me.

Estelle's dwelling is empty.

I turn the knob on the back door, not feeling too surprised when the door pops right open. Estelle's not one to lock things, especially in Orihia. This is her home. She feels secure in that.

I don't plan on *taking* anything, per se, just exploring and maybe borrowing a thing or two. I have every intention of returning whatever I choose to borrow.

The wooden floor creaks as I slink across the living room. I sneak over to the bedroom to make sure that the house truly is empty. I slowly push the door open. The bed is untouched and there isn't a soul in sight. I exhale a sigh of relief and head back into the living area. The black drape is right where we'd left it—when Felix so hastily told me to cover the shelves back up.

I whip the drape from its place and smile as rows upon rows of bookshelves appear before me. Whether it's an optical illusion or not, I still can't tell, but the feeling of awe remains as I walk up and down the aisles. There are so many choices that I can't decide what to read first.

My hand travels over the old, worn bindings as I scan the titles. I've had my fill of magick over the past week, so I land on a book entitled *The History of Trendalath.* Although Tymond enforced history lessons during my Cruex training, it wouldn't be surprising if I hadn't been told the whole story. And seeing as there's a banished book here specifically *about* the history of Trendalath, I decide it's a good place to start.

I slide the book from its indented place on the shelf. There's a heavy layer of dust on the pages, so I turn it over and give it a hearty shake. I take a seat against one of the shelves and begin to flip through the first few pages. I yawn, realizing how tired I am, but at the same time, I feel both energized and alive. I'm determined to find out whatever it is Felix doesn't want me to know.

After fifteen minutes of scanning the text and illustrations, I begin to wonder if there actually *is* something Felix and the Caldari are trying to keep secret, or if it's just something I've imagined in my head—wouldn't be the first time.

I spend a few more minutes scouring the pages for information, but I come up short. There isn't much in this history book that I don't already know.

I feel defeated until I absentmindedly turn to the next page. My eyes land on bold text that reads **The King's Savant**. My breath catches as I read through the paragraphs. I have to reread a couple of the sentences, mostly because I have a hard time believing them.

From what I can gather, the King's Savant has been around for ages and is the most powerful group of leaders, ancillary to the king. That part makes sense. The part that doesn't is where it mentions that the King's Savant is *illusié.*

Impossible. The king banished illusié from Trendalath a decade ago. Why would he have his own group of magick folk, especially when he has his hand-selected, highly trained Cruex assassins to do all of his dirty work for him?

I gulp as I continue reading, but I can't seem to fully absorb the words or their meanings. All I can think about is *why* the king would need the very thing he'd gotten rid of more than a decade ago. Unless . . .

Unless he knows the Caldari are still out there and needs a force more powerful to defeat them.

My heart leaps out of my chest at the thought. I decide I've done enough reading for the night and yet, I still turn the page, eager to know more.

I immediately wish I hadn't.

These pages are surprising. They have no text—instead, sitting between them, is a folded piece of paper. Gingerly, I take the paper between my thumb and forefinger. It feels like it could disintegrate at the slightest touch, so I unfold it with caution along the crease. I lay it out flat before me.

It's an old drawing of a group of men wearing dark

cloaks with an emblem of a serpent stitched into the sleeves. I take a closer look, realizing from what I've just read that they must be members of the King's Savant. I scroll over their faces, landing on one that stills my breathing. I try to tear my eyes away, but they won't budge.

This man in the drawing . . . he has my same pointed nose, same wide eyes. It's almost uncanny how much he looks like me. But that's not what is most disturbing. As I look his ensemble up and down, my eye catches what's in his hand.

A gold pocket watch.

RYDAN HELSTROM

A WEEK WITHOUT food, water, sleep, or social interaction really does have negative effects on the mind. Rydan can't seem to discern between his waking and sleeping hours, between hallucinations and real life. It all feels the same. Stuck in this miserable cell, in this miserable life.

But what's really driving him batty is not knowing what actually happened to Elvira. Seeing as King Tymond isn't one to be fickle with prisoners and their punishments, he's most likely already decided his poor friend's fate.

Nightmare after nightmare has visited him, and it's getting more difficult to tell whether they're real or just something he's made up in his head. He can only hope that the events in his nightmares are imaginary. For Elvira's sake.

With trembling arms and legs, Rydan presses against the damp stone wall to bring himself to his feet. Slowly, he takes one step at a time toward the cell door. It takes tremendous effort and, by the time he places his hands on the metal bars, he's panting, completely out of breath.

Food. Water. Elvira.

The only three things circling the confines of his mind.

Heavy footsteps echo from down the hall, as if two of his prayers have suddenly been answered. He tries to stay conscious, forcing his eyes to remain open, as a figure comes into view. The shadow moving toward him is thick and burly, and, for a moment, Rydan fears it's just the guard coming to take him back to the Great Room, back to King Tymond. His lips pull into a tight line at the thought.

But as the figure draws nearer, Rydan can see a tray in its hands, just like the one Elvira used to bring him. The thought of her sends sharp pains through his stomach, and he keels over, barely able to keep himself upright. But he manages to lift his head as the figure comes into the light.

Much to his surprise, it's a *woman.* Her face is full of wrinkles, ragged and tough. Her dark eyebrows are bushy and sprinkled with flecks of white. Her graying hair is pulled back in a messy braid, and she wears a uniform similar to those of Tymond's guards, although hers looks outdated by at least a couple of years. It doesn't take much for him to realize that this woman is Gladys.

His new handmaiden.

Without speaking, Gladys shoves the tray between the cell bars, the vegetable broth sloshing over the edge and landing at Rydan's feet. He takes the tray and mutters, "Thank you." The words come out as more of a croak. He eyes a canister of water and takes it off the tray, setting the rest of the food on the ground.

Gladys watches him with an unrelenting gaze, but Rydan hardly notices. He's too busy trying to get the food and water into his body so that he can feel somewhat human again. After keeping his hands steady enough to bring the food to his mouth, it only takes a matter of minutes before he's scarfed it all down. He purposely knocks the tray off his lap. Gladys doesn't move an inch as it clatters to the ground. He gives her a look, then picks up the tray and slides it through the cell bars. Gladys continues to stare at him, but doesn't move.

Feeling entirely uncomfortable, he scoots to the back of his cell and lays down with his back facing this strange woman; this woman who hasn't uttered a single word or sound. Perhaps she's mute? Or, perhaps the more likely scenario, she misspoke and King Tymond cut out her tongue as punishment. He wouldn't put it past his *Highness*.

Rydan closes his eyes, hoping that now that his stomach is full and somewhat satisfied, he'll finally be able to get some shuteye. He lies still for a few moments, eyes closed, but he can feel Gladys's gaze burning into the back of his head. He almost has the nerve to turn around and snap at her to leave, but thinks better of it. Despite his wishes, if this is going to be his new handmaiden, he may as well not make things worse.

"Thank you for the meal," he calls out, with his back still facing her. There's no response, but a short moment after, he can hear the shuffling of feet and the clinking of the tray. And when he finally decides to turn around, Gladys is gone.

DARIUS TYMOND

DARIUS SITS AT the round table in the Great Room amongst his Savant. Keeping an eye on Aldreda over the past couple of days has been exhausting, but she seems to be keeping to herself for the most part. Clive, too.

Good. He has enough to worry about anyway.

He gazes around the table at his men. Benson Hale, Conjurer, sits directly across from him, his hazel eyes poring into his own. His brown hair is unkempt and greasy, and it appears the poor lad hasn't bathed in months. Benson is a newer member, having only been with the Savant for two years. Tymond had searched for what felt like ages for someone who could conjure the elements—fire, water, air—and when he'd stumbled across Benson and his abilities in the Crostan Islands, he'd thanked his seemingly many lucky stars. Benson had accepted his invitation to join the Savant immediately and had moved to Declorath shortly after, no questions asked.

Sitting next to Benson is Landon Graeme. One of the older members of the Savant, Landon's abilities remain the most intriguing and one of Tymond's favorites. As a Curser, Landon has the ability to enchant objects, people—anything really—and produce highly negative effects. His skills have come in handy on more than one occasion. And, as his most trustworthy member, Landon has quickly become the king's closest confidante.

Across from Landon, and two seats down from Darius, sits his least favorite member of the Savant, Clive Ridley. But try as he might, Darius can't seem to justify getting rid of him. As a Caster, Clive has the ability to create illusions—ones that alter his enemies' senses and overall perceptions of their surroundings. A terrifying talent, surely, but Darius is almost positive he will need it for his own protection one day. That's the only reason he keeps Clive around. Otherwise, he'd be gone at the snap of his fingers.

Next to Clive sits Julian Enfield. A short, snarky fellow, he appears innocent and too plump to do any harm, but his capabilities make him incredibly powerful and dangerous. As a Multiplier, he has the ability to create lesser beings. With strength in numbers, he brings armies to life and is able to control them with his mind alone. A truly remarkable talent, and one Darius had jumped at when he'd realized the potential.

The king's eyes scan the last seat at the table, the one next to him. It's empty. His heart weighs heavy in his chest. The last member of his Savant has been missing for nine years—no one has seen him or heard from him.

His thoughts scatter as one of the Great Room doors creaks open. In walks Aldreda, looking marvelous as per usual. Her long blonde hair sits in loose waves below her shoulders, and her formal gown is much more formfitting than he's used to seeing. A royal purple corset accentuates her chest, and a bright ruby necklace adorns her neck.

The sight of her alone is breathtaking.

Darius notices that all eyes are on her, and for good reason. Normally, this wouldn't bother him—then again, normally her ex-lover isn't present. The breath of everyone at the table catches as she approaches. Without uttering a word, she takes the empty seat next to Darius. He begins to raise his hand in protest, but she quickly catches his wrist and gently presses it back down.

"I hope you don't mind my joining you," Aldreda purrs. Her eyes flit from Clive to Darius. "I haven't had a proper meal all day."

Darius clears his throat. "We were just about to discuss Savant business—"

"About the Eliri girl?" Aldreda cuts in.

Each of the men suck in a sharp breath at the last name, and Darius's eyes flit to the chair Aldreda is sitting in. Her blunt interruption catches him off-guard. "That, amongst other things," he says quietly, hoping she won't make a scene.

Her gaze is unwavering. "I would like to be in attendance. I believe I can add value to your discussion."

Again, Darius is about to protest—that is, until his least favorite person decides to pipe up.

"I agree," Clive says as he stands from his chair, goblet in hand. "We're still missing our final member and it's unlikely he'll even show up. Not to mention, no one knows where he is or where to even begin looking for him."

The men at the table nod, except for Darius. "I just think—"

"—You just think what? That because she's the *Queen*, she shouldn't be involved? I've known Aldreda for quite some time, and I move that she stays."

The words cut into Darius like a blade.

Silence fills the room.

No one says anything.

No one moves.

After a few moments of contemplating his choices, Darius finally gives in. Clive always seems to get what he wants. No use fighting it. “Fine. My Queen, you are permitted to stay.”

Aldreda leans back in her chair with a smug look on her face. “Thank you, My King.”

“Now, the first order of business . . .”

Darius somehow carries on with the meeting, even with Clive and his wife making eyes at each other the entire time. He promises to himself that he will dismiss the man from his Savant at some point, but deep down, he knows that there is no getting rid of him. As much as it pains him, Clive is here to stay.

For good.

CERYLIA JARETH

OPAL HAD INSISTED that Cerylia take a couple of days to prepare herself for the time travel. As much as she'd wanted to go back at that very moment, she knew the girl was right. Nausea, fever, and slight dementia are all possible side effects from time travel, and if one does not prepare for the strain on a mental, emotional, and physical level, the aftermath can be irreparable. Being so close to finally getting the answers, Cerylia decided it wasn't a risk she was willing to take.

But, after a few days of preparing and deep thought, she's ready. Delwynn will be in the vicinity with the healer when it happens—which gives her a certain level of comfort—just in case either of them needs tending to upon reentry into the present.

A knock on her bedchamber door startles her from her thoughts. Her heart thumps in her ears. She swallows, noticing how dry her throat is.

"Your Greatness, are you ready?" a voice asks on the other side of the door.

Cerylia nods, even though Delwynn can't see her. She tugs on the bottom of her tunic, feeling out of character in the clothes of common folk. She must admit, though, that it's much more comfortable than her robes and royal gowns, even on a good day. Her heavy boots clunk against the floor as she walks out of the room and down the corridor. Delwynn stays close behind her. She can hear him stifle a laugh as she struggles to pick her feet up.

"They make these heavy on purpose, don't they?" she jokes.

Delwynn finally lets out a hoot he'd been holding in. "They most certainly do not, Your Greatness."

"Well," Cerylia says as she reaches the door to Opal's bedchambers, "it's safe to say I have a newfound respect for the townspeople of Sardoria. No wonder everyone moves at a glacial pace—especially in the snow."

Delwynn seems to be at a loss for words, so he just smiles and opens the door for her. "After you, Your Greatness."

With a gracious nod, she enters the room. Opal is

standing by the fireplace warming her hands. She's dressed in similar clothes, her gaze steady on the fire. Embers crackle and pop. She seems mesmerized.

Delwynn clears his throat. "The Queen has arrived."

His announcement snaps Opal straight out of her daze. She looks Cerylia up and down. "Don't you look—"

"—like a commoner?" Cerylia finishes.

A wide grin stretches across the girl's porcelain face. "It's a good thing, I assure you. When we arrive, we don't want to raise any suspicion. Wouldn't want to seem out of place." She shrugs. "This is the best I could think of."

"You're the expert," Cerylia agrees.

Opal turns toward the fire and picks up a large canister of water. She dumps it over the flames, watching as they hiss and dissipate. Setting the empty container down, she walks over to a spacious part of the room and pushes a wooden chair out of the way, then rolls up the wool rug and places it in a corner. "Are you ready?"

Just as Cerylia is about to say yes, the door creaks open. She whirls around at the noise, feeling relieved to see that it's only the healer. "Now that we're all here, Delwynn, can you please secure the door?" She gives the healer a sharp look, feeling foolish for being so startled, as if she were doing something wrong. This is *her* castle, her Queendom. She can do as she pleases.

And do as she pleases she shall.

"Stay right here, no matter how long it takes," Opal instructs Delwynn and the healer. "We *will* be back. I just don't know exactly when."

The two men exchange nods. "We'll be here," they say in unison.

Opal turns her attention to Cerylia and extends her hand. "Shall we?"

Cerylia sets her hand gently in Opal's and nods.

"Here we go," Opal whispers as she squeezes the queen's hand.

Cerylia closes her eyes as a rush of wind surrounds them. Her stomach turns over once, twice, and, just when she feels as though she can't take it anymore, the sensation stops. When she opens her eyes, she's in a familiar place: Trendalath. From their discreet spot in the forest, she can clearly see the castle in all its glory, circa fifteen years ago.

Back when she and her late husband had ruled.

The thought makes her stomach turn again. She tries to choke her sadness down, but it comes out as a guttural groan.

Opal turns to her with a concerned look. "Your Greatness, are you not well?"

Cerylia can feel the color draining from her face. "I know we've only just arrived, but I need to sit for a moment."

Opal guides her to a nearby barrel of hay and sits beside her. She rifles through her bag and pulls out a large cylinder. “Drink this.”

Cerylia looks at her questioningly.

“It will calm your nerves,” Opal reassures as she presses the container into the queen’s hand. “Trust me.”

Cerylia pops the lid off and, without a second thought, gulps it down. Hints of rosemary, thyme, and other spices slide down her throat. It tastes awful. She removes the container from her lips and turns her head to spit some of it out, then shoves the vile concoction back in Opal’s direction. “That’s really something,” she says.

Opal lets out a small laugh. “I didn’t say it tasted good.”

Cerylia swivels back toward her. As much as she doesn’t want to admit it, she already feels better.

“There. The color seems to be coming back to your face.” Opal tucks the canister back into her bag before saying, “Follow me.”

She climbs through the forest, stepping over fallen logs and branches along the way. Cerylia follows, feeling grateful for her thick trousers and leather boots. She may look more common than she’s accustomed to, but she has to give Opal credit for suggesting they wear practical outfits on this rendezvous. Her delicate skin would have been scratched and torn to bits by now.

When they reach the edge of the forest, Cerylia notices that Opal begins to walk toward the back of the castle, not the front. "If you're looking for the front, it's the other way," she points out.

Opal shakes her head. "I know where I'm going. Trust me."

The queen doesn't say another word, just follows in Opal's tracks. They continue to sneak around the back perimeter of the castle, the ground growing muddier and harder to walk through. Cerylia's legs burn, feeling heavier and heavier with each step. Clumps of mud, twigs and leaves stick to the underside of her boots and bottom of her trousers, weighing her down even more. She's about to ask if they can sit once more when Opal stops in her tracks.

Thank the lords.

Without warning, Opal yanks the queen deeper into the forest behind the castle. She ducks behind a fallen tree and pulls Cerylia down with her. With wide eyes, she puts her index finger to her lips. Cerylia nods and imitates the motion. A few minutes go by until Opal peeks out from behind the log. She scans the area, then motions for Cerylia to follow.

Hoping that the coast is clear, she obliges. They don't get very far when Opal stops yet again, this time behind a large oak tree. Cerylia almost runs into her, but quickly realizes why they've stopped. In front of them is a brown tent, its flaps swaying in the breeze.

Muffled voices can be heard from inside and Cerylia wants more than anything to move closer to hear the conversation.

Opal seems to sense this and silently shakes her head.

Cerylia knows better than to disobey her—she's been right about everything so far—but her patience is wearing thin. She just wants to know the truth. She wants to know who killed her husband.

After what feels like an eternity, two cloaked figures finally emerge from the tent. They each have a set of bow and arrows on their backs, and speak in harsh undertones. Cerylia strains to hear what they're saying, but her efforts are futile. Their voices are too hushed.

Then, out of sheer fortune, one of the figures removes its hood to reveal curly copper hair and hazel eyes. He looks young, but at second glance, Cerylia realizes he's about her age, fifteen years ago.

Having no idea who he is leaves her feeling disheartened. She lowers her gaze to the ground. Perhaps she'll never know who killed her husband. Perhaps her quest for justice is just a waste of time.

Opal elbows her in the side, cocking her head toward the two figures. With a harsh glare then a sigh, Cerylia focuses back on the scene. As the man pulls his hood back over his head, the second figure's hood comes off. A braid of white-blonde hair appears, and

Cerylia gasps as the woman turns to the side, giving the queen a perfect view of her side profile. She lifts a familiar dagger from its holster and spins it in her hand. Her stomach twists and turns as the truth hits her like a ton of bricks.

Aldreda Tymond killed her husband.

BRAXTON HORNSBY

BRAXTON KNOWS HE'S headed east, but how *far* east remains a mystery. Over a day has passed since leaving Hanslow—wailing in pain, screaming in misery—behind. Braxton tries to block out the sounds bouncing around his skull, but his mind is cruel, forcing them to replay over and over again.

He stops in the middle of the forest, desperate for something—anything—to distract him. A bird soars overhead and, for a brief moment, he feels hopeful, like not all is lost. But as the bird comes into view, his heart sinks. It's a kestrel, not a black falcon.

Hanslow's desperate cries for help resurface. His

hands shoot to his ears and he presses his palms against them, harder and harder, as if the sounds are something physical he can block out.

How he wishes that were the case.

After a few minutes of frustration, he lowers his hands. His gaze lands on an exposed pathway in the distance. With nothing to lose, he takes off toward the open area, arms pumping at his sides. The cries seem to quiet down some as he runs, but he can't run forever. Eventually he has to stop.

Eventually they'll start up again.

He unintentionally zigzags across the forest. *When was the last time I ate? The last time I had water? The last time I slept?* Although the cries have quieted down, new voices plague his mind. *You're not going to make it. You're going to die out here.*

"No!" he shouts. He's panting, running for his life, running with no direction and no end goal.

Get away from the Savant. Far, far away.

He stumbles, tripping over his own feet, and tumbles to the ground. Although the forest floor is rigid and stiff, the bed of leaves and pine needles breaks his fall. He lies on his stomach for a few moments. His mind tells him to get up, but his body doesn't listen. He's gone far enough.

He stays there until, exhausted, he finally closes his eyes and succumbs to sleep.

Sunlight pours through the forest canopy. Braxton stirs, removing bits of pine needles and leaves from his chin and corners of his mouth. He has no idea what time it is, or how long he's slept, but based on the position of the sun, it's late morning.

Did I spend the night in the forest?

He pulls himself up to his knees, groaning as his joints crack and pop with the movement. A low whistle startles him, and he jumps, falling onto his rear at the sound. Frantically, he scans the forest until he spots a figure sitting at the base of a nearby tree. From the shadows of the spiked hair alone, he can tell who it is. He breathes a sigh of relief before saying, "Xerin, how long have you been here?"

Xerin shrugs and takes a bite of an apple. "Not sure, really. A while, I suppose."

"Why didn't you wake me?"

Xerin shrugs again, then tosses him an apple. "I tried. You were out. Stone cold. There was no waking you up."

Braxton feels his cheeks burn. "It's been an interesting couple of days." Images of Hanslow and the sound of his cries threaten to resurface, but he pushes them down. "What took you so long?"

Xerin raises an eyebrow, clearly amused at the question. "How do you mean?"

Braxton pulls himself to his feet, then walks over

to him. "You asked me if I wanted to join," he lowers his voice to a whisper, "you know, the Caldari. And then you left and didn't return." He takes a bite of the mealy fruit. "Until now."

Xerin throws his apple core to the side before standing. "I beg your pardon, but I do have *other* places to go and people to see besides you," he scoffs. "You are not my only priority. Actually, I'm not even sure you'd make the list."

His response angers Braxton, but he manages to keep his emotions at bay. "Well, I have an answer for you—"

"Let me guess," Xerin interrupts, "you'd like to join the Caldari."

Braxton closes his mouth, then nods his head.

Xerin gives him a coy smile. "I knew you would. What I don't understand is *why* you didn't jump at the opportunity when I first presented it to you."

"I had to think—"

"Don't give me that crap," Xerin barks. "You didn't have to think about it. You knew, from the moment I asked you to join, that you wanted to—that you were going to say yes." He raises an eyebrow. "So why didn't you?"

Braxton takes a step back. Even though he doesn't know Xerin that well, his harsh nature seems a little out of character, even for him. "Are you feeling okay?"

Xerin's mouth pulls into a tight line. "Answer the

question," he demands through gritted teeth.

Not wanting to see his dark side, Braxton does as he says. "Fine, I knew. I knew that I would join all along."

"Then why didn't you immediately accept?" Xerin presses.

"Because the thought of potentially facing my father again is too much to bear."

There. I said it.

A long bout of uncomfortable silence passes between them, making him wish he could take his last statement back.

Surprisingly, Xerin softens his tone. "Are you aware that your father has called the Savant?"

Braxton nods solemnly.

"Are you also aware that even if you didn't join the Caldari that you'd run into him again, one way or another?"

Braxton hesitates before nodding again.

"Good." Xerin inhales a sharp breath. "Now that that's settled, it's time for you to come with me."

Just as he's about to ask where, Xerin transforms into a falcon, flapping his wings until he's more than twenty feet in the air. The bird screeches and Braxton can only guess that, in bird-speak, it means *follow me.*

Xerin leads him even further east (which he hadn't thought possible) until they reach the end shores of Athia, where he morphs back into his human form and ushers Braxton onto a nearby ship. It's nearly nightfall by the time they set sail.

Braxton has no idea where they're headed, but, from the look on Xerin's face, he's almost certain he's about to make some new friends.

ARDEN ELIRI

I KNOW TAKING the book probably wasn't the best idea, but I couldn't put it back, not after I'd laid eyes on that drawing. For the third time that morning, I curse myself for not bringing my pocket watch with me on the Lonia mission—but how was I to know that it would be my last?

I sit at the desk in my dwelling, poring over the image with a hand lens, but it's too small and too blurry to make any sort of comparison. Not that I have anything *real* to compare it to—just the still image that's ever so slowly fading from my memory.

I grunt and throw the lens down in frustration. The man looks just like me *and* he has a pocket watch.

That should be sign enough, but then again, it may just be a coincidence.

I'm starting to feel like I'll never know.

A knock on my door startles me. Juniper is curled up in her usual place by the crackling fire, and doesn't stir in the slightest. I scurry over to my armoire and hide the book between some linen sheets, secure the cabinet, then walk over to answer the door. But when I open it, there is no one there.

Odd.

Just as I begin to shut the door, something presses against it. It's a strength greater than my own, and I start to panic as the door is forced open. I stop resisting and jump back in a fighting stance. The door swings open but still, no one is there.

A shiver creeps down my spine.

Dark whispers push at my mind, and the more I try to force them away, the louder they become. *Join us, Arden. It's where you belong.*

Without warning, I'm suddenly transported to a grassy meadow just outside Trendalath castle. It takes a minute to gather my bearings, but from a distance, I can see waves crashing onto a shore. A small figure near the water catches my attention.

Not knowing why, I make my way over to it.

A white-blonde head of hair comes into view. It's a young boy. He's fishing along the side of the castle. I feel the urge to tell him to run and get out of here—that it isn't safe here—but a stronger desire overcomes me.

Kill him and the terror will be over. The Tymond reign will cease to exist, the darkness whispers.

My lips pull in a grim line as I pull my chakrams from their holsters. The boy is only twenty feet away from me. His back is to me, and it seems that he has no inkling that I'm watching him.

Or that I could very easily kill him.

Don't listen to them, my mind urges. I attempt to pull the dark threads from my mind, but they're wound too tight. *What's done is done. Killing him won't do a thing.*

I want to listen—*need* to listen—to my own instincts, but I can't. Darkness has overcome me. I need to kill this boy, whoever he is. Just as I gear up to throw my chakrams, the boy turns around. Eyes the color of ice meet mine.

"Can I help you, Miss?"

I can only stare at him. It's blatantly obvious that I'm holding weapons, ready to strike, *and* that he is my target, but his innocent face reflects an eerie sense of calm.

"No," I mumble as I lower my weapons. I secure them back into their holsters. "I suppose not."

The boy smiles and turns back around to resume fishing.

I shake my head, closing my eyes to try to make sense of the conversation. When I open them, I'm standing in my hut, in front of an open door. With shaking hands, I rush toward it and slam it shut.

I stumble backward, eventually ending up on my bed. Juniper stirs and, with one look at my frightened expression, nuzzles up against my arm. I set her in my lap and stroke her white and black fur. My eyes stay trained on the door, but after calming my shallow breaths, my heart slows down and my breathing becomes normal again. I lean my head back against the wall and continue to pet the little marble fox.

Questions consume my thoughts. *What was that? Who was that boy? Why would killing him end the Tymond reign?* The interrogation swirls around in my mind, leaving me feeling exhausted and confused.

I'm not sure how long I've dozed off for when another knock sounds at my door. Juniper hops from my lap onto the floor and scurries into a corner. I rub the sleep from my eyes and, with a yawn, trudge sleepily over to the door. At first, I feel fine, until I recall what had happened earlier. Feeling wiser this time, I call out, "Who is it?"

"It's Xerin," a gruff voice answers. "Open the door. Hurry up!"

I do as he says. My gaze lands on Xerin, then quickly shifts to the man standing just a few paces behind him. Eyes the color of ice meet mine once again. My mouth goes dry as I realize who he is—who the young boy was in my vision.

King Tymond's son.

Without thinking, I lunge for him with ferocious intent and yell, "You!"

Braxton cowers while Xerin throws his arms up to block me, catching my wrists in his hands. He crosses my arms and flips me around so that my back is pressed against his chest. His fingers squeeze my wrists with so much pressure that I yelp a little. I writhe against him, but he has me in a stronghold. I start yelling again for no reason, unsure as to what's come over me, and, not long thereafter, I see Estelle and Felix barging through the back door.

Felix makes a beeline for Braxton, but Estelle comes straight at me. Her face is taut with fear as she looks from me to Braxton, then back at me again. "What in lords' name is going on here?"

At the sound of her voice, I stop writhing and Xerin loosens his grip enough for me to break away. I stumble forward into Estelle who shoves me onto the bed. My eyes catch Juniper, who's backed into a corner, eyes wide with fright.

Before I can process what's happening, Estelle climbs on top of me and clamps her hand down over my mouth. I don't even realize I've been screaming and yelling the entire time. She uses her free hand to press down on my left shoulder. "Shhh," she whispers, trying to calm me down. "It's okay, Arden. It's okay."

My chest is moving up and down at such a rapid speed that I feel like it's going to burst and splatter all over the room. I look into her violet eyes, into her soft expression, and slowly begin to calm my nerves. It takes some time, but eventually my breathing evens out, my hands stop shaking, and my heart resumes its normal pace. Slowly, she moves off of me and sits down next to me on the bed.

Xerin ushers Braxton inside my house, then secures the door behind them. He marches over to where I'm still laying and Estelle is sitting. For a moment, he seems so angry that he might backhand me, but Estelle stands up in my defense.

Xerin bumps into her, their noses touching, then growls, "What the hell was that?"

Estelle doesn't flinch. She places her hands on top of his shoulders. "Calm down."

Xerin inhales a sharp breath before swinging his hand to break contact between them. "I wasn't talking to you."

I know I've caused enough damage today, so I sit up, even though I still feel uneasy, and say, "I'm sorry, Xerin." My eyes flit to the older version of the boy in my vision. "And Prince Tymond, to you, I am also sorry. Regrettably so."

He looks at me with a pained expression. "Please, call me Braxton."

I nod. This exchange between us seems to lessen the tension. I notice shoulders drop and facial muscles relax as everyone moves to stand in a semi-circle. I rise from the bed and join them. It's hard to take my eyes off of Braxton, and I can tell that he feels the same way about me. I don't want to explain myself or defend my actions, but I can tell by the looks on everyone's faces that I need to. So far, I haven't made the best impression on the Caldari. If they were sensible, they would have kicked me out by now.

And yet, here I remain.

"I had a sort of vision," I blurt out, "and he, Prince Tymond, was in it."

Estelle tenses. "What kind of vision?"

I don't know how to tell them that the darkness speaks to me, nor do I want to, so I say, "I saw Prince Tymond as a young boy. He was fishing in the ocean on the side of the castle." My gaze flickers to him and his eyes grow wide, as if I'm somehow recalling one of his childhood memories. "I was told that if I killed him, the terror would be over." My voice croaks as the next words come out. "That if I killed him, the Tymond reign would cease to exist."

The room falls silent for a long while.

"Who told you this?" Estelle asks, her voice a mere whisper.

I shake my head, knowing better than to reveal my secrets. "I don't know." I look at her with sad eyes.

My answer lingers in the air. No one says anything. No one moves. Stillness surrounds us.

And then, in a surprisingly lighthearted tone, Braxton speaks up. "You probably should have done it then."

My head snaps up from the ground and I realize that he's *smiling*. Felix lets out a low chuckle, followed by a small laugh from Estelle. I'm relieved that Braxton isn't upset, and as much as I want to smile, Xerin's stone-cold expression stops me.

"We do not attack our own," Xerin says with extreme superiority.

"Our own . . .?" My words trail off as I realize what he's talking about.

Holy lords. The son of King Darius Tymond is one of *us*.

Illusié.

The realization is enough to make me lose my footing, but Estelle is right there to catch me. "Are you okay?" she asks.

I nod, even though I'm not.

The prince sighs. "I would really prefer if you call me by the name I've had for the past ten years, which is Braxton Hornsby. I don't want anything to do with the Tymond name. No association. Nothing."

I stay silent, but continue to stare at the prince. He looks so tormented, so sad. All I want to do is walk over to him and give him a hug and apologize over and over again. But I know my actions won't fix anything. Braxton's fighting his own demons.

Aren't we all?

I can tell Xerin wants to say something, but he keeps quiet. Just as I'm about to try and pull it out of him, Felix pipes up. "Well, now that the majority of us are here, I guess it's time we start on our training."

I look around at the group. I seem to be the only one wearing a confused expression. *The majority? Who are we missing? And what training, exactly?*

"Let's start first thing tomorrow morning. Be in the common area at 0700 hours." Xerin groans, but doesn't bother proposing a new time. Felix nudges him in the shoulder. "Oh, come on, Xerin. I would have thought you'd be the most excited to see what everyone can do."

I swallow the large lump that's formed in my throat as everyone turns to exit my house. Estelle's the last one out. She winks at me before shutting the door. And then I'm alone.

It's just me and Juniper.

I nestle back in the bed and pull the sheets tightly around me. Juniper hops up near my face and circles around my head until she finds a comfortable position.

My thoughts drift to tomorrow morning. In the past, I was never nervous whilst training with the Cruex. I knew my abilities, my strengths, and my weaknesses like the back of my hand. But this . . . this is entirely new to me. How can I show them what I can do when I don't even know what I'm capable of?

The thought sits with me until Juniper's rhythmic purring lulls me to sleep, reassuring me that it's tomorrow's problem.

RYDAN HELSTROM

VISITS FROM HIS new handmaiden have become less and less frequent, and Rydan finds himself desperately needing company, even if that company is of the strong, silent type like Gladys. When she does visit, she hardly ever speaks, just watches him with that unsettling gaze of hers. Normally, Rydan is babbling about something, droning on and on, just happy that he's being heard. He's never considered himself an extrovert, or even someone who enjoys social settings in the slightest, but after being locked up, for lords knows how long, with no one to talk to, he *craves* it.

So when Gladys enters his cell that evening with a

tray full of food, Rydan can't help but feel ecstatic. "Gladys, my friend! How I've missed you!"

As per usual, the handmaiden does not respond. She approaches his cell and, with what appears to be a small smile (although he may be imagining it), she pushes the tray through the bars.

Like a ravenous beast, Rydan scours through the food like a baby bear discovering meat for the first time. Gladys sits back and watches silently, as usual. Her gaze used to bother Rydan, but it doesn't anymore. Company is all he wants, no matter who it is.

And, speak of the devil, when he looks up, Gladys is no longer sitting outside his cell. Instead, eyes the color of fresh blood stare back at him. Rydan grimaces as images of a beheaded Elvira swirl around his mind. The crimson-eyed man rises and Rydan shuffles backward on his hands and feet.

Am I seeing things? Is this man really here?

If he hadn't just eaten, he probably would have written it off as another hallucination—he's had lots of them these days—but the food had quickly settled in his stomach. What he was seeing before him was *real*, not a hallucination.

"Rydan, is it?" The man's voice is smooth as silk.

For a moment, Rydan feels comforted, but then he looks back into the man's blood-red eyes. He doesn't say anything, doesn't nod. He fears that giving any indication as to who he is will lead to bad things. *Very* bad things.

"Don't look so frightened," he says. "Believe it or not, I'm here to help you."

Rydan continues to stare at him. Finally, he asks, "Who are you?"

The man chuckles. "My name is Xerin. Xerin Grey."

The name isn't at all familiar, which messes with Rydan even more as he tries to recall meeting someone named Xerin from his past; but he comes up empty.

"Let me help you," Xerin says. "You know my sister."

Rydan racks his brain for a girl in his circle of acquaintances with the last name Grey, but comes up short. His lips part to speak, but Xerin beats him to it.

"Elvira."

Rydan can feel his mouth drop as the words hit his ears. Everything Vira told him comes flooding back in a tidal wave of memories. She grew up in Chialka. The fires of Eroesa separated her family. She and her mother ended up in Trendalath, but her *brother* and her father . . .

The words come out as a croak. "You're her brother." Rydan scoots himself closer to the bars, trying to get a closer look at Xerin. Except for the blonde hair and pale features, they really don't look much alike, especially when comparing their eye color.

"Affirmative," Xerin confirms. He turns and walks

away from the cell, retreating back to the barrel of hay. He leans forward so that his elbows are resting on top of his knees. "I just spoke to her before I came in here."

The words are like music to Rydan's ears. "She's still alive? How is she?"

Xerin hits his tongue against the roof of his mouth, a clucking sound echoing through the dungeon. "It seems like you got her in a bit of trouble."

Rydan lowers his gaze. "I honestly didn't know I wasn't able to talk to her, or anyone for that matter." He raises his head. "No one handed me a rulebook for dungeon etiquette."

Xerin laughs. "Snarky one, aren't you?"

Rydan keeps his eyes trained on him. "How did you get in here? Where is Gladys?"

Without warning, a soft yellow glow suddenly appears around Xerin's body. Rydan's jaw drops as he watches him morph into the shape of Gladys—eyes, ears, mouth, hair. There are no differences to the naked human eye.

"Wow," Rydan breathes. "That's incredible."

Xerin-now-turned-Gladys doesn't say a word.

Rydan shifts uncomfortably under the gaze. "Okay, you can change back now. I get the point."

A smile graces Gladys's face, a rare sight indeed, and Rydan watches the transformation happen again. He claps his hands a few times. "Truly remarkable."

Xerin looks over his shoulder. "Do you have any

more questions, or can I say what I came here to say?"

Rydan straightens up, feeling slightly offended at Xerin's tone. Apparently, he asks too many questions for his liking. "Go right ahead."

"As I mentioned, before I came here, I visited Elvira. She's fine," he adds quickly, "but she may not be for much longer. It seems Tymond wants to make an example out of her."

"An example?" Rydan's hands curl into fists. Tymond better not be planning to execute her, or do anything at all to harm her. "So what is he planning to do?"

Xerin shakes his head. "It doesn't look promising for her. That's all I'll say. But I did give her some information to use at her disposal."

Rydan tilts his head before asking, "What kind of information?"

Xerin gives him a wicked grin. "I know where Arden Eliri is."

DARIUS TYMOND

IT'S EARLY MORNING when Darius awakens. Soft snores escape Aldreda's lips. She's in a deep slumber, so he does his best to slide out of bed as quietly as possible. He pulls on his robes and his shoes before opening the door to their bedchamber. He looks at Aldreda one last time to ensure she is still asleep before quietly closing the door behind him.

Sunlight pours in through the stained glass windows as he walks along the hallway. He turns right and continues to walk for a few minutes until he reaches the chambers in the far west corridor—the guest quarters. Without knocking, he flings open the first door. The bed is made and the room is tidy. It almost looks as if no one is staying there. He opens the doors to the next few bedchambers. Same thing, neat and tidy.

Good. His Savant is taking him seriously.

As he'd instructed, each member had left to search his respective territories. He'd given Landon the North quadrant, consisting of Volkharn, the Vaekith Mountains, and the Roviel Woods. In the Northeast were the Lirath Cave, Eadrios, and Sardoria, to which he'd given to Benson. Julian had been given the South, which included Declorath, Miraenia, and Chialka. And last, but not least, was the Southeast, consisting of Eroesa and the Isle of Lonia. He'd assigned Clive to this territory, knowing full well that it'd keep him as far away from Trendalath—and his wife—as possible. Clive hadn't seemed too fond of the idea, but he'd obliged.

Tymond had decided not to send anyone to Athia, seeing as some of his men had come from there on the way to the castle. They'd reported storming some inn nearby in search of the final member of the Savant, but to no avail.

Disappointing, really.

Darius leaves the far west corridor and briskly makes his way to the Great Room. Much to his delight, the room is empty. He strolls to a nearby table and pulls a piece of parchment that contains a map of the Lands of Aeridon from his robe. He runs his hands over the parchment in order to smooth its many crinkles.

One day soon, he hopes to rid each of the cities, making Trendalath the sole kingdom in the territory. His eyes flit to the Roviel Woods, then to Sardoria—*that* one will always remain a problem.

Queen Cerylia Jareth is quite formidable, even by his standards. A good-natured woman, surely, but Darius knew from the first day he met her that she had a dark side—one capable of perilous things. He'd rather squash that while he has the chance than find out what those things are.

He turns his attention back to the map. If his calculations are correct, then Benson should return first, followed by Landon, then Julian, and lastly, Clive. Unless, of course, one of them finds Arden. They'd been advised to send their carrier kestrel at the end of each day to report back with any news. If Arden is located, he'd directed them to detain her and immediately bring her to Trendalath castle.

We'll see just how inclined they are to follow my orders.

His thoughts scatter as one of the doors to the Great Room creaks open. Darius begins to roll the parchment up, but stops as he sees Aldreda enter the room. Her hair is unkempt and there are bags under her eyes. Apparently her slumber wasn't as deep as he'd originally thought.

"My Queen," he says with a polite nod.

She doesn't greet him, just walks forward with her hands resting on her lower abdomen, as per usual.

Darius notices the stoic expression on her face. "Is everything all right?"

Aldreda's face pales. "I'm not well."

Darius finishes rolling the parchment up and stuffs it into a pocket within his robe. "Please, sit," he says as he gestures to one of the chairs.

Aldreda shakes her head. "I won't be staying long. I just wanted to tell you that I'm not well and will be in our chambers for most of the day." Her eyes flit to the parchment sticking out of his pocket. "Has the Savant started their search?"

Darius immediately knows what she's getting at. She wants to know where Clive is. It's enough to make his blood boil, so he answers with a sharp "Yes," before strolling past her to leave.

She catches his arm. "Darius," she whispers.

He looks at his wife, her eyes full of longing and despair. "I know this hasn't been easy on you. But I want you to know that I am yours. I am loyal and faithful to you."

The words burn his ears. Images of Clive and Aldreda exchanging glances at the table resurface. But instead of getting angry, he just says, "I know."

She squeezes his arm tenderly. "I know you have plenty on your mind right now, but it'd be nice to take a day off from ruling the kingdom. Perhaps we could spend some time together." She gives him a hopeful smile.

Unfortunately, all Darius can see are lies, betrayal, and deceit. Disgust overcomes him, but this time, he can't hide it, nor does he have any desire to. "Perhaps when Clive returns, *he* can take a day off, seeing as his responsibilities are minimal compared to my own."

Aldreda removes her hand and takes a step back. "After everything I just said to you, about being faithful and loyal . . . about being yours . . . this is how you choose to behave? By lashing out at me?" She shakes her head in disappointment. "You're better than that, Darius."

Without thinking, he growls, "It's *My King,* to you." He can tell by the look in her eyes that he's gone too far.

"I'll be going now, *Darius.*" She clicks her heel and whirls away from him. As she reaches the door, she turns back around and places her left hand back on her bump. "I can only hope that you'll treat this child better than you've treated me." And with that, she swings the door open and slams it shut behind her.

Darius holds his breath for three seconds and then screams.

CERYLIA JARETH

SHE'D SEEN IT with her own two eyes. Aldreda Tymond. Plunging a dagger into her beloved husband's chest. Her heart wrenches at the thought as she rolls over onto her side.

It's only been a few days since she and Opal had traveled back in time—to fifteen years prior—but Cerylia has no plans to leave her bedchambers. Reliving the heartache and sorrow seems to grow worse, not better, with each passing day, and it's enough to cause concern.

Both Delwynn and Opal have visited her multiple times a day, but they never seem to make it past her closed door. She knows they mean well, and that they just want to check on her, but Cerylia knows what's best for her at a time like this. And right now, she needs to be alone. The sadness will pass, just like it always does, but that doesn't make it any easier or help to speed up the process. How she wishes it would.

She flips over again, but this time lies on her back. The bed seems to have taken the shape of her body, and she's almost positive there will be an indentation whenever she decides to rise from the confines of her mattress and actually leave the room. She gazes up at the ceiling, at the intricate paintings of angels and lords who are supposedly watching over her. Even though the sun is going down, the reflection of the paint twinkles, like brightly lit stars in the night sky.

Stargazing used to be one of her husband's favorite pastimes.

An image of his death reemerges once more, and she has to choke down the bile that creeps up her throat. No matter what she does, no matter what she looks at, she can't pull her mind away from the atrocity.

Enough.

Moping won't do her any good. And it certainly won't bring her husband back. She's better than this. She has to be.

Just as she's getting herself together and pulling her robes on, a light rapping on her door sounds. She finishes smoothing her hair, then walks to the door to open it. There stands Opal, looking just as distressed as Cerylia imagines herself to be.

I suppose our visit to the past has affected her, too.

"May I come in?"

The queen steps aside and ushers her in. "Where are my manners? Of course, do come in."

Opal stands in the middle of the room as Cerylia closes the door firmly behind her. "Please excuse me if this is out of line, but I wanted to see how you were doing after . . ."

Cerylia puts her hand up and nods slowly. "No need to rehash our recent travels. I am doing well. Not as well as I would like, but I think it will come with time."

The girl fidgets with the hem of her tunic. "I just wanted to tell you that it wasn't easy for me either." She raises her eyes until they lock with the queen's. "I know what it's like to lose someone close to you." She pauses, and Cerylia is surprised to see her tearing up a little. "Anyway, I'm here for you if you need me. Anything you need." She reaches out and places her hand on top of the queen's.

Cerylia hesitates for a moment, but decides to place her free hand on top of Opal's. "Thank you, my dear. Your generosity and kindness have been noted." She gives the girl a small smile. "And come to think of it, I think I know of a way you can help."

Opal regards her with large doe-eyes.

"My dear," Cerylia says, "I think it's about time we round up the Caldari."

BRAXTON HORNSBY

"DO YOU THINK I should try to go talk to Arden?" Braxton sits in the middle of Xerin's living room by the fire, watching intently as his new friend sharpens his weapons. Daggers, hunting knives, longswords, and the like are strewn about the kitchen table. Braxton has never felt fully comfortable around blades, but he has a feeling he's about to get real comfortable real quick.

Xerin ignores his question as he finishes sharpening a bronze dagger with an intricately designed handle. If Braxton had to guess, based on the bird-like features crafted into the wood, it's likely his favorite weapon.

He takes his silence in stride. “Why a falcon?”

At this, Xerin’s head pops up from his work. “They’re beautiful, majestic creatures that are renowned for their speed. While in flight, they can reach over 320 kilometers per hour.” He lowers his gaze again and takes a small rag to wipe the excess metal shards from the blade.

Braxton clears his throat before saying, “I’m going to step outside and get some fresh air.”

“You’re not going to talk to Arden, right?”

And just like that, Braxton has his answer. “No. Just going to take a walk.”

Xerin nods. “Very well.”

Braxton gathers his pack and throws it over his shoulder, along with his bow and arrows and makes for the door. He glances back one more time, but Xerin has moved on from the bronze dagger to the longsword and is wholly concentrated on polishing it. He shuts the door quietly behind him, then inhales a steady stream of fresh air.

For the sun just setting, Orihia seems pretty well lit. He walks along the stone path outside of Xerin’s dwelling, heading away from the rest of the Caldaris’ houses. Glowing orbs light the path before him, in reds, greens, purples, and blues. The walk is quite relaxing, and is much needed, given recent events.

After a while, he plops down on a giant mushroom. He extends his legs, surprised that his entire body can fit on the surface area with no problem. He gazes up at the canopy of intertwining tree branches. Insects hum their pleasant melodies and uniquely colored birds fly overhead. He closes his eyes, feeling serene and at peace for the first time in weeks.

He must have dozed off because the next thing he knows, a twig snaps and there's someone standing right in front of him. Braxton shoots up from the mushroom. Still sitting, he rubs his eyes, but it only takes him a few seconds to discern who stands before him. The one person Xerin told him not to talk to.

Arden.

"Would you like some company?"

She says it so casually, it almost makes Braxton feel as though they've been acquainted since they were children. Hardly the case. Xerin's warning pops into his mind, but he quickly shoves it aside. Something about Arden intrigues him, and if they're going to be training together and, ultimately fighting for the same cause together, then what's the harm in getting to know each other better?

Braxton scoots over, even though there's plenty of room on the mushroom, and pats the space next to him. "Have a seat."

Arden sits down next to him and he notices that a petite marble fox has been sidling at her feet the whole time. The fox jumps onto the mushroom and curls up beside her.

"Where'd you get a fox?" Braxton asks.

Arden shrugs. "Estelle gave her to me. She originally followed her around until I showed up."

"What's her name?"

Arden smiles as she pets the fox behind the ears. "Juniper."

He grins as he raises his hand to stroke the black and white fur. "That's an interesting name."

"She only eats berries. Juniper berries are her favorite."

He slides his index finger up and down underneath Juniper's chin. "Well then, I suppose I misspoke. It's a very fitting name, isn't it?"

"As long as you see the error of your ways." A coy smile tugs at her lips, and he senses that she's already becoming more comfortable around him.

He gives his best pouting face. "It would appear that the Caldari like you more than me. I didn't receive a welcome present."

Arden removes her gaze from Juniper and shifts it to Braxton. She rolls her eyes and laughs. "I'm sure they like us equally."

Well, if that isn't an opening, he doesn't know what is. He takes it without hesitation. "So, what's your story, Arden? Where do you come from? Have you always known you were illusié?"

"Whoa," Arden says as she puts both hands up. "Slow down there, tiger."

He blushes a deep shade of crimson. "My

apologies. Too much at once?"

Much to his delight, she laughs. "Just a little. Let's see, where do I start?"

"How about you start with where you come from?" Braxton prods.

Without warning, her tone shifts as a sort of darkness veils her expression. "Okay. I wish I could answer where I come from, but, in all honesty, I really don't know. Mother, father, sister, brother . . . I haven't a clue."

He swallows, immediate feeling like an inconsiderate jerk for asking such a personal question. *Strike one.*

But, much to his surprise, Arden keeps talking. "I grew up at Trendalath castle as an assassin, under your father's"—she pauses, realizing she's about to make a grave mistake—"I mean, King Tymond's reign. I was trained at a young age to be a part of the Cruex."

Braxton bobs his head up and down. *Ah yes, the Cruex. Formidable and daring.* At least that's what Tymond wants his enemies to think. As a child, he'd gotten to know a few of the older Cruex members, but he'd never seen Arden.

She must have been pent up on the other side of the castle.

He snaps back to attention as she continues. "As far as where I come from, I *think* Trendalath, but I'm not entirely certain."

"I was born in Trendalath," he chimes in. "At least, that's what I was told. Who knows if it's actually true."

Arden gives him a sad smile, then shakes her head. "And to answer your last question, no, I haven't always known I was illusié." She says the last word as if it's completely foreign on her tongue. "But, if I'm being honest, I'm quite pleased that I am."

Braxton raises an eyebrow, intrigued. "And why is that?"

Arden looks behind her at the many rows of dwellings. "Because now, I have a family."

Braxton nods his again, fully understanding what it feels like to not belong. To struggle with unfamiliar identity. To feel alone. It's something he's wrestled with his entire life, and it seems as though Arden has had a similar set of challenges. He looks at her, feeling their connection growing stronger by the minute.

"What about you?"

The question catches him completely off-guard. He's done so well hiding his identity and avoiding these types of conversations that he'd never prepared for the day if and when it ever actually arrived. But here it is, staring him in the face, begging him to let it all out. "Life as a young price wasn't as easy as most would think."

"I'm sure it was a lot easier than being a peasant," Arden scoffs.

"Excuse me," Braxton says, "but you lived in the same castle. You were fed the same food. I'd hardly call that being a peasant."

"Without freedom, I may as well have been a peasant," she says under her breath.

Braxton regards her with a concerned expression. "I suppose you have no plans to return to the Cruex?"

Arden shakes her head. "That is correct. I am done with the Cruex. Done with Tymond." She scratches Juniper behind the ears. "Plus being a member of the Caldari sounds pretty awesome."

Braxton nods his head in agreement. "Indeed."

"I'm sorry, I interrupted you. What happened after you decided life as a prince was too tiresome?"

He knows she's joking, but still rolls his eyes. "I ran away when I was ten."

The jovial expression on her face is quickly replaced with a troubled one. "Ten years old? How did you survive? Where did you go?"

Braxton sighs as he recalls the memory. "I'd saved up my coins from our travels to various towns. Made my way through the cities until I stowed on a boat to Athia. I stopped at the first place of business I could find and asked for a job." He can't help but shudder as Hanslow's cries resurface. "I stayed there and never looked back."

Arden is quiet for a few moments. "Wow. That is incredibly—"

"—stupid?" he finishes.

"I was going to say brave." A pink tint creeps

across her cheeks. "I actually admire you for it."

Braxton can feel his chest loosen. "Well, thank you. If I'm being honest, your response was completely unexpected."

"That's me," she says with a shrug, "always full of surprises."

He can't be certain, but by the way she blushes and looks away, he can tell that they both feel something. A deeper connection on a deeper level. Something elusive, but real.

"So, what's your ability?"

"Well, I have lots—"

Arden laughs. "I meant your illusié ability."

"Oh, right," he says, trying not to feel too embarrassed. "Xerin calls me a Deviator."

She eyes him curiously. "A Deviator? What's that?"

Braxton gives her a cockeyed grin. "Allow me to show you."

ARDEN ELIRI

I DON'T DARE take my eyes off of Braxton. Being a Deviator, whatever that is, has caught my attention and I find it incredibly intriguing—more intriguing than my healing abilities, anyway.

Braxton stands up from the mushroom we're both sitting on and gestures for me to do the same. I place Juniper next to me and push myself up onto my feet. Braxton walks a few paces away, then turns to face me. I start to follow, but he raises his hand in the air to stop me, so I just stand there, feeling awkward and a little on edge.

"Do you have your weapons with you?" he asks.

I look at him with surprise. "How did you know?"

"You're an assassin. Isn't it a cardinal rule to carry your weapons with you at all times?"

A coy smile tugs at my lips. "Touché, Prince. Touché."

At this, he shifts his stance. "It's Braxton."

"Understood. Sorry," I say quickly. *That was supposed to be a joke.*

"Don't worry about it." His ice blue eyes lock on mine. They're breathtaking. "Are you sure you're ready to see this?"

I keep my gaze hard on his. "You seem to have forgotten who you're talking to."

His eyes crinkle as he grins. "All right then. Pull out your weapons."

I do as he says, releasing the chakrams from their holsters. They feel good in my hands. I realize it's been a while since I've held them—a few weeks at the very least. My fingers slide along the smooth arc of the blades. "Next?"

Braxton nods. "Now I want you to attack me."

I'm immediately brought back to when Felix had ordered me to do the exact same thing. A cross between a laugh and a gasp escapes me. "Did you and Felix plan this or something?"

Braxton tilts his head, clearly confused.

"Never mind," I say. "Okay, if you're sure."

Braxton's voice is flat. "I am."

I take a step back, my chakrams at the ready.

With a grunt, I release them, feeling a part of me leave as I let go. I watch as they swiftly glide through the air, turning effortlessly in a clockwise motion right toward Braxton's head. My eyes widen as the weapons inch closer and closer and it dawns on me that I may have just made a horrible mistake.

Why isn't he doing anything? Why is he just standing there?

Just as I'm about to yell for Braxton to duck, something incomprehensible happens. Midflight, the chakrams come to a dead halt just inches from his face. In the middle of the air.

Fully suspended.

A wave of both awe and relief washes over me simultaneously. I watch, dumbfounded, as the chakrams rotate in midair so that the handles are facing Braxton and the blades are now facing me. I gulp as I realize what his ability is—what *Deviator* actually means.

He can return attacks back on the attacker.

There's no time to process what's happening—the chakrams are headed in my direction, straight for my skull. I squeeze my eyes shut and cringe, waiting for whatever painful end I'm about to meet, but after a few seconds, I'm still standing. I haven't fallen. I haven't been struck.

I open one eye, then the other. The chakrams are motionless, floating right in front of my face. I loose the breath I'd been holding in, the metal on the blades fogging up from the warmth.

Unbelievable.

My gaze shifts from the motionless objects in front of me to Braxton. I can tell he's focusing to keep the blades suspended. I snap my fingers, which distracts him, and the weapons drop at my feet.

"Deviator, huh?"

Braxton gives a timid smile. It's almost unsettling.

"I have to admit, that's a pretty impressive skill. But," I say as I walk closer to him, "you have to let them keep going."

Braxton stares at me with an alarmed expression. "Excuse me?"

"The chakrams. You should have let them slice me up." There's no inflection in my voice, and I can tell he thinks there's something *seriously* wrong with me.

Little does he know, he's right. But I won't give it away this easily.

"I'm a Healer," I clarify. "I can heal myself and others . . . I think."

Braxton storms over to me and grabs my wrist. "Don't ever say that someone should continue to attack you. Not illusié. Not Caldari. No one."

I roll my eyes. "Don't get your trousers in a twist," I say as I break free from his grip. "Maybe you didn't hear me before, but I'm a *Healer*, meaning I can *heal* people."

"You don't know how powerful you are," he

mutters under his breath.

"Oh, and you do?"

His face falls as he says, "I know that my father's called in his Savant to find you."

That shuts me up right then and there.

Estelle calls a meeting in the lower south quadrant of Orihia. Xerin isn't here yet, so Felix, Estelle, Braxton and I stand in a semi-circle staring somewhat uncomfortably at each other. It's obvious that Braxton and I are the newest members to the Caldari, which means that our training will be the most rigorous. If I have to guess, Felix and Xerin will most likely use this time to refine their skills, which means Estelle will be our full-time teacher.

I'm perfectly okay with that.

I gaze around at the scenery before me. Trees with multicolored leaves—shades of purple, pink, and yellow—tower over us. Small houses are built into some of the trees, and it makes me wonder if other creatures occupy them, or if the Caldari just use them as a means to escape when they feel like getting away.

My thoughts scatter as Estelle claps her hands. "Okay, time to get started, even though Xerin's not here."

By her tone, I can tell she's upset with him. "What

will we be doing today?" I ask, eager to get started. Juniper nips at my heels. She seems to be just as impatient as I am.

"You probably won't want to hear this, but we need to take baby steps. We can't release you into the world until we assess how powerful you truly are and understand what exactly you're capable of." She looks at Felix as if she's holding something back, then turns her attention back to Braxton and me. "So, we're going to start small, in a safe environment. Arden, I'm going to work with you today. We're going to have you heal any injured animals we may come across in Orihia. Braxton will be working with Felix." She turns her gaze to him. "Felix is going to send some seemingly harmless attacks your way. As you both master the easier tasks, we'll move into more difficult territory. Understood?"

I pout, knowing full well that my disappointment is written all over my face. Braxton gives me a quick nod, then jogs over to Felix. I watch as they disappear behind the brush. When I turn around, Estelle is standing right in front of me.

"You don't seem to be too happy after hearing your assignment for today."

That's an understatement, but I'm not going to tell her outright. Instead I just shrug and say, "We both know I can heal myself. You saw it when you first met me. I guess I just don't understand why I have to start at the very beginning—you know, with animals."

Estelle cocks an eyebrow. "Well, for starters, Juniper is hurt."

"What?" I give her a bewildered look. "No, she isn't."

Estelle points to the little fox. "On her stomach. See for yourself."

I crouch down to Juniper's level and gently roll her onto her back. She resists at first, but succumbs on the second try. There, along her stomach, is a vertical gash about an inch long. The blood has already started to cake in her fur, which is a good sign because it means it's healing, but I'm now worried that it could get infected. *How did I not see this?* My bottom lip starts to quiver as I place my hands on her belly. I've come to love this little fox, and I feel like a terrible fur-parent for not watching her more closely.

"Don't get upset," Estelle whispers from behind me. "Just breathe. And focus."

I press down a little harder, trying to be as gentle as possible. Juniper whimpers a little, and I swear I can feel my heart splintering in my chest. I take a deep inhale, trying to ignore the sounds she's making, and silently scold myself for not realizing she was hurt earlier.

What kind of person doesn't notice something like that?

I try to clear my mind, but it's no use. My guilt is piling up. Juniper will just be another dead body to add to the collection—yet another living thing I've killed. I remove my hands from her stomach and turn to look over my shoulder at Estelle. "I can't," I whisper.

She looks at me with grave concern. "Yes," she says as she moves next to me and places my hands back on Juniper, "you can."

There's a sort of comfort having her sit next to me and, slowly, I can feel my mind start to clear. *It's not my fault. None of this is my fault. You weren't born this way; you were made this way.* As I continue to repeat this in my head, my earlier feelings of guilt begin to dissipate. I notice I'm able to take normal, even breaths again, and Estelle seems to sense this as well because she removes her hands from mine.

"Focus," she whispers.

I do as she says. I close my eyes and search for the good within me. I have to go deeper than I remember, but I know it's there, somewhere. It feels like an eternity before I finally find it and grab onto it, but when I do, the results are instantaneous. My eyes shoot open and there are my hands, glowing in a soft white light. Just beneath that, I can see the color of Juniper's fur return to white. The scar stitches up on its own, the skin meeting in the middle as if nothing had happened. I continue to focus on the good, on the healing, and in just a few minutes time, the wound is nonexistent.

I let out a breath and lower my hands, the white light fading with the movement. "There."

Estelle pats me on the back. “Nicely done. Come on, let’s move to the next assignment.”

Next assignment? I’d forgotten how drained using my healing abilities makes me feel. Estelle pops up from the ground, but I remain seated.

“Are you coming?”

I put two fingers up in the air. “Just a couple of minutes.”

“Are you tired already?”

I try not to meet her gaze because I know she’ll see the exhaustion in my eyes. “Just trying to recoup a little. I didn’t sleep well last night.”

Estelle sits down next to me and tilts my chin up, forcing me to look at her. “Well, I’ll be damned. Healing such a small creature has drained you almost completely. Why didn’t you say so?”

I stay quiet as she tries to pull me to my feet, but my body acts as though it’s an anchor. “You could at least *try* to make an effort,” she says with a final tug.

I do as she says and, after expelling an enormous amount of energy, I’m somehow on my feet.

“Here,” Estelle says as she pulls some grains and nuts from her pocket, “eat these. You’ll feel better.”

She transfers the food into my palm. I stare at it for a few seconds, not recognizing any of the grains or nuts, but dump the lot into my mouth anyway. They’re surprisingly delicious and full of flavor. I reach for my canteen and guzzle some water. “Do you have any more?" I'm amazed at how much better I feel.

Estelle gives me a playful nudge. "What you just ate has some of the strongest healing properties in the world. You're strong physically, but weak mentally and emotionally." She senses I'm offended, then quickly adds, "It's normal when you're first starting your training. We all have strengths and weaknesses. At least now I know what yours are. We'll put you on a proper diet and take more time to train your mind and emotions. That way, you'll be strong in all aspects."

I don't dare argue with her, so I keep my mouth shut.

"Now it's time for something a little more challenging." She turns away from me and begins to walk deeper into the forest, in the same direction both Felix and Braxton had wandered off to earlier.

"Where are we going?" I ask as I fight off the many rogue branches in my path.

"You'll see."

We walk for about five minutes when Estelle comes to a halt—it's so sudden and unexpected that I almost bump right into her. I peer around her to see why we've stopped. My heart flutters as my eyes land on a fawn. Its little ears perk up and twitch as we move closer.

I expect it to run away, but I quickly realize that it's stretched out on its side. It doesn't move, and as I draw even closer, I can see that the coloring of its fur is off. Instead of a rich beige and taupe, the color is a dull shade of yellow.

Estelle stands beside me as I kneel to take a closer look.

"Is it sick?"

She shakes her head. "Not in the traditional sense."

I furrow my brows as I look up at her. "What does that mean?"

She sighs. "You've proven that you can heal external wounds, but I still question your ability to heal internal injuries."

I look at the fawn, then back at Estelle. "How do you know it has internal injuries?"

"The more time you spend as an active Caldari, the more you pick up on injuries that are of the natural world, and what injuries are of the magickal world."

I shift my attention back to the fragile animal. "The discoloration?" I whisper.

"Yes," Estelle answers. Her voice is soft, gentle.

I suddenly feel a rush of anger overcome me. "A Caldari didn't do this, right?"

Estelle shakes her head. "It was Tymond's Savant."

I can't help but grit my teeth. "Were they here?"

"It looks like it."

Without another word, I place my hands on the fawn's side. The animal seems nervous, almost frightened, but it doesn't move. Large black eyes stare at me, pleading to end the pain. I close my eyes and focus, once again trying to latch onto the pure tethers buried deep within me. I find some and reach for them, desperately, but they pull away, like a spider retreating to its web, at a moment's notice.

I open my eyes. To my dismay, there is no soft white glow. The fawn whimpers. I try again. Deeper and deeper I go until I'm surrounded by darkness. There is no light, nothing pure to latch onto. I must have used everything I had with Juniper.

I open my eyes again and remove my non-glowing hands from the fawn.

"What's wrong?" Estelle asks.

I don't want to say it aloud, but I know I have to. My eyes meet hers. "I'm not strong enough yet."

RYDAN HELSTROM

EACH DAY SINCE Xerin's visit, Rydan has to remind himself not to jump to conclusions when he sees Gladys. Secretly, he hopes and prays for Gladys to morph into the crimson-eyed man, but as of yet, no such luck. It feels as though time is ticking by ever so slowly, and each day without news is like another nail in Elvira's coffin.

His thoughts flit briefly to Arden. After Xerin had mentioned he knew of Arden's whereabouts, a flurry of emotions had come over him. The first was anger, for how she'd behaved during the Soames's mission. The second was betrayal, for when he'd woken up to find that she'd fled with their heads—his only proof to show

Tymond they'd actually been decapitated—and left him all alone. And the third was relief, for he now knew that she was okay.

Rydan bangs his head against the stone wall, his hands sliding along the damp, mossy floor. If he doesn't see Xerin today, he's almost certain he'll go insane. He'd left on a whim and hadn't thought to leave a semblance of a plan for Rydan. There's no sense of comfort, no inkling of security. Leaving his fate up to the Caldari?

What a foolish move.

Someone enters the dungeon. Even in the dim lighting, he can tell it's not Gladys. This shadow is much wider and much taller. Another large figure, of similar stature, appears behind the first. Rydan gulps as the figures approach him. Their methodical footsteps, perfectly in sync, are enough to cause serious panic. He scoots further back into his cell, knowing full well that they're coming for him, albeit he doesn't know the reason why.

"Rydan Helstrom?" a gruff voice asks.

He stays silent, hoping that maybe they'll take him for dead, or better yet, previously removed by another guard.

"Rydan Helstrom!" the guard repeats, louder this time.

It crosses his mind not to respond for a second time, but he thinks better of it. He pushes himself to his feet and scurries to the front of the cell. He winces as his chapped, calloused hands close around the icy bars. It stings.

He can clearly see the guards' faces now. One has steel gray eyes, bushy eyebrows, and a long brown beard that covers half of his face. The other is clean-shaven and has sharp, angular features. His hazel eyes bore into Rydan's.

"You're coming with us," the bearded one says.

For a moment, Rydan considers saying Xerin's name out loud. This could be him, plus one of his other Caldari, who have come to break him out of the dungeon; but something stops him. That look in their eyes . . . no, they're not Caldari.

They're Tymond's guards.

The bearded man unlocks the cell while the other readies the shackles. Rydan takes a sharp breath when the metal hits his wrists, but it doesn't stop there. The guard secures a chain around his waist, then moves down to his feet, where he locks more restraints into place. The metal is heavy on his skin. *How do they expect me to walk with these things on?*

The bearded guard leads the way and the other walks behind him, pushing him every so often for not moving fast enough. The stairs are the most brutal. It takes every ounce of effort for him to pull his legs up onto each steep step. When they finally make it to the top, Rydan is sure he's going to collapse, but the guard places his arms underneath his shoulders and holds him upright.

He eyes a canteen hanging off the front guard's belt. "Water," he says, his voice hoarse.

The guards exchange a look, but the one supporting most of Rydan's weight says, "Just give it to him. It'll make this a lot easier."

The other guard obliges and unscrews the cap to the water. He holds it just above Rydan's mouth and begins to pour until the water comes out in a steady stream. It splashes around his mouth as he tries to get every last drop and, before he knows it, the stream stops and the guard is replacing the canteen back onto his belt.

"Thank you," Rydan whispers.

"Now come on, you're going to be late."

Rydan looks over his shoulder to face the guard, suddenly feeling fully alert. "Late for what?"

The guard gives him a crooked smile. "Didn't you hear? Your trial's been moved up."

DARIUS TYMOND

TODAY IS THE day Clive is to return with his findings. After his meetings with Landon, Benson, and Julian earlier this week, Darius is anything but hopeful. Bad news seems to travel in threes, but his guess as to what Clive will bring back, if anything, is beyond comprehension. He'd sent Landon, Benson, and Julian to their chambers, not wanting to delegate yet another mission until his fourth Savant member returns.

It's well into the evening when a light knock sounds from behind the Great Room doors. Darius straightens before yelling, "Come in!"

Never in his wildest dreams did he think he'd ever

be happy to see Clive Ridley; but as the door opens wider, his glee—and the promise of everything he'd imagined in his head—fades. Clive is alone.

Which means he didn't find Arden.

Darius breathes in through his nose, hoping to appear calm and collected even though he is anything but. "Sir Ridley," Darius says with a nod of his head.

"My King," Clive responds with a polite bow. "I have good news, and I'm afraid I have bad news as well."

"Yes, I can see that," Darius mutters under his breath.

Clive takes a step forward and puts a hand to his ear. "My apologies, I didn't quite catch that."

Darius waves a hand dismissively in the air. "Commence with the bad news."

Clive removes his fur hat as he approaches the throne. "The bad news is that I didn't find the girl."

Darius sighs, even though this is exactly what he'd expected. "And the good news?"

"I think I have a better idea as to where the Caldari are stationed."

At this, Darius straightens up and leans forward. "Oh? Can you expand upon that?"

Clive wrings the hat in his hands. He looks nervous, anxious even, and it's a first for Darius to witness. "You see, My King, after searching for days for Arden without any promising leads, I decided I would leave a sort of trap. I found a fawn in the Thering

Forest and poisoned it with occinum."

Darius sits back in his seat. *Occinum.* It had been a while since he'd heard the term. One of the older Savant members had created a concoction of poisonous herbs and spices, then laced it with a magickal compound. Depending how much a person, or animal, was given, the effects could be immediate or drawn out for days.

Darius nods. "Continue."

"I left the fawn there for a few days and upon my return, checked its vitals." He clears his throat, but doesn't continue.

"And?" Darius presses.

He hesitates before saying, "And someone tried to heal its internal injuries . . . using illusié."

Darius can feel his palms start to sweat. He licks his lips as he digests the information. "Who in the Caldari has healing powers?"

Clive gives him a wicked grin. "To my knowledge, My King, none of them."

Darius rubs his chin as he processes the information. "I was hoping they wouldn't find her yet." Thoughts continue to swarm his mind as he taps his fingers together in front of his face. He brings them to the bridge of his nose and closes his eyes, looses a breath, then looks directly at Clive. "But it has to be her."

Clive holds his gaze. "How should we proceed,

Your Majesty?"

Darius lowers his hands into his lap. "Round up the rest of the Savant," he declares. "We have a lot of work to do."

CERYLIA JARETH

CERYLIA STANDS IN waiting just outside Opal's bedchambers. The suspense is killing her, but she has to remind herself to be patient. Opal promised she would call her in when the time is right, but it feels as though she's been waiting for centuries. If only Opal could speed up time and fast-forward through it all—now wouldn't that be something?

As if on cue, the door creaks open. Cerylia steps back as the girl's head pops out.

"We're ready," she whispers. She ushers the queen into the room and closes the door quickly behind her. "This way."

When Cerylia turns around, she almost loses her

footing. Blood-red eyes meet hers. She opens her mouth to speak, but not so much as a gasp comes out.

Opal comes to the rescue. "Queen Cerylia Jareth, this is Xerin Grey, the most senior member of the Caldari."

Xerin doesn't smile, doesn't nod, doesn't bow. He stands completely still and maintains unwavering eye contact.

Even though they've only just met, Cerylia senses that this is a power play. He wants to see her off her game, caught off-guard. She straightens up and takes a step forward, then, with the utmost confidence, extends her hand out and says, "It's nice to meet you, Xerin."

She's somewhat surprised when he returns the gesture, his firm grip meeting hers. "The pleasure is all mine, Your Greatness."

Cerylia lets go and allows her arm to float gracefully back to her side. "So, you're the most senior member of the Caldari? I never would have guessed."

A hint of a smile touches his lips. "Just one of the many perks of being illusié."

"I see," Cerylia remarks, returning the smile. "Has Opal filled you in?" The mood in the room shifts, and she fears that she's disrupted whatever positive energy was present before she'd arrived.

But Xerin's words slice right through the tension. "She didn't have to."

Cerylia furrows her brows as she looks back and

forth between him and Opal. "What does he mean?"

Opal opens her mouth to respond, but Xerin beats her to it. "I already knew. About Aldreda. Your husband."

The words crash down on her like sleet during a torrential blizzard. "You . . . *knew*?" Waves of anger churn deep within her and she fears if she doesn't leave the room now, she may unleash whatever wrath is growing inside of her. Her face tenses as her lips purse into a scowl. "Tell me how."

Xerin doesn't flinch at her harsh tone. "I'm the most senior member of the Caldari, remember? I see everything. I hear everything. I *know* everything."

His response angers her even more. Before she can think another thought, Cerylia is flinging herself at Xerin, hands balled into fists, mouth open in an ear-piercing shriek.

Xerin catches her by the wrists and pushes against her. He doesn't move, no matter how hard she tries. She shoves him, trying to get his back against the wall, but he's like a statue, strong and sturdy. Indestructible.

And then, something unspeakable happens. As she's seething and glaring into those crimson eyes, the color shifts, and suddenly she's staring into familiar hazel eyes with a ring of bright gold illuminated around the pupils. Cerylia's breath catches as she takes in the rest of the features. The elongated nose, the slightly puffy cheeks, the thin lips. The deep brown hair fastened into a low ponytail.

Her husband.

Impossible.

"Dane?" The word comes out as little more than a whisper.

"All is well, my love," Dane murmurs. "You can let go."

Tears prick Cerylia's eyes. "I can't. Not after what they—what *she*—did to you."

"You will only find happiness when you learn to let go."

"I can't," she says, her eyes welling with tears. "Please come back to me."

He shakes his head. "It's too late for that. Let go."

And then, as suddenly as he arrived, Dane disappears. Beautiful hazel eyes are replaced by crimson colored irises.

Cerylia frees the tension in her arms along with the rest of her body. Her muscles go slack. Xerin must sense this because he immediately releases her wrists. She drops to the floor and begins to hyperventilate. Her head falls into her hands.

"What did you do?" Opal yells as she rushes to the queen's side.

Xerin's hands are still halfway lifted in the air. He looks at them as if they've just committed a heinous crime. "I . . . I—"

"What did you do?!" Opal shouts again, louder

this time.

"I morphed into her late husband," Xerin stutters. "I wasn't even trying to—"

"Well, nice going," Opal snaps. "You've made her hysterical."

Sobs erupt and fill the room. Opal sits there with the queen, running her hands through her hair, rocking her back and forth—doing anything that might be soothing.

Xerin stays standing in the same spot, motionless. He's quiet for a few minutes before asking, "What can I do?"

At this, Cerylia finally raises her head to look at him. Another tear falls from her eye.

"Get out," she hisses. "Now."

BRAXTON HORNSBY

BRAXTON SITS BY a crackling fire, flipping through a book Felix recommended he read. The majority of the pages are filled with mind strengthening exercises, but the only thing that really needs strengthening, in his opinion, is his sleep schedule. Ever since running away from the inn, sleep hasn't come easy. Hanslow's cries for help fill his nightmares every night and consume his thoughts every waking hour. There's no getting away from it.

Having had enough, he slams the book shut and sets it on the wobbly wooden table next to him. He links the tops of his feet underneath the footrest and drags it a couple of inches closer, then sinks into the worn leather chair. Between the heat from the fire and the scent of pine trees just outside his window, it's the first time he's been able to clear his head. He takes a deep breath and closes his eyes.

It doesn't take long for the feeling of serenity to pass. The door swings open, and in comes an irate Xerin. He begins stomping around the cabin, muttering profanities left and right about something indecipherable.

Braxton runs a hand through his rich platinum hair. "Impeccable timing. I was just about to get some shuteye."

"You can sleep when you're dead," Xerin barks. He motions for him to stand.

Braxton groans and pushes the footrest away from the chair. "One day soon, I will get a good night's rest in Orihia. Even if the lords condemn me, it *will* happen."

Xerin ignores him. "I just left Sardoria."

"Sardoria? Why were you there?"

Xerin shifts uncomfortably from one foot to the other, raking his hands through his hair. "We have to go back. I need you to do something for me."

"Right now?" Braxton points to the window. "It's pitch black out there! And you want to cross the Great Ocean and then trek all the way to Sardoria? That'll take days!"

Xerin raises an eyebrow. "No it won't. How do you

think I got here so fast?"

Braxton shrugs his shoulders, too flabbergasted to speak.

Xerin morphs into a falcon to prove his point.

"Right, right," Braxton says as he waves his hand in the air. "The only problem is, I can't morph into anything."

A sly grin stretches across Xerin's face. "Who says you have to?"

Braxton squints as the wind whips against his face. He readjusts his grip on the scaly ridges of the creature's back, hoping that he doesn't fly off—or worse, get bucked off—into the cloudy abyss. Xerin, who's now in dragon form, roars, making Braxton hold on just a little more tightly. It's a good thing he does because the dragon nosedives but to where, Braxton can't tell.

He screams as they plummet toward the ground, then stops when they start to even out again. His heart pounds in his chest like a beating drum, and he can't tell if this is actually how dragons fly, or if dragon-Xerin is doing it on purpose. His gut tells him it's the latter.

It doesn't take long for them to land on stable ground. Even though they're surrounded by darkness, Braxton deliberately tumbles off the dragon, landing with a thud on the ground. He shields his eyes as a soft yellow glow illuminates around the creature. Within seconds, Xerin stands before him, buck-naked.

Braxton shields his eyes again, this time out of respect.

"Clothes," Xerin demands.

Braxton removes the pack and rifles through it, pulling out the trousers, tunic, and boots they'd packed earlier. He tosses them to his companion, making sure to keep his eyes lowered.

"Nothing you haven't seen before," Xerin mutters as he pulls the trousers on.

"Yeah, well, I need to focus on something to keep myself from hurling, and I'd prefer if it wasn't your manhood."

Xerin lets out a chuckle. "I also packed some crackers and water in the bag. They're in the side pocket. Have some."

Braxton pulls the canteen from the bag and guzzles some water. He pops a few crackers into his mouth, crunching loudly as if he hasn't eaten in days.

"Come on, we have to get going if we're going to catch the queen before she's in for the night."

Braxton stops mid-chew, crumbs spilling from his mouth. "The *queen*?"

Xerin laughs. "I may have left out that minor detail."

"Minor detail!" Braxton scoffs. "You said we were

coming here to talk to the last Caldari member!"

Xerin tilts his head back and forth, as if he's weighing whether or not the statement is truthful. "Well, we are. But we're also here to talk to the queen."

"You're unbelievable."

A crooked grin spreads across Xerin's face. "Let's go. It's only a half mile walk from here."

"Can't you turn into a horse or something?"

Xerin brings his hand to his mouth, as if something offensive has just been said. "I'm already dressed and don't have another change of clothes. Plus, you've already ridden me once today. Isn't that enough?"

Braxton's cheeks burn at the insult. "Fine, fine. I'm following you."

After fifteen long minutes, they arrive at the entrance to Sardoria castle. Xerin bangs the brass knocker against the wooden door, then scurries off to the side behind some shrubbery.

"What are you doing?" Braxton hisses.

"The queen and I didn't exactly get off on the right foot. So I think it's probably best if you greet her."

Braxton throws his hands up in the air. "What are you talking about? Xerin, I can't have you changing plans on me so last minute! It's confusing."

Xerin ignores him. "Someone's coming." He ducks behind the shrubbery so that not even the tips of his blonde hair are visible.

The door swings open.

Braxton whirls around to find an older man with a marble walking stick looking him up and down. "And you are?"

Braxton shakes his head, feeling entirely unprepared. "I'm here to see Her Greatness."

The man looks past him, surveying the perimeter of the castle. "At this late hour?"

"It's urgent," Braxton says, hoping the man will stop giving him a hard time and just let him inside.

The old man hesitates, then extends his free hand. "I'm Delwynn."

He grabs the man's hand and gives a firm shake. "I'm Braxton Hornsby."

"No, you aren't," the old man observes with a twinkle in his eye, "but I know who you are."

Another one?

The door opens a little wider and behind Delwynn appears a striking woman with deep-set brown eyes and chestnut hair. Braxton recognizes her immediately and lowers into a bow. "Your Greatness, I do apologize for the late hour." When he rises, her gaze is stone cold.

"Braxton Tymond. I never thought I'd see the day."

A lump forms in his throat. *Why didn't Xerin tell me she knows who I am?*

"Do come in," she demands. "I won't take no for an answer."

Braxton glances over his shoulder, but Xerin is nowhere to be found. He curses under his breath, then steps inside the castle, unsure as to what awaits.

ARDEN ELIRI

ESTELLE'S CALLED A meeting, but to what we owe the pleasure, I do not know. I'm the last to arrive, but I was also the last to find out. "My apologies," I say to everyone as I enter the room. There are no vacant chairs left, so I take a seat on the floor. Xerin and Braxton sit across from me, near the fireplace, and Estelle and Felix are to my left.

I look at Estelle. "May I ask the purpose of this meeting?"

Estelle bobs her head in Xerin's direction. "I'll hand it over to you."

My eyes flit between Xerin and Braxton. Goosebumps prick my arms. The windows are shut and the fire is burning. There is no draft. Suddenly, I feel uncomfortable. “What’s going on?”

Xerin takes a small step forward. He opens his hands in a wide gesture to greet the room. “Last night, Braxton and I visited Queen Cerylia Jareth of Sardoria.”

I notice Estelle shake her head and Felix make a popping noise with his tongue, but they both refuse to say a word.

“Is that supposed to mean something to me?” I ask.

Xerin raises his hand in the air to silence me. “King Tymond has my sister, Elvira. Her punishment, execution, will be carried out in exactly four days.”

“I’m sorry to hear that, but what do you want us to do about it? According to Braxton, Tymond’s called on his Savant.” I shrug, then continue, “If we try to free your sister, we’ll all be slaughtered.”

“My sister isn’t the only one Tymond has locked up,” Xerin retorts. “Does the name Rydan Helstrom ring a bell?”

I stare at him, unable to form a coherent sentence. I blink a couple of times and loosen my jaw, but no words come out.

Clearly, the shock is written all over my face, so thankfully Estelle jumps in. “It’s true, Arden. Tymond has Rydan and his trial has been set for the day after Elvira’s execution.”

Each time Rydan’s name is spoken, I feel as

though it's being pulverized into my brain. I wince, even though no one is inflicting pain, and open my mouth to speak. Soft wisps of air and a barely audible croak are the only things that come out. I crawl over to the corner of the room and pull a sheet from the bed. I surround myself in linen and begin to take deep breaths. I hear Estelle tell the others to give me a few minutes.

More like a lifetime.

I can see their shadows moving from behind the sheet, their figures flickering in the near distance. I pull the linen tighter and close my eyes. I need to fully comprehend what I've just been told.

Rydan's been locked up at Trendalath castle this entire time. If Tymond is bold enough to execute Xerin's sister, who knows what Rydan's punishment will be? Would Tymond really kill one of his own? One of the Cruex?

I continue to think about all of the mistakes I've made over the past month, what I could have done differently, and why I didn't act sooner. My pity party is interrupted as I feel the comfort and safety of the sheet being lifted. My eyes shoot open and right in front of me sits Estelle. The sheet is covering both of us so that we're secluded from the rest of the room.

For some reason, I feel more comfortable knowing that there's a barrier between us and the other Caldari members, no matter how thin it is. I don't bother lowering my voice. "Tymond has Rydan. What do we do, Estelle?"

Estelle takes my hand in hers and gives it a gentle squeeze. "Tymond has been killing illusié and other innocents for years. The time is coming where it'll be put to an end. And we'll be the ones to do it."

I look at her with wide eyes. The thought of facing Tymond again, as well as his seemingly terrifying Savant for the first time, makes my stomach turn. "*We*?"

Estelle squeezes my hand again. "The *Caldari*. Why else do you think we've all banded together and started training?" Her resolve is unwavering. "The Caldari will defeat Tymond and his Savant. It may not be today, or tomorrow, or even in the next couple of months, but it will happen. And we will be victorious—finally able to reclaim what's ours."

I nod my head, even though I feel more confused than before.

"Good. Now, let's get out from under this sheet. We look weird." She fluffs the linen around us until it falls to our sides.

When I look up, the rest of the Caldari are looking at us expectantly. Estelle rises and helps me to my feet. I stay quiet and allow her to take the lead.

"Arden is up to speed on everything. The information regarding Rydan came as a shock to her," she directs a harsh stare at Xerin, "so she needed a few minutes to process it."

Xerin's eyes meet mine. "I apologize for being so brash. I thought you already knew about Rydan. I'm sorry."

"It's okay," I say, holding his steady gaze. "Like Estelle said, the initial shock was overwhelming, but it's passed now."

Braxton steps forward and looks around at our group. "I hate to interrupt, but we need to discuss this now, seeing as we don't have much time." He holds up four fingers to emphasize the limited timeframe. "What are we going to do about Elvira and Rydan?"

Hearing Rydan's name again sends warning bells off in my mind. The words come out before I have a chance to stop them. "Did you ever to stop to think that maybe Rydan deserves to be in there?" I bite my tongue, but it's too late.

The damage is done.

"Isn't he one of your own?" Xerin hisses. "One of the *Cruex*?"

I can tell by the slits in his pupils that my statement struck a chord. A very *dangerous* chord. "All I meant to say," I struggle to find the words, "is that maybe there are things about Rydan you don't know. Just like you didn't know certain things about me."

"Oh, you mean like how you enjoy killing people?"

I slowly turn my head to the left. My gaze lands on Felix. "Excuse me?"

"You can't fool me," he retorts. "Whatever Rydan's

done can't be any worse than your deepest, darkest desires."

I can feel Braxton's eyes burning into me. From my peripheral, his face looks like it might contort into disgust, but it remains stoic. At least, I think it does. I don't dare look at him head-on.

Just as I'm about to say something to defend myself, Estelle jumps in. "That's enough, Felix."

Felix looks like he's on the verge of making some sarcastic remark, but after just a few seconds of being under Estelle's steely gaze, he seems to shrivel into himself.

"If we're going to do this, then we have to come together. As one unit. As the Caldari." She looks at each of us before continuing. "We can't do that by constantly pointing out flaws in others, picking fights, or maintaining a state of distress. We need to join together. And it needs to happen *right now*."

The room is silent for a few moments, the tension hanging thick and heavy in the air.

Braxton is the first to speak. "I'm in."

Xerin nods somewhat reluctantly. "Me too."

"I'm pretty sure this goes without saying, but I'm in, too," I say.

There's only one person who hasn't said anything. We all look to Felix. Estelle clears her throat.

Felix rolls his eyes and, with a sigh, says, "Fine."

"Good. Now that that's settled, I'll turn it back over to you, Xerin."

Xerin gives Estelle a small smile as he pulls something from the back pocket of his trousers. "Queen Jareth has agreed to provide a safe haven for us once we free both Elvira and Rydan, as long as Opal gets to stay with her."

I'm about to ask him who Opal is, when he marches over to the table and unfolds a large piece of parchment. "We only have four days to figure this out *and* strengthen our abilities. Not much time at all."

We all gather around the table and stare at the blank piece of parchment.

"Now," Xerin says as he dips his quill into a small jar of ink, "who would like the honor of getting us started?"

RYDAN HELSTROM

A COUPLE OF days have passed since Rydan was taken from one cell and thrown into another. When the guards had arrived, he'd originally thought he'd be going straight to the Great Room for his trial. He was more than disappointed when he found out that he was just being moved to a holding cell on the floor above the dungeon. That way, the guards would have easier access to him whenever Tymond decided to bring him in. The king seemed to change his mind a lot these days.

Rydan gazes around the brightly lit room. It sure beats the dank, dark dungeon he'd been living in for months. The food is slightly more appealing here, too, like the chefs actually empathize with the prisoners. Rydan likes to think it's their way of sticking it to Tymond—a way for them to get vengeance in an otherwise bleak, miserable life.

The cell across from him has been empty for days. As a matter of fact, he seems to be the only one in the holding cell besides old man Peters—although, he does just sit in his cell and sleep all day long—so Rydan may as well be alone.

Loud footsteps echo from down the hall. Rydan scurries to the back of his cell, a habit he's formed after his last interaction with the king. It's foolish to think that if they can't see him, they'll possibly forget here's there; but anything's worth a shot in such dire circumstances.

As the figure comes into view, he immediately recognizes it as Gladys. To her side, she's dragging someone with a bag over their head, wrists and ankles shackled. The chains clank against the floor as they draw closer. He realizes that the person Gladys is dragging along behind her is small, fragile. A girl.

Elvira.

Rydan jumps to his feet and moves closer to the front of the cell. Peeking out from underneath the bag is blonde hair.

It's definitely her.

Gladys stops in front of his cell. She pulls her prisoner around to the front and gets her to kneel. The bag is removed from her head. Sad blue eyes meet Rydan's.

"I was never here," Gladys grunts. She turns and walks away from the cell, but the footsteps stop just outside the chamber. He realizes she's guarding the door . . . *for* them.

Why is she doing this for me?

He shifts his attention back to Elvira. She's filthy—hair matted, dirt caked all over her face, clothes torn—and yet, she's still just as beautiful as Rydan remembers.

Her mouth twitches into a smile. "Fancy seeing you here."

Rydan knows it's supposed to be a joke, but it fills him with sadness. A low guttural sound escapes his throat. "Elvira, I am so sorry. I don't know how you can ever forgive me. This is all my fault."

She cocks an eyebrow. "Well, don't take all the credit."

Rydan can't help but grin. "Damn, the dungeon's really changed you."

She rolls her eyes. "I had to beg and beg and beg Gladys to bring me here. I need to talk to you, but we don't have much time."

"When is your trial?" Rydan blurts out without thinking.

Elvira lowers her voice. "I've already had it. My execution's tomorrow."

Rydan almost chokes on his own spit. She says it

so nonchalantly, as if being sentenced to death is something that happens every day. "Holy lords! Are you serious?"

Elvira tries to wave her hand in the air, but the chains weigh her arm down. "It won't matter though because they're coming for me—for *us*."

Rydan is sure the look on his face is one of pure bewilderment, but he doesn't even attempt to hide it. He's not sure whether to go along with it, or ask her what the guards have been feeding her. She looks dead serious though, so he asks, "What do you mean *they're* coming for us? Who is?"

Elvira looks over her shoulder before responding. "My brother visited me right after my trial. I wasn't in a good place then, but seeing him again . . ." She pauses, her gaze traveling to the ceiling. "I've never felt so happy in my entire life. To know that he's alive and well."

Rydan does a quick calculation in his head. Elvira's been locked in her cell this entire time. Tymond doesn't allow prisoners to have visitors. So how is it Elvira was able to see her brother? He wouldn't have made an exception for her. Unless . . .

The realization hits him like a ton of bricks.

Xerin.

Just like Xerin was able to morph into Gladys, he was probably able to morph into another guard and work his way in to see Elvira.

Sly bastard.

"Okay, so Xerin's your brother. I should have pieced that one together earlier," Rydan says as he scratches his head. "So what's the plan? Shouldn't they have broken us out by now since your execution is *tomorrow*?"

"Well, I don't know exactly what the plan is," Elvira admits. Her face turns bright red. "All I know is that they're coming for us. And I wanted to warn you so that you could be prepared."

"Prepared? How can I be prepared if I don't know what the plan is?"

"Shhh," Elvira urges. "I'm just letting you know to expect some sort of escape that will most likely happen tomorrow. Unless, of course, you'd rather spend the rest of your days rotting in one of these cells." She rolls her eyes. "You're welcome, by the way."

Rydan's palm meets the middle of his forehead. "I'm sorry, that was rude of me. I guess I'm just shocked. And nervous. I'm normally the one doing the planning, not the one the plan is centered around."

"Well, it's centered around the both of us."

A clearing of a throat interrupts their conversation.

"Gladys will be coming back in here any minute."

As if on cue, loud footsteps make their way back in their direction.

"Elvira?" Rydan sticks one of his hands as far out of the cell bars as he can.

She grabs hold of his fingers. “Yes?”

“Do you think this is going to work?” Rydan shakes his head, trying to find the right words. “I mean—do you trust them?”

Elvira gives him a reassuring smile. “It’s the Caldari, Rydan. I trust them with my life.”

Before he can say another word, Elvira’s face disappears as a brown sack is thrown back over her head. Gladys gives him a brief nod before dragging her prisoner away from Rydan and back downstairs to the dungeon.

Rydan watches until they disappear around a corner, his mind swimming with what-ifs and past regrets. There’s nothing he can do except wait for tomorrow and see what Xerin and the rest of the Caldari bring to the table.

If only he had as much faith in them as Elvira—it certainly would make things a hell of a lot easier.

DARIUS TYMOND

DARIUS IS ALMOST certain the members of the Caldari reside somewhere in the Isle of Lonia. After Clive's discovery of the partially injured fawn, he'd made an executive decision to send his most senior Savant member back to the Thering Forest. Clive hadn't seemed too thrilled with his assignment, but he'd bitten his tongue and obliged.

He'd tried to get Darius to go with him, but the king had been set on staying in Trendalath. After all, with Elvira's execution quickly approaching, what kind of king would leave, especially when he has every intention of making an example out of the girl?

"A coward, that's who," Darius mutters, answering

himself. He finishes polishing the looking glass Clive had given him just a few hours prior. Even though Darius wouldn't go with him to Lonia, he still wanted to keep an eye on things. This also gave him another excuse to keep Clive away from his wife for a little while longer.

A win-win.

He holds up the looking glass and repeats the incantation provided by Clive. A purple glow emanates from the glass, brightening around the sphere. He sets it down on the little stand in front of his throne and rubs his hands together with glee, then takes a seat and points his gaze at the mystical object. Like clockwork, Clive appears. He's walking on the outskirts of the town, right on the edge of the forest. He looks dreadful, like he hasn't slept in days, and he doesn't appear to be his usual snarky self. For a moment, Darius doubts his decision. Perhaps he should have let Clive rest for a day.

No, there wasn't any time. He had to leave immediately.

His internal battle carries on longer than expected until Clive ducking into the brush distracts him from his own debilitating thoughts. There seems to be a minor delay with what the looking glass is portraying and what is actually happening in Lonia. He rises from his throne and taps the glass, as if that's going to help it catch up to real-time.

He watches with curiosity as Clive wanders deeper into the forest, wondering where he's headed—but as the lapse in time grows larger, so does his frustration. Just as he's about to turn away and give up, Clive stops in his tracks. The looking glass has a chance to catch up, and Darius notices an animal just off in the distance. It appears to be injured.

As he draws nearer, Darius realizes that the animal is the injured fawn Clive had reported earlier during his search for Arden. Although he doesn't want to admit it, it's a smart move. For once, Clive has done something right.

Twigs snap. Leaves crunch. He moves to the edge of his seat, watching as Clive backs away from the fawn and hides in a shallow ditch nearby, behind a towering oak tree. He brings the sphere closer to his face, knowing full well that this won't improve his view. Psychologically, it satisfies some need.

Two shadowed figures come into view. From the high-pitched sound of their voices, he can tell it's two women, but whether or not they're Caldari, he hasn't a clue. The first one comes into view. Long black hair, violet eyes, and mocha colored skin. Darius has never seen her before, nor does he care. His focus is trained on the second figure. He catches a glimpse of emerald eyes and chestnut hair and inhales a sharp breath.

"It's her," he mutters to himself, then yells, "It's her!" He knows that Clive can't hear him, but that doesn't keep him from shouting, "That's Arden! That's her!"

"Is this the fawn?" the midnight-haired girl asks.

"That's it," Arden says as she approaches the injured animal. She kneels next to it, checking for vitals. "It's still alive."

She seems relieved.

Darius's gaze shifts to the shallow ditch that Clive is hiding in. "Why aren't you doing anything? That's Arden! Bring her to me!" he snaps, even though his demands are futile.

Arden gently places her hands on the fawn. *What is she doing?* The king's mouth drops as a soft white glow appears around her hands.

She knows of her abilities.

Anger roils deep within until he can't hold it in any longer. He smacks his hand down on the table, nearly sending the looking glass over the edge. He catches it just in time.

"Why aren't you doing anything!" he yells again, wishing more than anything that Clive could hear him. As if on cue, Clive appears and makes himself known. The midnight-haired girl steps in front of Arden and commands that Clive leave, but he stands his ground.

"Your friend comes with me," Clive says, his tone flat.

"By whose order?" the midnight-haired girl shoots back.

Clive narrows his eyes, his mouth twitching in

annoyance. "I don't answer to you."

"Well, we don't answer to *you*." The midnight-haired girl stays in front of Arden, blocking Clive from her like a giant, impenetrable wall.

Clive narrows his eyes as his lips turn upward into a half smile. Darius knows exactly what he's about to do—he's going to use his ability. As a Caster, he's able to cast and weave illusions to alter his victim's senses and perceptions of their surroundings. Having been a victim of one of these himself, numerous times over, he knows the shock and agony that comes with not being able to determine what's real and what's fake.

Arden pushes her way in front of Estelle. She draws weapons from her holsters, spinning the blades in her hands with ease. "I suggest you turn around," she hisses. "And don't come back *ever* again."

Clive raises one hand in the air. It appears as though he's about to surrender—until he flicks his wrist. Arden's once determined and daring expression turns into one of shock and fear. Even though Darius can't see what illusion Clive has cast around her, he knows exactly what she must be feeling—and it isn't the least bit enjoyable.

Arden tries to fight back, aiming her chakrams at emptiness while her friend screams, "It's not real!" He's not sure what the midnight-haired girl's abilities are, or if she even has any, so there's no use in worrying about her. For now, she's just a bystander.

The expression on Clive's face grows darker and darker as he weaves what are likely to be more elaborate—and terrifying—illusions around her. The thought alone is enough to make him shudder. Clive's mind isn't just bleak—it's downright twisted. His sense of right and wrong is completely warped. The affair with his wife is evidence enough.

He shoves the thought from his mind and focuses back on the looking glass. Arden seems to be fading. Any minute now, Clive should be able to shackle her and bring her back to the castle.

Just as Arden is about to fall to the ground, the midnight-haired girl flings a dagger right at Clive's head. It barely skims his cheek as it lodges itself into a tree. It does its job though—it's enough to distract him.

Darius watches with dread as the girl rushes to Arden and, suddenly, they're gone. "No, no, no," he mutters to himself. He taps the looking glass, hoping that maybe he's missed something, but no. He saw it with his own two eyes. The other girl is a Caldari. A Cloaker.

Damn invisibility—the ability for cowards.

It takes a few moments, but Clive seems to finally understand what's just happened. He throws his fists into the air, punching at the sky, then grabs the handle of the dagger and wrenches it from the tree. He shouts some profanities before turning around and

CERYLIA JARETH

"DO YOU THINK I should go with them?"

Cerylia knew the question would come eventually, but, even so, it still catches her off-guard. She glances at Opal, then takes a long sip of her tea.

"I don't know whether to take your silence as being deep in thought, or a flat-out no," Opal jests.

Cerylia regards her with a small smile. "I think you made the right decision by staying here," she says.

"I think you mean to say that *you* made the right decision in *making* me stay here." She's quiet, then adds, "Your Greatness."

Cerylia sighs. "The Caldari hardly even have a coherent plan in place. They're a bunch of rogue misfits trying to do good in a kingdom where they don't have the upper hand."

"Oh."

From the hurt look in Opal's eyes, the queen can tell she's gone a little too far. "I'm not saying you're a misfit, Opal—"

"But I'm one of them." She looks down at her hands, fidgeting with the edge of her plate.

"Aren't you hungry?" Cerylia asks, trying to change the subject.

Opal pushes her plate away from her before scooting her chair back. "May I be excused, Your Greatness?"

Cerylia sets down her teacup and gives the girl a pleading look. When she doesn't respond, the queen waves her hand in the air and says, "Yes, yes, you are excused."

The door shuts firmly behind Opal, leaving Cerylia alone with her thoughts, which isn't necessarily a good thing at the present moment. From the stories Cerylia had heard of the great Caldari, she'd always admired their tenacity and courage, their skill and prowess.

But after meeting with Braxton Tymond—or Braxton *Hornsby*, as he prefers to be called now—Cerylia can't help but feel as though the legends and tales she'd heard had been exaggerated to a higher degree. Their plan to overthrow King Tymond is not only disjointed and rushed, but the overall organization of their expertise and abilities seems, frankly, like a chaotic mess.

It wasn't at all what she'd expected, especially after working with someone like Opal. Opal had integrity, courage, and skill, yet she was also unforgiving and resilient—the way a Caldari should be.

She pours another cup of tea, blowing on the steaming liquid before raising it to her mouth. It goes down smooth, warming her to the bone. Opal's question repeats over and over again in her head. *Do you think I should go with them?*

When Braxton had shown up at her doorstep, she'd invited him in, albeit feeling hesitant to do so. It was well known around Aeridon that the Tymond's son, heir to the Trendalath throne, had run away at the young age of ten; so it was a given that Braxton despised both Darius and Aldreda just as much as she did.

Right out of the gate, he'd asked if Sardoria could be a safe haven for the Caldari. Seeing as she'd already had one of their members, how could she say no?

Braxton had presented the bare bones of their plan, and nowhere did it involve Opal's time-traveling abilities. At the time, Cerylia could sense the hurt Opal was feeling as she sat across the room and listened, completely removed from the conversation. Braxton had been in a rush to get back to the Caldari, so Cerylia had given him the answer he'd wanted to hear and let him go. Of course, she still plans to stick by it—she is, and always will be, a woman of her word, unlike so many others that have crossed her path.

Another long sip of tea has her feeling satisfied. She pushes her chair away from the table and rises. Her robes swish as she makes her way across the table to blow out the candles.

The room goes dark.

As she heads for the door, she stops mid-step. Tomorrow will be a big day. Best to put her mind at ease. She relights one of the candles as she surveys the room. Her eyes land on a bottle of red wine.

Yes, that will certainly do.

BRAXTON HORNSBY

BRAXTON'S CAUGHT IN a mid-afternoon snooze when loud shouts ring out in Orihia. He throws the covers off of him and stumbles out of bed, looking for his boots. He spots them in the corner of his room and pulls them on, then rushes out the door. He recognizes the voices to be Estelle's and Arden's, but the field outside his dwelling is empty. They're nowhere to be seen.

"Are you cloaked?" Braxton yells as he rubs the sleep from his eyes. "Estelle? Arden?"

The two suddenly appear just a few feet away from him, causing him to jump. "Lords, you scared me!" He shakes his head. "What's going on? Why are you shouting?"

Before they can answer, Estelle takes off toward Felix's dwelling.

Braxton gives Arden a confused look. "Should we follow her?"

Arden just shrugs.

"Grab Xerin!" Estelle yells over her shoulder as she swings the door open to Felix's place.

Braxton does as he's told as Arden runs in the opposite direction, toward Felix's. Braxton pounds on Xerin's door, waiting impatiently for him to answer. He glances over his shoulder, wondering what's gotten Estelle so worked up. When Xerin doesn't answer, he bangs on the door again, even louder this time. "Xerin!" he shouts.

No answer.

He forces his way in, quickly surveying the area. Bed made. Fire out. Window open. He rushes toward the window and pokes his head outside.

Still no Xerin.

His eyes scan the grassy meadow until they land on a tree in the distance. A bird is perched on one of the branches. A black falcon.

Feeling overwhelmed, he pulls his head back inside, cursing as he bumps it on the edge of the window, then darts over to the back door. He swings it open and runs across the back porch, flailing his arms in the air to try and get the bird's attention.

It works.

The bird cocks its head toward him, then hops from the tree onto the ground. A yellow glow appears around the animal, and Braxton taps his foot as the transformation ensues. A few moments later, Xerin's head appears above a haystack.

"You look crazed," Xerin says as he pulls a tunic over his head.

Braxton averts his gaze as he gets dressed. "Estelle and Arden are calling a meeting," he pants. He hadn't realized how out of breath he was until now. "They seem pretty shaken up, like they have something urgent they need to tell us. Come on."

Xerin tugs on the bottom of his tunic, and Braxton ventures around the haystack, pulling his sleeve to get him moving. They jog side by side until they reach Felix's house. The door is wide open, so they let themselves in. Estelle, Arden, and Felix are gathered around the table. They rise when Braxton and Xerin enter.

By the concerned looks on their faces, Braxton assumes they won't be bearing good news. "What's going on?"

Estelle looks right at him before saying, "It's time to set our plan in motion."

Braxton gulps as his gaze shifts from her to Arden. "Right now? Why? I thought we'd have more time."

Arden shakes her head. "Unfortunately, our

security is at stake."

He gives her a confused look.

She glances at Estelle, then raises her chin a little higher.

Braxton cringes, knowing exactly what's about to come out of her mouth. It's the one thing he's been dreading—the one thing they're not fully prepared for. *Don't say it. Don't say it.*

She says it anyway. "The King's Savant is in Orihia."

ARDEN ELIRI

I SPEND THE remainder of the evening ensuring that I've packed everything I need for our mission. Even though I haven't been in Orihia for very long, it's come to feel like my new home. I survey the space around me—the stone fireplace, the wobbly wooden table and chairs, the bed that Juniper and I fit perfectly in—and can't help but feel an overwhelming sense of sadness. Just when I was settling in, just when things seemed to be turning for the better, the King's Savant had to ride in and ruin everything.

I sigh as I secure my pack and throw it over my shoulder. Juniper is sitting patiently on the bed. I can tell she doesn't want to leave either. "Come on, girl," I say, patting my leg. She hops off the bed, but instead of coming over to me, she wanders over to the bookshelf. I try again to call her over, but to no avail. I give her an exasperated look before walking over to a nearby cabinet. I pull some juniper berries from a small rag I'd collected just a few days prior. I try once again. "Here, girl. I have a treat for you."

The little fox takes a few steps forward, then turns around with her tail in the air, and heads back to the bookshelf. I cross my arms. I will not let her temperamental behavior get the best of me. I try one more time, and I'm not sure if I'm seeing things, but I swear she just bobbed her head toward the bookshelf. I walk over to where she's sitting and kneel so that I'm eye-level with the lower shelf. The book I'd "borrowed" from Estelle stares back at me.

I scratch Juniper behind the ears. "You're too smart for your own good," I say as I grab the book and stuff it into my bag. I give her some berries and she trots happily behind me out the door.

"Don't fall behind!" Estelle yells from the front of the group. Her abundance of energy is truly astounding, but after realizing that even Felix and Braxton are having a hard time keeping up, I don't feel so bad. Xerin flies overhead, just a couple of paces behind Estelle. I'm at the back of the group, keeping an eye out for any signs of the Savant. Juniper's helping, and her little nose twitches as she raises it into the air.

After discovering that one of the Savant members had been in the Thering Forest, Estelle thought it best not to risk our safety. She recommended that we travel on the outskirts of the Thering Forest in order to reach Lonia bay. Felix has his ship docked there and ready for departure, so as far as I know, that's the first piece of the plan.

I reach into my pocket, feeling grateful for swiping the berries from my dwelling. After a few hours on foot, I know we should be nearing the bay soon, but my stomach won't stop rumbling. I pop a few berries into my mouth. Juniper looks up at me with pleading eyes, so I stop for a second to give her some.

"Better keep up, Eliri!" Estelle calls.

I roll my eyes as I tuck the food back into my pocket and jog over to them. I catch up to Braxton and give him a playful nudge in the shoulder.

He forces a smile. "Are you ready for this?"

"Do we really have a choice?"

Just as his smile meets his eyes, the falcon swoops down and Xerin morphs into his human form, pulling on pants as he walks beside us. "We're almost there! Five more minutes!" he shouts as he buttons them and runs to Estelle's side.

His calculations are eerily precise because we arrive on the edge of Lonia bay exactly five minutes later. We've somehow remained on the outskirts of town, trying to avoid any run-ins with the townspeople, or worse, the King's Savant.

I gaze at the familiar ship, docked in the same place as when I'd first arrived here. I never would have guessed I'd stay here this long. Without warning, Rydan's face drifts across my mind, and I have to shake my head to clear the image.

Estelle turns to face us. "We need to take turns," she says in a hushed voice. "We don't need to draw attention to ourselves." She taps her chin as she eyes each of us. "Felix, since it's your ship, we'll have you go first. Braxton and Xerin will follow shortly after. Arden and I will go last."

My throat suddenly feels dry. Normally, I wouldn't care what the order is, but today feels different. I want to get on that ship as soon as possible. I scoop Juniper up off the ground and trot over to where Estelle is standing. We watch as Felix begins his solo journey to the pier.

I elbow her lightly in the side. "Why are we going last?"

She grins so large that it almost swallows her face. "You know how men are. If they go last, something will go wrong. We'll never get to where we need to be."

I stifle a laugh, but fail.

Xerin turns around and rolls his eyes.

"Don't act like it's not the truth," Estelle says pointedly.

He turns back around and Estelle and I have to cover our mouths to keep from laughing out loud.

It doesn't take long for Felix to make it to the ship safely. Estelle prods Xerin and Braxton until they start moving. "Your turn."

"Okay, okay," Xerin says as he shoos her hand away. "We're going."

Estelle and I scoot closer to the edge of the forest as they walk casually across the sandy shores to the pier. Well, Xerin's walking casually—Braxton, on the other hand, keeps glancing over his shoulder, his head moving back and forth as if he's doing something he shouldn't be.

Real smooth.

"What is Braxton doing?" Estelle mutters. "He looks like a lost child with zero sense of direction."

"I'm sure he's just nervous," I respond. "You have to remember, he was living a pretty low-key lifestyle back in Athia. This is probably a whole new world to him."

"But he's royalty. I just figured he'd be a little more composed."

"He hasn't been royalty for ten years." As the words come out of my mouth, I can't help but feel shocked. I know a lot more about Braxton than I realized—certainly more than I've given myself credit for.

Estelle shoots me a sidelong glance. "Right. Well,

just a few steps more and they'll be there. Then we can go."

We watch as they walk along the pier to the ship. Felix waves them down from the upper level. I breathe a sigh of relief as both Xerin and Braxton disappear from sight.

Estelle turns to look at me. "Ready?"

I adjust Juniper in my arms and nod. Estelle leads the way. I follow her out of the brush, wincing as Juniper's claws dig into my forearm. It makes me wonder what's got the little critter so worked up. She whines and looks up at me, then lodges her claws into my arms again. They go deeper this time, causing me to fling her away from me. She lands on her feet, then scampers toward Estelle.

I look down at my arm. Pinpricks of crimson appear where her claws had dug into my skin. There's hardly any blood, but for some reason I feel woozy. I drop to one knee, then the other, but don't fall over. Somehow, I manage to remain upright.

Even though I don't want to, I look down again at my arm. An odd sensation comes over me—I feel queasy, but for some reason, I have a desire to look at the blood. My eyes take it all in. I can feel it coursing through my veins, pumping its steady rhythm, begging to be let out. It's then a familiar feeling washes over me.

The darkness.

It's here.

Slowly, my gaze travels up from my arm. Estelle and Juniper no longer stand before me. Instead, it's an all too familiar figure; the crimson cloak is especially vivid this time around.

"Hello, old friend," I say, the voice not my own.

The whispers begin to urge. *Come with us.*

They begin to plead. *You're not one of them.*

They won't stop. *Join us.*

Slowly, I rise from my knees and take a step forward. Then another. And another. Dark energy circles round and round my mind, consuming every inch of me. I can feel it pulsating in my temples, my heart, my very *being.*

It is the darkness. It is all that is me.

That's it, the cloaked figure whispers. *Keep walking.*

I do as my friend says, but my mind is elsewhere. I feel an indescribable tether binding us, something otherworldly. It drags me in and pulls me under, and there's nothing I can do to stop it. "I want to come with you," I say under my breath. "I know I belong with you."

You will join us then? The cloaked figure reaches for me, stretches its long, spindly fingers.

It's going to take me.

But, even in my trance, I recognize that this is a question. I have a choice. I've *always* had a choice. "Soon," I say, starting to feel a little more like myself again. “Real soon.”

Soon, the hood repeats. And then a first—a jagged yellow smile. Within seconds, the crimson cloak vanishes in a haze of gray and I find myself, once again, face to face with Estelle.

“Arden!” Her hands are on my cheeks, tapping and pressing, waiting for me to come back from wherever I’d just ventured off to. “Arden, are you okay?”

I snap out of my daze and focus on her violet eyes. I blink a few times until my vision clears. “Juniper . . . she scratched me.” I remove my hand from my forearm.

Estelle pulls my arm toward her, then gives me a concerned look. “What are you talking about? Your arm is fine.”

I furrow my brows as I blink a few more times, searching for claw marks that don’t exist. Estelle is right. My arm is fine.

She presses her lips together. “We need to get going if we’re going to make it to Trendalath in time.” She tilts her head and regards me with a slight frown. “Are you sure you’re okay?”

I nod, even though I feel anything but.

She pats me on the shoulder, then turns to walk toward the ship. Juniper scurries back over to me. I don’t pick her up.

When we make it onto the ship, it seems that the other Caldari have been eagerly awaiting our arrival.

Braxton approaches me and offers to take my bag. I feign a smile and hand it to him.

"Everything okay?" he asks.

I look around at my fellow Caldari on the ship, feeling too concerned to let them in on my visions. "No," I say, "but it will be."

RYDAN HELSTROM

IT WAS THE worst possible night not to sleep, but try as he might, Rydan couldn't seem to drift off. It's difficult to surmise how long he's been awake for, but if he had to guess, it'd probably be in the thirty-hour range. From the dryness of his eyes to the scratchiness of his throat, it wouldn't surprise him if it were longer.

Clomping footsteps sound from down the hall. Rydan scoots to the front of his cell and sticks his face in between the bars. Between the dim light and lack of sleep, the grim reaper could be approaching, ready and waiting to take him to his death, but it's only Gladys. He's not sure whether to feel relief or dread.

He waits for her to unlock his cell and replace his shackles, but she doesn't do either. Instead, she takes a seat on the haystack and glares at him. Rydan clears his throat before speaking, but his voice still comes out hoarse. "Will I be leaving my cell today?"

Gladys bites her lower lip as she shakes her head.

Rydan perks up. "But Elvira . . ."

"King's orders," Gladys says with a shrug.

Rydan's hands fall from the bars. He turns around, still sitting, so that the base of his head is pressed against the cool metal. *Why wouldn't Tymond want me to see Elvira's execution? Wouldn't it be greater punishment to have me watch?*

His heart picks up pace, a flurry of nerves erupting from within his chest. Thoughts of no one coming to save them swirl through his mind. *What if the Caldari are all talk? What if Elvira and I are both going to die?*

He tries to think of something else—anything else—but his mind is consumed with images of death and grief. In an effort to take his mind off of their potentially gruesome ending, he decides to strike up a conversation with Gladys, or at least try.

"So, how long have you been serving King Tymond?"

Gladys gives him a knowing stare before crossing her arms and turning her attention away from him.

Her behavior doesn't faze him in the slightest. "I've

been serving the king for as long as I can remember," he continues, even though she hadn't asked for his life story. "I think since I was a child. Really messes a kid up, you know?"

A hint of a smile cracks her stoic expression.

A-ha.

"It's not easy serving under him. I commend you. I really do."

At this, Gladys turns her head and locks eyes with him. "Elvira will be okay."

It's astounding how so few words can bring such great comfort.

Rydan looses a breath he didn't realize he was holding. He bows his head and raises his hands together in appreciation. "Thank you, Gladys."

Her expression returns to its stoic state and she becomes a statue once again.

Rydan studies her, seeing as there's nothing else to do and no faster way to make time go by.

They sit in silence for a long while.

Finally, a bell rings off in the distance.

Gladys looks at him again. "It's time."

Rydan knows she means Elvira's execution, or lack thereof, based on the conversation they've just had. The Caldari should surely be on their way, if they haven't already arrived.

Here's hoping.

DARIUS TYMOND

"WAKE UP, My Queen," Darius whispers as he shakes Aldreda's shoulder. "Today's the day."

Aldreda swats at him. She pulls the blankets tighter around her shoulders, then rolls over on her side.

Darius finishes gathering his robes, then stamps his feet as he marches to the other side of the bed. "My Queen, how is it that you're not bursting with excitement? Today's the day we get to make an example out of that poor little savage girl. Correct me if I am wrong, but these are some of your favorite days."

Aldreda groans. She mutters something inaudible from underneath the covers.

Darius strokes her hair, his fingers light to the touch. "Is it the pregnancy? A bad day?" He sighs when she doesn't respond. Silence usually means yes. "I'll leave you to it, but I don't want you to miss out." With a few long strides, he reaches the door, and waves his hand flippantly in the air, even though she can't see him. "Executions always ripen the mood." And with that, he shuts the door behind him and carries on toward the castle doors.

The halls are abysmally quiet for the day that lies ahead, but he doesn't let this affect him. His stomach rumbling, he decides to take a detour and swing by the dining hall to grab a small loaf of bread and an apple. On days like this, his appetite is rather large, but he's running late as it is. He'd rather have a smaller breakfast than miss out on a beheading.

He finishes the last of his apple, then throws the core behind him. His robes sway back and forth, stopping only when he opens the doors that lead to the outside of the castle. The sun beats down on his face as he walks over the drawbridge. Giant lungfuls of air soothe his nerves, but adrenaline continues to course through his veins.

Yes, it's the perfect day for death.

His guards, plus Landon, are waiting for him at the end of the drawbridge. The rest of his Savant has been put on Arden-duty, per his orders. Given past events, he prefers to keep one Savant member with him at all times, especially on an execution day, just in case something goes awry. Landon fits the bill. If all goes according to plan, it should be a day of little worries and great victories.

The guards bow at the sight of their king. Landon steps forward to shake his hand. "My King, you look rather," he pauses as he observes his superior, "exuberant this fine morning."

"It's execution day," Darius says for what feels like the eighteenth time that morning.

"Ah, yes," Landon agrees with a grin. "Always a good day."

Darius looks around him, wondering why they haven't started moving yet. "What are we waiting on?"

"Your wife, sir." Landon gives him a troubled look. "Will she not be in attendance?"

"It seems she may have fallen ill. It is in her best interest to stay in the castle and get some rest."

Landon doesn't ask questions, just nods before turning to the soldiers. "Onward! To the town square."

Darius pulls the sleeve of Landon's tunic. "Is it safe to assume that you've arranged to have the girl transported there?"

"Yes, Your Majesty. The prisoner awaits in the town square pending our arrival."

"Right," Darius says. "Onward it is then."

Landon helps the king into his carriage. He's about to shut the door, when Darius invites him inside. Seeing no other choice but to accept, he hops in. The carriage takes off at a startling speed, throwing both of them into the backs of their seats.

"First thing to do when I return to the castle," Darius mutters as he straightens his robes, "is fire the coachman."

Landon laughs. "Your Majesty, I don't think that will be necessary. I'm sure the horses were just spooked."

"Even so, it's nice to have fresh blood every once in a while. Keeps things interesting."

Landon doesn't laugh at this; instead he stays peculiarly quiet. Darius knows him well enough to presume he has something on his mind. "What is it?"

Landon sighs. "Is it that obvious?"

"I've known you for many years," Darius responds. A low chuckle fills the coach.

Landon's eyes crinkle up at the sides. "It may be that, or perhaps you're just observant."

"I'd prefer to think it's both." The king tilts his head, eyes blazing with questions. "So, what is it?"

Landon clasps his hands in his lap before saying, "It's about your prisoner, Elvira."

Although he doesn't mean to, the king tenses at the sound of her name. "What about her?"

Landon swallows. "What exactly is her crime?"

Darius narrows his eyes, trying to figure out where his subordinate is headed with the conversation. Instead of overthinking it, he simply says, "She was caught conversing with a prisoner during her duties as a handmaiden."

Landon raises a brow. "Let me get this straight. She's being executed for having a *conversation?*"

Hearing the words come out of someone else's mouth, Darius must admit it sounds quite foolish. "Not just *any* conversation," he quickly adds. "It was on a more . . . intimate level."

"I see." Landon rubs the stubble on his chin. "Well, if you ask me, that's a hefty punishment for such a trivial crime."

Darius's mood shifts instantly. "What are you implying? That I'm an unjust king?"

Landon's face falls. "I would never speak such words, Your Majesty." He bows his head in surrender. "I was just providing my counsel."

"Your counsel is not needed nor wanted here," Darius hisses. He averts his gaze to the small window within the carriage. Perhaps he was wrong about his Savant; perhaps they're not as loyal or as intelligent as he'd originally thought. Had they grown soft on him? Was inviting them to search for Arden a mistake?

The silence for the rest of the ride is palpable, and it feels like an eternity before the carriage finally comes to a halt. The coachman scurries down from his post to open the doors. Darius exits first, followed by Landon, who makes sure to stay a good number of paces behind him. The town square is already filling up with bystanders.

Good. A demonic smile stretches across the king's face. *This will be the best example yet.*

BRAXTON HORNSBY

BRAXTON STANDS IN the town square crowd, amongst the many unsuspecting bystanders. He wears a hood to ensure that no one will recognize him, even if it has been ten years since he's been in Trendalath. From the looks of it, nothing has changed. Still decadent and rich behind the castle wall; filthy and sullied in every other direction. It's enough to make his stomach turn.

He'd always hoped his return to Trendalath would bring him a sense of relief—that his parents had been so heartbroken by his absence that they'd change their ways. Being there, in the midst of it all, he could see his thoughts were far from reality. Things had only gotten worse, not better. A pang of guilt hits him in the stomach.

Am I the reason for Trendalath's undoing?

Braxton pulls the deep brown hood tighter around his head. He keeps his eyes cast down. White blond hair and ice blue eyes are not common in Trendalath. If anyone happens to recognize him, the Caldari's mission will be compromised. He may be the reason for Trendalath's undoing, but he won't be the reason for the Caldari's.

He sucks in a sharp breath as a bell sounds. He lifts his chin and looks to the right. The movement is brief, but he's able to see exactly what he needs: Xerin perched at the top of a nearby merchant's tent. He braves another look, eyeing the castle walls. Lined along the perimeter are hundreds of soldiers, bows and arrows pointed at the execution stage. He wouldn't expect anything less from his father.

The only upside to his father remaining the same? Braxton knows all his moves. He's predictable.

A hush falls over the crowd as Darius enters the stage. He opens his arms, gesturing to *his* people. Braxton can't help but scoff. His people despise him, yet there he stands, acting as though he's the lords' gift to them all. Their savior.

He says a few words, to which Braxton hardly listens. The only words he hears are "Let this be an example to you all!" Braxton lifts his gaze as the king makes his way across the platform to his throne. He notices the seat next to his father's is empty. *Where is my mother?*

His thoughts scatter as an ominous cloaked figure, in all black, steps onto the platform. Behind him is a guard dragging a petite girl who is shackled from head to toe. The executioner takes the girl from the guard and begins to move her toward the block. She doesn't seem to resist nor put up a fight; instead, she appears eerily calm, as if this is her path, her destiny.

The executioner leads her to the block and presses her shoulder so that she's forced to kneel. She doesn't look at the crowd, but up at the sky, almost as if she's expecting something.

Braxton sneaks another look to his right. His gaze meets that of the falcon. Within seconds, the bird takes off. It soars overhead toward the stage.

Showtime.

As they'd discussed, Braxton pushes himself to the front of the crowd. He flails his arms in the air and begins shouting profanities.

Elvira's head is lowered onto the block. The executioner sharpens his blade. Braxton shouts louder, pushing his way further to the front. The executioner swings the sword out in front of him. He's just steps away from the block, from Elvira.

Why isn't this working? Why is no one alarmed?

He spots the falcon land on a wooden post just

behind the stage. Any moment now, Xerin will morph into his human form. Any moment now, Braxton will have failed. He'd been given one job: to create a distraction.

It's then he realizes what he must do.

He spots a nearby column and darts over to it. He frantically climbs as high as he can go. *I can't believe I'm about to do this.*

When he gets to the top, he straightens on shaking legs and, with a deep breath, unveils his hood, revealing himself to all. "Father, you will not kill this girl!" he yells at the top of his lungs.

The entire crowd turns to look up at him. Darius shoots up from his throne and hurries to the front of the stage. The executioner's sword clatters onto the stage. Elvira's gaze shifts from the empty sky to Braxton.

Darius narrows his eyes. "Treachery! How dare you interrupt! Do you take me for a fool?"

Braxton tries to mask his panic, but he can feel his eyes widening against his will. "You've always been the fool, father." He focuses on the back of the stage where a guard is escorting Elvira away from the commotion. Eyes the color of crimson lock on Braxton's, and he breathes a sigh of relief knowing that Xerin is leading Elvira to safety. But his relief quickly converts to dread as Tymond's shouts echo in the square. "Seize him!"

Swishing fills the air. Braxton follows the source

of the sound, his eyes going up, up, up. Hundreds of arrows are about to rain down on him, as well as the many innocent people of Trendalath. Screams fill the air as the townspeople realize what's going on—tripping over one another, darting to and fro—desperate to find shelter. Seeing no other choice, Braxton focuses his energy on his ability. *I have to deviate the arrows.*

Townspeople continue to scream and shout all around him, ducking, running for cover, making it more difficult than usual to focus. He mustn't lose his concentration. His abilities depend entirely on the intensity of his focus; without it, he—and everyone here—will perish.

A deep stirring fills his chest as he homes in on the arrows with all the strength he can muster. He can feel the magick building, growing, little by little. His lips begin to quiver, his whole body shaking from what he's about to do. An estranged yell escapes his throat.

The crowd gasps as the arrows begin to change. The sharp, pointed ends move clockwise, slowly at first, switching direction in midair. Shouts ring out in the background, most likely his father throwing a fit, but he pays them no attention.

This is his game now.

Braxton lets out another disgruntled yell as he deviates the arrows and pushes them back in their original direction. The guards appear so stunned by what's happening that they don't fire any more arrows. Instead, they watch in awe as their weapons head back toward them.

Braxton briefly moves his attention to the stage. Xerin and Elvira are nowhere to be found. He realizes that they should have planned out their actual escape, but hadn't felt a need to since Xerin assured them he had it covered. *So where are they?* Just as he's about to succumb to his feelings of panic, a deafening roar fills the air. His mouth drops open as he gazes up into the sky. What he sees at that very moment can only be described by one thing.

Illusié.

It's stunning. The navy blue scales. The round orange eyes. The wing-tipped tail. Its colossal size. For some, it would be a creature from their nightmares—but not for Braxton. For him, this is a long awaited reunion.

At first glance, Braxton assumes Xerin has somehow morphed into the creature, even though dragons have been regarded as myth and folklore for decades. To see, with his own eyes, a real *dragon* flying directly overhead is almost too much to process. But it's when the creature starts to nosedive toward the crowd that he realizes who it's aiming for.

Xerin and Elvira.

Somehow, they've managed to make it to the top of an older dwelling. The dragon swoops down and turns, giving the two of them just enough time, and room, to climb onto its back.

Another realization dawns on Braxton. Elvira must be illusié. A Summoner.

She can summon dragons.

It's enough to make him lose his grip on the post. He falls to the ground, landing hard on his left arm. All around him, feet are stamping and people are still screaming. It's absolute chaos. Instead of standing and potentially making himself a target, he decides to crawl. He wriggles through the crowd of people, hoping that his sense of direction won't fail him at a time like this.

Finally, he reaches the outskirts of town, presses himself upward, and takes off into the forest. He doesn't get far when he notices an enormous shadow overhead. He slows, his footsteps coming to a halt. Above him is the mystical and illusive dragon. He stumbles over his feet as it begins to lower to the ground, giant wings and all. Its pointed tail flays back and forth, knocking a tree clear from its roots.

As the creature lowers, Xerin and Elvira come into plain sight. Xerin holds out his hand, and Braxton grasps it as he's pulled onto the dragon's back. Elvira sits between them.

"I thought you'd left!" Braxton yells over the loud flaps of the dragon's wings.

Xerin shakes his head. "We just had to get out of there. And now we have to get out of here!"

"Hang on!" Elvira shouts as the dragon rises into the air.

Braxton grabs onto the sides of the dragon, but it doesn't do much in the way of support. Elvira must sense this because she reaches behind her and takes his hands, placing them firmly on her hips. "Trust me," she says, "this isn't my first time."

Braxton's cheeks burn, but the feeling is quickly replaced by cool air whipping at his face. The dragon picks up speed and soon they're soaring faster than he'd ever thought possible. They fly over the Roviel Woods, the sight barren since the first leaves have fallen. His teeth chatter in the wind as they fly further north to the Vaekith Mountains.

Although it doesn't take long to reach Sardoria, Braxton is shivering by the time he dismounts the dragon. Opal runs out of the castle, her boots crunching in the snow, with bundles of blankets in hand. She hastily throws one at each of them. "Hurry inside," she urges. "I have a fire started."

Elvira starts after her, followed by Braxton, but when he turns around, Xerin is standing by the dragon, unmoving. "Aren't you coming?"

Xerin shakes his head, his cheeks flush with color. "My work isn't done yet."

Before Braxton can say another word, a soft yellow glow emanates from Xerin's body. "Stand back!"

Braxton pulls Elvira and Opal underneath the

castle's overhang as Xerin grows a tail, then a scaly body, followed by wings, and an enormous head.

"He's only been able to morph into things he's come into contact with," Elvira verifies, answering what everyone's thinking. "This is the first time we've seen each other in years." A smile radiates from her face. "What a wonderful reunion. For him to be able to morph into the one animal we always 'played pretend' as children."

Braxton breaks his gaze from Xerin-the-dragon to look at her. "Why isn't he staying? Where is he going?"

"Isn't it obvious?" Her eyes sparkle, even in the dim morning light. "He's going back for the other Caldari."

Braxton nods. "Right. They're his family."

She gives him a stern look. "*We're* his family."

He nods his head in understanding, then turns his gaze back to the dragon and draws the blanket up tighter for warmth. The creature flaps its wings, slowly lifting off the ground. In mere seconds, it's high overhead, soaring in the opposite direction. He watches Xerin take off into the clouds. He can only hope Arden, Felix, and Estelle are successful in their part of the mission.

All there is to do now is wait.

DARIUS TYMOND

"WHAT ARE YOU waiting for?" Darius shrieks as the dragon soars off into the distance. "Go after them!"

The executioner mumbles something inaudible, then hurries down the steps. Darius watches as he disappears into the crowd, ears burning as he turns to face Landon. "I wasn't only speaking to the executioner."

Landon bows his head. "My King, I can assure you, I am much more useful to you here. I have no doubt that one of the other Savant will catch them."

Exasperated, Darius throws his hands into the air. "You imbecile! How are they going to know? They weren't even here to witness the blasted mess!"

Landon tilts his head and eyes the king knowingly. "Perhaps this is just my opinion, but I'm almost certain the enormous dragon—a creature we all presumed to be extinct—flying overhead will tip them off."

Darius runs his hands over his face, his fingers catching in his beard. He closes his eyes. *This is just a bad dream. I'm dreaming, that's all.*

Landon opens his mouth to speak, and the king wishes right then and there that he would just disappear. Perhaps he'd sent the executioner off prematurely. "My King, that was," he pauses, then lowers his voice, "your son."

Ah, yes. His son. Braxton Tymond.

Liar. Conspirator. Traitor.

He's sure there are many other names he can add to the list, especially after this last incident—however, in that moment, all he feels is shame. Not for his poor parenting skills, but for Braxton's complete disregard for everything he's built over the past ten years, during a time when he wasn't even here—when he'd decided to run away and never return.

The thought is enough to send chills down his spine. As an image of Braxton shouting from the top of the post fades, another enters his mind—Aldreda.

Landon's said something, but Darius doesn't bother asking him to repeat it. He whirls around and makes his way over to the carriage that is parked just behind the stage. The coachman snaps to attention and scurries to open the door. The king slaps his hand away and opens the door himself, then climbs inside. "Onward!" he shouts, and in just a few moments time, the carriage jerks to life, the town square fading from view.

A short ride later, Darius kicks the door open and jumps down from the carriage. He marches across the drawbridge and through the giant double doors of Trendalath castle. They slam shut behind him.

"Aldreda!" he bellows, knowing full well that she can't hear him. The castle is so large that even as his voice echoes down the corridors, it's impossible it'd reach her rooms. He picks his robes up from the sides and begins climbing the many sets of stairs leading to the bedchamber. He picks up the pace, dashing down the corridor, panting the entire way. The door is cracked, and he bursts in without announcing his presence.

The bed is rumpled and unmade. Aldreda is not in it. His eyes scan the room frantically, his heart thumping in his chest. "Aldreda?" he says again, quieter this time.

Whimpering catches his attention, and he makes his way around the armoire. Aldreda is curled up in a ball behind it, weeping. Darius can't help but fall to his knees at the sight of her. "My love," he says as he reaches out to her, but she doesn't return the gesture. Her head remains in her hands. "My love, what is it?"

She slowly raises her head, her glassy eyes focusing on his. "I can't do this again," she croaks.

Darius shakes his head, not understanding her meaning. "Do what again?"

"This." She lowers her hands to her abdomen. "I can't have another child run away from us again. I can't bear the agony for a second time."

Darius bites his tongue. The urge to tell her about Braxton and everything that had just occurred in the town square is strong, but seeing her like this, so fragile and weak, makes him rethink his options. He scoots closer and puts an arm around her, pulling her in tight. He rocks her back and forth, just like she used to do when Braxton was a young boy. "There, there," he soothes. "Everything is going to be all right."

"I can't do it again," she whispers, burying her face further into his robes. "I just can't."

He sits there for hours, mostly in silence, with her body molded into his. At some point, her weeping ceases and she lets out a faint snore.

She's literally cried herself to sleep.

He breaks contact as gently as he can and carefully rises to his feet. Before she slumps over, he catches her and sweeps her up off the ground in one swift movement, then places her gently on the bed. He pulls the covers over her and blows out a lone lantern.

She doesn't stir.

Closing the door behind him, Darius looks at her one last time, then breathes a sigh of relief. He ensures the door is completely shut before beginning his stroll down the corridor. The castle is unusually quiet—an opportune time to get his thoughts in order. It doesn't take long for him to realize what he must do.

Arden is no longer his priority. Braxton is.

ARDEN ELIRI

EVEN FROM DEEP within the dungeon, I can hear people screaming and shouting outside. Executions are normally quiet—solemn—so the noise level outside indicates that something's gone terribly wrong. And, hopefully, that *something* involves Xerin and Braxton.

Estelle, Felix, and I huddle around each other, walking in sync as we head down the steps to the dungeon. Estelle has all three of us cloaked. It's a strange feeling, walking through the town and the castle, right in front of people, and not having them see you. It makes me feel invincible, and I wonder if this is how Estelle feels every day.

I gaze down at my hands, noticing their faint glow. What I am crosses my mind for what feels like the hundredth time that day: *Healer.* Honestly, after finding out I was illusié, I was sort of hoping my abilities would be on the more rare end of the spectrum. To be an assassin *and* a healer seems just a bit counterintuitive—like a constant, internal battle will wage on inside of me for the rest of my life.

Who am I kidding? That's the life I live right now.

The dungeon is dimly lit, and as we descend further down the stairs, I almost trip over my feet and fall into Felix, but Estelle catches my arm just in time. I look at her to say thank you, but she has her index finger pressed against her lips. Her eyes tell me not to say a word.

I don't know why we have to be so quiet; there doesn't seem to be anyone down here. But I trust Estelle enough to listen to her. We walk as silently as possible until we finally reach the bottom level. Voices echo throughout the chamber, but I can't discern whether they are those of prisoners or of guards. Why would prisoners be talking amongst themselves? Then again, isn't that what got Rydan into this situation in the first place?

I stay on Felix's heels as we round the corner. Estelle is right next to me, shoulder to shoulder. I can hardly hear her breathing. Felix pokes his head around one of the corners. He mouths, "Guards," and then lifts up two fingers.

Part two of our plan is about to commence.

Estelle releases him from his cloaked state, but she and I remain unseen. Felix takes a stroll around the corner, even having the nerve to whistle. I look at Estelle and roll my eyes. *Well, that will surely draw their attention.*

"Who are you?" a gruff voice demands.

"What are you doing down here?" says another.

Estelle and I slip around the corner, still cloaked. My eyes catch the cell at the far end, the one housing Rydan. A lump catches in my throat. I'm nervous, anxious, and irritated all at once. My anger hasn't faded in the slightest whenever I think back to that day in Lonia—if anything, it's grown worse. Especially knowing that he'd decided to head back to Trendalath even after I'd explicitly told him how I felt about King Tymond, and that the Soames' mission was just plain wrong. But he'd shown his true colors—he'd chosen to go back anyway.

Felix's voice interrupts my thoughts. "You have something I need," he says. He's standing in front of the guards now, just a mere five feet away.

"Hands behind your back," the lanky one orders as he rises from his seat, "and kneel."

A coy smile tugs at Felix's lips. "Oh, I don't think that will be necessary."

The other guard rises and they both unsheathe their swords. They head directly for Felix, but he just stands there, smiling. I feel a momentary flicker of panic, but it dissipates when the guards stop moving and drop their weapons. Their faces contort into expressions I've witnessed time and time again.

Complete and absolute fear.

Estelle nudges me in the side and mouths, "Now."

She goes after the lanky guard, who's clawing at his eyes, and I take the other, who seems to be frozen in time, petrified. Not much of a challenge, if I do say so myself. I begin to search him for the dungeon keys, but come up short. I snap my fingers once to get Estelle's attention. Her head pops up and I give a slicing neck motion to communicate that my guard is a dead end.

Felix keeps his gaze on both of the men. His hands begin to tremble and I can tell that the state of amplification is growing weaker by the minute. We don't have much time. I rush over to Estelle but, just as I arrive, I hear the jangling of keys. Felix releases the men from their amplified states, panting as the bodies drop to the ground. Whether they're unconscious or dead, I honestly can't tell.

"I can't see you," Felix pants between ragged breaths.

I feel a sort of veil lift off of me, and I can see both Estelle and Felix more clearly. She's released us both from our cloaked states. All three of us stand in the open, completely visible to the naked eye.

Estelle holds up the ring of keys and looks directly

at me. "Where's the cell?"

I point to the end of the hall. "According to Xerin, it's the last one."

Estelle and Felix rush down the corridor, but I stay behind. My eyes fall to the guards. Contrary to my belief that they'd be writhing in pain, they remain motionless. I bend down and pick up one of the swords. It glimmers, even in the dim chamber lighting.

As I'm standing there, alone, running my hand along the blade of the sword, something familiar approaches. I recognize it almost immediately.

No.

Dark energy circles around me, feeding off my desires. My "friends" have returned, just as I knew they would. *Do it*, the voices whisper. *Kill them.*

My mouth fills with a coppery taste. Blood.

I want this so badly.

The dark tethers pull at my mind as I position myself over one of the guards and raise the sword with both hands. It feels heavy and good in my hands. My fingers grip the pommel.

Do it. Kill them.

It's so easy. One swift movement and it's over. No one would be the wiser.

Just as I'm about to plunge the blade into one of the guards' skulls, the men suddenly disappear. I blink a few times, feeling disoriented. Slowly, I lower the sword and look to my right, then to my left. *Where did they go?*

Without warning, someone shoves me from behind, causing me to fall headfirst; but my hands catch me just in time. The sword scatters from my grip, and I watch with wide eyes as it slides along the damp stone. I flip myself over and look up at the perpetrator. It's Felix.

"What the hell are you doing?" he shouts. His eyes blaze with fury and his hands are balled into fists.

As much as I want to pull myself up and shove him back, I know better. My wrist throbs from landing on it, so I take my free hand and wrap it around the pain. I focus, trying to get it to heal, but Felix's incessant shouting isn't helping.

"The Caldari do not kill innocents!" he bellows. "We are here to do one thing and one thing only, and that is to free your stupid friend."

I nod. "I agree. He is stupid."

"That wasn't my point," Felix says through clenched teeth. "We don't kill *innocents*." The last word comes out as a hiss.

I breathe a sigh of relief as my wrist starts to feel normal again. I test it first before pushing myself up off the ground and dusting off my tunic. My trousers are now damp and dirty, thanks to this brute. I can feel my temper rising. I point at the area where the guards once lay. "They work for Tymond! They are not innocent!"

Felix chuckles. He shakes his head. "Have you

forgotten? So do you!"

I lurch backward as if I've just been hit in the stomach. "Did," I correct. "So *did* I. But I don't anymore."

"Well, from what I just witnessed, I wouldn't be surprised if you went running back to Tymond, begging him to take you back as an assassin."

My ears burn at the insult. Just as I'm about to strangle him, Estelle appears between us, her arms extended at full length. "Enough!" she shouts. She glances at Felix, then over at me with a harsh expression. "We need to be a united front. You can save your narcissistic pissing match for later." I can tell she's angry because I've never heard her talk like that before. "Now get over yourselves and follow me," she growls.

Without another word, Felix and I do as she says, trailing behind her to the end of the corridor. I grab one of the torches from the wall and hold it out in front of me as we approach the cell. A thin body is curled up against the back of it, a head of matted, ashen hair pointed directly at us. It doesn't look like Rydan, but then again, I haven't seen him in months.

I take the key ring from Estelle and bang it against the metal bars. The ashen head rises, and I expect to see beautiful, vibrant eyes, but pale yellow ones have taken their place. I gasp as his eyes meet mine, then take a step back.

His voice cracks. “Arden?”

The figure begins to crawl toward the front of the cell, eyes glued to mine the entire time. My mouth remains open, and all I can do is stare in horror. As he draws nearer, a wave of empathy washes over me.

The once fearless, strong man I’d come to know has been rotting away here in this cell, whittling away to nothing more than skin and bones. His rich black hair is now a sickly gray, long and tangled around his shoulders. His eyes, nose, and cheeks are sunken in, like the peasants we used to sneak loaves of bread to on the streets of Trendalath. His once brawny figure has disintegrated, and his bones look as though they might snap at any moment.

The image is gut wrenching.

“Arden,” he croaks again, “is it really you?”

“Yes,” I whisper, hands trembling as I start inserting different keys into the locks. “Yes, it’s me, Rydan.”

His lips crack into a smile, showcasing rotting teeth of the yellow and brown variety. “It’s so good to hear your voice.”

My heart picks up speed as I insert one key after another into the lock. I’m not as agile as I used to be. My emotions are getting the better of me. I can feel a minor meltdown coming on when a warm hand is placed atop mine. I raise my head to the right to see Estelle standing next to me.

“Allow me,” she says, her voice smooth as silk.

I pull one of the many incorrect keys out of the lock, then drop them into her open palm. “Thank you,” I whisper. She assumes my position as I move to the back wall of the chamber.

After a few less attempts than I’d had, the lock clicks. Rydan’s eyes have been trained on mine the entire time. Felix ducks into the cell and helps him to his feet. Rydan’s knees shake and his hands tremble as he rises, and he has to clutch the wall for support. Felix urges him to try and walk to test out his mobility. Still holding onto the wall, Rydan lifts his foot and takes a miniscule step forward.

“How the hell are we going to get him out of here?” Estelle asks. Her voice is strained as her eyes dart around the dungeon. “We need to leave. Quickly.”

“Oh, I’m sure we can leave. It’s the *quickly* part we’re going to struggle with,” Felix retorts.

Estelle leans her head against the metal bars. With a sigh, she mutters, “This is one part of the plan we should have fleshed out in more detail.”

I bow my head, not wanting to witness my previous Cruex partner dying before me. Even though I’m still disgusted by his actions in Lonia, I still care for him. He’s still Rydan. He’s still my *friend.*

And then I remember. *What am I doing just standing here?* I jerk my head up and rush into the cell. “Sit him back down,” I command.

Felix looks at me with resilient eyes. “But we’re

making progress."

I can't tell if he's joking, but if he is, now isn't the time. "Sit him back down. Now."

Felix lifts his brows at my tone, but doesn't argue. I'm actually surprised he's chosen to listen to me for once. He gently lowers Rydan back to the ground. I kneel and place my hands over his chest. "Close your eyes," I whisper.

Rydan cracks a small smile. "If I do, I'm not sure they'll open again."

The words send a pulsating pain straight through my heart. "Open it is then."

I know he's not going to like what I'm about to do—or to see what I actually am—but I don't see any other choice. I press my hands more firmly against his chest, trying to will away the memories of him speaking ill of illusié.

"What are you doing?" he asks, eyes flitting between my face and my hands.

I exhale. A soft white glow appears around my fingers. I release some of the pressure from his chest, scanning for signs of internal injury. Being a prisoner has done quite a number on him, and he probably doesn't even know it.

"What is this?" he asks again, his tone harsher this time.

I cock my head and Estelle appears across from me. She places her hand on Rydan's cheek and tilts it toward her. "Focus on me," she soothes. "And breathe."

"I don't understand what's going on."

Estelle shoots a look at me. I nod.

"We are Caldari," I say slowly. "Illusié."

Rydan's eyes widen, and suddenly I'm not sure that telling him was the best idea. But the distraction is working. His heart is beating faster. His injuries are healing.

"What are you doing to me?" he yells, although it comes out as more of a croak. He tries to thrash, but Felix is holding down his legs, Estelle his arms—plus he's too weak to make a harmful movement anyway.

The glow begins to disappear as I feel his energy bind together and grow stronger. I remove my hands from his chest and rise. I watch him carefully as Felix and Estelle help him to his feet. "For the time being, he should be able to walk, maybe even jog, if needed."

Rydan runs his hands over his chest and his arms, then through his hair. He shakes his legs and stamps his feet, as if he's a child learning his motor skills for the first time.

"Rydan, I'm illusié, a Caldari." The words feel foreign, yet satisfying, as they leave my mouth. "I'm a Healer."

Rydan looks at each of us with disgust. "What now? You expect me to come with you?"

I smirk, then turn around and walk toward the dungeon's exit. "It seems you don't have much of a

RYDAN HELSTROM

RYDAN CAN HARDLY believe how much better he feels. He's keeping up with Arden and the rest of the Caldari as if he hadn't been locked in a cell for months with little food, water, and sleep. He presses his hand to his chest, his heart beating steadily underneath his skin. His back, arms, and legs feel strong, but most surprisingly, his mind feels sharp—dare he say even sharper than before he'd been thrown into his cell.

What exactly did Arden do to me?

They'd left the castle with ease, only because Rydan had decided not to make a scene. As much as he loathes the Caldari and everything they stand for, he's certain he would have died in that dungeon cell. He had no choice—for his sake, and for Elvira's.

Estelle's cloaking ability is truly one for the books. It's a surreal feeling, being invisible and walking through crowd after crowd of unsuspecting bystanders. When they'd made it to the town square, Rydan had warned himself not to look at the execution stage, but had braved a look anyway. Where he'd expected there to be blood were planks of wood in their natural color—brown, not red—which meant one of two things. Either Elvira had escaped, or the execution hadn't happened yet. He sincerely hopes it's the former.

Nearing the outskirts of the forest, Rydan stops in his tracks. He can't keep going without knowing whether or not Vira is okay. "Arden," he says, tugging on the sleeve of her tunic.

She whirls around to face him, a concerned look on her face. "Is everything all right? Is the pace okay for you?"

He waves his hand in the air and shakes his head simultaneously. "It's not that. The pace is fine." He takes in a sharp breath, unsure how to phrase his question. It's strange being around her again. It feels different, but also the same—if that's even possible.

"Rydan?" she presses.

"Elvira." He casts his eyes to the ground. "Did she make it? Is she still alive?" The last word catches in his throat.

A slight frown graces Arden's lips. "Honestly, I don't know. I think so. But we'll know for sure soon."

Rydan nods his head, shoulders slumping. Not the answer he wanted, but it'll have to do.

"Hey," she says as she pats him on the back. "Come on. The faster we move, the sooner we'll know."

Rydan watches as she turns around to catch up with the others. He sighs and picks up the pace.

A couple of hours pass on their journey, but they don't seem to be making much progress. Felix and Estelle keep looking up at the sky, although Rydan doesn't know why. Every once in a while when they look up, he'll follow their gazes. Perhaps they're just using the sun to gain a sense of direction. Then again, they're Caldari—shouldn't they be able to conjure up *something* to help guide them besides what Mother Nature has to offer?

Regardless, it feels as though they've been walking in circles and Rydan decides it's time for a break. He spots a nearby rock and, without saying anything, meanders over to it. He plops down, surveying the area for a small stream or ripe berries. Honestly, anything will do at this point—he's parched *and* starved.

Arden seems to sense that he's no longer behind her. She calls out to the others to stop. They backtrack and soon, they're all standing around Rydan, looking down at him as if he's an injured animal.

"We've been walking for hours in what feels like circles. What in lords' name are we searching for?" Rydan asks.

Arden regards him with a confused expression. "What do you mean?"

He points to both Felix and Estelle. "They keep looking up at the sky. I want to know what we're supposed to be looking for."

Before Arden can answer, Felix cuts in. "It's really none of your business," he snaps. "Lords, we save your ass and we don't even get so much as a thank you?" His mouth curls into a sneer. "And Arden here, she *healed* you, so that you could walk, so that you could escape that death ridden cell. You sustained injuries that normally take years to heal, and she fixed them in a matter of minutes." He spits at Rydan's feet. "Tell me, *Helstrom*, why did we even save you in the first place?"

Rydan shoots up from the rock and marches over to Felix so that his chest is pressed against his. "Apparently, you're just a little servant boy who answers to Xerin's every beck and call."

"Enough!" Arden and Estelle shout at the same time.

Arden takes Rydan by the arms while Estelle grabs Felix's shoulders. Rydan tries to pull himself from her grip, but she's stronger than he remembers. "Do your friends have you in strength training or something?"

Arden's eyes ignite with fury as she slaps him across the face.

Rydan's hand flies to his cheek. He's never been slapped before, and it hurts more than he thought it would.

"I don't know what happened to you in there, or why you've suddenly become such a prick," she growls through clenched teeth, "but that ends right now." She pushes him away from her.

Rydan stumbles a little, shocked at how angry she seems, but he regains his balance quickly. He straightens his shirt before lifting his chin higher in the air.

Arden scowls. "Don't make me regret this, Rydan."

He shakes his head as a small laugh escapes his lips. "It seems you already do."

ARDEN ELIRI

JUST AS I'M gearing up to slap Rydan once more, an unnerving sound catches my attention. I look over my shoulder to see Estelle with her hand clasped over her mouth. I turn back toward Rydan and lower my hand. It balls into a fist. He gives me a sardonic smile and I whirl around before I change my mind. "What is it?" I ask Estelle.

"I'm a fool," she cries. She hits herself in the forehead. "I never released us. We've been cloaked this entire time!"

I rub my temples as I attempt to comprehend what she's just said. "So if Xerin's been looking for us—"

"—there's no way he could have seen us," Felix finishes.

Exasperated sighs fill the air.

I turn to look at Rydan, flashing him a look of warning to keep quiet. Surprisingly, he listens.

"I'm now releasing each of us from our cloaked states." As Estelle says this, I can feel the seemingly invisible veil being lifted, the sheen over my sight dissipating. Things become crystal clear. I'm disappointed in myself for not catching it earlier. If I had, Xerin would be here by now, and we'd be well on our way.

With slumped shoulders and frowns gracing their faces, I can tell the Caldari feel defeated. Disheartened. But I'll be damned if we allow ourselves to fall apart now. "It's okay. Let's keep going. Xerin can see us now, and I'm sure he's nearby somewhere . . ."

My thoughts trail off as a glimmer in the distance catches my eye. I race toward it, despite the conversation that's going on behind me. I hear my name being called, but I ignore it. As I draw closer, the object comes into view—a floating black orb with shimmering white and gold spots. It's stunning.

Has Xerin found more ways to shape himself?

"Xerin?" I ask. I reach out to touch it, but as I do, the orb moves backward, or at least it seems like it does. I furrow my brows and try again, but the orb retreats. I keep going, further and further into the forest. I finally reach a point where I turn around and can't see or hear anyone behind me.

A knot twists in my stomach as I turn around, a loud humming sound filling the space around me. It grows louder and louder at an alarming rate. I cringe and throw my hands over my ears, pressing my palms as tightly as possible to block out the sound.

I gaze up at the sky, at the source of the sound. My eyes widen at what I see. Hundreds of wispy black tethers come shooting down like arrows all around me. As they hit the ground, they dissipate to form a black fog. Eventually it gets so dense that I can't see. I'm coughing and gasping for air simultaneously and my eyes burn as the haze seeps into my pores.

Definitely not Xerin.

Darkness tears into me like a sword slicing through the middle of my body. I cry out in angst, feeling petrified and alive at the same time. Black tethers swirl around me like lightning in a torrential thunderstorm. It pulls at me, my feelings, my emotions, my mind. Pulls and pulls until I feel everything and nothing all at once.

"I knew you'd be drawn to it," a male's voice says. "The darkness, that is."

I squint, trying to discern where the voice is coming from. Even through the dense fog, a figure starts to take shape.

"We are one in the same, you and I," he says, "so why did you join them? Why did you join the Caldari?"

I open my mouth to speak, but nothing comes out. It feels as if my throat is lined with chalk and dust, dry and unrelenting. I begin to cough again, and the mystery figure clucks his tongue against the roof of his mouth.

"Such a pity, really. We could have used another one like you."

The man steps through the fog and, finally, I can see him clearly. He's tall and stocky—muscular, yet lanky. Copper hair wound in tight curls sits atop his head. Bright hazel eyes meet mine.

It's then I realize that he's one of the men in the photo.

I scan the images in my memory as I pull forward the photo of the King's Savant. He was standing next to the man with almost identical features to my own.

What is he doing here?

As quickly as it came, the fog begins to clear, but not in its expected fading fashion. Lines of black haze shoot back as if time is being reversed. I open my eyes wider as another figure comes into view. There is no mistaking who this man is. *This* is the man from the picture. The one that looks exactly like me.

My lower lip trembles as he draws nearer, but he doesn't fully approach me. Instead, he walks to the copper-haired man, who's currently on his knees, gasping for air. I look between the two men, trying to understand what in lords' name is happening, but for the life of me, I can't.

"Enough, Clive. She doesn't deserve this. Leave her be."

I watch in both awe and fear as the fog is seemingly sucked into a black hole the second man has somehow created. It doesn't take long for Clive to fall over completely. He lies on the ground, motionless, hands still clasped around his neck.

The man turns to face me. Emerald green eyes lock on mine. It's like looking into a mirror.

"Th-thank you," I sputter.

A longing smile touches his lips. "It's good to see that you're doing well."

I try to hide my confusion, but I'm sure my expression has contorted into a cluster of question marks.

"Casters are some of the most dangerous illusié," the man warns. "You'd do best to remember that."

I nod my head as he takes a step closer. I swear my heart might leap out of my chest.

"Let this token serve as a reminder." He tosses something at my feet, something strangely familiar.

My breath catches as I pick up the object. A gold pocket watch. I flip it over. *Eliri* is inscribed on the back. "How—?"

But when I look up, he's gone.

I grip the watch tightly, pick myself up, and run like hell back to the others. They're in the exact same place I'd left them, which is all the more confusing.

"Did you see that?" I yell, panting.

Estelle turns to face me. She looks even more confused than I feel. "See what?"

"Where have you been?" Felix cuts in, clearly annoyed by my disappearance.

I look at Rydan. "Did you?"

"Did I what?"

I repeatedly point to the spot in the forest. "See that? Did *anyone* see that?"

Rydan shakes his head. "Honestly, I have no idea what you're talking about."

"Argh!" I throw my hands in the air in frustration, momentarily forgetting about the watch. It slips to the ground.

It catches Rydan's eye, but just as he's about to pick it up, a strong breeze—one that almost knocks us all over—sweeps through the trees. I put my hand over my eyes and gaze into the sky. A giant creature hovers over us, then starts to lower.

"Look out!" I scream.

Everyone looks up. Once they've seen why I'm yelling, they dive off into different areas of the forest. The wind picks up as enormous wings flap. The leaves on the trees rustle, and the fallen ones scatter, dancing along the forest floor. The creature lands with a loud thud, the whole ground shaking, and I can't help but feel stunned. It's a *dragon.*

Holy lords.

I scan its body, working my way up until I reach its eyes. They're blood red.

"It's Xerin," I say.

The dragon makes a strange whinnying sound to confirm it actually is him.

There's no time for me to feel shocked or amazed. We have to get out of here. "Everyone get on his back. He'll take us to Sardoria."

Estelle climbs on first, followed by Felix. Rydan hops on next and holds his hand out to me. When I grab it, my fingers brush something cold and metallic. Before I can pull away, he wraps his fingers around mine. I can feel the circular shape pressing against my palm.

"I thought you never brought your pocket watch on Cruex missions," he whispers.

Good memory. I squeeze his hand tighter as he pulls me onboard. I swing my leg over the dragon, then look over my shoulder at him and say, "That's because I don't."

CERYLIA JARETH

CERYLIA SITS IN awkward silence by the fire with Braxton, Opal, and Elvira. It's been a few hours since Xerin left, but it might as well be an eternity. *Where are the rest of them? What's taking so long?*

Braxton sits across from her, eyes trained on the flickering flames. They dance and hiss, a mix of bright oranges, royal purples, and deep reds. Every time she looks at Braxton, she can't help but think of Darius. The boy is the spitting image of his father. Same blonde hair. Same ice colored eyes. But Braxton's face is kinder. Innocent.

Hopefully that will never change.

Her thoughts scatter as a throat clears. Both her and Braxton's heads turn toward Opal. She bites her lower lip as if she's weighing whether or not to speak. After a few moments, she gives in. "Sitting in silence isn't going to make time go by any faster."

A beat hardly passes before Braxton says, "I'm worried."

Cerylia gives him a reassuring smile. "No need to be. They're in good hands. Xerin knows what he's doing."

Braxton nods, but it isn't the slightest bit convincing.

"They should be back by now," Opal says. She's turned away from them now and is staring out the window. "It's entirely possible something's gone wrong."

"Don't talk like that," Cerylia scolds. "They are fine. They will be here."

Another hour passes with no sign of Xerin, Arden, Felix, Estelle, or Rydan. Cerylia can tell that both Braxton and Opal are growing restless, while Elvira's already drifted off into a deep sleep by the fire. *I need to take their minds off of this. Distract them somehow.*

She lifts her index finger to her lips and brushes them lightly. "So, Braxton," she starts, "you're new to the Caldari? If you don't mind my asking, what is your ability?"

This seems to catch him off-guard. "I'm, uh, what

they call a Deviator." He stumbles over the words as if it's the first time he's ever had a conversation.

"Which means what exactly?"

"That I can return attacks back to where they originated."

Cerylia leans forward. "Fascinating." She hesitates before asking her next question. "And when did you discover you had this ability?"

Braxton shifts uncomfortably in his seat. "When I was ten years old."

"Isn't that the same age you ran away from Trendalath?"

Opal regards the queen with wide eyes. "Your Greatness, isn't that a personal question?" Her gaze shifts to Braxton, whose eyes are now cast toward the floor.

Cerylia ignores Opal and waits for Braxton to respond. "Well?"

Braxton lifts his head. His eyes are glassy. "Yes."

Cerylia sits back in her chair. It dawns on her that she could seek vengeance on Aldreda by killing her only son. An eye for an eye, a love for a love. She's been told there is no love like a mother's love for her eldest son, but whoever said that had never met Cerylia and Dane. Their love could withstand anything.

Unfortunately, they were robbed of that opportunity.

No, she won't seek vengeance. Not yet, anyway. Braxton seems like a decent person, even for a Tymond. She'll have to find some other way—perhaps something worse than death.

Just as she's considering telling Braxton about the heinous crime his mother had committed, Opal speaks. "I don't think I ever had the chance to properly introduce myself. I'm Opal Marston. I'm also a Caldari—an Inverter."

Braxton looks at her with a blank stare.

"It means that I have the ability to travel back in time," she adds quickly. Cerylia can tell her nerves are kicking in because she's talking faster, and her voice has even raised an octave. "Actually, Cerylia and I recently—"

"—went for tea," the queen interrupts, realizing what Opal was about to bring up. "Do you like tea, Braxton?"

Before he can answer, she claps her hands three times. "Delwynn!"

Her advisor hobbles from around the corner into the den.

"That was surprisingly fast," Cerylia remarks with a small smile. "Would you be a dear and fetch us some . . .?" Her voice trails off as she notices the distraught expression on his face. "What is it?"

"You must see this. There's a . . . a . . . " Delwynn sputters, not quite able to get the words out.

Braxton shoots up from his seat. "Dragon?" he

finishes.

Delwynn's head bobs up and down. Elvira begins to stir from all the commotion. Her eyes flutter open, and Braxton takes her hand. "They're here." She and Braxton take off for the castle doors with Opal right on their heels.

Cerylia remains seated and waits patiently for her loyal advisor to turn his attention back to her. When he's finally focused on her again, he says, "My apologies, Your Greatness. I was startled."

Cerylia waves her hand in the air. "No apology necessary. Now, I'm thinking I could go for some ale. Be a dear and fetch me some."

"Ale? At this hour?"

"I said," Cerylia says again, this time through clenched teeth, "bring me some."

Realizing his mistake, Delwynn bows and nods his head, then hurries down the corridor.

Cerylia watches him go, then leans back into her chair. Yes, housing the Caldari and their friends will be anything but dull. And if she's to keep up, she may as well loosen the reins a bit.

BRAXTON HORNSBY

BRAXTON'S NEVER SEEN two people more excited to see each other. He watches as Rydan flings himself off the dragon straight into Elvira's arms. They hold each other close for a few moments, not letting go. From the corner of his eye, he can see Xerin, who appears to have a permanent scowl on his face, and Arden, who looks confused and almost hurt.

Braxton doesn't know the full history behind Rydan and Arden's friendship, but he's aware that they were in the Cruex together—probably even grew up together. That should make them like brother and sister, right?

Then why does Arden look so distraught?

Unless there's something more to her and Rydan.

His envy falters as a throat clears. Everyone hushes and turns toward the sound. Queen Cerylia Jareth stands in front of the doors to her enormously elegant castle. She opens her arms and, with a soft smile, says, "Welcome to the Queendom of Sardoria. I am so happy you've all made it here safely." As she scans each one of them, Braxton notices her lips turn down as her eyes run over him. "Delwynn is my most trusted advisor, and he will be yours as well for the duration of your stay. Anything you need, Delwynn will assist you."

Braxton can't tell if she's trying to push the Caldari off on Delwynn because she doesn't want to deal with them herself, or if Delwynn truly is the proper person to go to.

"I know in Trendalath, illusié was banished, but it isn't here. While in Sardoria, I request that you develop and hone your skills. Make yourselves stronger, more powerful." She walks down the steps, one by one, her hand sliding along the white and gray marble banister. "Delwynn will create a training schedule for each of you—but seeing as there's only one of him and seven of you, I may need to call in some minor reinforcements." She smiles. "That, however, will come with time."

Braxton is about to interject when the queen

turns and begins to climb the stairs.

"If you'll follow me, I'll take each of you to your chambers."

Rydan, Elvira, and Felix are first to jump in line, followed by Xerin, Opal, and Estelle. Arden joins last. Braxton strolls up beside her and nudges her in the side. "Well, this ought to be interesting, wouldn't you say?"

She nods, but doesn't make a sound. She's looking far off into the distance and is focused on something else entirely.

"What is it?"

She blinks before turning to look at him. "From one castle to the next," she says, biting down on her lower lip. "Will anywhere ever feel like home?"

Without thinking, he reaches over and grabs her hand. She seems hesitant, but her fingers close around his. He squeezes her hand gently. "Home is where you make it."

A smile graces her lips. She bows her head and nods a few times. "I suppose that's true."

They hold hands the entire way through the castle, but no one seems to notice—the other Caldari are occupied chatting amongst one another. They only break their grip once they reach their separate chambers.

"Goodnight, Braxton," she whispers.

"Goodnight, Arden." He waits until the door shuts firmly behind her. He taps the front of his door with his fingertips, trying to hide his smile, then slips into his chambers to settle in for the night.

ARDEN ELIRI

IT'S BEEN A little over a week since arriving in Sardoria. Tymond nor his Savant have come looking for us, which I suppose is a good sign. I feel safe in Sardoria—safer even than when we were in Orihia. I sigh as images of the beautiful tree village float across my mind. I was really starting to like it there, but I suppose I'm starting to like it here, too.

The queen already has us started on our training—the woman doesn't waste any time. I'm normally scheduled with Braxton, which I find comical. According to Delwynn and his many theories (trust me, he has more than I can count), Deviators and Healers are the ideal combination to train in tandem. I still don't quite understand this, but I let the little man do his thing.

I don't complain. I don't argue. I show up when it's required of me and do as I'm told. It's easier that way.

For the first time in my life, I feel like I can breathe without constraint. I'm not constantly being watched under a vicious dictator—I can make mistakes, I can mess up. I don't have to hit my mark every time. For an assassin, I thought this would be infuriating, but I actually find it quite refreshing.

Everyone seems to be settling in just fine, except for Rydan. We still haven't spoken in length about the past, about Tymond, about our Lonia mission. It's like he's tucked it into the far reaches of his mind, never to pull it out again.

Perhaps I have as well.

Braxton and I have just left our training for the day. I sit at the desk in my new room, devouring book after book from the Caldari's undisclosed library. I'd mentioned it to Cerylia when I'd first arrived, hoping that she'd send her guards to retrieve some of the texts, and she'd graciously obliged. Xerin had led the guards to Orihia—disguised as one of them, of course—and retrieved a large majority of the texts. When I'm not training, I spend a large portion of my time reading them. I soak it all in, hoping that it'll all make sense one day.

I yawn and pull the pocket watch from the corner

of the bookshelf. It's getting late. I shut the book in front of me and return it to its proper place. I look at the pocket watch again and the image of the man who gave it to me floats across my mind. It's a dream I've had often this past week, one I wish would go away. Perhaps one day we'll meet again and I'll be able to ask the many questions left unanswered. Or perhaps not.

Only time will tell.

Just as I'm about to wind down for bed, heavy footsteps race past my door. My curiosity getting the better of me, I hastily grab my cloak and wrap it around me, then hurry over to the door, opening it just a crack. A head of jet-black hair turns a corner.

Rydan.

I close the door behind me and sneak down the corridor, trying to hurry *and* be as light on my feet as humanly possible. Just as I reach the end, I peer down the hall to see Rydan turn yet another corner.

Where is he going?

I continue to follow him until we're just outside the castle doors. As he's about to descend the snow-filled steps, he seems to notice my presence. He turns around slowly. It's the first one-on-one encounter we've had since the Lonia mission. The same mission where I bashed him over the head with a lantern and left him by himself.

Alone.

He shakes his head, then asks, "Are you following me, Arden?"

I shrug my shoulders and smile. "It would appear so."

"Why?"

My face falls at his harsh tone. "Because we haven't spoken since Lonia."

His lips purse together. "It's probably better that way."

His blunt response stuns me a little, but his eyes say everything. They're cold and devoid of emotion. He hasn't forgiven me, and by the looks of it, I'm not sure he ever will.

I try to save face. "Rydan, you were the one person I could count on back in Trendalath. You were my friend." I swallow the lump that's forming in my throat. "How do we get back to that place?"

His voice is flat. "I'm not sure we ever can."

"Why not?"

"Because I don't trust you!" he lashes out. He throws his arms outward, then slams them back down at his sides. His hands curl into fists. He's shaking profusely.

I'm about to apologize when I smell something strange. I shift my gaze to the right. There's a tree next to me . . .

And it's on fire.

Even in the snow, it's *on fire.*

I slowly turn back to him. My eyes travel to his hands. They're glowing.

"Holy lords," I whisper. "You're illusié. You're one of us."

He stares at the tree for a moment, shocked, then looks down at his hands. He shakes them until the glow disappears.

A long silence stretches between us.

"Did you know?" I finally ask.

His breathing is rapid and his hands are still trembling. He shakes his head. "No."

"Don't you see?" I take a step closer. "You're one of us, Rydan. You belong here."

And just like that, his expression turns from shock to pure disgust. "I do *not* belong here. I do not belong *anywhere* with you. Not with someone who betrays one of their own."

His words sting. I wince, then scratch my cheek, hoping to play it off. "I didn't mean to leave you," I say, my voice strained. "I just didn't see any other choice."

"There's always another choice. We were supposed to be partners. You left me to fend for myself." His voice grows louder. "You left me, full well knowing that returning with a failed mission was punishable by death!"

I lower my gaze. I'm not sure how to respond to that, because he's right. But I was also right to stop him—because he's been killing innocents all this time.

We both have.

"I just want to get as far away from here as

possible," he hisses. "As far away from *you* as possible."

I bite my tongue, trying to keep my emotions at bay. I know what's about to happen next. It's Rydan's defense mechanism, the one thing he knows how to do best. *He's going to leave.*

"Give the queen my thanks for her hospitality, but it's about time I return where I belong."

I regard him with wide eyes. "Rydan, listen to me. You can't go back there. Tymond will *kill* you."

His mouth presses into a harsh line. "I'd rather be in the presence of a murderer than a traitor."

His words hit me straight in the gut. I shake my head over and over again. "Rydan, you cannot go back there."

"Why not? Tymond may be a murderer, but so am I. And so are you. You just happen to be both." His gaze is ice cold. "I'd rather be around someone like him than someone like you."

Murderer. Traitor. The words circle my mind, round and round they go. I throw my head back and gaze into the night sky. My past is already coming back to haunt me. I'm at a loss for words.

At a loss for anything, really.

"Good luck, Arden," Rydan says. "You're going to need it."

He whirls around and takes off into the snow with nothing more than a tunic, trousers, and light boots.

What a damn fool.

My eyes brim with tears. I blink them back. Everything in me tells me to stop him, to persuade him, to run and grab him and bring him back. But my legs are leaden. My feet won't budge. My heart is shattering, piece by piece.

And it's because I know Rydan well enough to understand what I must do.

I let him go.

Don't miss the second installment in the *Shadow Crown* series:

RENEGADE CRUEX

TURN THE PAGE FOR A SNEAK PEEK OF CHAPTER 1

ACKNOWLEDGEMENTS

This book was, by far, the most challenging for me to write. Writing for Arden was an emotional release, what with her constant battle between good and evil, and her aching desire to succumb to darkness, but ultimately choosing light. It's a struggle I think many can relate to, myself included.

First and foremost, I'd like to thank God. Waking up each morning to create my stories and put them down on paper is more than a blessing—it is my calling. I am so grateful to be able to do this each and every day.

To the incredibly talented cartographer, Deven Rue, for bringing The Lands of Aeridon to life. I still squeal with glee every time I look at the map. Thank you for being such a pleasure to work with!

To my cover designers at Damonza, thank you for going through round after round of revisions for this cover. I continue to be amazed by your beautiful work.

To my family—Erin, Mom, Dad, Paul, Rachel, Nana, and Papa—thanks for always being my biggest cheerleaders. Your support means everything to me, and I love each and every one of you more than you'll ever know.

To Kim Chance, Vivien Reis, Natalia Leigh, Lindsay Cummings, Mandi Lynn and our AuthorTube family—it feels so amazing to have finally found "my people". You guys are awesome in every way.

To my readers and fans—words cannot describe how grateful I am for each and every one of you. You make my heart so full. I love you all!

And to Jonathon—although we're no longer together, I could not have written this book without you. Only now do I realize how much Arden and Rydan's struggles so closely resembled our own. I know we will both get the endings we were meant for, even if it's not together. I wish you all the happiness in the world.

ARDEN ELIRI

I KNOCK ON the door to Braxton's chambers, knowing full well of the late hour. I don't expect him to answer, especially after the strenuous training Delwynn's put us through over the past week, but I have to tell *someone* about what just happened. That Rydan's gone.

That he's gone because of *me*.

The torch in my left hand flickers and dances as a cool draft sweeps through the corridor. I realize I'm barefoot and shivering, with only my cloak and this pathetic fire to keep me warm.

Fire.

My mind draws back to what I'd just witnessed outside the castle doors. Rydan losing his temper. His hands glowing. A tree bursting into flames. The shock and disgust on his face.

I squeeze my eyes shut to clear the image. I open them again and knock one more time. Just as I'm about to turn to leave, I hear footsteps on the other side of the door. I wait somewhat impatiently as it creaks open and Braxton's white-blonde head appears.

He rubs the sleep from his eyes with a yawn. "Is it time to train again already? I could have sworn I'd only fallen asleep an hour or so ago." He yawns again, then stops as his eyes land on my face.

"Can I come in?" I say under my breath.

He straightens, then nods, opening the door wider for me to enter. I place the torch in its holder, taking caution as I approach the center of the room. I arrive just a few feet from the hearth where I'm met with yet another reminder of Rydan. The fire dances to and fro, teasing me, taunting me.

I turn away from the fire to face Braxton. I'm shocked at what I see. No longer is he in his half-asleep state—he's now wide-awake, his eyes alight with curiosity and . . . something else.

Fear?

I realize that I must be the reason for his reaction, what with knocking at his door after-hours, all wide-eyed and dishevelled. I'm surprised he still has his wits about him. Perhaps he assumes I'm bearing bad news regarding the king—his estranged father. I quickly reassure him that this isn't the case. "It's not about Tymond."

Braxton looses a breath, then closes the door quietly behind him before joining me in the center of the room. He stands directly in front of me so that I can feel his warm breath on my face. He doesn't speak. Neither do I. The sweet scent of cinnamon and nutmeg lingers between us. Eventually, his eyes lock on mine as he says, "I know."

I regard him with a puzzled expression.my heart thumping in my chest. "You know what, exactly?"

Braxton takes a step back, his eyes traveling over the fire. "It's about Rydan, isn't it?" He doesn't look at me as he says this, and his tone is borderline distracted.

"How—?"

"I saw him take off into the woods." He shakes his head. "It's a shame, really. I wonder where he plans to go. Certainly not back to Trendalath, what with your history and all."

My cheeks burn at the remark as I recall our failed assassination attempt at the Soames' residence. I stroll over to an armchair and brush my fingers across the top. "Did you see anything else?" I ask gingerly, suddenly feeling the need to protect what little information I have left.

He cocks an eyebrow. "That's an odd question. I saw him leave. I didn't know there was anything else to see."

"There wasn't," I say almost too quickly. "It's just that . . . Rydan and I sort of got into a heated argument." I try to play it off like it's nothing. "I'd hoped that conversation was private."

Braxton shrugs, then gives me a small smile. "Didn't hear a thing. Just saw the poor sap leave."

I try to keep a straight face. Originally, I'd planned to tell Braxton everything, including Rydan's newfound abilities, but our current conversation has me thinking otherwise. Something seems off, and it makes me want to keep my mouth shut.

My thoughts disperse when he asks, "Should we alert the queen?"

I consider this for a moment, weighing the different scenarios. On one hand, if we tell Cerylia about Rydan's fleeing, it may raise questions as to *why* he left—questions I'm not willing to answer just yet. On the other, Cerylia seems to have a way of finding things out, and I wouldn't want to be seen as a traitor, not this early in the game—not ever, actually. I want to build her trust, as do the rest of the Caldari.

The decision comes easier than I would have thought. "We need to tell her."

Braxton nods in confirmation. "Tomorrow then?"

Just as I'm about to reply, a clang sounds from the bell tower. We exchange perplexed expressions, then rush to the door. Braxton pokes his head out first before stepping into the dimly lit corridor. I grab my torch and follow him, closing the door gently behind me. The bell sounds again.

We both head toward the front of the castle. The soft padding of our bare feet against the stone floors is the only audible sound. As we reach the entrance, we realize we're the last ones to arrive. Cerylia, Felix, Estelle, Xerin, and Opal stand before us. I'm not surprised at Rydan's absence, but I quickly realize there's someone else missing.

Elvira.

My heart sinks.

"Thank you for coming. Given the late hour, I'll make this brief." Cerylia glances sideways at Delwynn, who seems to be hurrying to make her a cup of tea. She sighs somewhat impatiently as he hands her the cup. I notice her hands are trembling as they fold around the fine china. She inhales, then continues, "It would appear both Rydan and Elvira have fled."

I shift my head slightly to steal a glance at Xerin. He doesn't look rattled at the news of his sister, but I notice a small tremor flicker just above his jawline—it's just enough to tell me that he's disconcerted. I turn my attention back to the queen.

"Does anyone have additional information that might help us to discern why these two have suddenly fled the premises?" My stomach lurches as her gaze travels across the group and lands on me. "Arden?"

My breath catches as I try to decide what to say. At first, I'm not sure why I'm being called out, but then I realize that I'm the only one who truly knew Rydan. I'm her best bet, and her best source, for information. But, unfortunately for her, I don't feel like giving it up. So I lie. "This is the first I'm hearing of this." Beside me, I can sense Braxton's discomfort. "Should we send a search team?"

The queen regards me for a moment with narrowed eyes. I don't dare flinch for fear that she'll see right through my idiotic ploy. I immediately regret lying to her, but I know it's too late to take back my words.

"Xerin," she commands, "I'd like for you to go on the search alone. Based on your unique abilities, I believe you'll have better luck spotting our two refugees from the air than we would on foot."

Xerin nods. "Yes, your Greatness."

"Then that's where we'll start," Cerylia says with a steadying breath. "I expect to see the rest of you at 0600 hours." She waves her hand in the air to dismiss us.

Estelle shoots me a knowing look as I turn to head to my chambers, and I have an unyielding sense that this night is far from over.

As I enter my rooms and begin to fold the sheets down from my bed, I feel some sort of presence nearby. I stop what I'm doing, keeping very still, as it draws closer. It doesn't feel to be a dark presence, but rather, one that is all too familiar. I'd know it anywhere. "You don't have to hide, Estelle. I know it's you." I glance over at my shoulder, eyes focused on the doorway as Estelle's wavy black hair appears. In the dim light, her violet eyes stand out even more against her mocha complexion.

"You'll stop doing that if you know what's best for you," she mutters as she finishes uncloaking herself.

I roll my eyes as I finish making down the bed. Juniper jumps off the seat of the armchair and hops up onto the end of the bed, circling multiple times, like a cat would do, before curling up into a ball. She falls asleep almost instantly.

"So, what's up?" I ask casually as I crawl into the bed, fluffing the blankets around me. I remain upright out of respect for Estelle, but all I want to do is lay down and go to sleep.

She approaches the bed and sits down on the edge of it, taking care so as to not wake Juniper. The little fox doesn't stir. "I need to know what you know." Her voice comes out just above a whisper, but even in the low volume, her words are still frighteningly intimidating.

I do my best to calm my thoughts and steady my voice before replying, "About what?"

"Don't play dumb, Arden. You're better than that."

Her words sting. She continues to stare at me with her relentless gaze until I finally muster the courage to speak. I decide to tell her exactly what I told Braxton—nothing more, nothing less. "I was there when Rydan left. We got into a pretty heated argument before he ran off into the woods."

Estelle looks at me pointedly. "What was your argument about?"

A lump forms in my throat. *Braxton didn't ask me that.* I freeze mid-thought, fearful that my expression is going to give away everything I haven't yet told her. Fortunately, she makes it easier on me.

"If I had to guess, I would say that it had something to do with your failed attempt during the Soames' assassination?"

This day is one giant reminder of my many mistakes.

"Is that a fair assumption?"

I nod my head, afraid that if I speak, I'll turn to stone. I've told enough lies and omitted enough information for one day, hell, probably for one lifetime. I grasp the blankets and tighten them around me, hoping that Estelle will get the hint.

"Well, if it's any consolation, I'm sure he's just blowing off some steam. He'll be back soon enough." I force a smile as she pats the edge of the bed and rises. "See you tomorrow, or I guess, technically, today."

I watch as she re-cloaks herself, wondering why she feels the need to stay hidden in a place that's been promised to us as a safe haven . . . unless it isn't?

I try to dispel the thought from my mind, but it lingers, just like the darkness around me. I pull the blankets tighter underneath my chin, but they don't provide much solace. How can they when I have not one, but two people out there who wish me dead?

Kristen Martin is the international Amazon bestselling author of the young adult science fiction trilogy, THE ALPHA DRIVE, and the author of the dark fantasy series, SHADOW CROWN. She is also an avid YouTuber in the BookTube community with hundreds of videos offering writing advice and inspiration, a writing coach and mentor, and founder of That Smart Hustle.

STAY CONNECTED:

www.kristenmartinbooks.com

www.youtube.com/authorkristenmartinbooks

www.facebook.com/authorkristenmartin

Instagram @authorkristenmartin

Twitter & Snapchat @authorkristenm